Prai
o

Soulbound

"A gritty, dark look into the world of magic.... Every character in *Soulbound* is written in a way that makes me feel like I must keep reading so that I can get to know them better.... If I ... had the next book in the series, I would have picked it up to read immediately."
—Fiction Vixen Book Reviews

"I was swept up from the very start, and just had to keep turning the pages." —Errant Dreams Reviews

"Fantastically dark and suspenseful paranormal romance with unique world building that had me completely absorbed." —All Things Urban Fantasy

"Lots of wonderful dark suspense, erotic passion, lighthearted humor, and magic that can make you gasp.... I already want to reread this book to see if there were any little clues or bits that I might have missed the first time." —Joyfully Reviewed

"Adams creates a story laced with tension, otherworldly action, and edge-of-your-seat suspense. The relationship between the heroine and hero crackles with sexual sparks, too." —*RT Book Reviews*

"Xandra Morgan is a strong, intelligent heroine."
—Smexy Books Romance Reviews

continued ...

The Dragon's Heat Novels

Forbidden Embers

"A steamy, exciting novel."   —Fresh Fiction

"An engaging tale of star-crossed love."
                                    —Genre Go Round Reviews

"A fantastic addition to the series that is filled with passion and intriguing characters."   —Night Owl Reviews

Hidden Embers

"[A] first-class, shape-shifting novel . . . filled with a fiery passion that's hot enough to set the desert sands aflame."   —*Romantic Times* (top pick)

"A super thriller."   —Genre Go Round Reviews

"A no-holds-barred epic romance where no emotion is left unscathed."   —Lovin' Me Some Romance

"Adams has created an enthralling, highly charged romance, complete with strong characters; hot, steaming sex; and fast-paced, suspenseful action, where no one is safe."   —Fresh Fiction

Dark Embers

"Written in a compelling voice, *Dark Embers* introduces a sexy and intriguing new world."
    —*New York Times* bestselling author Nalini Singh

"A blistering-hot, fast-paced adventure that will leave readers breathless . . . a romantic story that will captivate you and keep you turning pages long into the night."
    —*New York Times* bestselling author Anya Bast

"This darkly seductive tale will have you longing for a dragon of your very own."
            —national bestselling author Shiloh Walker

"A fantastic debut . . . that will take you on a scorching-hot adventure and leave you wanting more."
                —Among the Muses

"If you're looking for a fast paranormal read featuring suspense, hot shifters, and even hotter sex, then look no further."   —Smexy Books Romance Reviews

Also by Tessa Adams

The Dragon's Heat Novels
Dark Embers
Hidden Embers
Forbidden Embers

The Lone Star Witch Novels
Soulbound

Flamebound

A LONE STAR WITCH NOVEL

Tessa Adams

A SIGNET ECLIPSE BOOK

SIGNET ECLIPSE
Published by the Penguin Group
Penguin Group (USA) LLC, 375 Hudson Street,
New York, New York 10014

USA | Canada | UK | Ireland | Australia | New Zealand | India | South Africa | China
penguin.com
A Penguin Random House Company

First published by Signet Eclipse, an imprint of New American Library,
a division of Penguin Group (USA) LLC

First Printing, December 2013

ISBN 978-0-451-41505-9

Printed in the United States of America
10 9 8 7 6 5 4 3 2 1

PUBLISHER'S NOTE
This is a work of fiction. Names, characters, places, and incidents either are the
product of the author's imagination or are used fictitiously, and any resemblance
to actual persons, living or dead, business establishments, events, or locales is
entirely coincidental.

For Emily Sylvan Kim
You are, quite simply, the best.

One

"What are you doing?"

He doesn't so much as pause in the intricately difficult body movements that are part martial arts and part ancient Egyptian magic as he answers, "Preparing."

I take a moment to study him—I can't help it. He's so beautiful standing there, dressed in loose black pants and nothing else, his heavily muscled back gleaming beneath the sweat-slicked bronze of his skin. His long black hair is tied neatly at the nape of his neck and a series of black Seba tattoos dance across his shoulders with each movement that he makes. Directly in the middle of the ancient Egyptian stars is a gold circlet of Isis—proof that even the goddess knows he belongs to me . . . just as I belong to him.

Still a little uncomfortable with the thought—we've been an official couple for just over a week now—I focus on my end of the conversation.

"For what? World War Three?"

But even as I ask the question, I know the answer. It's been eight days since Declan found me onstage at the Paramount Theatre, eight days since the core of darkness I'd always sensed in him had been unleashed. He's barely slept since then. Barely worked, barely eaten. Every ounce of power he has is focused on revenge.

Not that I blame him. I understand his soul-deep anger. I even feel it myself. It's hard not to when the Arcadian Council of Witches, Wizards and Warlocks spent the first half of January tormenting, torturing and doing their best to kill me, all while framing Declan for my attempted murder and the murder of four other women—women whose only crime was that they looked like me. And as if that wasn't bad enough, they were also so afraid of the strength of Declan's magic, and the prophecy of my own, that they'd soulbound us without consent on the day I was born.

It's a clusterfuck of epic proportions, one I've spent nearly every waking moment thinking about these past few days. I've spent so much time on it, in fact, that my best friend and roommate, Lily, reminds me on a daily basis that Declan and I can't actually pit ourselves against the Council while they're at the height of their power—at least not without going up against charges of treason.

But it's not the fear of being labeled a traitor that stops me. It's the fact that I need peace even more than I need vengeance. I've spent my entire life latent, without magic, without power of any kind. Now not only do I wield more power than I ever imagined possible, but I also have access to the darkest emotions, the darkest deeds, known to man. Thanks to my magic, I see things, feel things, that shake me to the very marrow of my bones.

Perhaps if I'd grown up with these powers—if I'd learned from an early age how to live with them—I wouldn't be so shaken now. But I didn't and since it's been only a few days since a maniac tried to chop me into little pieces, and only a little longer than that since I lived through three separate psychic rapes, I think it's fair that I need a little time to recover. A little time to just get used to who I am now—and who Declan and I are together.

Declan doesn't see it that way, though. His rage is white-hot and deadly; his commitment to seeing the Council pay, absolute. I know it's because of me, because of what I suffered and what I still have to suffer by being soulbound to him, but that doesn't make it any less terrifying. Especially when he already lives in the shadows, already crosses the line between good and evil more than anyone should.

Oh, I know that his desire to take on the ACW stems from more than just a need for revenge. He wants to protect me, wants to keep me safe, and to hell with the consequences. And if I'd gone through what he had, maybe I'd feel the same way. Even though I had to suffer through the pain of the injuries inflicted upon me, at least I'd known that Declan was safe. That Kyle couldn't touch him. But he'd had to stand by while that lunatic tortured me.

Helpless to stop him.

Helpless to reach me in time.

Helpless to do anything but live through the pain with me.

For a man like Declan, who has controlled every aspect of his existence and his power for centuries, there is no worse blow.

But knowing that, understanding that, doesn't make it any easier to look into his fury-filled eyes. Especially when the dark is riding him like it is tonight.

So I don't.

Instead, as I take my first steps into his makeshift study, I do my best to look at anything *but* him.

I'm instantly awed by the power crackling in the air. Whenever Heka is performed, the ancient Egyptian magic usually leaves a stamp of its presence. In most cases, it's nothing more than a faint echo of the magic practiced there. But in Declan's case, that echo is a live wire of power that pulses in every molecule of the air around me.

I suck in a breath, and with it, just a touch of that magic. It zigzags inside me, lighting up my insides like a bonfire and bonding with my own magic, drawing it forth. It's still a strange feeling for me, this electricity inside me. I've spent so many years without it, and now that it's here, I'm not really sure what to do with it.

So, like so many other things in my life lately, I ignore it. Focus on the mundane instead. "Everything okay in here?"

He isn't even breathing hard from his exertions when he answers, "Everything's fine, Xandra."

"Good." I nod, but I'm not sure I believe him. The room is lit up like a beacon even though it's only four in the morning. I've had a difficult time being in the dark since my less-than-conventional magic kicked in. I wonder whether it's been the same for him. If every time he closes his eyes he remembers how close we came to losing each other.

Or maybe my fears are influencing him. I don't know if that's even possible, but it seems it could be. Some days I feel a grimness hanging over me, one that could come only from him. If that can happen, then it seems reasonable to think that my issues could become his as well.

I really hope that's not the case. Declan's existence is already so turbulent that I hate to think that I'm adding to it. But this soulbound thing is new for me, new for us, and I don't know if either of us is exactly certain of what it means. Of how it will change us. Or how we'll change each other.

Uncomfortable with the direction my thoughts are taking, I glance self-consciously around the room. It's huge, the largest in the lake house Declan bought three days ago—with cash—because he wanted to be near me. Which is why I'm here now, standing in the middle of what for most people would be the great room, but for Declan is a place of sweat and ceremony.

He hasn't done much to furnish it yet, just thrown down some mats for his rituals and brought in some of the magical objects that accompany him when he tours as a magician. He's known as the greatest illusionist of our time, but that's only because most of his audience doesn't realize that what they're seeing aren't illusions at all. Instead, they are magic in its most potent form.

"I like what you've done with the place," I tell him flippantly, wandering over to the twenty-foot-long credenza that stretches the length of the back wall. Yesterday I didn't have time to explore the changes he made while I was at work. He was too busy rushing me into the bedroom the minute I walked through the door.

"It's not much, but it's home," he deadpans as he does a particularly difficult combination. I watch him and try to keep my tongue from hanging out of my mouth at the way his muscles bunch and flow. He really is one incredibly gorgeous specimen of manhood.

Paying more attention to him than to anything in the room, I absently pick up one of the many athames lying on top of the credenza, then immediately wish I hadn't as terror—bone-deep and vivid—rips through me. Not mine. Not Declan's. I drop the magical dagger back onto the polished mahogany with a thunk.

I don't want to know. What Declan did before me isn't important. It's what he does now, when we're together, that matters. I grab onto the thought, repeat it like a mantra until I actually start to believe it. Until I forget the cloying taste of fear that ripped through my senses the moment I touched the ancient knife.

Making sure to give the rest of his stuff a wide berth— I'm not one to bury my head in the sand, but there are some things that even I'm aware I'm better off not knowing—I turn back just in time to see Declan stretch out his arms in a move that is all ancient warrior. I watch, fascinated, as his muscles stand out in stark relief and a bead of sweat drips slowly down his spine. Seconds later, fire explodes in a ring all around him, a blaze that starts out small but that grows to touch the ceiling in seconds.

Deep inside I recoil, my fear instinctive after I was nearly burned alive just days ago. But I work hard not to let my instant revulsion for the fire show. Declan is a fire element, the most powerful I've ever met, and I am afraid a rejection of the flame will somehow translate into a rejection of him. So I don't move, don't speak, barely even breathe, and watch with deliberately blank eyes as the fire winds itself around his chest and arms and legs.

He must sense my uneasiness, though, because with a flick of his hand he quenches the flames.

"You didn't have to do that."

He smiles—a slow, sexy curling of one corner of his mouth that melts my brain cells and my resolve.

"When you're in the room, I can think of any number of things I'd rather do than play with fire."

Dropping a quick kiss on my lips, he crosses to the minifridge and pulls out two bottles of water. Hands me one.

I watch him drink, mesmerized by the way his throat moves. By the way he— I shake my head sharply, determined to snap out of the sensual spell he casts without even trying.

It's easier said than done, though. Except for the time I spend working at Beanz, the coffeehouse I own down on South Congress, we've spent much of the last week in bed. Which has been fun and intense and sexy as hell, not to mention a million other things, but it hasn't exactly been conducive to talking. And today, I need to talk.

He leans forward to steal another kiss—a playful sweep of his lips across mine that quickly turns into something dark and dangerous and utterly mind-numbing. His arms link around my waist, pulling me closer, and before I go under completely, I slap a hand against his warm, bare chest and shove him away.

"We need to talk," I tell him, putting some distance between us so my nerve endings can stop firing . . . and so my brain cells can start.

He quirks a brow. "Aren't those the four most dreaded words in any relationship?"

"Only when they're followed by, 'It's not you, it's me.'"

He's silent for a second, then—"So is it?"

"Is it what?" I'm baffled by the guarded look on his face and by his sudden reserve.

"You, not me?"

I laugh, certain he's joking. But the look in his eyes is solemn. Though I only get a glimpse—Declan is a master at hiding his emotions—it occurs to me that the question might be real. That he's just as confused about this strange relationship as I am. And maybe as uncertain.

This time I'm the one who wraps my arms around him. I press kisses over his warm, hard torso, starting at the base of his throat and working my way straight down the center of his body until I get to the spot where his heart thumps heavily beneath my lips. I kiss him there, then rest my head on his chest and pull him even closer.

His arms tighten convulsively around me. "You make me crazy."

I look up at him through my lashes. "Believe me, the feeling is more than mutual."

He kisses me again, and this time I savor every second of it. He tastes like cinnamon and magic—dark, spicy-sweet and delicious. It's a flavor I'm quickly becoming addicted to.

His tongue sweeps out, traces my lower lip. Plays with the corners of my mouth. Dances across my top lip and the little indention right in the center of it. My arms tighten around him, and my mouth opens in a desperate need to get closer.

He nips at my lower lip, then sucks it softly to soothe the hurt away. I bite back, just enough to remind him that I have my own teeth, my own power. He groans deep in his chest, reaches for the bottom of my pajama top and whips it off. Then we're standing there, bare skin to bare skin, and it feels so good I forget every word of the carefully rehearsed speech I came in here to deliver.

His hands slide up my back to cup my head, his fingers tangling in the chin-length strands of my hair. He pulls my head back, tilts my chin up. And then he devours me.

His mouth is ravenous on mine, stroking, sucking, bit-ing, kissing. He explores every inch—every centimeter—of my mouth with his tongue, his lips, until I'm little more than a quivering mess of a woman. Only then, when my whole body is trembling with need and want and unchecked desperation, does he move on.

I moan a little in protest, try to hold his mouth to mine. But he has other plans. His lips skim across my cheek. He pauses for a moment to nibble at my earlobe—it sends shivers down my spine, like he knows it will—before kissing his way down my jaw and neck.

He stops at the hollow of my throat—his favorite spot—and licks and sucks until my knees go weak and my body feels like it will spontaneously combust at any moment.

Declan knows what he's doing to me. He knows that he has me now. Knows that I'll do anything to feel him inside me. Just like he knows that I'm seconds away from my legs no longer being able to support me.

Without raising his head, or his mouth, from the wicked, wonderful things he's doing to me, he sweeps a leg out and gently knocks mine out from under me. He catches me against him with one strong arm, then boosts me up so that I can wrap my legs around his waist.

This is one of my favorite things about making love with Declan. How strong he is, how easily he's able to manipulate my body into whatever position he wants me in. And how absolutely, ridiculously easy it is for him to pick me up as though I weigh almost nothing.

I sink down a little so that I'm resting against him, his erection hot and hard where it nestles against my sex. He groans a little, tilts his hips so that the tip of his cock is resting right against my clit and starts to move slowly, deliciously, against me.

Seconds later, his lips close over my nipple. I gasp, arch into him, and he bites down just hard enough to send pleasure shooting through every nerve ending in my body. He laves the little hurt with his tongue, then does it again. And again.

That's all it takes to send me over the edge I'm never very far from when Declan's around. My body trembles, convulses, and I cry out, hold on to him even more tightly. He kisses and soothes me through the surprisingly intense orgasm even as he shifts to find the spot that will take me higher. I come again, screaming, head thrown back and breasts thrust up like some ancient pagan sacrifice.

Declan accepts the offering, his mouth closing over first one nipple, then the other as he prolongs my climax until I'm a sweaty, shuddering mess. Only then does he let the primal need inside him loose.

Dropping to his knees, he slides me gently onto the exercise mat. Strips my pants from me. Does the same to his own. Then he's rolling me over onto my knees.

Wrapping an arm around my waist.

Pulling me back against him with less finesse than he's ever shown before.

Thrusting into me from behind.

It's primitive and possessive and perfect—so perfect that I climax again within seconds. Declan groans, his hands clamping down on my hips to hold me in place as he moves slow and deep inside me. Over and over and over again.

Eventually I cry out. My body is on fire, every nerve ending I have alight with so much pleasure that I can't breathe, can't think, can't function. There are no boundaries, no lines, nothing that tells me where I stop and he begins. It's exhilarating and terrifying and absolutely un-stoppable.

His power rises up, calls to mine, and I couldn't stop my magic from answering even if I wanted to. My power flashes out of me, slams into his in a mingling so intense that I feel it in my soul.

Declan gasps, his hands tightening on my hips as if he needs to anchor himself, and I know he feels it, too. Desperate, delirious, but determined to take him over the edge with me this time, I reach back, grab onto the firm muscles of his ass and pull him forward, hard, so that he slams—fast and deep—inside me.

He curses, then lets go in a potent flash of light and love. He pours himself into me and it sends me into one last climax, this one more powerful than those that came before because he's with me every step of the way.

Two

When it's over, Declan sags against me. His chest pressed to my back. His face resting against my shoulder. His body wrapped around mine.

I love it. Love the way he surrounds me, the way I feel him in every cell, every molecule of my body. Love even more the intimacy of being held so closely by the man I know I'm falling for.

I don't move, afraid to break the spell, and for long seconds neither does he. But eventually our skin grows sticky with dried sweat and the first fingers of dawn begin to creep through the wide, uncurtained picture window that makes up one whole wall of this place.

"I need to get to work." I should have left already. I was tired last night, and eager to see Declan, so I left without prepping the dough for the snickerdoodle cookies. It needs to be done soon or there will be a lot of disappointed customers this morning. The cookies are one of my biggest sellers.

"I know." He presses a soft kiss between my shoulder blades. "I'm sorry. You said you wanted to talk."

He helps me up and for a moment, just a moment, I get another glimpse of the vulnerability in his eyes. It's such an unfamiliar look for him that, like before, it takes me a moment to realize what it is. When I do, my heart melts just a little more. So often I feel like I'm the only one blundering around without a clue. Like Declan has all the answers to this mysterious connection we share while I don't have an inkling. It's nice to know that, steep as the learning curve is for me, I'm not in this alone.

"It's fine," I tell him as I head for the shower. "We can talk later."

I pretend, even to myself, that I'm not relieved at the reprieve. But I am. The last thing I want to do right now is fight with Declan, but I know that it's brewing. That it's just a matter of time before we have a knock-down-drag-out over the ACW.

He follows me down the hall to his bedroom, which is empty save the huge bed in the center of the room. The messed-up sheets and bloodred comforter pooled on the floor are testament to the fact that Declan and I didn't get much sleep last night. Not that I care. Being loved by him is worth any sleep I might lose out on.

"Are you sure? We can talk in the shower." The vulnerability is gone, replaced by a wicked gleam I know all too well.

I slap a hand on his chest, shove him away when he would have reached for me. "Dude, I know what your definition of shower is and it has very little to do with actually getting clean. I'm late. Plus, Austin's in the middle of a drought—"

"Which is why showering together is such a brilliant idea. We should do our part to conserve."

I snort. "Yeah, right. There's not enough water in the state for the games you like to play. You're on your own." I close the door on him, then lean back against it for a second to give my legs a chance to steady. As I do, I catch a glimpse of myself in the mirror. My skin is flushed, my eyes dancing, and there's a huge smile on my face.

It's a good look for me—beats the hell out of the bruised and battered one I was sporting for a while. Not that I don't still have bruises. I do, but thanks to time and Declan's ministrations, they've faded to almost nothing.

I don't look at them, don't bring the darkness into this one perfect moment. Being with Declan makes me happy, something I couldn't have imagined saying even two weeks ago. But he does. He makes me really, really happy and that's enough for now. Whatever this is between us, while intense and over the top, feels good and right—especially since the rest of my life is pretty much a disaster right now.

But I know it won't last. Not Declan, but the joy bubbling up inside me. It can't, not with the darkness that lives inside both of us. Not with the twisted maze of lies and danger that stretches before us. Between us.

I flip on the shower, brush my teeth as I wait for the water to warm. Tell myself that I need to enjoy every moment we have together before the evil intrudes. After all, these stolen days in Declan's arms are more than I ever thought I'd get when I was lying on that stage waiting to die. As long as I have him beside me, I can handle whatever comes next.

With that thought firmly in mind, I make my way toward the shower. But before I can set foot inside it, Declan is there—warm and naked, and suddenly I want nothing more than to crawl back into bed with all six and a half feet of him. And when he wraps his arms around me from behind, pulls me against his broad, hard chest, I can't do anything but melt.

At least until he puts his mouth to my ear and murmurs, "Let's talk. Is everything okay?"

The warmth leaves me in a rush. We need to have this conversation—I know we do. But I don't want to do it now. Not when I'm still loose and sated from our incredible lovemaking. And not when I want to savor the sweetness and the joy that springs up so unexpectedly between us for just a few minutes.

I'm not a coward, though, and I can't walk away from this conversation. I let Declan distract me earlier, just as I have every day since I've been out of the hospital. But that stops now. I need answers and he's the only one who can give them to me.

"What—" My voice breaks, so I clear my throat. Take a breath. Then try again. "What are you planning on doing?"

"I need to make some phone calls, deal with the wrap-up of the tour. Usually all that's done a week after the tour finishes, but I've been a little busy the last few days."

Taking care of me. That's not what he said, but it's what he meant. My cheeks flush with embarrassment. "I'm sorry. I didn't mean to take you away—"

"Don't," he tells me, right before he bends down and takes my mouth in a searing kiss. "Don't you dare apologize for what those bastards did to you."

"I'm not apologizing for *that*. But I am sorry I've taken up so much of your time when you need to be doing other stuff."

He stares at me for long seconds. "You just don't get it, do you? Even after everything we've been through, you don't understand how much you mean to me."

I don't. But I know how much he matters to me, and

the thought of anything happening to him because of me, because of our relationship, cuts like a knife.

Again, I think about running away. About heading into work without ever having this discussion. I've put it off long enough, though, and it's not good for either one of us to live in this kind of limbo where we're uncertain of each other's thoughts and intentions.

"When I asked what you were going to do, I didn't mean today," I tell him. "I was talking about the ACW. What your plans are regarding them?"

His eyes turn cold, flat, hard in an instant. "They need to pay."

The conviction in his voice is absolute, and it's exactly what I was afraid of. "What are you planning?"

"Right now?" He quirks a brow. "Nothing."

I nearly sag in relief. Thank the goddess he's being reasonable. I know how angry he is, but going after the ACW is suicide. Besides, I'm not ready to fight the war that such a move would invoke. Right now, I have more than enough on my plate just trying to get used to Declan and my new powers.

"You look shocked," he tells me.

"I am. I thought you'd be more . . . difficult about this."

"Difficult? Why would I be difficult?"

He's going for innocent, but all of a sudden I don't trust the look on his face or the shadows in his eyes.

"Declan, you can't . . ."

"Can't what?" Those eyes narrow.

I swallow nervously. Even after everything we've shared, it still overwhelms me to have all that gorgeous intensity focused so completely on me. "The Council is too strong. You need to let what happened to me go."

"Let it go?" He doesn't bother to hide the incredulity in his tone. "You think I'm just going to let it go?"

He steps away from me to pace the long, narrow length of the bathroom. Though I know it's stupid, I feel immediately bereft without his warmth wrapped around me.

"They don't get to do whatever they want. They don't get to play with people's lives—with *your* life—and get away with it."

"What are you going to do?"

"I don't know yet," he says in a harsh voice barely above a whisper. "But I'll tell you what I want to do. I want to rip them all apart. To kill every Councilor—in as bloody and as terrible a way as possible—for what they did to you. I want to shred the whole fucking lot of them, make examples of them so that no one, ever, thinks it's okay to come after you again.

"But I can't do that. Not now, not when you're in Austin. Because the only thing I want more than their blood is your safety. And this"—he gestures to the bruises still evident on my skin—"isn't safe. I would never do something that would double back on you. Never do anything that could make you suffer the way this has."

I hear what he's saying—of course I do, because I feel exactly the same way about him. But I also hear what he isn't saying. "Is that supposed to make me feel better? Knowing that if I wasn't around, you would kill every single one of them?"

"What do you want from me?" He's snarling now. "They *raped* you. They *tortured* you. They had every intention of *killing* you. And what? I'm just supposed to let that go? Let them get away with it?"

He whirls away from me, slams a fist into the wall. Pulls it back and does the same thing a second and a third time, until his fingers are swollen, his knuckles bruised and bloody. And still the rage pours off him.

He thrusts his uninjured hand into my hair, tightens his fingers into a fist and pulls me close, so close that I can see the silver flecks in his eyes. Feel the heat pouring off him. So close that we're breathing the same air.

Part of me wants to stop pushing. To bury my head some more and pray that it all goes away. But even I'm smart enough to know that's not going to work.

Gathering my courage, I take a deep breath. Close my eyes. And ask again. "What are you going to do?" Because he has a plan. I know he does.

He doesn't answer, which only makes me more concerned. "Damn it, Declan. Don't shut me out—you owe me that much. What are you thinking?"

In lieu of answering, he reaches for me. Pulls me into his arms. Then thrusts me away so that he can glide his fingers over my rib cage, my shoulder, the undersides of my breasts.

It takes me a minute to figure out what he's doing, that he's tracing each of the bruises and cuts I still bear from eight nights ago, when Kyle had me strapped to a table in some macabre offering to the sickness inside him and those he worked for. He presses kisses on them all—even ones that have faded or disappeared completely. He knows each and every one of them, and for the first time, I understand just how destroyed Declan is by what was done to me.

"Living like this, for revenge, isn't healthy." I brush my lips across his forehead.

"It's healthier than eating myself up every minute of the goddamn day, thinking that they're going to get away with what they did."

"They aren't going to get away with it. Kyle is—"

"Already dead. He just doesn't know it yet."

Horror seizes me, cold and all-consuming. "What did you do?"

"What needed to be done. He'll never stand trial for what he did, never get the chance to walk away from it."

I don't want to believe what he's telling me. "Then why all the safeguards? Why didn't you just let the ACW have him?"

The look he gives me is pure magic, dark and mystical and filled with unimaginable power. "And give them even a small modicum of peace of mind? Not going to happen."

I think of all the magic I know of, and all the magic I still don't understand. There are spells to do what Declan is suggesting—slow, insidious things that creep through the bloodstream and destroy a person from the inside out. I don't know how they work, have never given them much thought before as they are dark magic. Not black magic, not blood magic, but almost.

It shouldn't come as a surprise. I've known Declan walks the thin and shadowy line between white and black magic. But this, what he's talking about, is so close to stepping over that line that it might as well not exist.

My stomach cramps and for a second I'm certain that I'm going to puke. Panic, fear, even disgust well up inside me as I think about what he's done, what he will continue to do.

I don't want this.

Don't want to know this dark and driven side of Declan.

Don't want to understand the things he's willing to do and the lines he's willing to cross because of the shadowy rules he lives by.

"They've spent centuries fucking around with me, and that's fine. I'm used to it. But they will *never* touch you again." The words ring with conviction even though they're devoid of emotion. Or maybe because of it.

A hot and angry Declan is dangerous. A cold, emotionless one is terrifying. Not to mention deadly.

"You can't go up against the Council on your own."

He can't pit himself against the ACW; he just can't. Declan is powerful—terrifyingly so—but what he's talking about is suicide, even for him.

"Declan, I'm serious. That's treason. They'll kill you—if you're lucky—and hold you up as an example for every witch, wizard and warlock in existence of what happens to people who cross the ACW."

"For that to happen, there would have to be some Council members left alive. I'm not planning on that being the case."

Dear sweet goddess. "You think you can kill them all?"

"I'm *going* to kill them all."

"That's crazy, Declan! Even *you* aren't strong enough for that. Once they figure out what you're going to do, they'll do whatever it takes to stop you."

"It's not like I'm planning on sending them an engraved invitation to their deaths, Xandra."

I start to answer, but the words get stuck. I clear my throat, then try again. "It's not up to you to avenge me. Besides, I'm alive. I'm whole."

"But that's it. You'll never be whole again, at least not in the way you were. And it kills me, Xandra. It kills me that that bastard got so close to you. That you suffered the way you did."

"You saved me, Declan."

"Too late! I got to you too late. You saved yourself."

With help from him, but maybe he doesn't see it that way. "Does that bother you?"

"Are you kidding me? I'm so damn proud of you, some days I can barely see straight. But that doesn't mean they don't have to pay."

"That isn't what I want, Declan. Declaring war on the ACW. Taking them all down in some twisted sort of vengeance for me. That kind of darkness isn't what I need from you."

"Maybe it isn't. But I can't change who I am, Xandra, not even for you. Letting me do this, understanding that I have to do this, is what I need from you. Because I can't live in a world where a threat like that exists for you. Where they can decide, at any moment, that you're expendable. That I can't do."

He lowers his head then, presses his lips against mine. And I respond. I can't not respond.

Because there's something heady about being cared for the way he cares for me. And I need him more with each day and minute and second that passes.

But when his hand comes up to cup my breast, his thumb teasing gently over my nipple, I force myself to pull back. To look him in the eye and stand my ground. "Murder is wrong, Declan. No matter the reason. You have to know that."

"You say that because you're a princess of Ipswitch. You've been protected your whole life."

I laugh bitterly, gesturing to the bruises that cover so much of my body. "Does this look to you like I'm protected?"

"No." He cups my cheek sadly. "But you will be. I'll make sure of it."

"It's my power—"

He silences me with a soft finger against my lips. "A power you don't have if I'm not around." Again he brushes soft kisses over my bruises. "This is the Heka I know. This is the world I live in. They have to die, Xandra. Maybe not here, maybe not now. But they have to die."

Three

There's nothing to say after that—for either of us. No more teasing, no more kissing, no more joy in just being together. I pull into myself, trying to absorb everything Declan has just said. Trying to wrap my head around it and figure out what my next counterargument should be.

Declan senses my withdrawal, or maybe he's just as shaken by our conversation as I am. Either way, he presses a gentle kiss on my cheek and then walks out of the bathroom, leaving me alone with a bunch of thoughts that I would suddenly do anything to escape from.

It's not that easy, though. I may want to shed my fears like a snake sheds its skin, to leave them here in this bathroom and just walk away. But I can't. Because Declan isn't talking wildly. He isn't venting, isn't boasting. I don't know when or how, but one day he will bring the ACW members to their knees. And what comes after that will be a mess of epic proportions.

As I step into the shower and start to wash my hair, I try to figure out how to sway Declan away from his way of thinking about the Council and over to mine. But his position is so firm, his desire for vengeance absolute.

I am a princess of Ipswitch, daughter to a queen and

king who don't like or trust the ACW but who are closely allied with them for political reasons. If my lover is the one to bring them down, the political ramifications will be disastrous. It's why I haven't told my parents what happened here a week ago, why I haven't let them know who Kyle actually worked for. Because if they knew the Council tried to kill their seventh daughter, it would be an all-out war. Hundreds—no, *thousands* of witches, wizards and warlocks would die in the ensuing battle and, in the end, we'd be too weak to protect ourselves. Too weak to stand against any outside threats.

I don't know what to do, only that I have to somehow convince Declan that this isn't what I want. What I need.

Am I angry? Yes. Is there a part of me that wants revenge for what they did? Absolutely. But the truth is, all I really want right now is to catch my breath. To try to come to grips with the darker shades of magic that are becoming more a part of me with every day that passes. And to pretend, even for a little while, that the biggest threat to our happiness isn't the shadow that hovers over Declan and me like a storm about to break.

Hours later, I'm still struggling with what to do. It's early afternoon now and the lunch rush has finally eased off. I'm trying to catch up on my paperwork—with everything that's been going on lately I've been letting things slide—but all I can think about is the argument I had with Declan earlier.

Still, I open the ordering spreadsheet on the computer, start making notes of all the supplies we need for the upcoming week. If I can't solve the problems of my witch side, then at least I can keep the human side of my life going as smoothly as possible.

But that doesn't last long before Travis sticks his head in my door and says, "Nate's here."

I glance up from what I'm doing with a raised brow. "And this matters to me because . . . ?"

He sighs heavily and flops down in one of the chairs on the other side of my desk. "You know, Xandra, just because you and Declan are playing kissy face with each other doesn't mean you shouldn't keep your other options open. Nate's a great catch."

"Not to be obnoxious," I tell my best barista, "but shouldn't you be making coffee instead of planning out my love life?"

"Luckily for you, I can do both. Besides, I'm on a break." He makes a point of looking at his watch. "According to this, I've got thirteen minutes left before I have to report back to the front of the house. Which means I have plenty of time to help you freshen up a bit before you go out to the counter to serve Nate's coffee. Once I saw him come in, I told Meg to stall, so there's a little bit of a line."

"You think that's a good thing to admit to the boss?"

He rolls his eyes. "Honey, we don't have time for this." He crowds me as he scoots behind my desk. "Now, where's your purse?"

"What do I need my purse for?"

"You're still carrying that little emergency repair kit I made for you, right? It's nothing to be ashamed of. Every girl needs a little improvement now and again." He pauses to look at me. "Although, it's kind of hard to repair what was never fixed up to begin with."

"That's because I spent too long playing kissy face with Declan this morning."

"Of course you did. If I had that fine specimen of

manhood in my bed, I'm not sure I'd ever get out." He finds where I stuck my bag under the desk and starts rummaging through it.

"And yet you're still pushing Nate at me."

"Honey, guys like Declan don't stick around forever. Especially"—he eyes my jeans and fuzzy sweater with a look somewhere between dismay and disgust—"if you become one of *those* women who lets herself go once she's got a man." He hands me a raspberry-colored lip gloss. "Here, put this on. It'll plump up your lips. And maybe Nate won't notice those bags under your eyes."

I glower at him. "I *can* fire you, you know."

He snorts. "If you fire me, you'll have to be up front every morning, charming all the customers. And honey, you might be gorgeous, but charming you are not."

"Touché." I take the gloss from him and start applying it—not because I have any desire to primp for the homicide detective, who is my friend and former romantic possibility, but because Travis is like a dog with a bone once he gets an idea in his head. Nothing short of full compliance will get him to move on to something else.

"Since you're in your nasty mood, I want the record to reflect that I started the day with lipstick on."

He peers at my lips as if looking for the evidence. "Then what happened to it all? It's only two o'clock."

"Declan spent fifteen minutes kissing it off me."

"Now you're just tormenting me," he says with a groan.

"You deserve it."

"Really? I'm trying to help you here. It was a long, dry spell before Declan and I just want to make sure that doesn't happen again if you break up."

"What makes you think Declan and I aren't going to

make it?" I ask as he sweeps shadow into the crease of my eyelid.

"I said *if* you break up—"

"But you meant *when*. I'm not an idiot. It's written all over your face." I tense up instinctively as I wait for the answer. I'm obviously not the only one who sees the basic incompatibility issues facing Declan and me. Travis pauses to examine me, but I get the feeling that he's thinking more about my question than my questionable makeup choices.

"I believe," he says finally, "that you and Declan are in very different places in your lives. And that it's very difficult to make a relationship like that work."

"Difficult, but not impossible."

"No, sugar, of course it's not impossible. Few things are if you want them badly enough. But at the same time, you need to decide what it is you really want."

"I want Declan."

"Of course you do. What red-blooded human wouldn't? But is wanting him enough? I haven't been around him that much, but even I can see that he's haunted—and not by a ghost. That man has issues—dark issues that he's buried deep inside himself."

"He has a reason for them."

"Of course he does." He comes at me brandishing a mascara wand like a weapon. I duck, twist my head, but Travis only follows. "All the more reason for you to be careful."

"Haunted doesn't necessarily mean bad." I'm grasping at straws and I know it. And I still don't care.

"No. But it does mean difficult. Take it from someone who knows."

That's the thing. He does know—Travis is a magnet

for guys like Declan, minus the magic, of course. Maybe that's what this talk is really about—a cautionary tale brought on by the trouble in his own love life. I know it's wrong, but I can't help hoping that's what it is.

Deciding to poke around a little, I ask, "Still no word from Will, hmm?"

He drops the mascara and busies himself digging through the emergency repair kit for goddess only knows what. "Will who?"

I grab the kit, place it on the desk, then reach for his other hand. I hold on until he finally looks me in the eye. "First of all, if Will doesn't want you, then he's a fool. You're the absolute best guy I know and only an idiot wouldn't recognize that."

He doesn't answer, instead looking away. Travis can handle a lot of things without batting an eyelash—one of the many reasons I love having him in the front of the house—but he's never been very good at taking compliments on anything more important than his shoes. I know he wants me to let this go, but I'm not going to. I'm not sure what it is about the men in my life and their pathological need to dodge any kind of meaningful conversation. But, this is too important, and something that's needed to be said for way too long. So I wait patiently until he finally turns back to me.

"And secondly, I know it's hard to trust—believe me, I know." Trusting Declan, knowing who he is and the power he has, is the most difficult thing I've ever done—especially when the murkiness of his power threatens to rise up and overwhelm us both. "But no relationship is going to work out if you're constantly shopping for his replacement."

Travis swallows convulsively, studies his nails, taps his

foot. Then says, "Somebody's been reading too many pop psychology books lately."

I know it's the only acknowledgment he's going to give my words and since the snipe doesn't have Travis's usual bitchiness behind it, I give him a quick hug. Then decide, what the hell. I haven't seen Nate in a few days. It wouldn't kill me to give my best barista a thrill.

Shoving away from my desk, I stand and gesture to myself. "Do I pass inspection, oh wise guru of all things fashionable?"

"You need a little color." He pinches my cheeks, a bit harder than is strictly necessary, but I don't protest. I figure I have it coming. Then he steps back and surveys his handiwork. "Well, you won't win any beauty contests. . . ."

"Oh no. How will I live?" I pointedly glance at the clock. "I believe your thirteen minutes are up."

"Like I'd miss this? Hurry up." He shoos me out the door. "Meg's good, but she can't stall him forever."

Travis's words haunt me as I go to the front, but I shove them to the back of my mind. Declan and I are still in the getting-to-know-each-other phase, that's all. And our relationship has been a lot more intense than most new couples'—no wonder things feel so scary and off-kilter. That doesn't mean that they won't work out, right?

I approach the counter just as Meg is wrapping up Nate's favorite treat—one of the huge sugar cookies I make from scratch every day. I've thought about phasing them out for a more updated cookie, but I never have because I know how much he likes them.

"Just the woman I came here to see," Nate says as he catches sight of me. He's smiling and I do the same, though inside I'm still reeling.

"And here I thought you came for the French roast."
I fill a cup and hand it to him.

He takes it with murmured thanks, holds it up to his
nose and breathes deeply. "I can get coffee anywhere."
He takes a sip. "Maybe not this good, but there are three
Starbucks closer to the station."

Travis nudges me and I know he expects me to say
something, but I don't have a clue how to respond to
that—especially considering that Nate's been coming
here every day for well over a year.

Nate doesn't let things get awkward, though. Instead,
he nods to an empty table toward the back. "Do you
have a minute?"

I'm a little confused by his easy friendliness. Not that
Nate has ever been *unfriendly* to me, but things have
been strained between us ever since he suspected Declan of murder and tried to arrest him. Still, I've never
been one to turn a friend away, and Nate—despite Travis's hopes to the contrary—is a friend.

I wave away the money he holds out for his coffee,
and lead him to a table in the corner. As we sit, I become
aware of the grim vibes rolling off him—vibes I hadn't
noticed when he was chatting amiably with Meg.

"What's wrong?" I ask him as soon as we're settled.

"Something has to be wrong for me to want to talk to
you?"

"I can tell, Nate."

His smile freezes in place. "Oh, right. Because of
the . . ." He trails off and gestures a little awkwardly toward his head. I'm confused for a second, but then I remember how I explained my magic to him. When he
demanded a reason as to why I kept showing up at dif-

ferent murder sites, I told him I was psychic—which isn't exactly a lie, but it isn't exactly the truth, either.

"No. Not because of that." I smile at him reassuringly. "You just look . . . off."

"It's been a rough couple of weeks." He rubs a hand over his face and I realize, for the first time, just how much this job takes out of him. That may seem stupid—I mean, everyone knows it can't be easy to be a homicide detective with all the horrifying things they have to see—but at the same time, Nate always seems to handle it so well.

Then again, the black warlock–turned–serial killer who stalked Austin for the past few weeks pretty much defied human description. Poor Nate was stuck hunting him without having a clue as to what he was really up against. I'm a witch, soulbound to one of the darkest warlocks around, and I still have nightmares of being raped and murdered by that monster.

I look at the dark circles under Nate's eyes and wonder if he's having as much trouble sleeping as I am. I hope not.

"Where are you with Kyle?" I ask, breaking the uncomfortable silence that stretches between us.

"The D.A. has decided to seek the death penalty. He'll probably call you today or tomorrow to fill you in. He's planning on contacting all the victims' families."

When I don't immediately respond, he looks at me questioningly, but I'm not sure what to say to him. Especially since I'm too busy considering what that decision means to focus on an answer that won't give anything away.

I wonder if the prosecutor plans on contacting Declan, since he was the closest thing Lina, the first Austin victim, had to a family. If he doesn't, I'll have to tell him. Kyle was the Council's hired killer, and right now, Declan's magic is the only thing keeping them from stepping in and seeing that Kyle evades justice. But once they realize the death penalty is on the table, they'll up their efforts to break Declan's spell.

It's no easy task—the man has so much power it leaks from his every pore—but the Council is filled with some of the most talented practitioners of Heka in existence. It's not a stretch to think that together they'll find a way to circumvent him.

Hell, they've probably been working on it for the last eight days. Not because they actually care about Kyle—he was just a tool to them, after all—but because the Council has always stood firm on the fact that witches do not stand trial in human courts. Ever.

It's a carryover from the times when we were hunted, tortured, burned and hanged by people who didn't understand our powers and what we could do. And while I agree with the Council's stance in theory—humans do have a tendency to get a little excitable when magic is involved—I still think witches that commit crimes in human society deserve to pay for those crimes by human laws. Three of the four women Kyle killed had no power, and no way to defend themselves against what he did to them. He needs to answer for that. And while I've never believed in the death penalty before, I know the blackness of the magic that lives inside Kyle. Letting that magic loose—ever again—is not an option.

I shudder to think what Declan will do if the Council steps in, because not killing Kyle is already eating away at Declan's soul. I can feel it when he holds me, see it in his face when he thinks I'm not looking. And that eats away at me. I know he's trying to spare me the pain of it—my power is such that I feel the violent death by magical means of anyone within a certain number of miles from me (I'm not yet sure how far that power extends)—but I'm not so naïve as to think Declan won't step in if the Council tries to interfere with Kyle's trial and sentencing. By the time he's done, there won't be enough of Kyle left to recognize, let alone rescue.

"How are the families doing?" I finally ask, my voice breaking a little under the weight of my guilt. It's my fault those women died screaming, my fault they were taken away from the people who loved them.

"The funerals were this week. It was rough." He pauses, looks uncomfortable. I'm sure he's remembering that Declan was responsible for Lina's, that he saw both of us there. "How are you doing?"

"I'm fine." It's my standard answer. Just close enough to the truth that I can't be accused of lying. Kind of how I've lived all twenty-seven years of my existence up to this point.

"You look tired."

"So do you. Must be something about coming into close contact with a sociopath that makes it hard to sleep at night."

"Or any other time."

I laugh, but it doesn't hold a lot of humor. Because he's right. For me, the only thing that keeps the horror at bay is Declan. My only nightmare-free sleep comes after he's made love to me until I'm quivering with exhaustion.

Suddenly I need a break—this conversation is slowly leeching all the joy from me that I felt earlier after being in Declan's arms.

"Is that all you wanted to tell me? About Kyle?"

I gesture vaguely toward the tables around us, all of which are taken. It's three o'clock and the coffeehouse is filling up again.

Employees on their midafternoon coffee break.

Students finished with classes for the day, looking for a quiet place to unwind or study.

Tourists combing downtown, looking for a place to wait out the rain, which has turned the air cold and the sidewalks slick.

"Actually, that's not what I came to talk to you about at all." He reaches into his pocket, pulls out an envelope. "I should have gotten to this sooner. I know you're busy."

"It's fine." I watch as he slides the envelope across the table to me. "What is that?"

"I have a favor to ask. I know you don't normally do the whole psychic thing—at least not if you can help it. But—"

"Nate, no."

He holds up his hands. "I know, I know. It's uncool of me to ask. And I wouldn't, if it wasn't desperately important. There's a little girl. She's missing."

I want to slam my hands over my ears, to sing "la la la la la la" like a little kid who doesn't want to hear that it's bedtime. Because it's not that I don't want to help. It's that I can't help.

"It doesn't work that way."

"What doesn't?"

"My . . . gift." I barely stop myself from blurting out the word *magic*. "I don't see things that I concentrate on. I feel emotions. Pain. Violence. Fear . . ."

Death.

The truth is, I sense death and all the intense emotions that go along with it.

"Maybe if you look at her, you'll pick something up. She's got to be scared, right? She's been missing for four days." He grabs the envelope, slides a picture out of it and puts it faceup in the center of the table.

And despite my best intentions, I can't help but look.

She's a pretty little girl, maybe six or seven. In the photo, she's smiling, and there's a huge gap where her two front teeth should be. Her wide green eyes are bright and innocent and her long, brown ringlets are tied back from her face with purple ribbons that have white polka dots on them.

I stare at her for long seconds, mesmerized. I know I should close my eyes, should look away—the last thing I want is a picture of this lost little girl in my head. I can't help her, can't find her, no matter how much I wish I could. She'll just be one more nightmare for me to live with when the lights go out.

When I finally manage to pull my eyes away from her sweet, happy smile, I find Nate staring at me, his blond brow furrowed with concentration. "Did you . . . ?"

"I told you. It doesn't work that way." I look at him curiously, doing my best to ignore the sick feeling in the pit of my stomach. "How did you get involved in a kidnapping case anyway?"

"It's my neighbor's daughter. She was playing in the front yard with two friends after school. Her mom went to the back of the house to start a load of laundry and when she went to check on her about seven minutes later, Shelby was gone. She checked with the neighbors, but it turns out their mom had called them home about five minutes before. So sometime in the space of those five minutes, Shelby disappeared. Her parents are—" He breaks off, shakes his head. "They're a mess."

"I can't even imagine." The horror of it is pressing in on me, making it hard to breathe, hard to think. Pulling at me until I can feel myself spiraling downward, though I don't know why. It's a sad story, a terrifying story, but it isn't much different from a dozen others I'd heard about on the news in the last year.

Knowing I have to get away from Nate, from the picture, from the grief that seems to be closing in, I push my chair back from the table and stand up. I tell him, "I'm sorry. I can't help you find her."

"Are you sure?"

"Yes." Still, some instinct I don't even recognize urges me to pick up the photo. I slide it carefully into the back pocket of my jeans. "And you don't want my help. Because if I knew where she was, if I *could* find her, it would only be because she was already dead."

Four

I can't get the little girl out of my head. All day I think about her—while I'm running the register, while I'm mixing cookie dough, while I'm waiting tables. Her face is there every time I close my eyes, every time I pause for breath.

At first I panic, terrified that a compulsion is setting in. That the reason I'm fixated on her is because she's dead. As the day passes and I realize that I'm not going to be pulled out of my shop by some urgent need to find her, though, the fear begins to recede. But in its place grows a determination to do something, anything, to help her.

With that thought foremost in my head, I text Declan at five o'clock, as I'm walking out the front door of Beanz—just a quick note to tell him I'm going to spend the night at my own house tonight. I know it won't go over well, but I want to talk to Lily about Shelby. She has different magic than mine, and while she's no better at finding lost people than I am, she reads a mean tarot. Maybe, if she concentrates, she'll pick something up that can help Nate.

I drive the few short blocks to my house, praying the whole way that Lily will be home—and alone. I know it's not her boyfriend, Brandon's, fault that his brother is a crazed killer, but the truth is being around him now makes me really, really uncomfortable. It's another reason I've been staying with Declan since I got out of the hospital. Well, that and the fact that it's not exactly easy to convince him to let me out of his sight for longer than I spend at Beanz. And most days, even that is pushing it. I've grown used to looking up from my spot in the kitchen to see him ordering coffee or lounging at a table, a book in his hands.

I pull onto my street and breathe a sigh of relief as I spot Lily's car in the driveway, by itself. Brandon's car is nowhere to be seen. Thank the goddess.

I'm still reveling in my good fortune when I walk in the front door and find my best friend sitting on the couch, drinking a martini from an extra-large margarita glass and painting her toenails cyanide green. Neither is a good sign.

"What's wrong?" I demand, dropping my bag by the door and approaching her cautiously. When she's in this mood, there's no guarantee that she won't bite.

"Nothing. Why?" She reaches for the martini, takes a huge gulp of it, then goes back to painting her toes. All without once looking at me.

"Try telling that to someone who actually believes it." I hold up the bag of chocolate-covered potato chips resting next to her on the couch. "We both know these only come out in times of extreme trauma. As does the nail polish. So spill."

She blows out a breath, shrugs. "Brandon and I broke up."

I ignore the spurt of relief that shoots through me. Now isn't the time for a happy dance, especially when I get my first real glimpse of Lily's face and realize her eyes are rid-rimmed and swollen.

"What happened?" I ask after it becomes obvious that no details will be forthcoming.

She looks at me in disbelief. "Oh, I don't know. Maybe it's the fact that his nut-job brother tried to kill my best friend?"

"Yeah, but Brandon had nothing to do with that." Why am I defending him? Brandon's given me the creeps for a while now and I should be thrilled he's out of Lily's life. And I am. I really am . . . only I hate seeing her look so sad.

"Maybe not, but he insists on defending Kyle. He keeps saying things like it must have been a spell, that Kyle would never do something like that without a good reason."

My skin crawls. "He thinks there's a good reason that Kyle raped, tortured and murdered four women?"

"That's what I said. And then—" Her voice breaks. She grabs the martini and drains it.

"And then?"

"He said the Council must have some reason for wanting you dead. That maybe Kyle was only doing what had to be done. That's when I gave the sick fucking bastard the boot."

The boot? Knowing Lily the way I do, I'm a little surprised I didn't get a call asking me to help her bury a body. "I'm sorry," I tell her. "I know how much you cared about him."

"No, I'm sorry," she answers. "I'm sorry that I ever brought them into our lives. I can't believe I did that to you."

"That's ridiculous. Kyle was going to get to me one

way or the other. It's not like I trusted him more because you introduced us."

"But still. I invited that monster into our house. Made you double-date with him." She shudders as she finishes the second coat of toenail polish and recaps the bottle.

But when she reaches for the martini shaker, I grab it away before she can pour another glass and drink herself straight into oblivion.

She glares at me but doesn't say anything. It's proof that her bad mood is lifting a little. "So, how are things with you and Declan?" she asks. "I haven't seen you much the last few days, so I figure that has to be a good sign."

"They're fine."

"Really?"

"Yeah."

I must not sound very convincing, because this time when she reaches for the martini shaker, she pours the drink and hands it to me. "Then what are you doing here?"

"It's . . . complicated."

She laughs. "Sweetie, when you decide to tangle with a man like Declan, you'd better like complicated. It's pretty much his middle name."

"It really is. But that's not why I came over. I actually wanted to talk to you about something else."

"Oh yeah?" Her eyes narrow with interest. "Well, go ahead and spill then."

I take a long sip of the martini she handed me, searching for a little Dutch courage. The vodka burns on its way down my throat, but it takes only a moment for the fire to turn into a pleasant warmth. As it does, I settle myself on the couch beside Lily and reach for the tarot cards she always keeps in a basket on top of the coffee table. "It's not about me."

She eyes the cards. "So, there's another person's future you want me to tell you about?"

"Actually, yes."

"Declan's?" She sits up straighter, pulls the cards to her.

"No. Not Declan." I pull the picture of Shelby out of my pocket and lay it on the table in front of her. Then I tell her everything that Nate told me.

She has tears in her eyes before I'm halfway done. Lily may talk a good game, but she's the biggest softie in the book. Long seconds pass before she reaches for the picture of Shelby, runs her fingers over it once, twice. Then she sorts through the deck and pulls out the Sun card.

After laying it in the center of the table, she hands me the deck and tells me to shuffle.

"Why me? This is for Shelby."

"Yes, but you're the closest thing to a seeker we've got in this room, so you're elected. Besides, you know more about Shelby than I do."

"That's not true," I say, even though I'm already shuffling. "I told you everything."

"You think you did."

"What's that supposed to mean?" I set the cards down with a definite slap.

"You want me to tell you the future, right? I'm telling you the future as I see it, so shut the hell up and let me do my job." She picks five cards off the top of the deck and lays them out on the table—two on either side of the Sun and one crossing it.

"This is the World spread," she tells me. "It's the best place to start when looking for someone that's alive."

I nod, but my head is still whirling with what she said—and what she didn't. What did she mean about there being more for me to tell her? Am I missing something? And if so, what? I don't know Shelby, don't even know if it's possible for me to do this. But if it is, and if there is something I'm not seeing, I better figure out what it is pretty damn quickly.

I want to pepper Lily with questions, but she's already in reading mode. Her fingers linger over the Sun card for long seconds before moving on to the others. I don't know tarot very well—I have always relied on Lily for this part of Heka—but the spread doesn't look too bad to me.

None of the cards that I consider particularly menacing are there, at least none of the ones that normally pop up in my readings. I can only consider that a good thing since mine are usually so awful that I've made Lily stop doing them for me.

Still, I'm impatient. I want to know what she sees, but when Lily's reading tarot, she can't be rushed. The meaning of the cards mingles with something else inside her, some bit of foresight that allows her to get a really good grasp of the picture at hand.

"She's alive," Lily says after a minute. She's touching the first card in the spread—the Seven of Pentacles. "But everyone involved in the situation is frustrated. Her parents are terrified, the cops baffled because they have no real leads. Even the people who have her—" She closes her eyes for a second, concentrating. "I can't get a read on them, but they're also getting frustrated. Little Shelby is more trouble than she's worth. She cries all the time; nothing makes her happy. What are they supposed to do? If she doesn't shut up, someone will hear her."

A chill runs down my spine at the words, and the sing-songy way Lily says them. Her body's right in front of me, but I know that she's gone far away. I want to scream at her to come back, to tell her that it's dangerous, but she wouldn't thank me for it. This is what she does—what I asked her to do. It's not her fault that I'm suddenly filled with an overwhelming trepidation, a sickness in my stomach that warns me this reading isn't going to end as well as I had hoped.

She moves on to the second card. It's the Seven of Wands, the siege card that pictures a man defending himself against six other wands. "Whoever has Shelby is anticipating an attack. They will be the ones to start it, but whether they finish it is still up in the air. But their resolve is strong. They're determined to make it through, to win, no matter what they have to do or whom they have to kill."

The chill becomes a full-blown shivering. Dread starts in the pit of my stomach, a small ball that gets colder and more deadly with every second that passes. My palms and the bottom of my feet start to ache, and I know it won't be long before I have to listen as my hopes for Shelby crash and burn around me.

The third card, the King of Cups, is the contradiction card, the one that warns that things are not what they seem. As Lily talks about it, I try to puzzle out what is being hidden—besides Shelby herself. This is the card of ulterior motives and hidden agendas, and I can't help but wonder what we're missing. Is this not a straightforward kidnapping? And if it isn't, what is the real motive? Murder? Sexual abuse? Or something darker? Something involving black magic?

I know the odds are against the kidnapping being

magic related. This is a human child in the human world. And yet . . . something niggles at me. Some detail I've failed to pick up on or one I haven't yet learned. Whatever it is, there's more going on here than meets the eye.

The more I think about this, about Shelby, the more nauseated I get—until it takes every ounce of self-control I have to stay seated as Lily's hand brushes over the fourth card, the Three of Swords. This card is secrets—I know because it shows up in my readings a lot. It's not a bad card, has no harsh meanings associated with it, yet as I stare at it, I start to wonder.

No, please, no. I don't want to. I don't want to.

The voice comes out of nowhere, slams into me with the force of an eighteen-wheeler at top speed.

I won't. I won't. I—

I hear a high-pitched scream deep inside my mind and then a silence so ominous it scares the hell out of me. It's Shelby. I don't know how I know, but I do.

Helpless, hurting, I wait for more, for something else to come out of the unsettling quiet. It takes longer than it should, so long that I start fearing the worst. But then Shelby finds me again. She's whimpering now. Begging. Crying. Pleading.

Don't make me. Please don't make me.

I don't know what's going on, what they're forcing that poor child to do, but her fear is palpable inside me. And for the first time since my powers unlocked, I pray for them to come. Pray for that soul-deep compulsion that takes over my mind, my body, my very will, and drags me out into the world in search of evil.

I've spent the last few days terrified that I would feel it again, but now I want it. Now I'd do anything for it.

Suffer anything if it means finding the terrified little girl whose fear is ripping at the corners of my mind.

I reach for the card. I know better, but I do it anyway. Maybe if I can touch it, I can see her, find her. But my fingertips sizzle the second they come in contact with the Three of Swords and I yank my hand away. Damn it. Lily always warns me not to touch any of the cards once she lays them out in the spread, but I always thought that was just because she didn't want me to disrupt the flow of energy during the reading.

But that fire, that sear, was something else entirely. I turn my hand over, stare at the blisters starting to form on the three fingertips that touched the card. They burn, ache, and I know I should run some cool water over them. But the pain in my hands is nothing compared to the pain rising up inside me, slowly consuming me from the inside out.

With it comes fear of the most bitter kind. I'm not going to be able to find Shelby. At least, not until it's too late.

With this realization, the questions that have haunted me since I found Lina down by Town Lake rear their ugly heads once more. Why do I have this power? Why do I see these things, if I can't do anything but relive them after they've happened? What's the point of living through the pain, if I can't do anything to stop what I see?

What's the point of seeing little Shelby if she's doomed to suffer anyway?

Lily reaches for the last card, and even she seems hesitant. She's staring at the burn on my hand, trying to puzzle out what it means. I can tell from the look on her face that in this one moment, she is as lost to the darkness as

I am now. It's a sobering realization, especially considering we've always been careful not to tread too close to the shadows.

That care is gone now, and—I'm afraid—so is the light.

How can it not be after what I've seen since my gift came to me? After what I've seen and done? Even Lily's been affected by the stain working its way through me. But at least she can still find her way back.

The thought comes out of nowhere and makes me shakier than I already am. Part of me wants to end this now, to run screaming out of the room as if my hair's on fire. But that won't solve anything.

Plus, the reading still needs to be finished, the spread closed. And maybe, just maybe, a clue can be found that will help Nate. I hold on to that thought, keep it in the forefront of my mind, going over it again and again like a chant.

Or a prayer.

The last card is the Ten of Swords. I'm shuddering before Lily even picks it up, the fear overwhelming now. It's inside me, pinging around. Ripping at me until I can barely think, barely breathe.

There's a part of me that recognizes this feeling. There's no compulsion, no need to go tearing out of the house in search of something—someone—but the rest is the same. The sickness, the horror, the plea deep inside me for this to be something, anything, other than what I think it is.

The Ten of Swords is an ending, not a beginning, and now that I understand where it's positioned, it seems so much more menacing than I originally gave it credit for. This is the warning, the finale. The card that suggests there is no more to know, no more to learn, nothing else to find. If this is the advice position—what we're supposed to do to help find Shelby—then it's pretty much as nefarious a card as I have ever seen. It implies there's nothing else. No chance to save Shelby. No chance to set things right.

But I won't accept that. I can't. Otherwise, what's the point of having power?

Lily intones a few words—ritual words in ancient Egyptian—as she closes out the spread. Then she turns to me, face white and eyes alarmed. "Xandra, are you all right?"

I try to tell her that I'm fine, but my teeth are chattering so badly that I can't get the words out.

"Damn it!" she yells, reaching for the blanket off the back of the couch. "You're freezing."

She throws it over my shoulders, starts to wrap it around me, but before she's done much more than close the two sides together, a powerful knock sounds against the wood of the front door.

Lily jumps and I can see the indecision on her face even through the pain wracking my body. Should she open the door or not? Normally, we'd let it go, but whoever's on the other side sounds like he or she means business. She looks at me, but I'm in no shape to make the call. I'm a trembling, aching mess currently one step away from being scared of my own shadow.

Seconds later, the choice is taken out of our hands. There's a loud pop followed by a wrenching noise. The door flies open to reveal Declan standing at the threshold.

And he doesn't look happy.

Five

"What the hell have you done to yourself?" he demands, storming through the small foyer and into the living room. A careless flick of his hand has the door slamming closed behind him while a second flick has the tarot cards flying off the table like confetti.

He's at the couch now, all tense and brooding and completely pissed off as he stares down at me. "This is what you blew me off for?" He picks me up as if I weigh nothing and starts to carry me down the hallway toward my room.

Lily runs behind us. "Is she okay?" my best friend asks anxiously.

"She will be." Declan barely glances at her. "I'll take it from here."

Lily doesn't argue. I think Declan intimidates her way more than she wants to admit. So I start to protest—he can't just barge in here and take control whenever he wants—but the warmth of his body seeping into mine feels so good. So safe. Already the chills are calming down to a more reasonable level. And the pain, while not completely gone, is a lot better as well.

"What are you doing to me?" I finally ask. My teeth are still chattering, but at least the words are recognizable now. "How can you—"

"I'm taking care of you," he answers. "Which I would have been doing all along if you'd told me what you planned to do."

He sets me down on my bed without another word, crosses to my bathroom. Seconds later, I hear him turn on the bathtub tap.

Then he's back, stripping off my jeans and shoes and sweater like I'm a child. Or an invalid. Again I think about protesting, but it feels good for him to be in charge, just feels good to let him handle the details when my brain and body are so overloaded I can barely remember to breathe.

When I'm finally naked, Declan picks me back up and carries me into the bathroom. The water hasn't gotten very high yet, so he grabs a towel and wraps it around me. Then he sits on the thick edge of my bathtub with me on his lap, and starts to rock. He croons wordlessly to me as he does.

"I'm okay," I tell him. Not that I want him to stop, but as we sit here, I realize that I'm not the only one shaking.

"I know." He grinds the words out between clenched teeth.

I struggle against his hold a little, sitting up so that I can look into his face. It's drawn and tight, cheeks hollowed out and eyes burning. He looks like a different man than the one I went to bed with this morning—he's frazzled and worried and completely stressed out. It hurts me to see him this way, especially because I know I'm responsible. My magic, the way I live my life, is doing this to him.

"I'm sorry." Now I'm the one holding him.

For long seconds he doesn't answer, just presses me against him. He holds me tighter, then slips the towel from around me and lowers me gently into the bathwater.

It's hot—really hot—and it feels good. The last of the achy, cold feeling leaves me, a strange, floaty lethargy taking its place. My eyelids want to drift closed, but I don't let them. I need to talk to Declan about Shelby, need to tell him what I felt. What the tarot cards said. See if he can help.

But first I want to know how he knew that I was in trouble. We're soulbound, yes, but I can't sense him when we're apart. I don't know his mood or what he's doing or if he's in danger. So how did he know that I needed help, needed him?

I ask him, and his first response is a searing look and an even more searing kiss. "I felt your distress. I didn't know what was causing it, didn't know if you were in danger, if you'd found another body, if someone was hurting you." He closes his eyes and shudders as his hands reach for mine.

This time, I do let my eyes close as I settle against the back of the bathtub. He needs a minute to regain his equilibrium and so do I. I hate how vulnerable I always appear to Declan. I want him to think of me as strong and smart and capable, not some damsel constantly in need of being rescued.

And yet I have to admit that it feels nice. Not the being rescued part, but the knowing someone cares, really cares, about what happens to me on a very different level than my family or my friends.

Declan shifts, slides over, and I open my eyes just in time to see his still-jean-covered legs slide into the water on either side of my shoulders. Then he's leaning down, pressing kisses against my temple, over my hair. "I need a minute," he says softly. "To convince myself that you're really okay."

I don't move, don't breathe, terrified of doing something to end this moment. Declan is never unsteady, never exposed, never vulnerable. Not in front of me or anyone else. The fact that he is now, and that he's sharing it with me—even if it's only because he can't help himself—is a huge concession on his part. I want to savor it. Not because I enjoy seeing Declan shaken up and worried, but because I know this is another step toward intimacy, another step down the path Declan and I are destined to walk together.

I don't know how things are going to end between us—though there's a big part of me that is sure this will end badly—and for once I don't care. Everything in me yearns toward him, wants to protect him. To share with him. To love him.

The word catches me off guard, freaks me out a little, so I shove it down deep inside me. I'm already feeling vulnerable and confused. The last thing I need to do is try to deal with feelings like that in addition to the others that are ricocheting around inside me like bullets gone terribly awry.

Eventually Declan raises his head and the iron grip he has around me slowly loosens. I bite my lip to keep from whimpering, from begging him to hold me just a little longer. I expect him to move away, to complain about my carelessness or the fact that his jeans are soaked up to the knee.

He does none of the above. Instead, he reaches for the bath gel I keep on the shelf that runs beside the tub. It's homemade—a relaxing blend of lavender, rosemary and ylang-ylang made especially for me by my sister Rachael.

She's the healer in the family, and the one who makes herbal shampoos and lotions and a million other things.

Declan squeezes some of the bath gel onto his hands, rubs them together. Then he leans forward and glides those hands all over me. He starts at my neck, skims down my back and then up my arms to my collarbone before going lower to tickle my ribs and belly button.

My pulse quickens—I can't help it, can't control it. I never can when Declan is touching me—even now, when I know what he's doing is meant to soothe and relax me. My whole body goes on alert, my sex softening as my nipples harden.

I know he sees my response, feels the restless way I start to move in the water. But he doesn't pause what he's doing. He soaps his way over my stomach and up my rib cage before gliding his hands up and over my breasts with the utmost care.

I gasp, arch into his touch. I can't help it. Even upset, I long to feel his hands on my breasts, long for him to cup the weight of them while he pinches my nipples just the way I like.

He doesn't do that, though. Instead, he skims over them like they're just another part of my body. Then he moves lower to soap up my thighs and knees and calves. He's gentle with me, tender, careful not to press against any of the fading bruises left over from my encounter with the madman. I know it drives him nuts to see them, but tonight he doesn't show his angst by so much as an uneven breath or muffled curse.

When he's washed every part of me—even my toes— Declan turns the water back on and rinses me thoroughly. Then reaches for the plastic cup I keep on the same shelf and fills it up.

"Scoot down," he tells me in a voice filled with gravel, the first indication I have that he isn't quite as unaffected as he's trying to make me believe. I do what he says, and he tips my head back before slowly, carefully pouring the water over my hair.

He squirts some shampoo into his hand, then begins gently combing it through my hair. The last of the panic and confusion ebbs away under his tender ministrations, utter relaxation taking the place of those feelings. My eyes start to close, but I force them open, keeping them fastened on his.

Lying here in this bathtub as he cares for me, I feel more vulnerable than I ever have in my life. And also more protected. Declan's face is only a few inches above mine, his eyes locked onto mine as he washes my hair with a gentleness I didn't know he had in him. In their depths I see him, really see him in a way I'm not sure I ever have before.

There's torment there, a dark fire he doesn't even try to hide.

Strength, more of it than I think even he realizes.

Rage, a slow burn that blankets everything going on inside him.

And deep inside, locked behind the few emotions he doesn't mind showing, is love. Kindness. Tenderness. For me. I know it's all there for me.

I know he feels it, too. This nebulous connection between us, different from the soulbound thing but no less powerful for all of its delicate fragility.

He starts to rinse my hair out and I reach a hand up because I can't stand the pain of not touching him for one more second. I brush my thumb over those insanely perfect lips of his, cupping his cheek with my hand. His breathing hitches, stops. Then he turns into my touch and presses a warm, lingering kiss in the center of my palm.

"Declan. I . . ." I don't know what to say, don't even know what I want to say.

"Sssh." He places a wet finger against my lips. "I've got you, Xandra. I swear I've got you."

The emotion in his eyes grows more raw and powerful with each second that passes and still I don't look away. I can't. I'm trapped like a moth around a flame, desperate for whatever part of him he'll let me have.

I know it's in my eyes, know he must see my own vulnerability and desperate need as clearly as I see his. And in this one tremulous but perfect moment, it feels right. In a world spinning so rapidly beyond my control, it feels . . . good.

He conditions my hair with the same care that he washed it and by the time he's done, I'm shaking all over again, this time for very different reasons. He pops the drain, helps me stand, then dries me off before sweeping me back into his arms and carrying me to my bed.

Then he moves to my dresser, one of the few things that didn't burn in the fire I set last week with my less-than-stellar magic. He pulls out a nightshirt. But when he comes back to me and tries to slip it over my head, I rip it from his hands. Throw it across the room. And reach for him. Just him.

He meets me halfway, slams his mouth down on mine in a kiss so intense, so powerful, so *possessive* that it feels like a brand. Which should offend my feminist sensibilities but doesn't because the kiss I'm giving him is exactly the same.

Lust—raw, carnal, overwhelming—rises up in me. I

reach for the hem of his T-shirt and fumble the thing over his head before going for the button on his jeans. They prove to be more difficult, not just because my hands are shaking so badly, but because the bottom half of each leg is wet and heavy and clinging to his calves.

He curses as he wrestles with them, his voice a low, guttural growl. Seconds later he gives up the fight, mutters a spell that has the jeans disappearing into thin air. Any other time I'd probably be awed—transubstantiation is a rare gift in the Hekan world, and a difficult task no matter how talented the practitioner. But right now all I care about is that Declan is naked and aroused and pressed intimately against me.

I wrap my arms and legs around him, desperate— starved—for the feel of him inside me. He has other ideas, though, and as he presses slow, sweet kisses to my throat and shoulders, I know he plans another long, drawn-out seduction.

I can't take that, though, not now when my entire body is threatening to spontaneously combust. Bracing a foot on the bed for leverage, I roll us over until I'm the one on top, looking down at him.

His eyes are dark and bottomless, filled with the same urgency that's tearing at me with razor-sharp claws. I push myself into a sitting position, then sink down on him in a move so smooth and quick, it has me moaning and him jerking beneath me.

Desperate—delirious—with desire, I start to move, settling into a rhythm that has Declan's body arching beneath mine and his eyes rolling back in his head. One of his hands goes to my breast, pinching and plucking at my nipple, while the other fastens itself to my hip in a gesture so possessive it takes away what little breath I've managed to hold on to. And then he's lifting his hips, driving himself deeper inside me.

The tension is building inside me, hotter and sweeter and more desperate than ever until nothing matters but Declan and the way he feels inside me, the pleasure that slams through me with every stroke, every touch, every breath.

Declan is close, too. I can feel it in the rock-hard thighs that have gone rigid beneath me and the strong fingers that clutch my hips so tightly that I may very well have new bruises when this is over. I don't mind—it's exhilarating, not to mention sexy as hell, to know that I've driven him to this—that I've brought a man of Declan's strength to the brink of mindlessness.

Sensation swamps me at the thought and my eyes drift closed. I'm right there at the edge, my body poised to explode with just one more—

"Xandra."

My eyes spring open at the dark command in Declan's voice and once again lock onto his. It's what he wanted, what he needed. And—I'm not surprised at all to realize—that it's what I so desperately needed from him as well. Proof that there's a connection between us.

Declan chooses that moment to slide his hand up from my breast to my collarbone, his long fingers circling my neck in a moment of utter domination, utter possession that might have felt threatening if it was anyone but him holding me like that. But it is Declan, and his touch feels both as hot as hell and as natural as breathing to me.

His thumb comes up, rubs over my lips again. This time I bite him, hard, and that's all it takes. His hips slam into mine and I shatter. He's right there with me, and as his body pulses against mine—as he empties himself into me—the pleasure swamps me, takes me over.

For long, endless seconds there is nothing but Declan and me and the soul-searing ecstasy we bring each other. And though I know better, though life has taught me better, I can't help thinking that I want it to be like this between us forever.

Six

For long moments, I just lie there on top of Declan, too drained to move. Usually when we make love it energizes me, makes me feel like I can take on the world. But tonight I don't want to move, don't want to think, don't want to do anything but lie here and pretend the whole world away. I want, just for a little while, for it to be only Declan and me.

No ACW. No Shelby. No worries about being soulbound. Just two people who like and respect each other—two people who just happen to catch fire the moment they touch.

Yet even as the wish flits through my head, I know it's not to be. It's been seven years since our first kiss, but only two weeks since we met again, even less than that since we've become an actual couple, and there is so much I don't know about him. So much I don't want to know. So many questions I'm afraid to ask.

But that's on me, not on him. As are these overwhelming, all-encompassing feelings for him that well up inside me when I least expect them to. I can't help the way I feel, though. I can't help the hold he has over me any more than he can help the one I have over him. And it's not just the soulbound thing. It's the way he looks at me.

The way he touches me, as if I'm fragile, important, *precious*. It's the way he respects my strength and my right to do things on my own, but is always there to pick up the pieces when I hit the wall. And I've hit that wall a lot since my powers have kicked in. I can't forget that Declan's been there, every time, to put me back together.

Part of me knows it's dangerous to feel so much for him, especially when things are so uncertain between us, when it would be easier for him to kill me than to live with this tie between us. Oh, deep inside, where logic has no place, I know he'll never hurt me. I know he would rather die than let anything bad happen to me. After all, he's saved me from death twice in the last two weeks. If he'd wanted me dead, it would have been easy enough to just walk away when I needed him most.

He didn't do that, though.

And still, I'm afraid. Not of him so much as the forces that surround us and make my feelings for him so improbable, so impossible. There's a darkness in him that I can't touch, and though he keeps it under wraps, I know it's there. I can feel it in him as surely as I can feel his skin hot and slick against mine.

And still I cling to these moments of peace with bloody, battered fingertips. Declan's right about one thing—I do feel fragile right now, as if I'll crack if one more rug is pulled out from under me.

Declan sighs, his hand tangling in my short, razor-cut hair. I can feel his need to speak just as I can feel his hesitation. Maybe, like me, he is unwilling to shatter the quiet between us. Maybe, like me, he knows just how much we need it.

The minutes tick away as I listen to the steady thump of his heart beneath my ear. I should get up, take a shower, let him breathe. But he's still inside me, still hard, and I find myself unable to break this most tangible connection between us.

Eventually, though, he says, "Tell me about Shelby."

I don't ask how he knows her name—sometimes I think he knows everything. Or at least is powerful enough to get whatever information he wants or needs with a flick of his metaphorical magic wand.

"I don't know much," I answer, lifting my head to look at him.

"Tell me what you do know." He presses my head back to his chest and wraps his other arm around my waist so that I'm anchored to him. So that I can't move away. Not that I have any plans to try.

I tell him what Nate told me and what Lily's tarot cards said. He listens in silence, interrupting only to ask pertinent questions—many of which I don't know the answers to. When I've finished relating what I know, he doesn't speak for the longest time.

I do squirm away now, the anxious feeling building inside me again as I think about Shelby, scared and alone. I can feel my mind drifting, can feel it trying to connect back to her again. It's the first time I've ever had a conscious awareness of my magic taking control— usually it just grabs me by the throat and drags me wherever it wants me to go—and I wonder if I'm finally getting a grip on it. Or if the control is simply because I'm so close to Declan, whose command of Heka is no less than terrifying.

Whatever it is, I'm grateful. I know that I can't leave Shelby there alone, suffering, if there's any way that I can help her.

Declan doesn't protest when I scramble off him, just

follows my progress across the room with watchful eyes. I grab my sleep shirt and tug it over my head, then go into the bathroom to clean up. If I'm going to try to connect with Shelby, or whatever the hell I did earlier, I'm not going to do it all sex-mussed and naked.

When I come back into the bedroom a couple of minutes later, Declan is sitting, cross-legged and nude, in the middle of my bed. For a second I can't do anything but stare. He's so damn gorgeous that it freezes me in place, and even though I'm completely satiated, I feel a familiar heat start low in my abdomen.

He smiles at me and raises an eyebrow in a wicked invitation I have absolutely no intention of accepting. And just to make that clear—to Declan and myself—I grab a pair of old and very unattractive sweatpants out of my oh-so-comfortable-but-never-to-be-worn-in-public drawer. Only after I've yanked them up my legs and into place do I dare to settle myself on the bed.

Amusement flashes into Declan's eyes—making him look a million times younger—but it disappears so quickly that I barely have a chance to process it. Unfortunately, it's not the only thing to disappear. Seconds later, I watch in astonishment as my pants melt right off my legs and into nothingness.

"Are you freaking kidding me?" I yelp.

He just shrugs. "I like your legs." Then he leans over, trails a finger up my calf, over my knee and around to my upper thigh. He plays with me for a second, rubbing up and down my sex before circling my clit a few times.

I press into his hand despite my best intentions, let my knees fall wide. He smiles in delight and now that he's proven his point—that he can make me want him with almost no effort at all—I think he'll take his hand away.

But he doesn't. Instead he increases the pressure until I'm gasping, stroking and circling until he sends me straight over the edge into another orgasm.

I'm still trembling when he pulls me into his arms, brushes soft kisses over my hair and forehead. "Was that strictly necessary?" I ask when I can find my voice again.

"I'm sorry. Making you climax is rapidly becoming an addiction." He strokes a hand down my arm, holds me close until I finally recover.

"You don't sound all that sorry."

I feel him grin against my hair. "Maybe sorry is the wrong word for it."

"You think?" I grab a pillow and smack him with it.

The next thing I know, I'm flat on my back and he's looming over me, his eyes laughing as he finds a ticklish spot on my ribs. "No!" I gasp, wiggling and writhing as I try to escape. I almost make it when my breast brushes against his palm and distracts him, but seconds later he intensifies his attack, refusing to stop even when I'm a giggling, squirming mess.

In self-defense, I try to tickle him back, but it turns out there's not a single ticklish spot on him. So then I try to roll him over, but he's so much stronger than I am that he's not budging unless he wants to. Finally I decide to fight dirty—since he obviously has no problem doing so—and I deliberately wiggle so that my breasts are pressed against his chest and my legs are tangled with his.

I can tell the moment he registers what I've done, because the laughter leaves his eyes. Is replaced by the intensity I know so well. And then he's inside me once more.

This time is slow and sweet and gentle, him easing me

to completion rather than hurtling me there. And when it's over, when he slips out of me before pulling the covers over my nearly comatose body, it occurs to me that I never tried to connect with Shelby.

Forcing my impossibly heavy eyelids open, I plan on telling Declan what I want to do as soon as I can muster enough energy to lift my head from the pillow. And find him watching me with wary, worried eyes. Too tired to do more than brush a comforting hand down his cheek, I snuggle against him and decide that we can talk later.

It's not until I'm drifting off to sleep that the truth occurs to me. That Declan deliberately distracted me with sex and tickling and that strong, beautiful body of his for the express purpose of keeping me from using my powers.

For the express purpose of keeping me from trying to find Shelby.

One more thought flits through my brain before exhaustion takes me over. What does he know that I don't?

It's dark.
   I'm scared.
   Cold.
   Hungry.
   Please, mister. Please don't turn the lights off. Please don't put me in the dark again. I promise I won't do it again. Please. I don't like the dark.

The voice in my head is young and feminine and scared. So scared. I try to figure out who it is, where it's coming from, but nothing is making sense. I was with Declan, at my house—

Please! The little girl is crying now, and in pain. I try to pinpoint the pain, to see what's causing it, but there's so much of it. Everything hurts. Everything burns, aches, throbs.

It's okay. I try to speak to her. *Honey, it's okay. Stop crying now. It's okay.*

She doesn't hear me.

Sweetie, please. I make my voice louder, more forceful. *Tell me where you are. Tell me how I can help you.*

She still doesn't answer.

The pain is getting worse—hers, mine, I can't tell. Everything's all muddled and I'm having a terrible time thinking straight. I know something is wrong, with the girl, with me, but I can't figure out what it is.

Sweetie. I try again. *Where are you? Tell me where you are and I'll come get you.*

She doesn't stop crying, but I hear her inhale sharply and I know that my voice has finally gotten through.

Who are you? she asks.

My name is Xandra. What's your name?

She sniffles a little and I get the impression that she's wiping her face. *I'm Shelby.*

The name strikes a chord in me. I wrack my brain, try to figure out how I know it—how I know her—but nothing comes. It's like everything before this moment is a totally blank slate.

I know I should be concerned by that, but for some reason I'm not. *It's nice to meet you, Shelby,* I say after a few moments of trying to get a handle on what's going on.

It's nice to meet you, too. She sniffles some more, but at least she's not crying anymore.

Can you tell me what's wrong? Maybe I can help.

I want my mommy.

Of course you do, sweetheart. Can you tell me where she is? I can get her for you?

She's at home.

Where's home?

Two-four-seven-one Sycamore Street. Her singsongy words are the musical recitation of a small child who has just memorized her address for the first time.

And where are you? Are you near Sycamore Street?

Fear.

Confusion.

Tears.

She's crying in earnest now, harsh, heartbreaking sounds that rip at me with each shaky inhalation she takes. I feel terrible, don't want to push her, but I need any help she can give me.

I don't know. I don't know where I am. It's dark. I'm scared. Please get my mommy. Please, Xandra.

Her confusion becomes mine, her fear tearing at me like the sharpest claws.

Oh no!

What's wrong? I snap out, responding to the increased urgency in her voice.

He's coming back.

Who's coming back?

She doesn't answer. *Shelby! Shelby! Are you okay? Who's coming back?*

No, no, no! She's wild now, hysterical. Pain drips from every syllable.

Shelby! I try to reach for her, but there's a wall between us, one I can't get through no matter how hard I batter at it. *Shelby!* I call again, but there's still no answer. Terror swamps me, threatens to pull me under. I fight it, but it's nearly impossible—especially when the pain starts. Deep, agonizing, a razor-sharp blade raking across my upper thigh.

Blood wells. Gushes from the cut—thick, red, viscous. More screams. More pleading.

Rough hands on my back, rolling me over. Rolling *her* over. I struggle to remain apart, not to get sucked into Shelby's tiny body. I can't help her then. But it's hard, impossible. Because I can feel him touching her, touching me. His hands positioning me on my side on the edge of the bed.

A whole new horror swamps me, but he doesn't touch her again, except to pull her leg forward and over. There's a drip, drip, drip sound as the blood hits something metal. The bed frame. No. A container. A chalice.

Oh goddess. Oh goddess. Oh goddess. No. No. No! It's me screaming now, not Shelby. She just feels the pain. She doesn't know what this is, doesn't know how much worse it's going to get. But I do. I do.

Shelby! I scream her name. *Answer me! Shelby, are you there?*

There's no answer. Just a low, ceremonial chant that registers only on the edges of my consciousness. I strain to hear the words, but they're soft and muffled, nearly indistinguishable. I know the rhythm, though. Have heard it before, though I don't know where or when or why. This kind of magic is far blacker than anything I have ever experienced.

Xandra! Xandra, help me!

But I can't help her, can't do anything but lie here as—

Burning agony explodes through my face, through the whole left side of my head. My ear rings and my eye feels like it's going to pop right out of the socket. I try to hang on to Shelby, to the connection between us, but everything is mixed up. Chaotic. Like I'm three steps behind where I should be and can't quite figure out how to catch up.

Xandra! Xandra! Xan—

And then there's nothing.

Seven

I wake with a start. Alone. Confused. Shivering. Terrified without knowing why. Reaching out an arm, I search for Declan's warmth. But his side of the bed is cold, empty. He's gone.

Not just gone-to-the-bathroom gone or in-the-kitchen-making-coffee gone. But well and truly gone. I can't feel him. He's not here, in my bedroom or in my house.

More confused than ever, I push myself into a sitting position, then immediately wish I hadn't as my whole body protests. It hurts. Goddess, it hurts so much. But why? I don't understand. I was fine when I went to bed, fine—

Xandra!

It's a psychic scream and it grabs me on a visceral level, wraps itself around me and squeezes until my heart feels like it's going to explode. And then my dream comes flooding back. Shelby. Blood. Pain.

Shelby! Now I'm the one screaming her name—and on a psychic plane I didn't even know I could reach. There's no answer. *Shelby! Shelby! Shelby!*

Nothing.

Totally freaked out now, I push the covers back and

swing my legs around to the side of the bed. Everything aches. Still, I have to get up. I need my phone, need to call Declan. I don't have a clue what's going on, but he might. Surely he can at least tell me if it's even possible that I connected with Shelby or if it was all just a nightmare brought on by my concern for her.

Before my powers kicked in, I'd never been prone to night terrors, but lately I've been getting them every night. Sometimes two or three times a night. Yet another reason why it's so strange that Declan isn't here. He knows how bad the nightmares get and he never leaves me alone while I'm sleeping, never leaves me to face them by myself. Especially when it's still dark outside. Which it is.

I glance at the clock. It's barely one in the morning. Which means I've been asleep about three hours. I think about my last encounter with Declan, how I was so sure that he had distracted me in an effort to tire me out and get me to stop asking questions. If that's true—and it's hard to imagine that it isn't—what reason would he have to do it? He might be dark, but he has a surprisingly large heart. I can't imagine a lost little girl not touching him.

Shelby. I call to her again, determined to find out if this is all just a figment of my overactive imagination. There's no answer.

I shove out of bed, determined to find my phone. And I end up falling flat on my ass, my legs completely unwilling to support me.

What the hell?

I grab onto the nightstand and shakily pull myself back up. My head is pounding, my leg throbbing, and the rest of my body is filled with dull aches and pains that weren't there when I went to bed.

I put my hand on my right thigh, start to massage it. Then I pull up short when I feel a long, thick scar stretching all the way down to my knee. Images from my vision tumble through my mind and I start to race to the bathroom. But I manage to take two steps before I'm on the floor again. *Damn it.*

Once again, I pull myself up. But the room's spinning around me, the dizziness and nausea from earlier back with a vengeance. Concerned now, I reach an unsteady hand out to the wall. Then I lean on it for support as I make my way slowly, slowly, into my bathroom.

By the time I get there, I'm pale, sweating, and my nausea has reached a critical stage. Dropping to my knees, I vomit the meager contents of my stomach, then continue with dry heaves for long, unpleasant minutes. Finally, it stops. Shoving away from the toilet, I try to get up.

I can't. I'm too weak to even get to my knees. Frustrated, angry, I press my forehead against the cool blue tile of my bathroom floor and wait for this—whatever it is—to pass. I'll try again in a minute or two.

But it turns out, I don't have to wait that long. The bathroom light flips on and I catch a glimpse of cyanide green toenails before I clap a defensive hand over my eyes.

"What the hell, Xan!" Lily crouches down next to me and lays a soft hand on my forehead. "Are you sick?"

"I don't think so," I croak. "I just—"

"Oh my God! What happened to you?" She helps me into a sitting position, then scoots me over a little so I can rest against the wall. "Did someone die? Did you go to another murder scene?"

"I've been in bed all night."

"Then what the hell happened to you?" Her eyes narrow. "Did Declan do this?"

"Do what?"

She grinds her teeth even as she fumbles around on the counter for a second. Then she's shoving my small, standing mirror in my face. "That. Did Declan do *that*?"

One glimpse and I suddenly understand her concern. The entire left side of my face is one big bruise and my left eye is nearly swollen shut. "No! Of course he didn't. He would never hurt me."

I reach a trembling hand up to poke at the bruises, then immediately wish I hadn't. Pain radiates from my temple to my jaw. My stomach sinks as I remember Shelby and the sudden agony of being punched. I pull my nightshirt up a few inches to stare at the long, jagged scar that runs the length of my right thigh. It's pink and raised and looks newly healed, as if the skin has just started to mend itself.

"What the hell is that?" Lily demands, leaning over me. "Dear goddess, Xandra. You're covered in cuts and bruises all over again. Are you sure nobody's dead?"

She's remembering the times I came home covered in injuries after finding Kyle's victims. Part of my gift—or curse, depending on how you think about it—is that I relive what the victim went through. While I don't suffer the broken bones and open wounds that they do, I do get bruises and marks that mimic those injuries.

Except Shelby is still alive. I was connected to her. I heard her cry, listened as she begged for help, felt her pain as it was inflicted. Unless . . . unless all that was posthumous and I just didn't know it.

The nausea's back with a vengeance. I lunge for the

toilet, barely making it before the heaving starts all over again.

An hour later, I'm sitting at the kitchen counter, a mug of tea liberally laced with whiskey cupped between my freezing hands.

"Try Declan again," Lily tells me as she ladles some chicken soup into a bowl for me.

"I just did. Still no answer."

"That's so weird."

"You're telling me." He's been so protective since that last incident with Kyle. I've barely been able to walk from point A to point B without tripping over him. Even when I'm at work, he calls or texts me a few times a day—in addition to stopping by for lunch. So for him to just disappear like this, with no warning, no phone call, nothing, is completely out of character. I'm beginning to think it's my turn to start worrying about him.

Except I already do. All the time. Which is another reason why this absence is freaking me out so much. The only reason for him to go AWOL like this is if he's doing something he knows I won't like. And since I'm a pretty open-minded kind of girl, the list of things I don't tolerate is pretty damn small—it starts and ends with black magic. Well, that and cheating on me. And since I doubt Declan's sleeping with anyone else, I can't help but wonder if what he's doing has something to do with the soul-deep scars and shadows that haunt his every move. I don't know what those scars are, but I know they're there. Just like I know there's a lot about his life before me—before us—that I don't know. That I may never know. I'm trying to be okay with that.

"Okay, then," Lily says, handing me the soup as she settles across the table from me. "Let's think this thing through."

"I've been doing nothing but thinking for the last hour," I tell her as I spoon up some soup. "I'm no closer to finding the answer than I was when you found me."

"Yes, but you're cleaner and steadier now. And you aren't trying to puke your guts up—all three things help with the advent of rational thought."

She has a point, so I just shrug. Take another bite of soup. It's not very good, but its heat slowly warms up my frigid center.

"Still no compulsion to go crashing out the front door?" Lily asks.

"None."

"Well, that's a good thing, right? Because if Shelby was actually dead, shouldn't you be able to feel it since you now have a connection to her?"

"I still don't know how my powers really work. I mean, Austin doesn't have many violent deaths, but there are some. However, I didn't have a compulsion to find that guy who was murdered here the other day."

"But he was never missing. The killer left his body in his house for his wife to find when she got home from work."

I think about her words. "You think my powers only kick in when people are lost?"

"It makes sense, right? Otherwise you'd be chasing after a dead body every night, depending on where you lived. But the way it works, how you have to stay with the body until it's not just found, but actually removed from its dump site makes me think the lost thing is a valid theory."

"Shelby's lost."

"She is." Lily nods. "She's lost and alone. She's scared. And she's being hurt. Why wouldn't you be able to sense her?"

"Because that's not what I do." I push away from the table, carry my half-full bowl of soup to the sink. Suddenly, I'm not very hungry. "I connect with people who have died violently. It's what my magic does, what it is."

Lily just snorts. "No offense, Xan, but you just said you don't know what your powers do. And how could you? You've had them for all of three weeks."

"So?"

"So you know as well as I do that magic changes, matures, the more you use it. Add to that your connection with Declan and frankly I'm a little surprised you aren't getting a new talent every day."

"That's not funny," I tell her, with a frown.

"It wasn't meant to be. Maybe when your powers first kicked in, you could only sense dead bodies, but things change. You've spent the last three weeks in almost constant contact with Declan freaking Chumomisto—and much of that contact has been pretty damn intimate if the noises I heard coming from your bedroom earlier meant anything."

"Lily!"

She holds her hands up in mock surrender. "I'm just saying. All that power, all that passion . . . Why wouldn't things start changing for you? It only makes sense. You know as well as I do that magic responds to all different kinds of energy. And sexual energy is one of the most powerful kind."

"I get it," I tell her with a mock scowl. "You don't have to keep harping on my sex life, you know."

"Sorry, I can't help it. We single girls have to get our thrills where we can find them."

"You've been single for less than twelve hours. I really don't think one day without sex qualifies you as in need of a thrill."

She snorts. "That's because you have no idea just how bad Brandon was between the sheets. If you did, you'd probably loan Declan to me for a night on purely humanitarian grounds."

I laugh. "No, I wouldn't."

"Well, that's not very BFF-like," she answers, pretending to pout.

"Sure it is. Because if Declan so much as looked at you that way, I'd have to kill you both. This way, I get to keep my BFF alive."

She thinks about my logic. "Well, when you put it that way . . . Good call."

"That's what I thought. Though I am sorry about Brandon being such a loser all the way around."

"Not your fault I picked a dud. But maybe, when the weirdness of your new life settles down a little, you could introduce me to Declan's very sexy brother."

"You're interested in *Ryder*?"

"You don't have to sound so surprised. He's pretty damn delicious. I wouldn't mind taking a couple of bites out of him."

"Well, when you put it like that . . . ," I tease, tossing her words back at her. "I'll make sure to introduce you the next time he's in town."

"Excellent."

Suddenly Shelby flashes back into my mind and the last trace of levity drains from me. How could I laugh with Lily—even for a second—when a little girl is out there somewhere, being hurt. Or worse.

Lily notices my shift in mood, and reaches out to squeeze my hand. "She's alive, Xandra."

"You don't know that."

"No, I don't. But I believe it. And you need to, too."

"Why?"

"Because it will break your heart if you don't. And, honestly, I'm not sure how much more heartbreak you can take."

Again, she has a point. Besides, how could it hurt? Thinking of finding Shelby alive might be the only thing that gets me through the next few days. Because, whether she's dead or alive, after speaking with her the way I did—after feeling her pain and her fear—there's no way I can just turn my back on her. I *am* going to find her. And when I do, I'm going to tell her that she's the bravest little girl I've ever met.

I should have told her that before, when we were talking. A sudden realization hits me, one that makes me believe, really believe, that Shelby actually is alive. "I talked to her."

"What?" Lily asks, looking up from where she's making another pot of tea.

"I talked to Shelby. It wasn't a dream. Obviously," I say, gesturing at the damage to my leg. "I never did that with any of the others. I felt their pain, lived through their deaths with them, but I never talked to any of them. I couldn't."

"Because they were dead."

"Exactly." Relief, pure and overwhelming, rushes over me. Because as much as I hate to think of Shelby suffering at the hands of some monster, I hate more to think of her dying alone and terrified. "And she isn't."

"That's what I like to hear!" Lily settles back down at the table, a big smile on her face. "So what are we going to do to find her?"

"We?" I ask.

"Hell, yeah, we. You got to do all the heroics last time. This time, I definitely want in."

"I'm not sure being tortured is actually heroic, you know."

"It is if you end up capturing the murdering bastard in the end." She pops a cracker into her mouth, chews pensively. Then she says, "What do you think we should do first? Do you want to try to reach out to her again?"

"I've already tried a couple of times. Nothing's happened. I think whoever hit her"—I gesture to my bruised face—"probably knocked her out." I deliberately refuse to think of other, worse scenarios.

"So, we just wait?"

"No." I reach for my phone, scroll through my contacts. "I think we should call Nate."

"And tell him what?"

"The truth. He already thinks I'm psychic—that's why he asked for my help. The fact that I've connected with Shelby shouldn't even have him raising an eyebrow."

"Maybe you're right. But you do realize that it's two o'clock in the morning, don't you?"

I freeze, my thumb suspended over his contact information. "Good point. But don't you think he'll want to know? He is the one who asked for my help, after all."

Still, I don't press SEND. Maybe Lily's right—maybe I

should wait until morning. I don't actually have much information for him. Maybe if Lily and I work at it—

That's when it hits me, a wave of power so all-encompassing that it sends my phone skittering out of my hand and across the table.

"Xandra?" Lily asks, leaning forward, a concerned look on her face.

Before I can answer her, another wave hits. This one actually picks me up and slams me back down into the chair with enough force to shatter the thing into a thousand wooden splinters.

Eight

"What the hell?" Lily scrambles around the table to help me up, but I throw out an arm to ward her off. Whatever is happening to me isn't good and I don't want her anywhere near it.

She freezes in place. "Xandra?"

"Give me a minute." I'm on the floor now, in the midst of the debris from the shattered chair. I have just enough time before the third wave hits to thank the goddess that I don't have a bunch of splinters in my ass. This one knocks me flat on my back. Then it lifts me up again, arching my back even as it spread-eagles me five feet off the kitchen floor.

"Xandra!" Lily wails.

I hit the ground again, this time even harder than before.

Totally disregarding my warning, Lily rushes toward me. She drops to her knees next to me, her hands going immediately to the back of my head, where she feels for bumps and bruises. "Are you all right?" she demands.

I try to answer her, to tell her to get back because the electricity is still zinging around inside me and I have a sick feeling that this—whatever this is—is far from over. But that last hit was so strong that it knocked the wind out of me. I've got absolutely no air, and no matter how hard I try to force my lungs to expand, nothing's happening.

"Xan?" The alarm on her face turns to full-out panic. "Oh dear goddess. Are you paralyzed? Are you dead?"

I shake my head, try once more to inhale. This time it works, and I suck in huge, noisy gulps of air. After a minute, I ask, "Do I look dead?"

"Kind of." Lily sags with relief, rests her forehead on my shoulder as she takes a few deep breaths of her own. "Don't ever do that to me again!" she says finally, her voice so high-pitched she sounds more like Alvin the chipmunk than my best friend.

Before I can answer, I feel the next wave building inside me. It's welling up, the power growing more and more massive with every second that passes. Alarmed, I scramble backward, away from Lily. Something tells me this is going to be the worst one yet and I don't want to hurt—

Flames break out on my arms and legs, ripple over my skin in waves. They don't burn me—at least I don't think they do—but I'm too busy trying not to catch anything else on fire to pay much attention to what's happening to me.

Lily screams, then does a fast crawl across the floor to the kitchen sink. She pulls out a fire extinguisher, but before she can fumble the key out of it, I'm being lifted again—this time so high that I can touch the ceiling without much effort. Even with the fire still licking over my skin, the only thing I can think is that this time it's really going to hurt me when this thing—whatever it is—drops me.

Sure enough, the fire winks out one second before I plummet to the ground. I try to curl myself into a ball in an effort to protect my spine, but I'm seizing before I hit the floor, my whole body jerking and convulsing in the throes of what I'm sure looks like a grand mal seizure, but it feels like something else entirely.

Even as it's happening, I'm completely aware of everything going on around me. Lily is screaming as she launches herself at the phone to dial 911. She's got it on speaker, so I can hear the emergency operator giving her instructions in between Lily's terrified screeches. I want to tell her that I'm okay, that I'm in here and I'm just fine, but my body is completely out of my jurisdiction. Whatever magical force has glommed on to me has got me completely under its control and it's not letting go until it's good and ready.

Time passes—seconds, minutes, I can't tell which— and then, finally, the energy flows out of me in one long, smooth wave. The seizing stops and my entire body just seems to collapse in on itself.

"Xandra?" Lily whispers, crawling back over to me. "Xandra, are you okay?"

My eyelids feel like they weigh a hundred pounds each, but somehow I manage to force them open. Lily's face is only inches from me and she looks like hell, like she's aged ten years in the space of the last five minutes.

I try to smile at her, but it must come out looking like a grimace because she squeaks, "Dear goddess. Is it happening again?"

"It's over," I assure her in a voice that sounds like I gargled with razor blades.

"Are you sure?"

"Yeah."

She collapses, stretching out on the floor next to me. "The paramedics are on their way."

"You should probably cancel them. I don't think there's anything in the medical books that covers what just happened to me."

"No shit. The 911 operator asked if there was any sign that something was wrong before you started to seize. Somehow I didn't think telling her you were doing a damn fine impression of the *Exorcist* would go over well." She sighs. "Still, I think you should let them check you out. You hit the ground pretty fucking hard."

"It feels like it," I grumble. "Declan's going to kill me. He leaves me alone for a couple of hours and I'm right back to where I was a week ago, covered in bumps and bruises and aching in places I didn't even know it was possible to hurt."

"Yeah, well, when he gets back, I'm going to give him a piece of my mind. This is his job, not mine."

"I think you handled yourself pretty well."

She snorts. "That's 'cuz you don't realize how damn close I came to peeing my pants. You caught on *fire*, Xandra."

"Oh yeah. With the seizure and everything, I forgot." I glance down. "Am I burned?"

"Amazingly enough, no. Like I said. Freaky. Freaky. *Freaky*. Exorcist. Shit."

Just then, the doorbell rings. Lily groans but rolls to her feet. "You're going to need to let them check you out."

"Are you kidding me?" I gesture to my face. "They'll drag me to the hospital for an MRI or CT scan or something."

"Maybe you should let them."

I growl at her, but she just blows me a kiss on her way to the door.

Reluctantly, I climb to my feet as well. Ignoring the pain in what I swear is every single muscle in my body, I walk into the family room, where Lily is letting two very nice-looking paramedics into the house. Hopefully, if I'm on my feet and lucid, they'll be more likely to believe that I'm all right.

But I've barely said hello to them when a fire truck pulls up behind the ambulance, lights and sirens blaring. Shit. Our neighbors are going to kill us.

It takes the paramedics about ten minutes to check me over. They do their best to convince me to let them take me to Brackenridge, but I think that has more to do with the bruises on my face and the broken chair in the kitchen.

My vitals are fine, and except for a goose egg on the back of my head, the rest of me is also relatively fine. Still, they seemed very concerned about whether I'm safe in my home, and while I really do appreciate it, I'm going to lose my mind if they don't get out of here ASAP. Because five minutes into their exam, it occurs to me why we might be having so much trouble reaching Declan. While I admit that I still don't know how this soul-bound thing works, it doesn't seem out of the realm of possibility that if something happened to him, it would definitely affect me as well. Which means that all of that weird stuff that just happened could have been my own magic's reaction to something going wrong—really wrong—with Declan.

The second I close the door behind the paramedics, I dive for the phone. But Declan's cell just rings and rings. Where is he? Why isn't he answering? I try not to panic, but it's hard—especially when everything just feels off. Even my skin feels too tight.

Sitting here worrying isn't doing me any good, though, so I might as well make myself useful. Lily is cleaning up the mess in the kitchen and I get up to give her a hand. I am the one who caused it, after all.

I've only taken two steps toward the kitchen when it hits me. I stumble into the wall, grab onto the door frame to keep from falling as my whole body starts to shake.

"Oh shit!" Lily yells, dropping the broom and rushing over to me. "Not again!"

"I'm fine."

"Yeah, you look fine." She reaches for her purse. "That's it. I'm taking you to the hospital."

I shake my head as fear wells up inside me. "I can't go."

"Bullshit. You're going."

"It's too late."

I stumble back to my bedroom, every step a battle against the energy raging inside me. *Please don't let it be Declan,* I pray. *Please, Isis, I beg of you, not Declan.*

I reach for a pair of jeans, yank them on. Then slip my feet into the first shoes I find—the pair of purple cowboy boots my mother foisted on me the last time I was home. Then I'm grabbing a jacket from the coat rack in the hall and tearing down the hallway to the front door.

"Where are you going?" Lily demands, standing in the middle of the living room, her hands on her hips and an exasperated expression on her face.

"It's happening," I tell her.

"What's happening?" Then her eyes grow wide. "Oh shit. No way!" She dashes down the hall to her room. "You're not going out there alone. Let me get dressed and I'll go with you."

"Hurry," I tell her, knowing it's useless to argue. Besides, I don't really want to do this on my own. If it is Declan's body I find . . . If it is him, I don't know how I'll survive.

The sick feeling inside me is growing with every second that passes. It's an itchiness, a low-grade vibration running through my veins. It's not bad yet, but I know from experience that this is only the beginning. But if Lily doesn't move it, I'm going to be in a world of hurt before I even step out of the house.

Seconds later, the electricity starts. Small, painful sparks that travel along my nerve endings—pop, pop, pop—one after the other. I can't take it anymore. I throw the front door open and head down the steps to the driveway. Once there, I bend over, brace my hands on my knees and concentrate on pulling deep breaths into my lungs.

The nighttime air makes it a little bit better, but with every second that passes, the compulsion is getting worse. The need to move, to search, to find, is taking me over a little more with each electric jolt that sweeps through me.

Turning to the left, I start to walk. Even as I tell myself to wait for Lily—even as my brain orders me to stop—my body keeps moving. I've waited too long. I'm firmly in the grip of the compulsion now and nothing can stop it, stop me, short of finding the body that caused all this.

I hear Lily slam the front door behind me. A string of inventive curses rings through the night air as she realizes I've taken off without her. Again I try to stop, or to at least turn, but it's no use. My body's been hijacked and I won't get it back until I've done what I need to do.

Seconds later, Lily's car engine starts up. Seconds after that, she's in the street, driving along beside me. "Damn it, Xandra, get in," she tells me, her voice hoarse with the same fear that's ricocheting inside me.

I don't argue with her, just jog around the car and hop into the passenger seat. "Thank you."

She just shakes her head. "I swear to the goddess, you're going to give me a heart attack one of these days."

"I know. I'm sorry. Turn right at the corner."

She follows my directions all the way through downtown Austin. I don't know where we're going, only where the compulsion tells me to turn—at least until we make the last turn. Then, suddenly, I know.

How could I be here again?

How could this be happening again?

Last time I'd had to charm the hell out of a cop to get on the grounds, and frankly, after how that turned out, I don't think I have a chance in hell of ever doing it again—even if I wasn't sporting enough bruises to qualify as an MMA fighter.

"Pull over," I tell Lily, who parallel parks in the first available spot.

"So, where are we going?" she asks.

I just point before climbing out of the car and heading toward the end of the street. The compulsion has me now and it's not letting go. The electricity has gotten wilder, hotter, until every breath I take is pure agony. I waited too long, took too long to get here. I pick up the pace, start to jog down the deserted street. I want, need, the pain to stop.

"Are you freaking kidding me?" Lily demands as she runs to keep up. She's about five inches shorter than I am, so the pace I'm setting is brutal for her shorter legs. I know it, even feel bad about it, but there's no way I can stop. The compulsion is pulling so hard that I'm afraid that any second it will yank me right off my feet.

"How many damn people die at the Capitol grounds anyway?"

"Too many, obviously." But seconds before we get to the driveway in front of the huge Austin Capitol, I veer to the left. Head down the sidewalk to the small parking lot for employees on the side of the grounds.

"Someone's dead back here?" Lily whispers loudly.

"I don't know. I guess." *Please,* I repeat for what has to be the millionth time, *don't let it be Declan. Don't let it be Declan.*

We reach a small patch of grass and flowers that stand outside the gate. There's a historical sign marking it as something—I don't bother to look at it—and a bunch of other signs that give directions to various places on the Capitol grounds. At first I think I'm meant to follow the signs to somewhere, but every time I take more than a step away from the center of the garden, the pain intensifies.

"This is it," I tell Lily. "It has to be."

"Right here?" she demands.

"I think so." I glance around, reach into my pocket for my cell phone and turn on the flashlight app. "Do you see anything?"

"Not unless you count that group of very drunk, and very much alive college students who must have wandered off Sixth Street." She points to the group of guys in question.

"I definitely don't mean them," I tell her, lowering my voice so we don't attract their attention. It's not that I think they'll try to hurt us—they look harmless enough. Besides, I'm pretty sure Lily and I can handle a few drunk twenty-year-olds. But if they come over to investigate, it's that much longer before I can figure out what the hell is going on. That much longer before I know if Declan is okay.

"Then I got nothing."

"Neither do I."

Just then, my phone pings. I glance at it, and nearly melt into a puddle of relief when I realize that Declan is the one texting me.

Sorry. Had something to take care of. On your front porch. Come let me in.

Something to take care of? Could he get a little more vague? Suddenly, I'm beyond annoyed. I've been to hell and back tonight worrying that something has happened to him and all he's got to say for himself is "Had something to take care of?"

Before I can type out an answer, my phone pings again.

Where are you?

My eyes narrow. The man is in serious need of a lesson, but now is not the time or place for me to give it to him. Especially since the compulsion's getting worse, the electricity zigging and zagging through me in an effort to hurry me up. Too bad it can't clue me in, because I have no idea where to go from here.

I text Declan back quickly, telling him where I am, and then I head over to the ornately carved bench Lily is standing beside.

The closer I get, the more the pain eases off, thank the goddess. "Did you find something?" I ask.

"No," she says with a shake of her head. "But I just remembered something I heard in a class once. I didn't pay much attention to it at the time, figured it was just a wild-goose chase."

A sliver of unease works its way down my spine. "What is it?"

"You know how nobody knows where the ACW's headquarters is?"

The sliver becomes an avalanche. "Yeah?"

"There are a few main theories, right? Alexandria, Cairo, Paris—"

"So what? What does that have to do with this?" I know I sound impatient, but the compulsion hurts. I just want to find this body, call Nate and let him deal with it.

"Well, my professor said that some people think the ACW's headquarters is in Austin."

"Yeah, and some people think it's on the moon. But we all know it's in the Egyptian desert somewhere, probably close to Luxor."

"Well, what if that's just what they want us to believe? My professor said that the Council moved to Texas over a hundred years ago, when the whole witch-hunt thing started to heat up over there."

"I didn't realize they had." I can't help looking at her a little askew. Lily's read a book or taken a class on just about everything at least once, which is one of the reasons I usually pay close attention to what she's saying. But this doesn't make any sense. The Egyptians, while definitely monotheistic now, have a deep and abiding pride in their heritage. I can't imagine that changing if they found a few practitioners of Heka.

Lily shrugs. "Me neither, but supposedly there was a rash of killings a number of years ago that sent the whole Hekan community scrambling for cover. The perpetrators were eventually found, and condemned to death, but by then a lot of the witches and wizards had gone underground."

"Underground," I repeat. "Not moved to *Texas*."

She holds up her hands. "I'm just telling you what I heard—that the ACW moved their headquarters to Austin and hid it somewhere downtown."

"Downtown. As in the Capitol grounds downtown?"

"You're the one who brought us to this little patch of grass. You tell me."

"That's the most ridiculous thing I've ever heard." I throw my arms up in defeat. "But if you think you can find it, who am I to stop you?"

"I didn't say I could find it. Just that it might be here." Still, she squats down, starts poking around. "What do you think an entrance to the ACW's headquarters might look like?"

I have no idea. But if Lily's right, we need to find it soon. Before I end up electrocuted by all this damn energy inside me. "Shouldn't it be big and decked out in gold and powerful stones or something? They aren't exactly the kind to hide their lights under a bushel."

"They are when they're being hunted."

It's a good point. So even though I'm pretty sure it's a waste of time, I start to look. But ten minutes later, we've still had no luck and I'm in worse shape than ever. The compulsion is riding me hard, ripping me apart from the inside out until I feel like I've been scraped raw, right beneath the skin. It's a weird feeling, an excruciating one, and I'm not sure how much longer I can take it without screaming.

I must look as bad as I feel, because Lily is suddenly by my side, easing me down onto the closest park bench.

"You okay, sweetie?" She reaches into her bag and pulls out a small bottle of water. She hands it to me.

I take it gratefully, but before I can do much more than twist off the cap, Declan steps out of the shadows and into the glow of the nearest streetlamp.

"What. The. Fuck. Are. You. Doing. Here?"

Nine

He looks angrier than I've ever seen him. Which is fine, because I'm pretty damn pissed myself. After the night I've had, the absolute last thing I need is for him to come in here and play the big alpha he-man with me. I know he warned me not to go wandering off without him right now, not when things with the Council are so uncertain, but he knows I can't control the compulsions. Besides, if he wanted to come with me, he shouldn't have snuck out of my bed the second I fell asleep.

"I could ask you the same question." I keep my voice deliberately calm, refusing to give him the response he's looking for.

Declan's eyes narrow and Lily sucks in a loud breath. I half expect her to run for cover—which is fine, I've got this—but instead she puts a hand on my shoulder in obvious solidarity. And people wonder why she's my best friend? There's nobody else I'd rather have at my back. Except the enraged man in front of me, but he pretty much screwed that up when he left without so much as a note letting me know what was going on.

"I came because you told me you were here."

"Hmm, that was nice of me. Telling you where I was so you wouldn't worry. How very mature of me."

His jaw clenches and I can all but hear his teeth grind together, but I'm not backing down. Not this time. "This is really how you want tonight to go?" he asks, coming closer in what I can only assume is an attempt to intimidate me. Too bad it isn't working.

"You don't get to blame me. This is your choice, not mine."

"I told you. I had something to do."

"Yeah, well, now I have something to do."

"Right here?" He crouches down on my right side, and with a quick squeeze of my shoulder, Lily steps back. I don't blame her. It's all I can do to hold myself up to the crushing dominance of his personality right now. Lily doesn't stand a chance, especially considering she doesn't have the same soul-deep belief that he won't hurt her that I have.

"It appears so." I'm not giving an inch.

He reaches out, gently circles my right wrist with his fingers. Then slides his hand—slowly, slowly—up my arm and shoulder, until he reaches the bend where my neck meets my shoulder. He rests his hand there for long seconds, before continuing the journey up to my cheek. He strokes his fingers softly over my jaw, his eyes ablaze with emotion, and for the first time I realize it's not anger motivating him. It's fear.

That knowledge brings my own anger down a few notches as I try to put myself in his place. After everything that's happened to me in the last couple of weeks, is it any wonder he freaked out when I wasn't at home? Yes, it could have been avoided if he'd just answered his phone—or if he hadn't left to begin with. But that doesn't mean I can discount his concern.

"Look at me, Xandra."

It's no less a command for the fact that he whispers it, and while I might have ignored him just a couple of minutes ago, understanding tempers my reaction. Besides, if I'm honest, I want to look at him. I want to see in his eyes the truth of where he's been and what he's been doing. I don't have a claim on him, I know that, but I've also spent the better part of the last couple of hours worrying if he was injured or dead. Common courtesy doesn't take much.

I turn my head, finally prepared to explain what is going on, but I never get the chance. Because this time it's Declan who loudly sucks air in through his teeth.

"What the hell?" he demands, fear at my disappearance forgotten. He moves in front of me, slides his fingers around to the other side of my jaw, probing delicately. "Who did this to you?" His voice vibrates with fury, with power.

It takes me a second to remember what he's talking about—so much has happened tonight that I actually forgot that the whole left side of my face looks like someone took a baseball bat to it.

"Xandra." It's another command, one I might feel inclined to defy if I didn't already feel the healing warmth flowing in from his fingertips. The ache I've carried since I woke up from the dream about Shelby slowly dissipates under his oh-so-tender ministrations.

"It's been a rough night," I finally tell him.

Behind me, Lily snorts. "Yeah, you could say that."

"Tell me."

"Later." Declan's touch muted the compulsion for a couple of minutes, but now it's back, worse than ever. I feel like I'm going to jump out of my skin—or worse, claw it off my body—if I don't figure out what this small, plot of grass is trying to tell me. "I have a body to find."

Declan freezes. "What, here?"

"It appears so. Goddess knows the compulsion won't let me move more than three feet in any direction. But we can't figure out where the victim is hidden."

Declan steps back, pulls me gently to my feet. "You're sure it's here?"

"Pretty sure."

"Fuck." His hand wraps around the back of my head, pulls me closer as he leans down and presses his forehead gently to mine. For long seconds he doesn't move, doesn't do anything but stand there—as if he's gathering strength from me even as he's loaning his to me. The last of my anger abates. It's hard to stay mad at a man who literally trembles at the idea of me being hurt.

"We're going to talk about everything I missed tonight later."

"I'll show you mine if you show me yours."

"Somehow I figured that was how it was going to be with you." Still holding me tightly, he takes a few deep breaths—it's probably fanciful thinking, but I swear it feels like he's drawing my scent deep inside himself. Goddess knows, that's what I'm doing. The wild cinnamon scent of him is a gift to my senses even after the night I've had.

Eventually, Declan pulls away. "I think I know where your body is."

"Goddess, I hope so. Because I'm about to jump out of my skin here."

"I'm so sorry you have to go through this, baby." He kisses me softly, sweetly, then steps back. He walks over to the historical sign I paid absolutely no attention to, then turns to look at Lily. "I'm not really sure how this works. Go stand near Xandra and both of you stay back for a little bit. Just to be safe."

"What are you doing?" I ask. "We've already looked over there. There's nothing."

"You wouldn't believe me if I told you."

I glance at Lily whose eyes are wide, but probably no wider than mine at this point. She looks about to swallow her tongue and I don't blame her. Because insane as it sounds, I'm beginning to think that maybe—just maybe—she was onto something earlier with that whole ACW headquarters spiel.

Declan lifts his hands to about shoulder height, spreads them wide. And then he doesn't move again for what feels like forever. Seconds become minutes and I'm starting to wonder if he's entered a trance, when it occurs to me what he's doing. Safeguards. He's unraveling safeguards. Holy shit. Lily was right.

Finally, finally, Declan drops his arms. He glances back at us—to check on us or make sure we're both following orders or maybe both. Once he's satisfied that we're staying out of trouble, he starts to chant, loud enough that I can tell he's speaking Ancient Egyptian, but not so loud that I can decipher what it is he's saying.

Intrigued, I step closer. I may not have had my powers very long, but I've spent my life around Heka—and most of my adolescence trying to be the überwitch my mother so desperately wanted me to be. If he's working an actual spell, and not something he's just put together himself, I should recognize it. I want to recognize it. Because what we're doing now is *Twilight Zone* stuff and I want to know how it happens. How I can do it on my own if I ever need to.

Admittedly, my magic isn't like Declan's. I can't just mutter a spell and have it work. He has a real talent for those things human beings refer to as magic because they don't know any better—transubstantiation, moving from one place to another by manipulating the time-space continuum, creating things from nothing, inter-preting safeguards.

I'll never be anywhere near as talented as he is in those areas. But that doesn't mean I can't practice, can't learn how to do the basic stuff. Goddess knows, on nights like tonight, it would really come in handy.

Not that I think what Declan is doing is basic. The ACW is made up of nine of the most powerful witches, wizards and warlocks in existence. If, by some miracle, Lily and I have actually stumbled upon their mystical headquarters, then I have no doubt the wards they have protecting them are the most potent, most dangerous in existence.

And yet Declan thinks he can get around them. No, I tell myself as the ground beneath his feet starts to trem-ble. He *is* getting around them. Unbelievable.

Moments later, the whole area starts to shake. My knees go weak, as if they're going to collapse beneath my weight at any second. But as I look down, I realize it's not my knees that are the problem. It's the ground I'm standing on. It's bucking and rolling, just like it does when there's an earthquake—I remember from when I was caught in one in Los Angeles years ago.

Lily whimpers, throws an arm out to help keep her from falling. I grab onto it, pulling her in close even as I plant my feet firmly on the constantly shifting grass. I might be the one wearing all the bruises these days, but she's always been the one with major balance issues.

Wrapping an arm around her shoulders, I let her borrow some of mine.

The rolling stops as suddenly as it starts. Lily breathes a sigh of relief, starts to pull away. But before she can get more than a step or two, the ground starts to shake violently. It's mimicking a different kind of earthquake, one I've never been in. And though it seems more violent, and harder to stay upright, I try to comfort myself with the knowledge that it's the rolling quakes that cause the most destruction. The shaking ones just scare the hell out of people.

Goddess knows, it's scaring the hell out of me. Lily, too. Declan's the only one who seems unaffected as he stands upright in the middle of the small garden, completely calm and cool as the earth beneath us does its worst.

"Are you two okay?" he calls over his shoulder.

Before I can answer, the wind picks up, going from almost nothing to slapping against us with the force of a stage-one hurricane.

"Shit," Lily gasps, bending nearly double to protect herself from the leaves and twigs and rocks the wind has transformed into missiles. "Your boyfriend sure has pissed someone off."

"It's a talent of his."

She looks around, nearly gets a twig in the eye for her trouble. "I guess." She opens her purse, fumbles around for a minute. "Why didn't I bring my sunglasses?" It comes out as a wail.

"Because it's the middle of the night and neither of us was anticipating playing the role of Wicked Witch of the East."

She looks confused. "Don't you mean the West?"

"The East is the one who got caught in the tornado and had Dorothy's house land on her."

If possible, Lily ducks even more. "Great. Now I have to look for flying houses," she mumbles under her breath.

"Flying houses might be the least of our problems," I tell her as huge, angry-looking storm clouds move in directly above us. Though no rain is falling, lightning is flashing and thunder rumbling. "You need to get out of here, Lily." I give her a little shove back toward the car.

"And what? Leave you here? I don't think so."

"I'll be okay."

"Then so will I, because I'm sticking right next to you."

Scared for her, and for the man who has come to mean so much to me in so little time, I scream his name to be heard over the wind and thunder. "This isn't safe. You guys need to get out of here."

"I'm almost done," he shouts back at me. "It'll be fine in a minute."

His definition of fine must be very different from mine. Because at that moment, a huge lightning bolt shoots out of the sky and slams into the earth only a couple of feet from where Declan is standing. The next thing I know, he's hurtling backward through the air.

"Declan!" I take off running straight at him, Lily right behind me. Has he been electrocuted? What kind of shoes is he wearing? Is he—

"Stay back!" he shouts, sounding a little worse for wear.

Still panicking, I ignore him. But the closer I get to him, the more my feet start to tingle. That's when I remember that I'm wearing boots instead of tennis shoes— the ground must still be holding on to some of the charge.

It doesn't hurt, though, doesn't burn, so I keep going. By the time I reach him, Declan's pushed himself back to a standing position. I glance down at his feet. Thank the goddess. He's wearing thick, rubber-soled hiking boots.

"I thought I told you to stay back," he tells me even as he wraps his arms around my shoulders.

"Yeah, well, you aren't the only one who doesn't listen to directions."

"Obviously."

"What the hell have you done, Declan?" Lily yells from a few feet behind us. "Unleashed Armageddon?"

"Close enough," he answers, reaching out for her wrist and yanking her—and me—behind him, just as another bolt of lightning strikes the garden. "Hold on."

"What now?" Lily demands.

He doesn't answer, just turns his back on the spot where he'd unraveled the safeguards, wraps his arms around us to shelter us. "You don't want to know."

"What's that supposed—"

Before I can finish, a loud crack sounds, ripping through the night air. It silences the thunder, stops the lightning and the wind, even stills the shaking ground. Then, before Lily's and my astonished eyes, the ground in front of us splits wide open.

Ten

"What. The. Hell. Is. That?" I demand, pointing to the gaping hole in the ground. "And how the hell has no one called the police on us yet?" Yes, it's the middle of the night and this part of downtown is just about completely deserted. But still, there are a few people around. A few cars on the street. What I just witnessed is abnormal enough to have attracted the attention of anyone in the vicinity.

"They can't see us, right?" After clearing her throat a few times, Lily finally manages to get her vocal chords working again. "Because of the safeguards."

"I thought Declan unraveled the safeguards. Isn't that what all this fuss was about?" I pull against the strength of Declan's arms until he finally gets the hint and lets me go reluctantly.

"There are different levels of safeguards. Those meant to keep humans from discovering this place and those meant to keep witches out."

"You left the human safeguards in place."

"I did."

Now that all the excitement has died down—and now that there's a clear path laid out in front of me, the compulsion is stronger than ever. I walk straight up to the opening in the earth.

"Xan, wait," Declan cautions. "You don't know what might be waiting for you down there. Let me go first."

What he says makes sense. I'm not one to hide behind a big strong guy, but these are extenuating circumstances. Goddess only knows what we're walking into—especially considering the only thing I know for sure is that somewhere down there, somebody is dead. And not from natural causes.

I open my mouth to tell him to go ahead, but what comes out is, "No, I need to go first."

There's a long, narrow staircase leading down into the hole, and I head down it without another word. Behind me, Declan and Lily curse. But Declan, who has seen me in the throes of these compulsions before, knows there will be no arguing with me, no turning me from this course until I find what must be found.

"Aren't you even going to ask what this place is?" he demands as he follows so closely behind me that I can feel his breath on the nape of my neck.

"Headquarters for the Arcadian Council of Witches, Wizards and Warlocks," I answer.

There's a stunned silence. "How do you know?"

"How do you know? More importantly, how did you get this place open? I'm not sure even my mom or dad could have done it."

"They've done it before. This is where most ACW meetings take place, after all. Although, in those cases, getting in is a little different."

"You mean because they're invited instead of breaking in?"

"Pretty much."

"Speaking of which," Lily says from where she's pulling up the rear. "Our entrance isn't exactly what I'd call subtle. What's going to be waiting for us when we get to the bottom of this staircase to hell?"

"It wasn't subtle for us," Declan answers, "because I invoked a couple of very powerful spells. But down here, they probably didn't even notice."

"How is that possible?" I turn to look at him. The light is dim down here, but there's enough for me to see his eyes—and the grim smile he's wearing.

"Because the ACW is nothing if not arrogant. They believe firmly in their own supremacy, so they can't imagine that anyone could breach their security without them knowing."

"Even you?"

"Even *you*, Xandra. You're the reason we're here, after all."

I don't really agree with that, considering he's far more powerful than I will ever be. Still, the compulsion is riding me hard, making me walk faster, so I move on to other questions. It feels like I have a million of them, after all, and I'd like to get the most important ones answered before we get to the bottom of the steps. If we ever get to the bottom. We've already done about a hundred steps and there's no end in sight.

"What about this staircase? They don't know when it's been activated?"

"This isn't their staircase. It's mine."

"You mean, you built this?"

He inclines his head. "In a manner of speaking."

"Huh." I walk even faster. Without the compulsion, I never would have stepped foot down here—I don't know how Declan and Lily are doing it—but knowing that Declan created this never-ending staircase somehow makes me feel better. It's still a little terrifying, but I know—despite his darkness—that he'd never do anything to put me in jeopardy.

"How do *they* get down to the pits of hell?" Lily demands. "Their broomsticks?"

Declan laughs. But the sad thing is, I'm not sure she's joking.

"Do you want to go back up?" I ask. "You don't have to come down with us if it freaks you out." She's done more than enough for me tonight. I wouldn't blame her if she decides that enough is enough.

But Lily just snorts. "Yeah, because what I really want to do right now is brave the Little Garden of Horrors all on my own. No thanks. You're stuck with me for the duration of this."

We continue on in silence. I started counting the steps a couple of minutes ago and we're on step one hundred forty-three, not including however many we did before I began ticking them off in my head. But if I were to guess, I'd say we're closing in on two-hundred and fifty steps. Maybe Lily's right and this really is the stairway to hell. Goddess knows, I expect molten lava to start spewing around us at any moment.

"Not to be a party pooper," I say into the pensive silence, "but how the hell are we going to get back out of here? I mean, does either one of you know how to create a magic elevator?"

"How hard could it be?" Declan asks. "A little steel, a few cables—" He winks at me when he sees me staring back at him over my shoulder. "Just kidding."

"Yeah. You're a freaking riot," I deadpan. "How much farther does this thing stretch?"

"I don't think it's much farther," Declan says, wrapping one large, warm hand around my upper arm and pulling me to a stop. "Let me go in front."

There's a part of me that still wants to argue with him. While I understand his fear, even sympathize with it, I'm still annoyed with how he left me. He seduced me into sleep and then took off to do goddess knows what. I don't care that he had something to do on his own—it's not like I want to be joined at the hip with him. But what he did smacks of secrecy and that I don't like. All he had to do was be honest with me and everything would have been fine.

"I've got it," I answer, and even I recognize the snap in my voice.

"You don't know what you're going to be dealing with when you get to the bottom."

"And you do?"

"I have a pretty good idea, yes."

"And why is that? I wonder," I demand archly. "Are you leading an entire secret life that I'm not aware of?"

"You're being ridiculous."

"Maybe. But you're hiding something and I don't like it."

He grinds his teeth. "Get behind me, Xandra, or I will pick you up and put you there."

The threat rubs me the completely wrong way. "I'd like to see you try."

"You sure you want to go there, baby?" he asks, one brow lifted in that ridiculously hot way he has. He looks like a complete badass standing there, an impression that is backed up by everything I know about him and every action he's ever made in front of me.

Despite the anger that still seethes inside me, a shiver

of awareness sparks. I can't help it—he's looking at me the way he does in bed, right before he does something completely delicious to me.

Right now he looks like he wants nothing more than to push me up against the wall and prove to me and everyone else that I belong to him, that he can keep me safe. And under normal circumstances, I might have been willing to let him. But the timing couldn't be more inappropriate for this—on both our parts. We don't know what awaits us in the depths of this place. Besides, Lily's right here, her eyes wide as saucers as she takes in the exchange between us. Guess my BFF didn't realize just how volatile Declan is—or how volatile I am when I'm around him.

I send her a reassuring smile along with a bunch of this-is-no-big-deal vibes, then turn and start heading down the staircase once more. The second I'd stopped, the compulsion started burning hotter and hotter, until every breath became an agony.

And still I can't let my conversation with Declan go. Not if our relationship—excluding the whole soulbound thing—has any hope of working. "And don't call me *baby*," I toss over my shoulder. "I'm not a child."

"Then stop acting like one." He's seething at the challenge, something that makes me aware of just how often I've let him have his way in our partnership. Normally, it makes sense—he knows a lot more about this stuff than I do, not to mention that he has more magic in one flick of his hand than I can imagine possessing in my whole lifetime. But not this time. I'm the one who knows where we're going. I'm the one who—

I freeze as I circle around what turns out to be the last

bend in the staircase. Lying on the ground right in front of me are two wizards. I note two things about them immediately.

One, they're obviously security for the Council.

And two, they are obviously dead.

Eleven

"Well, it looks like you've found your bodies," Lily tells me so flippantly that I know she's fighting her gag reflex with everything she's got. The more she's upset by something, the less she lets it show.

"Looks like it," I answer, but I'm not so sure. The compulsion, while it's let up a little, doesn't seem ready to release me quite yet. It's pushing me to pass these two men who are lying in pools of their own blood, eyes staring sightlessly, throats cut. Normally, I'd be down there, checking for pulses, reliving their deaths whether I wanted to or not. But while I feel a small tug toward them, a need to do just that, most of the pull I feel is for somewhere else. For *someone* else.

"You okay?" Declan asks, rubbing a hand down my spine, a gesture that is both soothing and supportive. Our spat, if you can call it that, is completely forgotten in the face of what we now have to deal with.

"I don't . . . This isn't . . ." I shake my head, at a loss to put into words the feelings ricocheting around inside me.

His eyes narrow with sudden concentration. "This isn't what, Xandra?"

Just then, a new wave of compulsion slams into me. It bows my back, sizzles along my spine. Then wraps itself around me like an invisible cord. For all of its invisibility, this compulsion is the worst one yet. It feels like the sharpest razors are cutting into me wherever the cord touches—my arms, my upper torso, even my neck.

It must look like that, too, because Lily suddenly gasps. "Xan, you're bleeding!"

I don't answer her, I can't. Not when I'm nearly jerked off my feet by the force of this magic. Knowing it's no use, I give up trying to fight it and simply let it pull me along—out of this huge room and down a dark and winding hallway.

Declan moves swiftly, positions himself in front of me. He doesn't try to touch me—he knows how dangerous it is at times like these. But he's determined to be in front. Determined to face whatever threat might be waiting for us around the next bend first.

In some distant part of my mind I'm aware of Lily following us, her phone the only thing illuminating the path in front of me. Though to be honest, I kind of wish she'd turn the damn thing off. This place is creepy enough in the dark. Being able to see the magic carvings in the ceiling—not to mention the cobwebs hanging from wall sconces that don't look like they've been lit in a hundred years—is not exactly making this any easier. Especially when there's a new, uncomfortable facet to this compulsion that I've never felt before. And it is really freaking me out.

I'm always cold at times like this, on a physical and soul-deep level that just adds to the misery of the experience. Tonight, that chill is still there, but with a little something extra. Frigid air blowing against my left ear and the back of my neck like the iciest of breaths. With every step I take, it gets more noticeable, more overwhelming, until the hair at my nape is standing straight up.

Every ghost story I've ever heard is running through my head, but I refuse to go there right now. If I do, I'm afraid I really will lose it and that's just not an option. Not now, when I've just fought Declan for my right to do this without his interference. And certainly not when losing it will get me nothing but a one-way trip to the local mental hospital. I can't leave—there's no way the compulsion will let me go until I find what it wants me to find—and if I let my imagination get the best of me, I'll never be able to do what needs to be done.

Locking everything down deep inside me—the fear, the pain, my evolving magic—I force myself to keep going, to put one foot in front of the other. Whatever is down here can't be as bad as what will happen to me if I don't keep going. I just need to remember that.

We come to a fork in the passageway and Declan steps to the side, where he waits. I know he thinks it will take me some time to figure out which way to go, but I don't even hesitate. The body at the end of this trail is practically screaming for me to find it, the compulsion so great that I take off running.

Behind me, both Lily and Declan curse, but I have no time to explain—and no words to give them anyway. Everything I am, everything I have, is focused on getting to the end of this trail.

The floor is slanting downward now, and it's rougher than it was up above—as if I'm sprinting along barely paved rocks. Somewhere close by I can hear the sound of rushing water, like a waterfall, but that makes no sense, so I don't bother worrying about it. Not now, when I'm so close. So close . . .

We meet a dead end, with the choice to go left or right. I go left, then make an immediate right followed by another left. And then I'm there, right there.

It's dark, so dark that I can't see three feet in front of my face, but I know that I've found him. And it is a him. I don't know how I know that, but I do.

I stop short so suddenly that Declan and Lily, who were hot on my heels, end up slamming into me. The impact knocks me forward and I start to fall. Declan snags me and pulls me up against his chest.

Lily's flashlight app is doing its best to light up the room, but the place is huge, cavernous, and her little iPhone can only do so much. I want to keep moving forward—the compulsion is pushing at me even though I know how stupid it is to go any farther until I can see— but Declan keeps a tight arm around my waist, refusing to let me move so much as an inch away from him.

Then, his breath hot against my ear, he mutters one of the most basic Hekan incantations there is—the one for fire that most children master before they're a decade old. I was twenty-seven before I could use it to create so much as a spark, and then I nearly burned my entire house down. Just one of the many, many reasons this Heka thing is not for me.

Fire flares to life in Declan's open palm, caressing him like a lover. He bends his fingers—works it, shapes it, until it's a glowing sphere of light. It takes a minute or so, but once the orb is created, he sends it spinning out into the middle of the room, where it grows and grows and grows.

Within seconds, the entire room is bathed in the warm, soft light of Declan's fire. And that's when I see him, when we all see him at the front of this plush, well-appointed room that is very obviously a Councilor's office.

In the very front of the room, over what was once a desk but now has very much become an altar, is what is left of ACW Councilor Viktor Alride. And it isn't pretty.

His first glimpse of the murder scene has Declan cursing, low and long and vicious. Lily gasps, and then it's her turn to be sick. Declan conjures up a container and hands it to her before she can make a mess.

I know I should be shocked, repulsed, horrified, by what I'm seeing, just as they are. And there's a part of me that is. But that part isn't in control right now. Instead, the compulsion still has me and it's dragging me across the floor until I'm inches from the desk. And inches from the body suspended in midair over it.

Councilor Alride did not have an easy end.

"Xandra." Declan comes up behind me, rests his hands on my shoulders. "What are you doing?"

"I don't know." I sound lost, confused. I don't feel that way, but then I'm not feeling much of anything right now. The compulsion has finally eased and now I just feel . . . empty. Like I don't have anything to fill up the void it's left behind.

"Fuck!" he mutters under his breath, then turns his voice low, soothing, as he addresses me. "Come on, baby, let's step back a little. You don't want to mess with the integrity of the scene."

Oh. Right. The integrity of the scene. So that Witchcraft Investigations can get to work finding out who did this to a mighty Councilor.

"We need to get out of here. Xandra, please." Lily looks at me with pleading eyes. "We have to leave."

I look at her in surprise. She knows I can't leave until

the body has been taken care of. Until it has left the scene.

"We should call someone," I tell Declan. The only problem is, I don't know whom to call. Austin's Witchcraft Investigations department? Though Austin is a lot bigger than my hometown of Ipswitch, the WI department here is pretty much a joke. Except for the Council—whose headquarters most people don't even know are here—Austin is pretty much a witchcraft-light city. In fact, I know only about ten members of my coven who actually live here. Which means Austin is not exactly a hotbed of witch-on-witch crime. No crime, no WI.

"They must have security headquarters down here somewhere." I walk closer to the desk, reach for the phone. "There must be some kind of internal—"

"Don't touch that!" Declan's voice cracks like a whip. "We can't call anyone, Xandra."

"We have to. We can't just leave him here. There are things that need to be done."

Things like cutting him down. Things like—

I freeze as a new observation penetrates my shock. I stare at the body, horrified, even as I allow Declan to guide me a few steps back. Only then do I ask him, "Do you notice anything strange?"

"You mean, besides the fact that there's a man spread-eagled and strung up in the front of the room? And that he's been completely eviscerated?"

"Yes. Besides that."

Declan looks at me like I'm insane. And maybe I am. Goddess knows, I'm not sure where this bizarre sense of calm is coming from. There's a part of me that's freaking out, that's screaming. I'm staring at a man whose abdomen has been so deeply sliced open that his internal organs have fallen out of his body—all thanks to gravity and the heavy-duty hooks and chains that are keeping him suspended from the ceiling.

Yet there's another, darker part of me that looks at this as karmic justice. Maybe I should have more pity for him, because, goddess knows, he suffered. But as I stare up at Councilor Alride, all I can think is that he still didn't suffer as much as Lina did. Or Amy. Or the other two girls Kyle tortured, raped and murdered at the Council's behest.

Why shouldn't he have died like this?

Why shouldn't he suffer the way he ensured others did?

The thoughts are so black, so unlike me, that I feel a little nauseated just having them roll around in my brain. Nobody should die like this. Nobody should suffer this way.

And yet, there's a righteousness about it too. . . .

The two different feelings war within me, until I'm confused, conflicted—like there are two separate people inside me taking this all in. Two separate moral codes that are making very different judgments.

That makes no sense, especially considering I don't suffer from multiple personality disorder. Or at least, I never have before.

"Xandra, darling." Declan's voice intrudes on the strange fog that seems to have enveloped me. As it does, it snaps me back from the edge of whatever crazy cliff I'm standing on.

Horror overwhelms me—at my own moment of callousness as much as at the sight of Councilor Alride—and I stumble backward, hand pressed against my mouth.

"Are you going to be sick?" Declans asks.

"No." But I bend over, let the blood rush back to my head. Better safe than sorry.

He's right there, rubbing my back, all concerned eyes and worried voice. As I struggle to pull air into my tortured lungs, it occurs to me that this is the reaction he's been looking for. What he's been expecting all along—a minor freak to show just how incapable I am of handling the darker aspects of this gift he's brought into my life.

Once I can breathe, I look up. See the guilt shining in eyes as dark as obsidian.

It straightens my spine, pulls me back from the edge in a way nothing else could have right now. "It's okay," I tell him, running a hand down his back.

Then I turn to my best friend. "Lily, are you okay?"

She stares at me with haunted, incredulous eyes. "Are you kidding me?"

"Take her into the hall," Declan tells me. But even as he says it, we know it's not going to happen. I won't be able to move from this room until Councilor Alride has been cut down.

"I'm fine," she tells us. "Just do whatever you have to do so we can get the hell out of here."

I don't bother to tell her that it doesn't work like that. I'm too busy staring at the body at the front of the room again. Now that I have my feelings under control, my earlier impressions are all ricocheting back—one thought chief among them.

"Declan?" I ask, looking over the carnage with the most impersonal eyes I can manage.

"Yeah, baby?" I can feel his resistance in every breath he takes, every word he doesn't say. He wants nothing more than to gather me up and take me as far away from this place as we can get. The fact that he can't—that it simply is not possible—is ripping at him the same way the compulsion ripped at me earlier.

It's another realization, another by-product of our relationship that I'll have to think on later. Because right now, my mind is occupied by just one thing—the bold and terrifying truth staring back at me out of Councilor Alride's unseeing eyes.

"There's no blood."

Twelve

"What?" Declan snaps out the single syllable, but I can tell he's looking at the scene with new eyes.

"Oh God," Lily moans as she comes to stand next to me. She wraps an arm around my waist—as much to comfort as to take comfort.

"He's been cut open, his internal organs have literally fallen out of his abdominal cavity and he's hanging from the ceiling." The place should be drowning in blood, but it's not. There's almost nothing, just a scattering of drops on the desk. "So where's the blood?"

It's a rhetorical question. Whoever murdered Councilor Alride bled him dry first, and took the blood with him when he left. There's only one reason for that, and it isn't a good one. The darkest magic, the blackest form of Heka in existence, uses blood magic. The strength of the spells, of the power, depends partially on the practitioner and partially on the blood.

The blood of a Councilor would make some very, very powerful magic.

On the heels of that thought comes the realization that we need to start tracking his blood. I'm not sure that's even possible, but if it is, someone needs to do it.

The alternative—that all that blood, all that power, is just out there for someone to tap into—is terrifying.

Bleeding someone out—

How did you get here? You need to leave immediately. Councilor Alride's voice booms through my head, blocking everything out but the deep tenor of his words. The fact that they echo Declan's so closely has me blinking, confused, at the angry man looming over me. The very angry, very alive man.

When I don't answer, he continues. *What are you doing? Stay right there. Don't come any closer. I'm calling security.* He reaches for the phone. *I'm—*

The crack of a whip sounds over his angry posturing. Pain—sharp, focused, hot—rips through my hand. My arm.

That's when I understand. He's not talking to me. He's talking to his killer. It's never happened like this for me before. I've never been allowed to see or hear or feel anything before the attack and death occur.

Another crack rips through the air like a gunshot. More pain licks over my chest and side this time.

How dare you! Councilor Alride's uninjured hand shoots into the air and I can feel the magic building inside him, feel him gathering it from the world around him.

There's a flash of light, and then nothing. No pain. No sound. No fear. Just an utter blankness that doesn't make sense. In the back of my head, there's a voice calling to me, but I can't reach it, can't hear it. It's distracting, annoying, so I shut it out. Then I turn into the black.

I push through the darkness, searching for Alride. Searching for anything that might tell me what happened to him. How a Councilor of his power was so completely overwhelmed. And by whom?

For a long time, there's nothing. Just darkness. And then—shooting pain. In my ribs. Again and again and again.

I grab onto the sensory memory, hold it tight to my chest even as the pain spreads through me. I have to see, have to know. . . . It's a new compulsion, one that grows stronger with each passing moment.

Metal. Sharp and cold and thin, so thin, as it presses against my jugular. A quick nick of pain, then blood—warm and liquid—welling above my collarbone. More warmth. A finger catching it, smearing it a little. The finger disappears. I hear the muted sounds of someone sucking.

My whole body tightens in revulsion, in rejection. I try to shove my attacker away, but my hands won't work. No one licks my blood, takes my blood, without my permission.

Laughter—a little wicked, a little mocking—washes over me. *How does it feel, Viktor? How do you like being on the other side of the game?*

I don't know what you're talking about.

Tsk. Tsk. I've never been very fond of lies.

Another cut. This one a little deeper. It stings more, bleeds more. I can feel the blood leaking slowly down my chest. The finger is back, playing in it. No, not a finger. A tongue. There's a mouth on my chest—lips running over the bloody trail, tongue licking it up drop by drop by drop.

I yell for help. No sound assaults my ears, but I can feel the scream in the twinging of my vocal cords and the sudden hoarseness of my throat.

No need to panic. The voice is low, a whisper. I try to tell if it's a man or a woman, try to see the face it belongs to, but there's nothing there. Just the voice, just the tongue, just the pain.

More metal, more cold. Not a knife this time. Handcuffs around my wrists. No, not handcuffs. This is thicker, tighter. Two inches thick, it wraps around my wrist. Squeezes so tightly that it pinches the thin layer of flesh that rests right over my bones.

What are you doing? I ask again. My voice is no longer steady, my confidence—in myself and my abilities— shaken. No, not me. Viktor. This is all happening to Viktor, I remind myself.

It's strange, muddled. Hard—so hard—to tell the difference now.

I'm moving, being pulled up, slowly, slowly. There's grunting, a mocking laugh. A breathless admonition for me—for Viktor—to lose weight. A promise to help him with that.

And then I'm hanging, my arms stretched wide above my head. *I don't understand. I don't understand. Why are you doing this?*

No answer now. No sound at all but the harsh breathing of physical exertion. I reach for my magic. I mutter an incantation so old it has been forgotten by nearly everyone. I need my hands for it to work well, but I still have my fingers. Maybe that's enough—

Pain. Overwhelming, this time. My entire system is overloaded with it until I can't breathe, can't think, can't do anything but endure. Endure. Endure.

Finally, it ends.

I kick out with my feet, hit something hard but human. A murmured curse, than another kiss of the knife. This time from my neck to my belly button, slicing my shirt to ribbons and digging a furrow into my flesh as well.

Another swipe of the hand—I try to focus on it, but I can't get a picture. It's like the killer is somehow blocking any reception of him or her that I might get.

Strangely muffled voice.

No image of him to lock onto.

Nothing but the pain he gives me. Viktor. Me.

The confusion grows worse.

More words. Hard to hear. Harder to focus on. Like I'm underwater and everything is muffled, muted. I know the words are important—I can sense it if nothing else and strain, strain, to make something out.

For just a second the spell slips and I hear three words: *Close doesn't count.* Then everything grows muffled again and I'm out of luck.

Close doesn't count. I turn the words over in my mind, trying to make something of them. Something's there, hovering around the edges of my brain. But every time I reach out to grab it, it flutters away. *Close doesn't count.* I've heard that combination of words before. The more I repeat them, the more sure I grow. I know the rhythm, the—

Agony. Excruciating, omnipresent, eternal. My whole body, one long unending shriek.

Intellectually, in the small part of me that is still Xandra, I know that this is it. This is the death blow that slowly—oh so slowly—killed Councilor Alride. It happened to him—it isn't really happening to me. And yet I can't stop myself from clutching at my stomach.

I swear to the goddess I can feel the squish of my intestines between my fingers, smell the metallic earthiness of my blood, hear the sound of that same blood ping ping pinging into the metal trays set up directly below me.

At least that answers the question of where the blood went—as if I had any doubt.

Time passes—I don't have a clue how long—and I feel myself growing weaker, more tired. The pain is still there, but it's dull now. Background noise to the lethargy that is creeping over me a little bit more with each second that slips by.

I can hear voices again. Not the killer's, not that evil, indistinguishable hiss, but real voices. Loud, urgent, desperate. I try to respond, but I'm too far under. The pain, the vision, the magic, has stripped everything else away but Viktor Alride's last moments.

The wheezing starts, the gasping, and then he's slipping away from me.

Slipping.

Slipping.

Gone.

Only silence remains.

"Xandra!" I hear Declan calling my name, feel his hands cup my face. It's the first time I hear him, though I get the sense that he's been trying to reach me for a while. Is his the voice I heard when I was under? Was he the one trying to reach me? Or was it something else—something much more sinister?

Either way, I'm me again, thank the goddess. Viktor Alride is long gone from this plane of existence.

"Damn it, Xandra!" Declan sounds panic-stricken and I realize this is the first time he's ever really seen me like this. Though he's been with me at other murder scenes, he's always come after. He's never seen the whole show before.

"Come back to me, baby. Open your eyes. Come on, Xan. Look at me."

I struggle to do what he asks, but it's so hard to get my body to cooperate. So hard to do anything but lie here in a stupor.

"Xandra!"

The urgency in his voice finally gets through to me and I force my eyes open. Only it's not Declan's concerned face I see hovering above me. It's Lily's tear-streaked one.

"You have to stop doing this to me!" she tells me in a shaky voice. "One of these days you're going to give me a heart attack."

"Sorry." I look from her to Declan. He hasn't said a word, but if possible he looks even more freaked out than my best friend does.

I reach a hand up, cup his face. His fingers grab onto mine, squeezing so tightly that I feel the circulation cut off to my fingers. I don't protest. How can I when I know I've put him through hell a dozen times in the last few weeks?

It takes a minute, but his grip finally loosens. Blowing out a long breath, he says, "We need to get you out of here."

"Like right now," Lily agrees.

I nod, even as I answer, "You know I can't go."

Declan's mouth forms a grim line. "You *will* go." His arm slips behind my back, presses me gently up into a sitting position.

"The compulsion doesn't work that way. Until he's been cut down and taken away, I won't be able to leave this room."

"Yeah, well, we can't stay here. Do you know what will happen if they find us in a murdered Councilor's office?"

It's a mess of massive proportions. Even strung out and exhausted from the past few hours, I know that. The queen and king of Ipswitch's daughter found at the bloodiest crime scene in ACW history? That would be bad enough. Now add in the fact that I have a grudge against them—as does my lover. I figure even if we aren't found here, we'll be on the short list of suspects that WI puts together.

That doesn't matter, though. Logic and self-preservation never do. Not when my magic is involved.

But just because I'm screwed, that doesn't mean Declan and Lily have to be. Pushing shakily to my feet, I tell them, "You should go. I can handle this on my own."

They stare at me, looks of utter noncomprehension on their face.

"I mean it. You two need to get out of here while you still can. Those two guards out there aren't going to go undiscovered for much longer."

"What are you saying? That you want us to just walk out of here without you?" Lily demands incredulously. Declan doesn't say anything. He's too busy glaring at me from eyes turned incandescent with rage.

"There are three dead bodies down here. Even if, by some miracle, the compulsion lets me walk away from Viktor, there's no way I'll make it out of here. Not with the guards lying so close to the entrance."

"I'm not leaving you."

"You have to." I wrap my arms around his waist, rest my head on his rock-solid chest. "The ACW has been looking for a way to execute you for decades now. If you're found here, you'll give them exactly what they've been wanting."

His stubborn-as-hell jaw locks into place. "I'd fucking love it if they came after me. It'll give me the chance to get rid of them once and for all."

"Be reasonable."

"This is as reasonable as I get, baby." At that moment, the antique grandfather clock in the corner starts to chime. Before it falls silent, it's clanged four times. My need to get them out of here becomes urgent. I had no idea that much time had passed—I must have been out of it longer than I imagined if nearly an hour has passed since we got down here. No wonder Lily and Declan both looked so freaked out when I came to.

"I'll be fine," I tell them again. "The ACW won't hurt me. Not when they have my parents to deal with."

"Uh, I hate to point out a flaw in your logic, Xan, but the ACW just spent weeks trying to kill you," Lily answers with a shake of her head. "Finding you here is pretty much the answer to their prayers."

"But they did that under cover. This would have to be blatant and in my parents' faces. They won't risk that. Not yet." I give her a little shove toward the door, then cross to the desk and lift up the receiver of the old-fashioned phone that resides there. "Go," I tell them right before I dial the operator.

"Put the damn phone down, Xandra." Declan looks more pissed than I have ever seen him—and that's saying something.

I ignore him. When the operator answers, I say, "There's been a break-in in Councilor Viktor Alride's office."

"Who is this?" the operator demands.

I don't get the chance to answer. Declan's across the

room in a flash, ripping the phone out of my hand and throwing the whole thing against the wall. "You need to get out of here!" I tell him urgently.

"Fuck that!" He places a gentle hand on my head, murmurs something. And for the third time tonight, everything goes black.

Thirteen

This time when I wake up, I'm in the backseat of a car. At first I think I'm with Lily, but a quick look around tells me I'm in Declan's BMW. He's driving, his shoulders tense and his hands clenched on the wheel. I might feel bad for him if I weren't so annoyed at basically being kidnapped against my will. He always wants to take care of me, but he never gives me the chance to take care of him. It's just one of the many inequalities in our relationship and it is beginning to severely tick me off.

Not to mention that I'm getting damn sick of waking up not knowing where I am—or what the hell happened to knock me out. It's one more thing I plan to talk to Declan about. The way he just takes over when he thinks he knows better, whether I need him to or not.

"How are you feeling?" Declan asks from the front seat.

I haven't moved, haven't made a sound, so I don't know how he's so certain I'm awake. Except he's Declan and I'm beginning to think the man knows everything. Or at least is damn good at faking it.

"Fantastic, considering I've been kidnapped." I sit up slowly, glare at him in the rearview mirror. Then wish I'd stayed where I was when my stomach pitches and rolls.

"I prefer to think of it as extricating you from an increasingly sticky situation." He grins at me.

"Of course you do." I rest my head on the seat in front of me, try to ignore the fact that my head feels like an entire flock of very busy woodpeckers have taken up residence behind my eyes.

He turns serious between one breath and the next. "You okay?"

"Yeah." No. Everything hurts. My head. My stomach. My muscles. Even my skin feels too tight, like one quick move will split me wide open. It's an unfortunate analogy, considering where we just came from, but it fits nonetheless.

It's the compulsion, my punishment for ignoring it even though I didn't have a choice. And it gets worse with each mile we travel from the murder site.

Declan turns the corner quickly—too quickly—and my uneasy stomach revolts. "Pull over!" I tell him, already reaching for the door handle.

Thank the goddess it's so early and no one is on the normally crowded downtown streets. Declan yanks the car over to the curb within seconds, and before he can even turn the thing off, I'm leaning out the door, getting sick.

Another thing I'm very tired of. And another black mark against Declan on my list. I know he's just trying to help, but sometimes I don't want his help. Don't need it. These are my powers and I have to learn to deal with them on my own. Counting on him to always be there to do it for me is not an option. Not when he can disappear on a whim—for hours or years—and not when he doesn't feel what I feel. See what I see.

Ceding control of my powers over to him is a stupid

move, any way I think about it—especially with the darkness that is so much a part of him. I felt a little bit of that darkness when we were down in the ACW headquarters, and while I understand where it comes from, I don't want it inside me, affecting my powers. Not now. Not ever.

Declan opens the other passenger door, crawls in beside me and holds my hair away from my face as I empty my stomach of the last of the water I drank before leaving home tonight. Then I'm back to dry heaves. So. Much. Fun.

"I'm sorry, baby," he tells me as he tenderly strokes my hair. Then he's murmuring again, and though I can feel a soothing warmth seeping out of his hand and into my head—a warmth that eases the worst edges of my headache—I knock his hand away.

"Stop that!"

"You're sick."

"Because of your damn magic, so excuse me if I don't want any more of it."

He stiffens and I know I've struck a direct blow. I feel bad, but not bad enough to try to take the words back.

"Xandra, be reasonable," he says, still trying to touch me. "Why should you suffer when you don't have to?"

"Because it's my choice! My body! My life!" I stop because I'm heaving again, which pisses me off more—especially considering how it underscores his point.

He grinds his teeth, but he sits back. Let's me finish being sick in peace.

When it's finally over, I close the car door and lean weakly against the seat. Declan hands me a bottle of water, waits patiently while I rinse my mouth a few times and then drink thirstily. I know it's killing him, but he doesn't touch me, doesn't try to heal me or help me or do anything else that might set me off. And in doing so, he manages to calm the anger that's been batting around inside me since I woke up in this goddess-forsaken automobile.

Exhausted despite my magically induced nap, I lean against Declan. I sigh as his heat finally manages to permeate the cold that has enveloped me so long I've begun to think of it as a permanent fixture.

Declan relaxes slowly, inch by inch. I cuddle closer, and—with a sigh—he wraps his arm around my shoulder. Pulls me against his chest. Drops soft kisses over my hair and forehead.

"You scared the hell out of me tonight."

I snort. "And you weren't even around for the main attraction."

"So Lily told me." His grip tightens. "I'm sorry I wasn't there."

"That's okay. I'm not sure I'd want you to see me seizing in the middle of the kitchen floor anyway."

"Fuck. Is that what happened?"

"Kind of." I tell him as much as I can remember—some of it is blurry because of the convulsions, but Declan definitely gets the gist of it. I can tell by the way he grows more and more grim.

When I'm finally done telling my story, he drops his head until his forehead rests against my temple. "I don't know if I can take it if your empathic magic gets any stronger."

"I don't understand. You think my magic turned against me?"

I really hope that's not the case, because if it is, experiences like that will only get worse as my power gets

stronger. And I'm smart enough to know that if Declan
had been there, if he had seen what had happened to me,
he wouldn't handle it well. Though I'm terrified of the
darkness I feel inside me, darkness that can only come
from him, that doesn't mean I want to lose him. After all,
he left me once for my own good, and though he's prom-
ised never to do it again, I'm not sure I believe him. The
man who would take on the ACW to keep me safe, who
would risk being accused of a Councilor's murder rather
than leave me alone, is more than capable of walking
away if he thought it would keep me safe. Especially if
being near him is what grows my magic, which in turn
ends up hurting me the most.

But the thought of going back to my old life—latent,
free of coven politics, without Declan—doesn't appeal to
me. No matter how much my life sucks at present—and
let's be honest, it sucks a lot—it's still better than living
without him in my life. He broke my heart the first time
he left and all he'd done was kiss me, hold me, talk to me.
Now that we've made love, now that he's let me see the
man behind the mystery, I can't imagine waking up every
day to a life without him in it.

"I think your magic gives you the ability to tap into
the power all around you. Those seizures, the fire . . . You
know that Alride was a fire element, too, don't you?"

I didn't. I ponder his words for a moment, try to figure
out what he isn't saying. When it finally hits me, I break
out in a cold sweat. "You think what I felt was Viktor
dying?"

"Alride had a great deal of magic at his disposal.
When he died violently, struggling, that magic shot out
into the universe and glommed on to the first magical
empathy it could find."

"Me."

"You." He nods solemnly.

My stomach clenches all over again. I didn't like Alride when he was alive, and the thought of his magic latching onto me, tearing through me, makes my skin crawl. I don't think he should have died the way he did—no one should go through that—but that doesn't mean I want any part of him inside me.

My expression must reflect my revulsion, because Declan pulls back. "Are you all right? Are you going to be sick again?"

"I'm fine," I tell him. "Everything's going to be fine." I refuse to think of it any other way.

"I know." More kisses, this time on my brow and along the line of my jaw. "I just wish you didn't feel so fragile against me."

"There's nothing about me that's fragile." I'm a little insulted that he thinks there is.

"Baby, *everything* about you is fragile." He runs a deliberate hand over my wrist, which is small and—admittedly—one of the most delicate things about me. "It's why I'm so astounded by the strength you show over and over and over again."

"You don't really mean that." How can he when he's constantly swooping to my rescue?

"I've never meant anything more. You're amazing. I thank the goddess every night that you're mine. Maybe I'm too harsh, maybe I don't show it enough, but, Xandra, every day you find a way to astonish me. To thrill me."

I melt. There's no other word for it. The last of my anger at his high-handedness dissolves and I press myself against him. Hold him tight.

He holds me just as securely.

Long minutes pass where neither of us moves. Finally, as the first hypnotic colors of dawn start creeping across the sky, I pull away. The ache inside me—the one that pushed and shoved at me in an effort to force me back to the ACW headquarters—has dissipated some. Viktor's been found. Thank the goddess.

And while I would sooner roast over an open pit than admit this to Declan, it's nice to know that I can survive if I turn my back on the compulsion. It isn't pleasant, and I'll definitely need help—no way can I do it on my own—but it can be done. That has to count for something.

"Do you think you'll be okay if I start driving again?" he asks cautiously.

I nod. "Lily is probably worried about us anyway."

Long seconds pass as he continues to hold me. Finally, reluctantly, he moves away. Climbs out of the backseat and into the front.

After putting on my seat belt, I lean forward, rest a hand on his shoulder. For a brief moment his hand comes up and covers mine. Then he's starting the car and pulling back onto the street.

We get to my house about ten minutes later. Lily is in the family room waiting for us. Every light in the house is on. Poor baby. Tonight traumatized me. I can only imagine what it did to her.

Once she makes sure Declan and I are home safely, she drops a kiss on my cheek, warns me never to put her through anything like this again, then makes a beeline for her room. I'm right behind her, so tired and grubby and miserable that all I want is a shower and a bed. Usually, I'm just getting up at this time, preparing to head into work to get started on the baking.

But right now, all I can think of is sleep. I don't need much. Just a couple of hours to recharge my batteries and get the horrors of tonight out of my head. Then I'll worry about work. Travis will be there to open in the morning, along with two other longtime employees. Together, they're more than capable of holding the fort.

Though my body craves sleep like a junkie needs a fix, I walk straight past my bed and into the bathroom and turn on the shower. With all the sweat, puke, blood and tears I've been through tonight, it's all I can do to wait for the water to warm up. I'm desperate to feel clean. To *be* clean.

And the first order of business is brushing my teeth. I reach for my toothbrush and toothpaste, start to scrub vigorously.

Declan follows me. He begins stripping off before he even hits the bathroom. I glance at him in the mirror—because I'm tired, not dead—then freeze as I get my first good look at him since he tucked me into bed hours ago.

His back has a long scratch down it—from left shoulder to right hip—and his chest and stomach are splattered with . . . blood?

"What happened to you?" I demand, rinsing out my mouth before walking closer so I can get a better look at the damage. I'm tired enough that it's entirely possible I might be delusional.

But the way he reacts—stiffening and turning away from me like he has something to hide—sets off a whole cacophony of warning bells in my head.

"Declan? Answer me. Whose blood is that? How did you get injured?"

"Don't make a big deal of it, Xandra."

"Don't make a big dcal? I get a little bump on my

head and you act like it's the end of the world. You're scratched up and covered in blood and I'm not supposed to be concerned? That's bullshit."

I'm close enough to touch now, and I run my fingers over a particularly wicked-looking portion of the scratch. He flinches away. "You need to take care of that," I tell him, "Or it will get infected."

"It's fine."

"It's not fine." I bend down, look at his pants. And I realize, with horror, that they, too, are splattered with blood. "Whose blood is this?"

He shrugs. "It must be Alride's. Or those guards'."

"No way. You already know that Alride's scene was almost completely bloodless. And you didn't go near the guards. You certainly weren't near enough to get this kind of spatter off two dead men."

He sighs, runs a hand over his eyes. "Look, Xandra, can we not do this now? We're both exhausted, both have had one hell of a night. We'll talk about it tomorrow."

Part of me thinks he's right, that we should just shower and go to bed. Daylight and a good night's sleep make everything look better. And yet, I can't just let it go. How can I when the man I love, a man who has made no bones of his dislike for and determination to break up the ACW, is covered in blood—on the same night that one of their most important Councilors is dead?

I think of Alride. Think of the missing blood and the hideous way he died and that more is to come—there has to be more to come. Otherwise, why the blood? Why Shelby? Why any of this?

A sinking feeling starts in the pit of my stomach. Even as I pray it isn't true, I'm reading the writing on the wall.

Putting two and two together and coming up with the most terrifying four imaginable. "Did you do it?" I whisper. It feels like everything we are, everything we have depends on this answer. It isn't true—at least I don't think it is—but after our conversation yesterday, I need to hear him say it. Need to hear the word no fall from his lips.

He thrusts an impatient hand through his too-long hair. "Did I do what, Xandra? You're going to have to be more specific. Did I find you when you were in danger? Did I get you back here before you could be arrested for an unspeakable crime? Did I cover up the fact that we were in that damn room to begin with?"

He stops once he gets a good look at my face. From what I've seen these last few weeks, Declan's typical modus operandi is to go on the attack, to make whoever is opposing him feel and look so foolish that they back down rather than pursue their line of questioning. He isn't going to do that with me. Not now. Not on this.

"Did you *kill* Councilor Alride?"

He stares at me for several long, inscrutable seconds. His face is blank, his eyes as guarded as I have ever seen them. And I realize that the old Declan is back, the one I met eight years ago and the one I met again eighteen days ago. Not until his reappearance—not until this moment when distance once more yawns between us—did I realize how much Declan has softened in the last couple of weeks. How much he's let me in.

With that thought comes regret, real, powerful, overwhelming. "Declan—"

"No. Don't back down now, Xandra. You can't accuse me of killing Alride, and then take it all back like a bad case of buyer's remorse." Without looking at me, he steps into the shower. Starts to wash.

My spine stiffens at his tone. "You don't have to be obnoxious about it. You're covered in blood. We just came from a murder scene where the victim was bled out—a victim who you have to admit is on a list of people you have every reason to hate. It's not so far-fetched for me to imagine that you might have killed him."

"Not so far-fetched? After everything we talked about yesterday, it's not so far-fetched?" he repeats as he scrubs himself. The blood is gone. All that's left of it is the pink-tinged water that is even now circling the drain. Well, that and this conversation. A conversation I wish I'd picked any other day, any other time, to have. It's not like I'm at my most lucid right now, and, exhausted or not, Declan's proving to be a lot more adept at arguing than I am.

"Let me get this straight," he says a couple of minutes later into the silence that yawns between us. He's shut off the shower, grabbed a towel, and is now in the process of drying himself off. He's gorgeous like this—all damp and dark and pissed beyond belief. My magic rises within me, responds to him even when my human side is frustrated, furious. Suspicious.

"You've been through hell tonight. You've had ridiculously awful nightmares that you awake from bruised and battered, you've had a seizure—after prolonged agony—in the middle of your kitchen floor, and then you ended up chasing after a dead guy in the middle of the night and reliving his murder, complete with pain and side effects.

"It's been hell for you to suffer and hell for Lily and me to watch you suffer. And yet you're going to stand there and accuse me of deliberately doing that to you. Of caring so little about you that I'd let you endure that and not even bother to be here to make sure you were okay."

"I didn't say that."

He prowls toward me and I've never been more aware of the spatial limitations of this room more than I am right at this second. Because Declan is all wounded, enraged male animal and I'm the one who caused it. Not to mention the only one currently in his sights. "You said exactly that."

"No. I didn't."

He's in my face now and I shove against his chest. He doesn't budge, doesn't back up, so I have to. Even as tired and messed up as I am right now, I still can't think when he's that close to me. "I asked a very legitimate question. I didn't accuse, I didn't condemn. I simply asked."

"If I had killed Alride. If I had disregarded everything I know about you and what being in the general vicinity of murder does to you and just went for it."

"Not everything's about me, Declan."

"Yes, goddamnit, Xandra, it is. In my life, it is all about you. How could you not know that?" He brings a hand up, rests his palm on my shoulder while his fingers gently stroke the line of my neck. It's a possessive hold at the best of times. Right now, with his onyx eyes blazing into mine, it's a claiming of the most intimate kind, a declaration of intent that manages to be both comforting and sexy as hell. It's taking every ounce of strength I have not to give in. Not to just melt against him and say to hell with my suspicions. To hell with anyone or anything that isn't right here, right now.

"You walked away from me once."

"You were a child."

"I was nineteen."

"You were a *child*. You didn't see yourself in that forest. You were terrified, traumatized. What else was I supposed to do?"

"Tell me the truth."

"Really? I'm telling you the truth now and you don't believe a word I'm saying."

"I didn't say I didn't believe you."

"No, but it's written all over your face." He puts his hands on my shoulders, pulls me close until his face is only inches from mine. "I didn't kill those guards. I didn't kill Alride. And I sure as shit didn't bleed him dry. I have spent nearly your entire existence trying to protect you. And now that you're mine, there's no way I would ever do anything to hurt you like that."

He steps back and for just a second, his guard drops. I see past the anger to the hurt my accusation has caused him. Remorse fills me, but it's too late. He's stepping back, clothing himself with a wave of his hand.

"Get some sleep," he tells me. "I'll call you later today."

Then he's gone, walking out—walking away from me—without a backward glance. And stupid me, I just stand there and watch him go.

Fourteen

I'm exhausted, but I can't sleep, can't do anything but toss and turn as I try to get comfortable despite the bruises. And try to figure out why I was stupid enough to just stand there as Declan walked away.

There's a part of him that scares me—and a part of who I am when I'm with him that scares me—but that doesn't make him a murderer. Yes, he lives in shadows and yes, he straddles the line between good and evil every day of his life. And yet, this man, who for so many years has lived on the fringes of eternal darkness, has a more fixed moral code than anyone I know. He sees things, even himself, in black and white. No excuses, no apologies, no such thing as extenuating circumstances. And yet when it comes to me . . . when it comes to me, he isn't exactly rational. Those lines become even more defined, until anyone who puts so much as a toe over them won't be tolerated.

The ACW put a whole hell of a lot more over that line than their toes.

Finally giving up on sleep, I push back the covers and stumble into the kitchen for a cup of coffee. Normally I play around a little, foam the milk, make a cappuccino, but today I don't care about fancy. Don't even care about taste. I just need a caffeine-delivery vehicle.

Lily stumbles into the kitchen a few minutes after I do. I pour her a cup and hand it to her—a dollop of cream and two sugars, just the way she likes it—and try to decipher the garbled words that come out of her mouth.

"You're speaking in tongues again," I tell her, pouring myself a second cup of coffee.

She flips me off, then goes back to mainlining her coffee. Finally, after another cup and five minutes of total and absolute silence, she pins me with eyes that are surprisingly bright and sharp after the night we had.

"Why did Declan leave last night?"

Trust Lily to cut right to the chase. "We had a difference of opinion."

"You argued? How the hell did you have the energy left to form words, let alone argue?"

"It wasn't an argument so much as a total inability to merge life philosophies."

"At four in the morning?" She stares at me incredulously. "After everything that happened last night? What gave you the idea that you could merge *anything*, let alone life philosophies? What the hell is wrong with you?"

And that's one of the many reasons I love my best friend so much. She has a way of putting things in perspective without even knowing she's doing it.

"I freaked out. Completely lost my mind, I think."

"Do tell." She gets up and pours herself a third cup of coffee, then reaches into the top cupboard for the secret stash of mini chocolate doughnuts. She doles out four of them for each of us because "It's definitely a four-doughnut morning."

I couldn't agree more.

She settles back at the table, coffee in one hand, doughnut in the other, and just looks at me. And looks at me. And looks at me.

I scramble to get my thoughts in order, to try to find a way to explain the jumble of emotions at work inside me. In the end, I settle for just letting the words tumble out in whatever order they want to. "I'm crazy about him and terrified of him all at the same time."

She cocks her head, studies me. "You think he'll hurt you?"

"Yes! But not in the way you're thinking."

"I'm not thinking anything, except that that man is devoted to you. You should have seen him last night when you were doing your trance thing. I thought he was going to lose his mind."

"That's part of the problem. The feelings between us, they're just so . . . intense. More intense than anything I've ever experienced."

"And that's a problem because?"

"Because I've never felt like this before. But we're so different, we look at the world in such opposite ways. I mean, Lily, he thinks murder is an acceptable way to end a disagreement!"

Her eyebrows practically touch her hairline. "Alride?"

"He says no—"

"And you don't believe him?"

"No, I do." That was one of the conclusions I came to as I stared up at the ceiling in the early morning hours. "But it very easily could have been him."

"So now we're condemning guys based on what we think they're going to do?" She shoves a whole doughnut in her mouth, contemplating while she chews. "I've got to tell you, Xan. That's not the best idea you've ever had. How am I supposed to ever get laid again if I'm constantly worried about something the guy might or might not do six months or six years down the road?"

"I'm not talking about some mythical maybe, Lily." And then I tell her everything Declan has told me in the last few days.

When I'm done, she does the last thing I expect. She kicks back in her chair and says, "I knew there was a reason I liked that man."

I gape at her. "He told me he has every intention of killing people, Lily."

"People who had every intention of killing you. Declan's an eye-for-an-eye kind of guy. You didn't really expect anything different from him, did you?

"Think about if someone tried to kill him. If they beat and tortured and emotionally devastated him. How would you feel?"

I'd want to fry the bastards. I don't say as much, but from the way she bursts out laughing, I'm pretty sure she can read the expression on my face.

"Still, wanting to do it and actually doing it are two very different things," I insist.

"I'm sorry, but has he actually killed anyone to avenge you? Even Kyle's alive and that sorry excuse for a warlock should be wiped off the face of the earth. To be honest, I'm a little disappointed Declan hasn't taken care of that already."

Her vehemence shocks me. "You don't mean that."

"Yeah, I really do. If I could figure out how to do it without getting caught, I'd probably end him myself."

Silence falls between us as I really don't have anything to say to that. I think of my earlier thought, about wanting to destroy anyone who hurt Declan. I wonder if I was too harsh on him last night. If I used my fear of his darkness as nothing more than an excuse to push him away.

After all, he was dark when I fell for him.

"When I was looking at Alride's body," I say slowly, "there was this moment when I was glad that he was dead. Glad that he had suffered."

"That seems perfectly understandable to me."

"But it isn't. Understandable, I mean. Even as I was feeling that way, I knew something was wrong. I could sense it, feel it. Like there was a darkness pressing down on me, taking me over." I shudder at the memory.

"You think that darkness came from Declan." Again, Lily is nobody's fool.

"Maybe. The more I think about it, the more I think it might be the whole soulbound thing."

"Because your souls are connected, you think Declan's bringing you into the dark?" She tilts her head as she thinks. "But that theory only works if you're also bringing him into the light."

"I don't think so. Remember what you said when you were researching what it means to be soulbound?"

"That was just one book. It doesn't have to be that way."

"I think it does." Being soulbound sounds like a good thing, but the fact of the matter is, it's pretty much the worst thing that can happen to two people. An Anathema born of the darkest magic possible, the only way out is death or the complete and total destruction of one of the pair's souls. It's why Declan planned to kill me all those years ago. He obviously didn't follow through with it, but that just means we have this problem now.

"The longer he and I are together, the worse it's going to get," I tell her.

"So, what are you going to do? Be apart? That didn't work for either of you and you know it." She reaches across the table, squeezes my hand. "There are some things you're going to be able to fight, Xan, and some that you aren't. There's nothing you can do about your connection to him. It's time to accept it and try to live with it."

"That's the whole point—only one of us is going to be able to live with it! And Declan won't hurt me. Not like that. He'd never allow me to lose my soul."

"That's a two-way street, Xandra. He would never do anything to harm your soul and you would never willingly destroy his. That's a good thing. It's why I believe you're both going to make it out of this and have an awesome future together."

"That's the point. We don't *have* a future. I can already feel him going darker. That's what I felt at the Council's headquarters last night and that's what I sensed in him when we got back last night. He had blood all over him, Lily. Even if it wasn't Alride's, it was somebody's."

"What did he say when you asked him about it?"

"Nothing. That's another problem—he won't talk to me, really talk to me, so we can try to figure this out. I know he thinks he's protecting me, but . . ."

I can feel tears welling up, but I refuse to let them fall. Tears won't help Declan, won't help us. So they're worthless to me right now. "He's so much stronger than I am, Lily. So much better at magic. There's no way I'll be able to fight him when things start to get worse. No way . . ." My voice breaks. I take a deep breath, force the words past the sudden tightness in my throat. "No way that I'll be able to save him."

And there it is, my worst fear, worst nightmare, out on the table for everyone to see. This is the terror that has haunted me for the past eight days, the nightmare that comes even after I've banished thoughts of Kyle and the ACW and what they've done to me. It's not just my fear that Declan's own shadows will overwhelm him, but that being soulbound to me will cast him irretrievably into the darkness. I could see it in him last night and it terrified me. That's why I pulled back from him. Not because I was afraid of him, but because I was afraid for him. The longer we're in contact, the closer we get, the faster one of us will be destroyed.

"I can't hurt him like that, Lily. I can't. It will end up destroying me as surely as I'll have destroyed him."

For a long time, Lily doesn't say anything. Not that I'm surprised. There's not much she *can* say. I've spent the last eight days examining the problem from every side I can think of and I've got nothing. I know Declan, who is so much more accomplished in Heka than I am, has done the same thing. If he'd come up with a solution, he would have said something. He hasn't. Which leads me to believe that there really is no solution.

"It's not done yet, Xandra."

"You're the one who told me there was nothing I could do about the Anathema, nothing anyone could do. You did the research."

"I know. But those are just old books. What do they know?"

I stare at her, my mouth open and eyes wide. "Okay, who are you and what have you done with Lily?" My best friend is a historian through and through, one whose powers are linked to her constant quest for knowledge.

Currently working on her PhD in ancient symbols, she all but worships books, and we both know it.

"I'm serious," she tells me. "Yes, in the past, no one's managed to undo an Anathema like this. But then, there's no proof that it's ever been used on people with the kind of power you and Declan have. You're the seventh daughter of the seventh daughter of the most powerful priestess who ever lived. You have more talent, more magic, in your blood than anyone else living today. And Declan . . . Well, he's just Declan. He can do anything. Who says he can't do this, too?"

"Don't." I get off the couch and cross to the window. Stare outside where it's starting to rain yet again. With the gray sky and grayer clouds, it looks almost as dark and bleak as I feel. "Please, don't give me false hope. I can't take it."

"It's not false if there's a chance."

"But there isn't."

"There could be." She sighs gustily. "Are you feeling weaker? Is Declan?"

"No, of course not, but that's the whole point. When we're near each other, being soulbound amplifies our power right up until—"

"No until. So your magic is good and so is Declan's. How about your soul? Do you feel like it's fracturing?"

"I told you about the darkness last night."

"How do you know that wasn't just you? After what they did to you, you have every reason to want Councilors dead. Maybe that's what you were feeling."

"And maybe pigs can fly." But she's got me thinking, hoping. Which is somehow a million times more painful than accepting.

"Well, how do you feel now? Do you feel dark? Broken?"

"I feel exhausted."

"Of course you do. But that's not the same thing."

"What about Declan, Lily? There's so much darkness in him already. And now, with this revenge thing, it's just getting worse. But is that because of his anger or because of me? Does he have a handle on it or is it spinning out of control because of our connection? I can't tell the difference. The only thing I do know for certain is that he won't tell me if he's in trouble."

"So what? Are you going to spend your life waiting for shit to happen? Like that chicken?"

I turn to stare at her. "What chicken?"

"You know, the one with the sky. She ran around screaming that it was falling, except it wasn't. It was an acorn or something."

"Are you talking about Chicken Little?"

"Yes! Chicken Little. She wasted her life worrying that the sky was going to fall. Don't be Chicken Little."

"Lily?"

"Yeah?" She looks so proud of herself that I almost hate to burst her bubble.

"In the end of that story, they all died."

"They did?"

"Yep. A fox ate them all because they were so worried about the sky falling, they forgot to be afraid of him."

"Are you sure?"

I nod. "Pretty sure."

"Well, fuck. That didn't turn out the way I thought it would. Stupid chicken." She thinks for a second, then reaches for the doughnut bag. "Well, if the sky really is going to fall, you might as well load up on fat and sugar."

I laugh because the alternative is crying and I've already done enough of that to last a lifetime. Then I decide what the hell. I take the bag and scarf down a couple more doughnuts.

Lily joins me and soon the entire bag is empty. Now I'm feeling even sicker but for totally different reasons. I'm not sure if that's better or worse.

Pushing back from the table with a sigh, I say, "I need to get going. Travis will only hold down the fort so long before freaking out."

Lily stands up as well. But it's obvious her mind is a million miles away. I'm halfway down the hallway to my room before she speaks. "He hasn't killed anyone, you know."

I don't pretend to misunderstand. "You don't know that."

"Yes, I do. And so would you if you'd just let yourself believe what's right in front of your face."

She's right. I know Declan hasn't gone that far into the darkness. At least not yet. "That doesn't mean he won't."

"But he hasn't yet. He's holding on. And that means you have to as well. If you can't hold on to anything else, hold on to that. Hold on to him."

I nod, because she's right. I have enough trouble in my life right now without borrowing more. Declan's taking things one day at a time with me. It's about time I do the same with him.

Fifteen

I've just pulled into the back parking lot at Beanz when it hits me. Half in the car, half out of the car, I feel the world starting to spin around me. I sink back into my car seat and try to figure out what the hell is going on. And then it's too late. The damn blackness sweeps over me before I can even begin to fight it.

Xandra! It's Shelby's voice and she's screaming my name, her little hands reaching for me as tears pour down her face.

I'm here, Shelby.

Where did you go? You were gone for such a long time.

I'm sorry, sweetheart. I'm here now.

Don't leave me, Xandra. Please don't leave me here alone! Not again.

I'll try not to. I promise. I only hope I can keep that promise. This connection with Shelby is different from the compulsions, different from the way I slip inside the victim and experience what he or she experiences. With Shelby, I've done that, but more often than not it's this strange voyeuristic thing, where I'm looking at her instead of looking out at the world through her eyes.

I try to glance around the room, to pick up some clues about where she is or who might have her. But I can't see anything but her, can't feel anything but her. It's like she's in a vacuum—one I can't hope to breach.

Tell me where you are, Shelby. Give me some clue and we'll come find you right now.

I'm scared. She's mean.

She? It's a woman who has you?

Yes. And a man. He's mean, but she's worse. She tries to act like she's nice, like if I do what she says, she won't hurt me. But I don't believe her. She has really mean eyes.

Good. Don't believe her, Shelby.

I want my mommy.

I know you do, baby. Can you look around the room? Or tell me what you see out the window? I know it's high, but maybe there's something out there—

Suddenly, I'm no longer in my car, no longer in the parking lot at all. Instead, I'm in that dingy little room, with the skinny cot and threadbare blanket and tiny window close to the ceiling. It lets in a little light, but not much—especially on a grim-looking day like today. I can't see much more than the plain white walls, the dark wood floor.

And Shelby. I can see Shelby, though she isn't talking to me anymore.

I can see her face clearly despite the dim light. Her pretty face has lost its color. The small smattering of freckles on the bridge of her nose stands out in startling contrast against her pale skin. Her eyes are dim, unfocused, and she's no longer squirming. No longer crying. No longer doing anything but staring sightlessly toward the center of the room.

My heart stutters in my chest for a few impossibly long seconds. She's dead. Oh dear goddess, they've bled her out, too. Killed her, too. Hysteria rises up inside me—terror and confusion and sickness all mix together in a way they didn't when I first saw what had been done to Councilor Alride.

That's enough. The words are snapped out, the voice deeper in pitch than Shelby's, but still feminine in nature. *Don't kill her. We may still need her.*

Strange rustling sounds, the clang of metal—like a handle hitting a bucket. And just that simply I'm pulled out of the room . . . and into Shelby.

My thigh hurts and my head hurts and I'm cold. So cold. A warm hand strokes my cheek. It feels good, though it doesn't chase the chill away. Or the pain.

Dear goddess, it hurts.

No, I remind myself violently even as the thought forms. I'm not cold. I'm not hurt. Shelby is.

This isn't happening to me. I repeat the thought like it's my new mantra, determined to hold it together. I have to hold it together if we have any hope at all of finding Shelby before it's too late.

Locking out the pain, the cold, the fear that is a ravenous monster inside me—inside Shelby—I try to focus. To see not just her, but the room around her. To see through her eyes. The room. The man hurting her. The woman who seems to control everything.

It's the first time I've ever tried anything like this and I don't have a clue what I'm doing. It's hard, impossibly hard, because everything seems to be muffled. The woman's voice. The eyes I use to look at her. Everything. Nothing is as it appears.

Shelby! I try to separate myself from her, from the pain that is coming in waves now. From the cold that seems to get deeper and more frigid with every second that passes. *Shelby! Answer me.*

I'm here, Xandra.

Can you give me something? I repeat. *Can you see anything out the window? Can you see the woman's face? Can you hear any noises? Construction? Traffic? Water?*

My head hurts.

I know, sweetheart. I'm sorry.

I'm sleepy. My legs hurt. There's a strange clicking noise that I can't identify, until I realize that it's her teeth. She's shivering so much, her teeth have begun to chatter. Poor, poor baby.

I know, honey. That's why I want to come find you. So we can get you some medicine. Your mommy will help me take care of your head and your leg. Provided the monsters who have her don't bleed her dry before then. But I need to know where to look. Is there anything—

Shelby turns her head and I get it. A quick picture, just a glimpse, of the top of a building outside her window. And not just any building. One with tall, glass-paned, triangular turrets on the top. And a clock built in right below one of the turrets.

I've got it, Shelby. I've got it.

Okay, Xandra. Okay. Her voice is fading. *I'm so tired now.*

I know, sweetheart. I know. Just hang on for me. Can you do that? Can you hang on just a little longer?

She doesn't answer. Panic rears its ugly head, but I beat it back down. She's asleep, I tell myself as I climb out of my car. Just asleep. Not dead.

I grab my purse and cell phone, head into Beanz. As I do, I can't help looking up at the small part of the Austin skyline I can see from where I'm standing. The Frost Bank Building, with its glass turrets and imbedded clocks facing out in all directions.

Travis hits me as soon as I make it through the door, lobbing questions at me about my bruises and cuts and whether I need him to take me to the hospital. Within seconds, my other employees—all of whom feel more like family than anything else—gather around me. Marta makes the biggest fuss, insists on helping me back to my office and bringing me a cup of tea and some oatmeal.

I let her because it makes them all feel better—I probably should have tried to put some makeup on to cover these bruises before heading out this morning—and because it suits my purposes to be alone in my office for a while. I want to call Nate, to tell him what I found out about Shelby.

Goddess knows, it isn't much, but there aren't that many places in Austin with a bird's-eye view of the Frost Bank Building. Even fewer with that particular angle. Surely Nate will be able to do something with it, even if it means searching every building in the area.

But when I call, I end up getting his voice mail. Disappointed and more than a little worried—I'm not sure how much longer Shelby is going to be able to last—I leave an urgent message. Then I stare at my phone and contemplate calling Declan. He hasn't called me this morning, but then, I am the one who flinched away from him last night. Who let him leave. Maybe that means I should be the one to call him.

But what if he doesn't want to hear from me? After all, Declan isn't much of a game player when it comes to this kind of stuff. If he wants to talk to me, he'll talk to me. Maybe I should—ugh! I barely resist the urge to slam the phone, or my head, into the desk. This is why I don't do relationships. Trying to figure out the other person's intentions makes you bat-shit crazy.

Deciding to hell with it—if he doesn't want to talk to me, he doesn't have to pick up—I search through my contacts for his name. But before I can press CALL, my phone starts to ring. It's my aunt Tsura and, while I adore her, I can't help thinking about sending the call straight to voice mail. Because while she's my favorite aunt, she's also my mother's twin sister and accomplished spy. Oh, she'll hand me some crap about wanting me to send her some of my special French roast coffee beans—because nobody has better coffee than I do—but the truth is she's probably on a reconnaissance mission for my mother.

But in the end, I pick it up. If I don't, she'll just keep calling. And soon enough, my mother will join the game, too.

"Hi, Aunt Tsura. How are you?"

"Fine, baby. How'd you know it was me? Are your powers chan—"

"Your number's in my phone. I looked at the caller ID."

"Oh, right. Of course." She sounds disappointed. Not exactly a surprise. "How are you doing, Xandra? Is Austin treating you well?"

"Absolutely." I sit gingerly in my desk chair, try to ignore the pain that swamps me with each little move that I make. "The coffeehouse is busy, but that's how I like it."

"Of course it's busy! You make the best coffee around. In fact, that's why I'm calling. I need you to send me five pounds of your French roast beans. I just can't get coffee like that around here."

"I'll be happy to. Are you at home in Ipswitch or are you in New York?"

"I'm in New York right now, but I'll be home in a few

days. You can send the coffee to Ipswitch. Or better yet, you can come visit and bring it with you."

I sigh, glance at the clock. It took her less than two minutes to get around to my mother's dirty work. Must be a record of some sort. Usually she has a bit more finesse. "I was just home a few weeks ago for the solstice. Remember? Mom tried to poison me?"

"I'm so sorry to have missed that!"

I choke on a sip of tea. "You sound disappointed."

"Only because I would have healed you right up, darling. Rachael is a great healer, but she's still learning the craft. There's a lot she doesn't know, including different ways to treat poisoning." She clucks her tongue. "I still can't believe Alia tried to do that. Sometimes I wonder about why she was gifted with all that power."

So do I. But that's my mother for you. Macchiavelli had been talking about her when he wrote that the ends justified the means. She doesn't care whom she hurts as long as the end result is the one she wants.

"Speaking of healing, how are you feeling? Are you all right?"

I shift uneasily, then wish I hadn't when my leg starts to ache—exactly where Shelby's cut is. "I'm fine. Just working hard. You know the drill."

"I do." She laughs lightly. "But everything's healed up from a couple of weeks ago? No complications?"

"I'm good. Honest. You and Declan did a great job fixing me up."

"Yes, well, he's got quite a talent for healing himself. Which is a surprise, since healers are usually drawn to the light." She sighs. "Oh well. The goddess works in mysterious ways, doesn't she? I've seen that over and over again with the way things have turned out in this family."

"She really does."

"Speaking of which, I heard you might have run into a little trouble down there in Austin last night."

"What do you mean?" She can't know about Viktor Alride's death yet, can she? I've been keeping an ear to the ground, so to speak, all morning, and nothing has come across any of the usual magical channels. So far, it seems the ACW is keeping the Councilor's death locked down pretty tightly. Surely I would have received a call from my parents if it was otherwise. Between my magic and the implications of his death . . . I guarantee my mother would want to check on me.

"You didn't sense anything *strange* last night, did you?"

Then again, maybe that was what this was—my mother's way of checking on me without really checking on me. Thinking about that, trying to figure this out, I know I sound wary when I answer, "That depends what you mean by strange."

Silence comes from the other end of the phone and I know my aunt is trying to puzzle out my reticence. I'm not normally one to play cat-and-mouse games, but this is my aunt, my mother's sister. She's a wily one, just like my mom, and I can totally believe this conversation is more of a fishing expedition than a simple chance to check up on me. And maybe I should tell her what's up—tell her about Alride and everything that happened before and since—but all that will do is worry my family. Considering it took every ounce of persuasion Declan had to convince my mother to go home a few days ago, the last thing I want—or need—is something that will send her scrambling right back here.

At least not if I want to keep my sanity.

And not if I want to protect Declan. Yes, he told me he didn't kill Alride. And yes, I believe him. But that doesn't mean anyone else will.

When the silence continues to stretch between my aunt and me—she's waiting me out, I can tell—I finally decide enough's enough. "I've got to go, Aunt Tsura. One of my baristas just stuck his head back here and told me we were getting slammed." I cross my fingers against the little white lie.

"Of course, of course. I shouldn't have called during your business hours." And still she makes no move to hang up the phone. Instead she says, "You know, Xan, if you need me ... if you get into trouble ... you can always call me. I'll come."

I can't help but soften toward her. The sincerity in her voice, the obvious love, is just one of the reasons she's my favorite of my mother's six sisters.

"I'm good. I swear."

"You sure about that? Declan's treating you right?"

"Declan's doing everything he can to keep me in bed and out of trouble."

I didn't catch the double meaning in my words until my aunt burst out laughing, and then my cheeks flushed even though she couldn't see me. "I meant—"

"I know what you meant, darling girl. But I'm sure Declan's doing *everything* in his power to keep you in bed."

"And on that note ..."

She was still giggling when she said, "Well, I'm glad you're doing so well, sweetheart. I know you're busy, so I won't keep you any longer. But please, consider coming to Ipswitch for a visit. I miss you terribly. You're my favorite niece, after all."

I laugh. "You say that to all of us."

"Maybe I do. But I really mean it when I say it to you."

"I'm glad." Even though I know she says that to everyone as well. "Because you're my favorite aunt."

"I hope so—close only counts in horseshoes, after all. Besides, all the gray hairs you've given me through the years better be worth something. Take care, Xandra. And come home, soon."

"I'll think about it."

"Do more than think about it." And with that statement—which sounded a lot more like a royal decree than a request—she hangs up the phone.

Yep. Definitely acting as my mother's stooge. Which is fine. Because if I can help it, it will be a long time before I step foot in Ipswitch again. My mother might have sat by my hospital bed a week and a half ago and sworn that she'd turned over a new leaf, but it'll take more than a few words to convince me to believe her. That belladonna poisoning was one for the record books.

Before heading to the kitchen, I take a couple of minutes to finish up my tea and enter the receipts that came in after I left the shop yesterday. I want to get started on my muffin batter before Travis leaves for class in an hour and I have to take over the front of the house. Then again, considering the way my staff responded to my bumps and bruises, maybe I'll let Marta handle it. Scaring customers away is not on my short list of things to do today.

I sink gratefully into the routine of baking. I've always loved to cook, but lately it's been more than just a creative outlet and a job. It's been a way for me to keep my sanity.

Baking is so orderly, so precise. You have to measure the ingredients exactly, add them in a certain order, mix them to a certain consistency. The more jumbled and chaotic my world gets, the more I appreciate the precision of these moments in my kitchen.

I manage to get two batches of banana chocolate chip muffins in the oven and am just filling the tins with the batter for my best-selling strawberry cream cheese muffins when Travis pokes his head into the kitchen. "Nate's here. He's following up on your phone call."

"Awesome. Tell him I'll be right out."

I finish up the muffins, get them in the oven and set the timers so Marta and Jules know when to take them out. Then I make a quick chicken panini sandwich for Nate. I plate it up with some chips and fruit and grab his favorite iced tea. I know the way I take care of Nate whenever he comes in annoys Declan, but I do it for all my friends. And these days, Nate needs the TLC almost as much as Declan does.

He grins when I slide the plate onto the table in front of him, but his smile quickly fades when he gets a look at my face. "Xandra! What happened?" he demands, his hands clenching into fists.

"It's nothing," I tell him.

"That's nothing? You look like someone mistook you for a punching bag." His hand comes up and probes gently at my jaw, in much the same way Declan did when he first saw me last night. With Nate it feels a little uncomfortable — we're friends, but we were once on our way to being more than that, before Declan came to town.

It must feel weird to him, too, because he drops his hand after only a second or two. "Who did this?"

"It's not what you think."

"Did Declan—"

"No! Of course not!" I answer impatiently. "I told you it wasn't like that. I got this looking for Shelby."

"Shelby? Why would you go looking for her by yourself? Why didn't you call me? Why didn't—"

"Because," I interrupt before he can work up a whole new head of steam. "I didn't actually go out looking for her. That's not how it works."

"Oh." He settles back in his chair, watches me carefully. "Right. So how did you get that black eye if you weren't physically searching for her?"

I explain as much as I'm able, leaving out the magic but keeping everything else in. By the time I'm done, Nate looks completely sick. "Xandra, I'm sorry. If I'd known what it was like for you, I never would have asked."

"Then I'm glad you didn't know. To be honest, I wasn't sure how it was going to work out, either. I've never connected to someone who's alive before. But we need to get to her quickly. I'm not sure how much more time she's got. She's hurt pretty badly."

The words galvanize him to action. As he eats, he calls the detective I assume is in charge of the case and relays the information I gave him. But he doesn't stop there. Within fifteen minutes he's got an entire search party organized. I learned a couple of weeks ago what a damn fine cop Nate is, but standing here, watching him mobilize to find a little girl who isn't even technically his responsibility, drums it home all over again.

He gets up to depart, and I slip out from behind the counter so I can catch him before he leaves. I can't tell him that the people who have Shelby are magic, can't tell him that they are actually evil. But I can't just let him walk in there blind, either.

"Hey, Nate. Do you have a second?" I call as I come up behind him.

"For you? Always." He looks at me quizzically, his green eyes calm but his body filled with nervous energy. He's more than ready to go out on the hunt.

"These people who have Shelby. I don't know who they are, but I've seen enough to know they're bad news."

"I figured that when you told me she was in bad shape."

"No, I mean, it's more than that. More than hurting a defenseless little girl. They're dangerous, Nate. You need to be careful. You need to be really careful."

His eyes narrow and the smile slips from his face. "What aren't you telling me?"

Too much, but he wouldn't believe me if I tried to explain. "I just get really bad vibes from them. They've killed before, and it's not just kids. Just please, don't go storming in once you find the place. They'll hurt you and I don't want anything to happen to you."

At my words, everything about him softens just a little. "Thanks, Xandra. I'll be careful." He gestures to my face. "I'm really sorry about what it cost you."

I touch my cheek. "This is nothing. Not if it means Shelby gets to go home."

"I'll keep you posted on what we find. And if you manage to connect," he says, using the word awkwardly, like he's still uncomfortable with it, "to her any more, please let me know."

"Of course I will."

He pulls me in for a quick hug, drops a kiss on my uninjured cheek. I return the friendly gesture, then step back. As he turns to go, I look past him for the first time — and right into Declan's dark and shadowed eyes.

Sixteen

Nate says something else to me on his way out the door, but I don't hear it. I wouldn't even be aware of him exiting except he passes right by Declan, on whom I'm hyperfocused. I try not to respond to the deliberately bland gaze he shoots Nate as the detective sweeps by him, but it's hard—especially when hot color creeps slowly up my neck.

I don't know why I'm so nervous. It's not like I did anything wrong. I helped a friend who asked me, and in doing so maybe helped a terrified little girl as well. I should be proud of what I did, not worried about how Declan is going to react.

Except it's not the part where I helped Shelby that I'm worried about. Then again, there doesn't seem to be any reason for me to be worried at all. Declan doesn't seem upset by what he witnessed, so why should I be? Except—except his eyes are a little too calm, his face a little too composed.

Of course, I could just be projecting my own issues onto him. I'm not sure how well I'd take seeing him hugging one of his old romantic interests only a few hours after his perceived rejection of me.

When he makes no move to come toward me, I raise

a hand in a tentative greeting. He waves back, a two-fingered kind of thing that is totally Declan. And totally annoying. Maybe he's more upset with me than he's letting on.

Deciding to give the lion a few minutes to chill out before I beard him in his den, I return to the counter and take drink orders from the small line that formed there while I was talking to Nate. Once the line is down to a trickle and Declan *still* hasn't moved from the spot against the wall where he's carelessly lounging, I start to get annoyed. Since he went to all the effort of showing up here, the least he could do is make it to the front counter to talk to me. Especially since I can feel his eyes on me even when my back is turned to him.

More customers come in and I wait on them, too, getting more and more irritated the longer this absurd standoff between us goes on. I've just about resolved to ignore him completely—that's the least that he deserves—when it occurs to me that this whole situation might very well be my fault. He came to see me, and yes, he hasn't actually made it to the counter, but I've been busy filling orders pretty much the whole time he's been standing there. If it was anyone else, any of my other friends, I would have done for them what I did for Nate—made up their favorite sandwich, grabbed their favorite drink. . . . How ridiculous am I that I'm too proud to do the same for the man I care about more than any other? The man I want to call my own.

Screw it. I head back to the kitchen where Marta and Lisa are just finishing cleaning up from the lunch rush. Both batches of my muffins are cooling on the counter and—after sending them out to work the register—I snag a strawberry one, put it on a plate. I add some of the pasta salad Declan likes so much and dish up a big bowl of chicken noodle soup to go with it.

After carrying the dishes back to my office, I go in search of Declan. He hasn't moved from where I left him, but his head is bowed, his eyes closed, his fingers pinching the bridge of his nose like he's trying to relieve a headache.

Sorrow pours from him and it's such a change from the usual vitality and rage that it hits me right in the gut. Makes me feel a million times worse about letting him leave last night than I already do. I needed time to come to grips with everything that has happened, but when I accused him of murder, I obviously hurt him and that's the last thing I ever wanted to do.

Heart bruised with love for him, I start across the room. I'm still several feet from him when Declan senses me, looks up. Our eyes meet, hold, clash, and somehow I know that it's taking every ounce of self-control he has not to bound across the restaurant to me. Not to sweep me up in his arms and take over the way he's so damn good at. But he doesn't do it. Instead, he waits for me to approach him. He gives me that control even though it's totally out of character for him.

Looks like that game of wills I thought we were playing really was all in my head.

I step closer and want nothing more than to pull him into my arms, to hold him and comfort him the way he's done for me so many times before. But not here, not in front of all these people with their prying eyes and inability to understand everything that Declan and I have gone through.

So I reach for his hand instead. He clasps it like a lifeline, and for the first time it hits me that he needs me

as much as I need him. I don't know why it's such a revelation—we are soulbound, after all—but this is so much
more than that. This is Declan needing me, Xandra, not
just the Anathema at work.

I lead him back to my office, close the door. And wrap
my arms around him.

He buries his face in the curve of my neck, shudders.
And takes the comfort I so desperately need to give.

When he finally lifts his head, those dark eyes of his
find mine, hold. He's looking for something in my gaze. I
don't know what, but I'm determined to give him whatever he needs.

"I'm sorry," I tell him. "I should have asked you to
stay last night."

"I'm the one who's sorry. You'd just had the worst day
imaginable and all I did was add to it."

He reaches up, strokes his fingers down my cheek. I
turn so that my mouth lines up with his palm and press
a soft kiss right in the middle of his hand.

"I made you something to eat."

"Thank you." He settles on my visitor's chair. "Will
you eat with me?"

"I'm not—" I break off at his long, steady look. He
might have been shaken earlier, but Declan is still Declan. "Okay. The strawberry muffins are my favorite."

I lean against the desk, but Declan whips his hand out
and grabs my wrist. Then he tugs until I'm sitting, curled
up, on his lap. "How are you supposed to eat soup like
this?" I demand.

"I'll manage." He breaks off a piece of the strawberry
muffin, feeds it to me. I let him, because I can sense that
he needs this. He needs to take care of me, comfort me
in a way I wouldn't let him early this morning.

As he does, we talk of silly things. Travis's new haircut. A new cookie I want to try out. The traffic jams that rain always brings to Austin.

Before I know it, I've eaten the entire muffin and half of the pasta salad—all from Declan's hand. When he goes to feed me yet another bite, I moan in protest. "I can't," I tell him. "You've stuffed me."

"Good." He looks me over. "Your color's better."

"I think that has more to do with you than the food." His eyes go impossibly darker and I grab his hand, pulling it to my heart. "Thank you."

My gratitude is for a lot more than the minutes he spent feeding me, and he knows it. I might not agree with everything he does, I might be scared of the parts of him he keeps hidden beneath his oh-so-calm surface, but I know he's got my best interest at heart. No matter what he's doing, no matter how he's doing it, I know that what he really wants is to protect me.

"You're welcome." Another long, steady look. "What did Nate want?"

Knowing what it cost him to ask that, I answer immediately. Hold nothing back. "I had another dream about Shelby."

He stiffens. "Oh yeah? Did you find out anything else?"

"She's close. When she looks out the small window in her room, she's got a view of the Frost Bank Building."

"What kind of view?" he asks, suddenly alert.

I pull back, wary of where his line of questioning is going. "Why are you so interested?"

"A little girl's been stolen from her parents, is being tortured by goddess only knows who. And you think I shouldn't be interested in finding her?" He's stiffened up again, his voice as cool and remote as it was when he walked out of my bathroom last night.

"I didn't mean it like that."

"I think you did. But it's fine. I'm used to it."

The words are a slap in the face, as is the way he lifts me gently off him and settles me on my desk chair. "I should probably go. I have a number of things I still have to get done today."

"You didn't eat."

"I'll get something at home."

My stomach tightens uneasily. I hate the tension that stretches between us, the stilted conversation that's polite but not much more. Again, I'm assaulted by the knowledge that my inability to trust him completely is ripping us apart. But how can I trust him when the shadows around him grow darker with each day that passes? When he admits with no compunction that he's already set things in motion to kill one man? That he plans to kill more?

Then again, how can I not trust him when he's proven, over and over again, that he'll do anything for me?

When Declan leans down to brush an impersonal kiss across my cheek—the same cheek that Nate kissed just a little while ago—I turn my head so that his lips connect with mine instead.

I wrap my arms around his neck, pull him closer. Then I suck his lower lip between my teeth, nipping gently at it.

At that first soft bite, it's as though a dam bursts inside him.

His hands go to my hair, twist and tug until my head is at the angle he wants it. His mouth opens against mine, his tongue delving in to stroke, to taste, to plunder. It's an old-fashioned word, one I never thought I'd use in reference to a kiss, but it fits perfectly. Declan plunders me, takes everything I have to give, then looks for more. Demands more.

Which is completely fine with me. My own hands find their way into the cool, ebony silk of his hair. My tongue meets his in an intimate caress. My body, my bruised and aching body, arches against him in a desperate plea for his touch.

He doesn't take the hint. Instead, he pulls away, stumbles back a step or two like he doesn't trust himself not to touch me. His lips are swollen, his eyes hazy with desire, his hands shaking with his self-imposed restraint.

"Why are you stopping?" I demand, my own body trembling with need for him.

"Do you want this?"

I stare at him incredulously. "Doesn't it feel like I do?" I take his hand, press it to my breast. He groans as his thumb strokes over my hard nipple, once. Twice.

"Declan, please." I need him, need to prove to myself that the connection between us is still there.

But he stops, his palm resting directly over my heart. I know he can feel it thundering beneath his touch.

Declan closes his eyes, makes a sound that's a cross between desire and devastating pain. I reach for him, run my hands over his washboard stomach and narrow hips. Revel in the hitch of his breath, in the fine trembling he can't control.

And still he doesn't take me.

"What's wrong?"

When his lids lift again, his eyes are midnight black, and I swear I can see small flames flickering in their depths.

"I need to hear you say it," he tells me in a voice that is all smooth whiskey and starry nights. "I need to know I'm not influencing you, that all this heat isn't just the soulbound thing at work." He takes a deep breath. "Do you want me, Xandra?"

His restraint makes no sense, not when we've made love dozens of times in the last week and a half. And yet it makes perfect sense, because Declan will never take anything from me that he isn't sure I want to give. Our fight obviously shook him up, too.

Wanting to erase the doubt I can see in his beautiful face, I reach for him and wrap my hand around his neck. I tug until his mouth is only inches from mine.

"I want this, want you, more than I want my next breath. More than I've ever wanted anyone or anything in my life.

"Kiss me." I brush his lips with mine.

"Take me." I stand, rub my body against his.

"Love m—"

His mouth crushes down on mine before I can say another word, and then he's lifting me up, grinding himself against the very center of me. I moan, wrap my legs around his back for better access. Scratch my nails gently down his back.

He mutters a curse against my lips, something dark and dirty and oh so sexy. Then he's turning, backing us up against my office wall. Thrusting against me until I feel like I'm going to lose my mind if I can't feel him hot and hard and naked against me. Inside me.

I fumble with his shirt, desperate to pull it over his head. But his hands are in my hair, on my breasts, and he won't let go long enough for me to get the damn thing off.

"Please," I tell him, arching my back in a desperate need to get closer, to feel the heavy weight of his body against my own.

A flick of his hand and the shirt is gone. And so are the rest of our clothes.

"I'm beginning to really like that trick," I murmur against his mouth.

He grins, though he doesn't stop kissing me, even for a moment. "Me, too." Then he's reaching between us, his fingers stroking around and over my clit before dipping down to test my readiness.

"Fuck. You're so tight. So hot."

"So ready for you," I tell him, hitching my legs a little tighter around his waist. "Please, Declan, don't make me wait. I need you."

"I thought you liked foreplay?" he whispers as he trails hot kisses over my cheek, down my jaw.

"Fuck foreplay!"

I feel his grin against my neck. "I'd rather fuck you."

And then he does, slipping inside me so easily, so perfectly. This is what it means to be meant for someone, this glorious, wonderful, perfect fit. Not just in our bodies, but in our souls. I can feel his dark, wild spirit tangling with my own, the connection between us locking more tightly into place with each breath we take. With each slide of his body into mine.

I turn my face away, but his hand comes up, grasps my chin. "Look at me, Xandra. Please. Look at me."

I do, because I can't say no to him. Not when he uses that gravelly deep voice of his. And not when every moment, every movement, fuses our souls more deeply together. My eyes lock on his, and in their depths I see the same joy and terror that I know he can see in mine.

I've never felt more vulnerable in my life, and there's a voice, deep inside me, that's urging me to look away. To hold myself back. Not to give him everything when our future is still so uncertain.

I ignore it, shove it back down as pleasure races up my spine and nearly overwhelms me with its intensity. Because no matter what pain the future brings, no matter what danger or disaster is waiting for us, this connection between us is completely and utterly worth it.

I love you.

The words tremble in my soul, hover on my lips. But before I can say them, before I can give him the reassurance we both so desperately need, Declan slams his mouth down on mine. He strokes one thumb over my nipple, another over my clit. And with a final thrust of his hips, he sends me hurtling over the edge into a climax so electric it's like magic itself.

Seventeen

Once we can both breathe again, I expect Declan to lower me to the ground. I'm not sure my legs will support me after that, but I'm willing to give it the old college try. Only Declan doesn't pull away, doesn't even pull out of me. Instead, he just leans against me, eyes closed, forehead pressed to mine, and just breathes.

"Am I too heavy?" he finally, reluctantly, asks.

I tighten my arms around his shoulders. "You're perfect."

He grins. "It's about time you figured that out."

"And so modest, too."

"Modesty is overrated."

"Obviously." I press kisses along the curve of his shoulder. "You know," I tell him in between soft, sweet smooches, "our fight might be over, but we still need to talk out the points we disagree on."

He groans and shifts a little, though he doesn't pull away. The slight movement sets off a bunch of sensations deep inside me and I gasp. Tremble, despite myself.

His laugh is low and sexy as he moves again. This time he shifts so that his palm rests against my lower abdomen, his fingers curling possessively over my sex. It's different from the other times he's touched me, though, because the heat I'm feeling is more than just sex. It's a fine, electric vibration that originates in his fingertips and works its way—slowly, sensuously—over my skin, and then through it, to what lies beneath.

"What are you—" I break off as a wave of pleasure slams through me, before finally gasping, "What are you doing?"

"If you don't know, I must be doing it wrong," he teases as he leans in for a kiss. As he does, another shock wave of pleasure shoots through me, this one bringing me to the very brink of orgasm all over again.

"You're not—" I gasp, twisting my hips to maximize the sensations sparking inside me, then try again. "You're not going to distract me with sex this time."

His lips smile against my own. "Hate to be the one to break it to you, but I think I already have." I feel another shock of electricity—this one longer and more intense than the ones that came before.

I scream a little, claw at his back in a desperate need to get closer. "Finish it," I demand when I can think again.

"What if I don't want to?" Yet another pulse sets my nerve endings jangling. "I kind of like you like this, all sexy and demanding."

I grab his hair in my fists, yank his head back. "I'll show you demanding! Finish it!" I growl against his lips.

"What's the magic word?" he asks, even as he slides one of those magic fingertips of his against my clit.

"Please!"

"I was thinking more along the lines of *abracadabra*, but *please* works, too." He bends his head, pulls one of my nipples into his mouth. And with another jolt of electricity straight to my sex, sends me tumbling into a second orgasm.

It takes me even longer to come down this time, because Declan keeps petting and kissing and touching me. Every time I think I've caught my breath, another wave crashes through me until finally, in self-defense, I sink my teeth into his heavily muscled shoulder.

He jerks against me with a groan. I like the sound, so I do it a second time, relishing the way such a simple touch from me can send him spiraling into another release as well.

"Now," I tell him after our heart rates settle and he finally stops kissing me, "it's time to talk about the ACW."

With a groan, Declan pulls back and lets me slide slowly to the floor. He keeps an arm around me—just to make sure I'm steady on my feet, even as he conjures our clothes back up.

"That's a pretty parlor trick," I tell him as I grab my jeans out of thin air. "Ever thought about including it in the show?"

"To do that, either I'd have to get naked or I'd have to strip a member of the audience. Neither seems an optimum choice for my career."

"You could get a really cute assistant. Strip her down on stage. I'm sure the male contingent of your audience won't mind."

"Maybe not," he answers with a smirk. "But transubstantiation only works if I'm really motivated. Maybe if you were up on stage with me . . ."

It's my turn to smirk. "Dream on, buddy."

"Oh, I will." My bra is dangling from his fingers when he swoops in for another kiss.

After he's dressed and I've snagged some more food for him from the front of the house, I settle down behind my desk and try to figure out the best way to launch into the conversation we need to have. In the end, Declan does it for me.

"You can try to reason with me all you want, Xandra, but when it comes to the ACW, I'm going to do what I see fit."

"Even if what you see fit to do causes a major war?"

"Hard to have a war if all the players are dead," he says, taking a huge bite of the steak sandwich I made him.

"Well, that's impressive reasoning." My tone says it's anything but. Declan just grins at me and forks up a bite of pasta salad.

"Right now we have a bigger problem than what happened to me. We both know that the Council, even now, is scrambling to figure out what happened to Alride so that they can annihilate the threat."

"That's all I'm trying to do, too, you know. Annihilate the threat to you."

"Yes, but you don't have the full backing of Hekan law behind you. They do," I tell him with a roll of my eyes. "But that's a different story. It won't take them long to start running through the list of people who would want a Councilor dead. And once they do that, it will take even less time for them to land on your name. Or mine."

"Don't kid yourself. They've already landed on our names. I'm expecting to receive notice of a command performance any hour now."

Just the thought makes my stomach hurt. "What are we going to do?"

"Not much, besides go see them."

I stare at him incredulously. "Are you kidding me? Tell me you don't honestly want to walk straight into the belly of the beast—knowing its claws and teeth are aimed straight at you."

"I already told you what I wanted to do," he answers with a sardonic lift of his brow. "And you didn't seem any more impressed with that plan than this one."

He's right. I know he is, know I'm being impossible, but I don't know what to do. I'm a princess of Ipswitch, have been surrounded by the dark power struggle that accompanies politics all of my life. If my powers weren't forcing my involvement, none of this would be all that new. No, Councilors haven't been murdered in my lifetime—all part of the power and stability my mother brings to the throne—but it isn't the first time in history this has happened. And it probably won't be the last.

But that doesn't mean I want Declan, my family or myself to be caught up in it in any way. Because when things like this go bad, they go really bad, really fast.

"We need to stop this," I tell him.

"Kind of hard to stop it now. Alride's already dead."

"Yes, but there's no guarantee another Councilor won't follow. We need to figure this out before someone else dies."

There's an urgency to my tone that I know Declan hears, but for the first time in forever, he doesn't respond. Instead, he just leans his back against the wall and watches me, his arms crossed over his chest. Though he doesn't say anything, I know him well enough—even after only a few weeks—to recognize a *hell no* gesture when I see it.

"We can't just let them all die."

"No one's saying anyone else is going to die. This could be a one-off thing with Alride."

"You don't really believe that."

"No."

"Then we need to do something."

He lifts a brow. "Why? Seems to me whoever's doing this is taking care of a problem. I'm more than okay with that."

"Taking care of a—they're killing people, Declan."

"People who need to die. I already told you I have no compunction whatsoever about that. I'm not a hypocrite, Xandra."

"I never said you were. But we're talking about people's lives here—"

"The same people who had no problem fucking around with your life. The same people who actually hired someone to kill you. I'm not going to forget either of those things just because you want me to."

He bends down, starts yanking on his boots while I search desperately for something to say that might change his mind. Even as I do, I have a feeling I'm too late. In his head, Declan condemned these people to death—even the innocent ones—the moment he realized they were responsible for what Kyle did to me. The fact that someone else is killing them might bug him—knowing, as I do, that he wants to do it himself—but at the same time, it must be kind of nice. He gets the outcome he wants without having to face me after doing something unforgivable.

"But what happens to the Council?" I finally ask. "If all the Councilors are dead, what happens to the whole Hekan community?"

"Same thing that always happens. They'll be replaced by more corrupt witches and wizards and the whole thing will start all over again."

"Exactly."

"So, what's your point?"

"The point is, killing them isn't going to solve any-thing."

"Yeah, but their gruesome deaths will stand as a warning not to mess with you."

"Who else is going to mess with me? It's not like my birthright doesn't offer me some protection."

Again, Declan doesn't look impressed. "The world's a fucked-up place, Xandra, filled with fucked-up people who will be drawn to a power like yours. The Council went after it once and it's only a matter of time before they go after it again. Once that rabbit's out of the hat, it won't take long before every asshole with a little magic and a plan comes calling.

"What's so special about me? I've been latent for twenty-six years and now that I'm not, I can see dead people. It's not exactly a power that's in high demand."

"I keep telling you. You don't know what your magic is yet. Yes, communing with the dead is the first power to have woken up in you. But there's a lot more still buried. When they come out, you'll be more powerful than your mother ever dreamed of being."

His words strike a chord deep inside me, send me reeling, though I work hard not to show it. "You don't know that."

"Yeah, I do."

"How?"

"The same way you can sense my magic. I feel it deep inside you."

"And you think my magic makes me a target?"

He gives me a no-shit look. "I know it makes you a target. Otherwise, the ACW never would have come after you. Their deaths will prevent that from happening again—especially if I kill one or two of them."

His words send terror skittering through me. "You have to stop thinking like that," I tell him firmly. "Self-defense is one thing, but revenge is totally different. You can't actually sanction the killing of eight people just because you think it will keep me safe."

He's never looked more serious than when he says, "I'd let a lot more than eight people die to keep you safe, Xandra. If you don't know that, then you don't know me at all."

"That's ridiculous! I'm not that special, Declan."

"You're that special to me. I told you yesterday. Nobody hurts you and lives."

The shadows are back, and in that moment I see him more clearly than I ever have before. It shakes me to my core as understanding, true understanding, of his perspective, seeps in for the first time.

We see things differently—magic, the world, ourselves and each other—will probably always see things differently. For some people and some things, that's fine. I don't care if he likes red wine while I like white or that he's a night person while I'm definitely all about the day. Those differences don't matter. But our magic, our power, those differences, change everything.

I understand Declan's anger. I do. If someone tried to hurt him, kill him, I'd hunt the bastard myself. Take great joy in watching him rot in prison forever. But vengeance of the type Declan demands? Sanctioning violent, premeditated murder? Or doing it himself? That I can't understand—or get behind.

He doesn't say anything as I think this through, just sits there watching me with implacable eyes. There's a part of me that wants to throw myself into his arms and beg him to see reason. But there's another, bigger part that knows that he won't. That he can't. Not as long as the darkness surrounds him like a cloak.

As the realization sinks in, I want to scream, to cry, to beg the goddess to—what? Beg her to do what? I ask myself a second time. To take the soulbinding away? To take Declan from me? Because if I can't accept him, walking away is the only route left to me.

No! It's a soul-deep cry, an instinctive claiming that goes deeper than black and white or right and wrong. I will never ask the goddess for that because I will never let him go. Declan is mine. Above and beyond the soul-binding, above and beyond family and duty, magic and mayhem, he's mine and he will stay mine.

If that means the shadows that are so much a part of him eventually become a part of me ... well, then, I'll deal with that when it happens. Because anything else is nonnegotiable.

Declan knows what I'm thinking. It's in every implacable line of his face, every steady breath he forces himself to take. He must be a hell of a poker player, because he's giving away nothing. But for me, that's his tell. Because lately when he looks at me, there's so much emotion in his eyes, his face, that I can't help but know what's going on inside him.

I pull him close because I can't do anything else, press soft kisses to his eyes, his cheeks, his forehead. With each press of my lips, he relaxes a little more, that terrible rigidity draining out of him inch by inch. By the time I get to his lips, he's ready for me, his hand tangling in my hair as he holds me in place. Then he ravages me, using his lips and teeth and tongue to brand me in a way I won't soon forget.

I'm gasping when he finally pulls away, my body shaking with need and love and a bunch of other emotions I'm too wired to identify. Reaching up, I grab fistfuls of that wild black hair of his and tug, waiting until his eyes meet mine. "We're not done talking about the Council."

"You can talk all you want."

I make a frustrated sound deep in my throat. "No. *We'll* talk." I narrow my eyes at him, knowing that if I give in now, it's just an invitation for him to walk all over me later in our relationship. And while my feelings for him are often overwhelming, I'm no pushover. Better that he know that now. "I mean it, Declan. I don't want you doing anything without talking to me first."

He watches me closely as he says, "Fine. We can talk. But that doesn't mean I'll end up agreeing with you. And in the end I'm going to do what needs to be done. They will not hurt you again."

Determined to stay on task, I brace myself not to melt at the concern and possession evident in his words. "That's fine. I'm all for them not getting near me again. All I'm asking is that we take a little time to figure out what that is before you turn all avenging angel on me."

"I'm no angel, Xandra."

"Yeah, don't I know it." I lean over and kiss his cheek. "But you're no devil, either."

"I could be." He grabs me, tumbles me into his lap. "I've been on my best behavior for you."

I can't even imagine a universe where that's true. And if this is his good behavior, what on earth does it look like when he's being bad?

Choosing not to go there for now, I watch him finish his sandwich. Then say, "I don't believe everyone on the ACW is corrupt. You want to kill them all because you think they're all involved in the soulbinding and in what happened to us. But some of the Council members are new—they might not know anything about what's going on. You can't tell me you honestly think they should die, too."

"If you lie down with dogs . . ."

"It's not the same thing."

"Sure it is."

"No. It's not." Determined to win this battle, I try to stare him down. But Declan just looks at me, the left corner of his mouth lifted in a half grin that tells me he's not budging. He looks hot and I want to jump him again, even as a part of me wants to strangle him.

"Look, can we at least think this through? Try to figure out who's doing the killing? Because I don't believe everyone on the ACW is corrupt and I can't stand the idea of someone innocent dying when there might be a chance that we can stop it."

For long seconds, he doesn't say anything. Just looks at me with that shit-eating grin. Then, with a shrug, he says, "Okay."

"Okay?" I narrow my eyes at him. "After all that fuss, that's all you have to say?"

"Pretty much." He breaks off a corner of the cookie I brought him and holds it out to me.

I eye him suspiciously. That agreement came way too easily. "Really?"

"Why do you look so skeptical? I am capable of being reasonable, you know."

"Oh yeah. Reason is your middle name." I continue to watch him distrustfully.

"Fine." He reaches for my hand, squeezes tight. "You said we. I liked the sound of it."

"Enough to give my way a shot?"

He shrugs. "Yeah. Sure. Why not?"

His concession is the last thing I expect to hear. But as I watch him, see the pleasure in his eyes that he's no longer trying to hide, it hits me. Declan is one of the most powerful, most feared warlocks in the world. But that kind of power isn't exactly conducive to a real relationship— any kind of relationship. No wonder he's so close to Ryder. For centuries, his half brother has probably been the only one he can count on to see beneath the power to the man.

"Just so you know, I like the sound of it, too." More than I ever thought I would.

Eighteen

After Declan leaves for a meeting he "can't miss," one that he promises won't end with him splattered in blood this time, I head back out to the front of the house. Help out brewing coffee, as the predinner crowd is just beginning to descend. As I do, I work hard to keep the just-got-laid smile off my face. I think I succeed, too—at least until Travis, who is working a split shift today, puts his tongue firmly in his cheek and points out that my shirt is on inside out.

So much for Declan's transubstantiation skills.

After ducking into my office to fix my shirt, I switch places with Lisa, who's working the kitchen orders. Actual food orders are slow right now and will be for the next hour and a half or so—which makes this the perfect time to prep my dough for the morning. Each day, I make four different kinds of cookies, two kinds of muffins and a couple of different cakes. Lots of people have told me it's too much work, that I need to streamline or hire the baking out, but the fact of the matter is, I enjoy it.

Back before my magic kicked in, this was the only kind of potion making I got to do—mixing ingredients and creating beautiful, delicious treats for people to enjoy. Then again, who am I kidding? Even with my new powers, this is still the only mixing I get to do. Potions are really more of my mother's thing. Hence the reason I know so much about them. When I was younger, and still trying to be her, I struggled with hundreds of different potions, desperate to get one right. Just one.

It never happened, though, and eventually I moved to Austin to get away from the craziness of being the only latent princess in Ipswitch's history. I was a huge embarrassment to my family—a reminder of how things could go terribly wrong—so I figured it was best to get out of town. Plus, here I can live my own life, relatively safe from my mother's interference. At least some of the time.

Of course, now that my powers are kicking in, things are getting weird on that front on a whole new level. My mom wants me back in Ipswitch, even though my life is here. Now that I finally have magic, she expects me to claim my rightful place in the family, but the fact of the matter is, I'm in no way ready to go back to the restrictions of that life. Especially not now that I have Declan.

After I prep the chocolate chip cookie and sugar cookie dough, I set about making the red velvet cupcakes I try to do a couple of times a week. I'd have them every day—they're big sellers—but they're my favorites, too, and if I have too much access to them, I completely lose the ability to fit into my jeans.

As I'm whipping up the batter, I try to ignore the fact that I may not be able to stay in Austin much longer. Oh, I have no intention of giving Beanz up—I love this place—but it's only a matter of time before my mom and dad get wind of what really happened here a couple of weeks ago. So far, Donovan has covered for me—telling them that my involvement with Kyle came only from my magic and not because he was hired by the Council to kill me.

He's convinced I should tell them the truth, and I know it's only a matter of time before he takes things out of my hands. But if they had a clue what was really going on, we'd end up at war with the ACW. And while Ipswitch is the biggest seat of Hekan power in the world, going up against the Council is an act of treason (something I keep trying to remind Declan of). Without absolute proof, and probably even with it, my parents would end up locked in a power struggle of epic proportions. And if that happens, there's no guarantee how it will work out. Yes, my mom and dad are among the most powerful practitioners of Heka on the planet. But so are the Council members.

The only thing about the outcome I am sure of is that it wouldn't be a fair fight.

So, no, I won't let my family get pulled into this until I have no other choice. It kills me, already, all the agony that Declan has had to suffer through the years. Letting the Council get their hooks into anyone else that I care about is not going to happen. Not if I have any say in it.

I pop the cupcakes in the oven, set the timer. Start in on the batter for my chocolate chip brownies. And think back over my discussion with Declan. Maybe he's right. Maybe we should just step back and hope that whoever's gunning for the Council gets them all. Hell, maybe we should help them. We could figure out who the corrupt Councilors are and then just take care of—

Horror sweeps through me as I realize what I'm thinking about. What I'm contemplating. It doesn't make sense, not when I've been so determined to keep Declan from violence.

So where are the thoughts coming from? My stomach clenches, rolls. I press my hand to it, try to breathe through the nausea that isn't really nausea. It's something else, something darker. I don't feel sick exactly, but I don't feel normal, either. It's like there's something else creeping through me, a darkness whispering through my veins and staining everything it comes in contact with.

Before I can do anything with that knowledge, Travis sticks his head through the kitchen doorway. "Hey, Xan, couple more guys here to see you."

"Who are they?"

"They didn't give their names. But they're determined to talk to you."

I wait for more—more description, a few pithy observations, something—but Travis is strangely subdued. Not concerned, exactly, but not comfortable with this newest development, either.

His discomfort is what gets me moving. I quickly wash my hands and strip off my apron before heading to the front of the shop. If Travis is disconcerted, something major must be going on.

Two men in dark suits and sunglasses are standing next to the counter. They don't look impatient, exactly, but they don't look like they're willing to wait much longer for me, either. Not that I'm surprised. After all, I know who they are the moment I lay eyes on them. They aren't exactly subtle.

They're members of the ACW's version of the Secret Service—only a hell of a lot meaner and more powerful than the guys who guard the president. My parents have a few of them in their employ—less now that we're adults and more able to take care of ourselves—but enough of them that I know that if they want to talk to me, I don't have a choice. So much for Declan's master plan of getting the hell out of ACW headquarters last night before anyone noticed we were there.

"Ms. Morgan, we're going to have to ask you to come with us."

That's it. No identifying themselves. No asking if this is a convenient time. Just that flat, dead tone that matches their faces exactly—and refuses to take no for an answer. "Of course," I tell them. "If you'll give me a few minutes—"

"Now, Ms. Morgan." The tall one tells me through clenched teeth.

"Excuse me." Travis steps forward, goddess bless his protective little heart. "Is everything okay here?"

"I'm fine, Travis. These gentlemen are friends of my father."

He looks at me like I'm crazy and I don't blame him. If there are two men on the planet less likely for a sane father to sic on his daughter, I haven't seen them. Neither, apparently, has Travis.

"Can I talk to you for a minute?" he asks, motioning with his head for me to step aside with him.

The short ACW guy—who bears a striking resemblance to old paintings I've seen of Napoleon—opens his mouth to object, but I cut him off with a look. They might be from the Council, but I am a princess of the most powerful Hekan coven in the world. I might be a princess about to be accused of murder, but I am still a princess.

He nods and I step aside with Travis. As I do, I wrack my brain about what to say—and how to say it. Travis is a savvy guy, one who knows me pretty well after working with me for the past couple of years. I don't want him to see how tense I am about these guys, because he'll feel honor bound to intervene and that's the last thing I want. These guys play hardball, and while I know they'll do their best to keep the whole witch thing under wraps—it's ACW law, after all—they'll have no problem doing whatever it takes to keep Travis from becoming a problem, either. I can't let that happen.

"What do they want?" Travis demands the second we're out of earshot of the others. "And don't give me that bullshit about your father."

"It's fine. They're private detectives. They work for my dad and they just want to go over a few things that happened last week."

"They're being awfully insistent for men on your father's payroll." Travis is too suspicious to just let it go that easily.

"Yeah, well, my dad is a results-oriented kind of guy. I'm sure he's riding their asses."

"Over what? I thought you said that Kyle guy was working alone?"

"He was," I say to soothe. "But my dad's overprotective. He wants to make sure nothing else is going on before he stops worrying about me over here in the big, bad city." I put in a shrug for good measure, my version of *what-can-I-do?*

Travis laughs, exactly as I intended. Austin is growing by leaps and bounds, but the crime rate is still really low. Which is a good thing, as I don't want to spend my life being compelled from one murder scene to the next. I can't help but wonder about witches who have powers like mine and live in major cities like New York or L.A.

or Houston. I don't even want to imagine the horror of dealing with the sheer number of homicides in places like that.

"You sure you want me to let you leave with them?" he asks after a second.

I nearly laugh. Travis is an awesome guy—smart, inventive and with a wicked sense of humor—but he's no match for the two men currently standing next to my cash register. They'd eat him for a midafternoon snack and barely even notice.

"I've got this," I assure him. "I'm just going to get my purse from the back."

My heart is pounding double time as I grab my bag. My cell's tucked into the front pocket and I pull it out, fire off a quick text to Declan. I don't know where I'm going, but I'd feel better if he at least had an idea of what was going on. But when I get back to the front, I see Travis on the phone—and the look on his face speaks volumes.

If I had to guess, I'd say he's talking to Declan right now. And that he's even less pleased than Travis is about my leaving with these guys.

"Can you tell me how long this interview is going to take?" I ask the agents as I approach them. "I have plans in a couple of hours."

"It'll take however long it takes, Ms. Morgan," the tall one tells me.

"Can you at least tell me where we're going?"

"I think you've got a pretty good idea."

I don't actually, unless they're bringing me back to ACW headquarters. Which, now that I think about it, they just might be. What better place to grill me than at the scene of the crime, after all?

We walk outside and it's raining again. I swear, these last couple of weeks Austin has confused itself with Seattle. I slip a little on a slick patch on the sidewalk and throw an arm out to catch myself. But the shorter agent is already there. He wraps a hand around my upper arm to steady me — or at least that's what I think he's doing — and then I feel a weird tugging movement. Not so much on my arm as on my entire body. Dizziness swamps me and for long seconds, the world goes black.

Which is strange. Really strange. Because I'm awake, alert, but it's as though all my senses have been stripped from me. I can't see, can't hear. I can't even feel the cold rain falling onto my skin anymore. It's like everything has just stopped.

Then suddenly it all comes back, in one excruciating rush. Pain slams into me like a sledgehammer, and I gasp. Stumble backward. I expect to feel the rough rock of Beanz's outside wall behind my back, but instead I feel a soft cushion. Which doesn't make sense. Except, when I open my eyes — I don't even remember closing them — I'm not on the busy downtown street in front of my business. Instead, I'm sitting on a couch in a low-lit room, staring at shelf upon shelf of ancient Hekan artifacts.

I don't bother to gasp, or demand to know where I am. I must be somewhere at the Council headquarters, after all — that much is obvious by the décor of the place. As for how I got here? My first experience with a travel spell that very few witches can master. Declan has — it's how he escaped when he was trapped at the top of the UT tower last week — but I've never met anyone else who could do it before now.

This blatant demonstration of power makes me even more uncomfortable. Sliding my hand into my pocket, I reassure myself that my cell phone is still there. The second I get the chance, I'm sending another text to Declan—and this one will have 911 attached to it.

"Can we get you something to drink, Xandra?" the tall one asks me. He's looming over me, and not for the first time, I realize how vulnerable I am.

I spring to my feet. "What happened to Ms. Morgan?" I demand, going on the attack.

I expect him to step back, but he doesn't. Instead, he spreads his arms in the most totally useless attempt to appear nonthreatening that I've ever seen. Now that we're out of my coffeehouse and away from all the normal mortals on the street, menace rolls off him in waves.

Still, he keeps up the façade by saying, "I was trying to make you more comfortable."

"You'd make me more comfortable if you stepped back a little and told me who you were and where you've taken me."

"Of course. I'm John." He gestures to the shorter man. "And this is Larry. And you're in one of the parlor rooms at the ACW."

John? Larry? Two names that sound less Hekan I have never heard. As the parlor, it seems more like a place designed for torture than one where people drink tea and eat crumpets. Or whatever the hell a person is supposed to do in a parlor.

"Better?" John asks me.

Not even a little bit. "What do you want from me?"

"Why all the hostility?" Larry asks as he closes the distance on my other side. Suddenly I'm all but surrounded by the two of them. It freaks me out even more than I already am, and I reach into my pocket for my cell phone. Screw subtle. I need Declan, now. He's the last person in my call log, so if I can just hit SEND—

I never get the chance. John rips my phone out of my hand and sends it flying across the room. It smacks into the harsh stone wall, then plummets to the ground with a sickening crack.

Nineteen

And they wonder why I'm feeling hostile? I stare at the remnants of my iPhone and try to figure out what the hell I'm supposed to do now. Deep inside I feel my magic start to well up, but it's not enough. Not even close to enough, considering I still don't know what to do with it. So far, my experience with power has been much more about it driving me than me channeling it.

I reach for it anyway, try to grab onto it the way I did during Kyle's attack on me. But I can't get a grip, can't get anything but a little spark, no matter what spell I try to recite. And judging from the looks on John's and Larry's faces, they know it, too. Damn it.

"Come on, Xandra. You don't want to do this the hard way, do you?" Larry gestures to the sofa. "Have a seat."

"It feels like we're already doing this the hard way."

John grins and it's a terrifying sight. "Only because you haven't seen how much harder it can get."

I sit.

"Good girl. Your mother would be proud. Now, tell me what you know about what happened to Viktor Alride."

I think about lying, about trying to bluff my way out of this. But the fact of the matter is, we didn't leave any evidence of our presence behind. So if they know I was in Alride's office last night, they *know* it. Denying it won't do anyone any good.

"I don't know much. Only that he died badly."

"Badly? That's one way of saying he was drawn and quartered, isn't it?" John leans forward, and suddenly there's a knife in his hand. He doesn't bring it anywhere near me, but its presence is threatening enough.

I meet his eyes. "Yes."

"Now, Councilor Alride wasn't the nicest guy I've ever worked for," he continues, "but he wasn't a bad sort, either. And the number of people he might have pissed off enough to do something like what was done to him? It's small. Very small."

"Good for him." I can't take my eyes off the knife. He's tossing it into the air a little, turning it end over end so that his fingers grab onto the handle, then the tip of the blade, then the handle again.

"Maybe. But not so good for you, as you and your boyfriend definitely make the short list."

"Then it must be a pretty long short list."

"That's the thing. It really isn't." He grabs the knife by the handle, flicks a finger over the tip of the blade. I watch, horrified, as a drop of blood drips from his fingertip onto my hand. I'm dying to wipe it off, but I don't want to take the chance of setting him off so that he uses that knife on me.

"I didn't kill him."

"No. Now why should I believe that, considering your history with Councilor Alride?"

"We don't have a history. He knows my parents, obviously, and I've met him a few times, but that's it."

The knife is against my throat in the space of one

breath to the next. "Don't play stupid, Xandra. We both know what the Council did to you. The only question is what do you plan on doing to the Council?"

I lean backward, straining away from the knife, but John follows me with it. He even lets me feel the bite of it against my skin, followed by the warm dribble of something down my throat.

"Nothing. I swear." He presses harder. I feel a sharp pain followed by the sensation of more blood leaking down my neck.

"Why were you here last night?"

I don't know what or how much to say. But I don't have anything to hide. Not about this. "I felt him die," I finally say after a long silence.

"Because of your connection to the warlock?" Larry demands, getting in on the inquisition for the first time.

"Because of my connection to Alride. It's what I do, how my magic works."

"And how about Chumomisto's magic? How does that work?"

"I don't know."

The knife digs deeper and I cry out, despite my resolution to be stoic. "You can cut me all you want, but it's not going to make me change my answer. I don't know how Declan does what he does. And I don't know who killed Viktor Alride."

"So it looks like we're back to the beginning then. What do you know?"

My throat stings from the little—and not so little— cuts he's inflicted on me while my body aches from how rigidly I'm holding it. Even worse is the sudden knowledge that no matter what I say, this isn't going to end well for me.

When I agreed to come with them, I figured Declan would find me pretty easily. And even if he didn't, I didn't actually think they would harm me. Not when my parents sit on the most powerful Hekan throne in the world.

But somewhere along the line I miscalculated—either about how afraid the ACW members are of this unknown killer and how desperate they are to apprehend him or about their feelings for my parents. For all I know, it could be both.

I've spent the last week and a half scrambling, trying to keep my parents from figuring out exactly what went down here with Kyle and the Council. I wanted to protect them, to keep my coven and my family out of war. But maybe all I did was make them appear weak, like they couldn't mount a challenge against the ACW even after their youngest daughter was tortured and nearly killed.

"Alride was bled out. Which means someone plans on doing some pretty dark magic to tap into his powers."

"Good. Now we're getting somewhere." The knife lifts a couple of centimeters away from my skin. "And this dark magic. Is it something your boyfriend is planning on doing?"

"No. Goddess, no."

The knife is back. "You sure about that?"

"Declan didn't kill Councilor Alride and neither did I."

"I thought you didn't know who killed him?"

"I don't. But it wasn't Declan." As I say the words, the last little doubt that haunted me drops away. I don't know where Declan was last night and why he came home scratched and bloody, but he wasn't here.

"I'm sorry, but I'm just not as certain as you are.

Maybe if we could talk to Chumomisto, we'd be convinced, too."

My entire body recoils at the thought of telling them anything about Declan, or where to find him. They must feel my resistance, because the knife disappears—only to be replaced by John's hand stroking slowly down my arm.

My throat tightens and my heart beats wildly inside my chest as I begin to panic. I jerk away, but he follows me. Continues to rub his hand up and down my arm in a way that is so much more terrifying than the knife to my throat.

I know he's doing it on purpose, know he's going there to bring back memories of the rapes Kyle committed, but rationalizing it doesn't make being touched by him any easier to handle. Because while I wasn't physically raped by Kyle, every time I relived one of those women's attacks, it certainly felt like I was.

John's hand trails up my arm to the back of my neck. I know I shouldn't react, but before I can stop myself, I shrug him off. He grins and brings it right back. Only this time, his fingers creep up my scalp, tangle in my hair, and tug until my head is tipped back and my face is only inches from his.

"Tell us more about Chumomisto and I'll stop."

"And if I don't?"

"If you don't, you're going to end up getting much more closely acquainted with Larry and me." He reaches out with his free hand and swipes at a trickle of blood running down my neck. Then lifts the finger to his mouth and licks my blood off it as his other hand tightens in my hair.

I lose it completely. Screaming, I jerk away from him,

ignoring the pain of pulled hair. He follows me, trying to keep his grip, but I lash out and catch him in the nose with the heel of my hand. At the same time, I drive my booted foot straight into his groin.

He sinks like a stone.

But I'm not free yet. His hand is still tangled in my hair, dragging me down with him, and Larry is right there, too. Frankly, I'm not sure which one of them looks more pissed off, and I brace myself as Larry cocks a fist and plows it straight into my jaw.

Pain explodes through my skull, knocks my head back so hard that it smacks right into the wooden edge of the couch. Dazed, I look up just in time to see Larry's fist coming at me a second time. If he hits me again, I'm done. I know it — already the cartoon birds are circling around my head.

Ducking just as his fist comes toward me, I spot the discarded knife lying next to me on the floor. I grab it in my left hand and slash out at Larry with it. I catch him right across the upper thigh and he screams as blood spurts everywhere.

"You bitch!" John growls, his hand once again tightening in my hair. I don't let myself think. Instead, I jerk the knife through my hair, chopping off inches of hair and making some powerful slices into his fingers as well.

It's his turn to howl and before he can recover, I'm lashing out at him again, driving the knife straight into his bicep. Then I'm clambering to my feet and running full tilt for the door.

Twenty

Once I make it out of the room, I turn right and keep running. I don't know where I'm going, don't know if I'm heading toward the exit or if I'm just getting myself deeper into the tunnels. And I don't care. All that matters right now is putting some distance between them and me.

I think I have a couple of minutes—I'm pretty sure I sliced into Larry's artery and I'm hoping John will stop to save his life instead of immediately coming after me. But I'm not sure, so I lay on the speed. If he catches me now, I know there's no way I'm getting out of here alive.

The hallway I'm in dead-ends in a few feet and I'm going to have to go left or right. Again, I don't know which way to turn, but I don't want to take the time to puzzle it out. So I turn left and hope for the best.

I hear footsteps behind me now, John calling my name as he pounds through the underground passageways looking for me. I keep running, praying that I'll run into a staircase, an elevator, anything that might get me to the surface.

But there's nothing. No matter how far I run, no matter how many corners I turn, I can't find anything that might point me to an escape route. I'm gasping for air and though I can normally run a lot longer than this, fear is making my chest ache and my breaths come in choppy little bursts.

I turn another corner and nearly scream in frustration as I realize it's a dead end. I'm trapped.

Afraid, angry, determined, I turn so my back is to the wall and prepare to fight. I don't have much of a chance against his magic, I know that. But I have to try.

Less than a minute passes before he appears at the end of the hallway. He's bleeding pretty badly from where I stuck him with the knife, but it doesn't seem to be slowing him down much. He's got a crazed look on his face and a gun in his hand—a gun that's pointed straight at the center of my chest. Suddenly this whole back-to-the-wall thing doesn't seem like a good idea.

He advances slowly, and I can tell from the look on his face that he wants me to beg. But I'll be damned if I'll plead with the sick fuck for anything—even my life— and I tilt my chin up. Refuse to back down.

"Don't be stupid, Xandra." His voice rings down the corridor. "There's nowhere for you to go. The only chance you've got is to give up Chumomisto. Tell me where he is and I'll let you live."

Not for one second do I believe that. And I wouldn't give Declan up even if I did. But before I can tell John to go to hell, there's a flash of light in front of me. Suddenly two strips of fire are racing down the hallway straight at John. He stares at them, shocked, then stumbles backward. But it's too late. The fire's already on him, flames climbing up his legs, wrapping themselves around his calves, his thighs, his waist.

He screams, once, twice, and starts to flail wildly. In the mayhem, his gun goes off and I brace myself for the impact of a bullet. It never comes. Instead, Declan is there between John and me. He wraps himself around me as he lifts me into his arms, covering every inch of my body with his. And then we're barreling through the flames.

I close my eyes and hang on tight, and try to pretend not to hear John's screams as the flames devour him inch by painful inch.

"Are you okay?" Declan asks as he careens around a corner. "Did he hurt you?"

"I'm fine."

"Good." He makes a sharp left, then a right and another left. Suddenly a staircase looms in front of us and he runs for it, flat-out. Fire alarms are going off and people are stirring—I can hear shouts echoing down the corridors. I can't help freaking out.

"One more minute," he tells me. "We just need one more minute."

I glance over his shoulder to where people are staring after us. "I'm not sure we're going to get it."

"Oh, we'll get it." He takes the stairs three at a time and the second we're fully above ground, I feel it—that strange, shadowy tugging again. It's the last thing I feel before things turn black for the second time in an hour.

This time the effect on my senses isn't as dramatic and it doesn't take as long. I'm not sure why, but I think it has something to do with Declan. When I can see again, I'm standing in the middle of my living room with Lily hovering over me.

"Is she okay?" my roommate asks Declan.

"I'm fine," I answer.

"Oh, good. So then maybe you can explain to me

how you materialized from nothing? One minute I'm watching Netflix, wondering if you're planning on coming back here after work, and the next minute you two are in the middle of the freaking room. And you were looking," she adds critically, "a lot worse than you did when you left the house this morning. And that's saying something."

I turn to Declan. "Can you tell her what you did? Because I'm not sure—"

I break off at my first good look at Declan. He's pale, ashy, weak. Some instinct I didn't know I had has me reaching for him, but I'm too late. His knees give out and he hits the ground, hard.

For a second it's so shocking that all I do is stare. But as he falls face-first onto the carpet—his arms spread wide—I fall to my knees beside him.

"Baby! What's wrong?" Even as I ask the question, I see the blood seeping onto the hardwood beneath him. I flash back to that moment when the gun went off, right before the flames swallowed John, and I know what's happened. Declan's been shot.

"Call 911!" I shout to Lily as I rip at his jacket and shirt, determined to see the wound. There's a lot of blood on my floor and it's only been a few seconds. I can only imagine how much blood he lost while he was running through the underground passageways of the ACW.

"I'm fine," he grates out from between clenched teeth. "I just need a minute—"

Neither Lily nor I pay any attention to him. Lily because she's on the phone and I because . . . because I've just uncovered the wound. It's a huge hole that goes straight through his shoulder, leaving nothing but raw, jagged flesh in its wake.

"Oh my God. How did you carry me with this? How did you run?"

"It looks worse than it is."

"Somehow I doubt that." I place one hand on the front of the wound and one on the back and then press. I'm desperate to stop the bleeding.

Declan blanches, mutters a string of curses. But then he reaches up with his uninjured arm and places his hand over mine. A wild heat spreads from his hand to mine and I watch in fascination as the blood flow becomes sluggish.

"You can heal yourself?" I whisper as he arches into the warmth. It's a rare ability, one that few healers ever develop. Rachael, my sister, can heal little things on herself, but nothing on the scope of a gunshot wound.

"Not me," he grates out. "You."

"I can't heal."

He doesn't answer me, just presses down a little harder on my hand. Within a couple of minutes, the bleeding has stopped completely. The wound has begun to heal, and though it's still red and angry-looking, it's nothing compared to how it had appeared even five minutes before.

"Cancel the ambulance," Declan says hoarsely, finally letting go of my hand.

"You need to be checked out."

"Too many questions with a gunshot wound. What am I going to tell them?"

I know he's right, but it kills me to just go along with him when it's obvious he needs medical attention. "What about infection?"

"The healing takes care of that."

I turn to Lily. "Can you help me get him up?"

"Yeah. Of course."

Together we wrestle Declan to his feet. He sways a little, but once upright he seems a lot more in control. Which is good. An injured, dependant Declan is a terrifying thing. Not because I don't want to take care of him, but because it kills me to see him in pain.

"I've got it from here," he says, and begins the painful trek down the hall to my bedroom.

Rolling my eyes, I plaster myself to his uninjured side and drape that arm over his shoulder. "Don't you want to sit down?" I ask, glancing behind me at the sofa.

"I need to take a shower before I bleed all over your house."

"Do you think I give a shit? You're who I care about."

He smiles at me, a real, genuine smile that lights up his whole face and has my heart hitching in my chest. "Yeah, well, I think we've done enough damage to the place in the last couple of weeks, don't you?"

I know he's talking about the fire I started and the windows I've broken as I tried to seize control of my magic. "So far, I've done all the damage. Now it's your turn."

He shakes his head. "Shower."

I all but growl in frustration. Goddess deliver me from big, strong, alpha he-men.

But in the end, I help him strip off his clothes. Even help him with the shower before drying him off and tucking him into my bed. "You need to rest."

He grabs onto my hand. "I'll rest a lot more if you're in bed beside me."

"If I'm in bed beside you," I say with a snort, "I doubt you'll get any rest at all."

His smile is wicked. "I won't tell if you don't."

"Go to sleep," I answer severely. "Or at least rest while I get you something to eat."

"First tell me what happened. Who was that guy?"

"You rest first. Then we'll talk."

"Xandra."

I look away, refusing to be drawn into the dark dominance of his gaze. "That's the deal. Take it or leave it."

He grumbles under his breath, but in the end he takes it because I don't give him any other choice. And I'm glad I don't, because in the time it takes me to make him some soup and fill Lily in on what happened, he's fallen fast asleep.

I don't wake him. Instead, I stand by the bed and watch him until long after his soup grows cold, and try to pretend that I'm not terrified. But I am. I almost lost him today, and though it's been only three weeks since Declan walked back into my life, I no longer want to imagine what my life would be like without him. In a very short time, he's become incredibly important to me.

With that thought first and foremost in my mind, I gently crawl into bed beside him. Then I curl myself around his uninjured side and drift slowly into sleep. The ACW can wait, for a little while at least.

I wake up slowly, hot and thirsty and completely out of sorts, though I don't know why. I'm curled up against Declan, whose body is radiating so much heat that it feels like the middle of August instead of January.

Once the heat registers, fear assails me. Rolling over, I press a hand to Declan's forehead and nearly shudder in relief when I realize it's definitely cool. He's not running a fever.

I've been around Hekan healing my whole life. I

know how it works and I trust it for myself, no problem. But, it turns out, trusting it for Declan is a lot harder. Especially when we're talking about a bullet wound.

Sliding my hand down, I push the covers off his shoulders and press my fingers gently against the rapidly healing bullet wound. There's no sign of infection and though the skin around it is tender and a little pink, it isn't red or irritated-looking.

Content with the knowledge that Declan is doing better, I shove off the covers and climb out of bed. Part of me wants to go back to sleep—I'm still exhausted after everything that happened last night—but something is still niggling at me. Stopping me from relaxing.

Plus I'm hot. Really, really hot.

I walk into the bathroom, splash cold water on my face. It doesn't help, so I hold my wrists under the freezing water and wait for the chill to work its way through me. That doesn't happen, either.

Not sure what else to do, I wander into the kitchen and get a glass of ice water. Drink the whole thing down in a couple of long swallows. Then contemplate sticking my head in the freezer. Surely that will stop the strange, uncomfortable burning that's overwhelming me from deep inside.

I'm just getting another glass of water—after reluctantly deciding against climbing into my deep freeze—when it hits me. The heat shoots up exponentially, becoming a spinning, boiling cauldron of fire centered right in the middle of my midriff. Completely freaked out by it, I bend over. Brace my hands on my knees and take a few deep breaths in an effort to fight off whatever this reaction is.

It doesn't work.

Instead, pain swamps me — the burn turning from uncomfortable to excruciating between one second and the next. I claw at my stomach where the heat is centered, so desperate to get free of it that I don't care what damage I do. I'm literally gouging at the skin now, and as my fingers curl into talons, flames break out along my skin.

They race from my hands to my elbows, over my biceps to my shoulders and torso before climbing up my neck to my face and hair. Damn it. Not again.

I rush to the sink in an attempt to extinguish the fire, but it's gone before I even get there. I start to slump in relief, but then the second wave hits me and I'm seizing. It's last night all over again — only better because I can prepare for it and worse because I know what's coming.

Sure enough, my legs go out from under me and I slam into the ground, convulsions shaking me until my teeth rattle and my eyes roll back in my head. It's hard to think in the middle of shakes, to try to figure out what to do, but I force myself to stay calm. Maybe if I just let the energy take control instead of fighting it, I won't end up feeling like I was hit by an eighteen-wheeler when it's all over.

It's a good theory, not so great in practice. But at least I don't do the whole *Exorcist* thing and levitate this time around. Instead, I just flop around on the ground for a while. I end up thrashing around so much that it's a miracle I don't give myself a concussion — especially considering the knot I gave myself yesterday. Without Lily around to clear things away from me, I end up banging into the kitchen table, a couple of chairs and even the center island.

When it's finally done — when the energy has left as quickly, but nowhere near as easily, as it came — I curl up into the fetal position on the cold wood and shiver end-lessly. I want to move, but I can't. My muscles, already stressed from yesterday's episode, are in full revolt. They wouldn't hold me up right now even if I wanted them to. Which I don't. I'm so tired that I'm happy to lie right here for the rest of the night. At least I'm no longer in danger of being burned alive.

I'm not sure how long I'm sprawled out here waiting for my body to recover. Not thinking, not moving, doing my best not to feel. But eventually the second half of the night's entertainment kicks in—just like I was afraid it would—and a powerful compulsion rips through me.

Here we go again.

Despite the pain, despite the fatigue and my deep-seated need to curl up in bed with Declan, I'm on my feet in seconds and heading for the front door. A part of me wants to head back to the bedroom, to grab my purse and a warm sweater. To wake Lily up and tell her where I'm going.

But she'll only insist on coming with me and I don't want to drag her into this again—not when she still hasn't recovered from last night. Waking up Declan is also out of the question. The healing may have begun, but he was shot tonight. Because of me. There's no way I'm going to forget that any time soon.

Besides, this compulsion is stronger than any I've ever felt before. When I try to walk down the hall to my bed-room, it stops me flat-out—as surely as if I'd slammed into a brick wall. I barely have time to slip on my boots and jacket from near the couch in the living room before it's propelling me out the door and down the front walk.

I'm mentally prepared to head back to the Capitol grounds, though I have no idea how I'm supposed to slip in—or out of them again, after this afternoon. But to my surprise, I turn left at the bottom of the driveway instead of right.

Those first steps are the beginning of a long and lonely hike through the freezing January night. I try to be grateful—at least it isn't raining today and at least I'm dressed for it in flannel pajamas and a warm coat—but it's hard to feel that way when every step is fraught with agony. And when I know what's waiting for me at the end of this journey.

Funny, isn't it, that I know what I'm going to find even though I don't know anything else. Where the body's going to be. Who it's going to be. What I'm going to blindly be walking into. I don't know any of that and maybe it's selfish, but I hate it. I hate this power and I hate the pain that comes with it.

I started this week hoping for peace. For a chance to assimilate to all the changes that have so quickly happened in my life. Instead, I'm in the middle of another murder investigation, this one equally as deadly as the one I just lived through. I know it's wrong to complain, to feel sorry for myself when someone is dead and I am still very much alive. But I'm tired and I'm hurt and I just don't want to do this anymore.

And still I must continue. I turn corner after corner, walk street after street until I'm utterly lost. I have no idea where I am, only that I'm on the right track. I can feel it in the electricity zinging through me with each step that I take and the compulsion pressing against my back, urging me to go faster and faster.

This isn't the way to the Capitol grounds or the way to anywhere famous downtown. And yet, when the compulsion jerks me to a stop in front of a plain little house, buried among hundreds of others in one of Austin's oldest neighborhoods, I know immediately that it's the right spot. Power throbs in the air all around me, brushes against my skin, works its way down my spine. And that's when I know for sure. Though I'm off the beaten path, and though it makes absolutely no sense, I am positive that another Councilor lies right beyond the gray-painted front door.

Twenty-one

Though every part of me strains against it, I nevertheless begin the short walk up the flower-lined path to the front door. Within seconds, I'm up the stairs and on the porch, staring at a door that is just slightly ajar. Not enough for the average passerby to see from the street, but more than enough to indicate that there's a problem. That someone has been here.

But I already know that, don't I? Still, I pause a second, knock on the door. As expected, no one answers, so I take a deep breath and gingerly press the door open just wide enough that I can slip inside.

The second I set foot in the small foyer, I can smell it. Death has a particular scent, especially a violent death. Cold and metallic, with an underpinning of something smoky I have no idea how to identify, it's smelled the same each and every time I've stumbled across it. Tonight is no different.

Dreading what I'm going to find, I step gingerly across the black-and-white patterned tile of the foyer and start down the narrow hallway that stretches the length of the house. On either side of me are the living and dining rooms, but both are in pristine condition. There's no sign of a struggle at all, and a small light has even been left burning on one of the end tables.

I use the light to guide my way into the depths of the house, careful not to touch anything. Not that it really matters, I suppose, as it's not like I'll be sneaking away from this before someone comes to clean it up. Not when the compulsion refuses to release me until the body has been taken away.

As I walk the shadowed hallway, I think back to last night when Declan knocked me out in order to get me away. Is that why I'm in so much pain today, why the walk here seemed even worse than usual? Is it some kind of psychic payback?

The sickening scent gets stronger the closer I get to the back of the house, and I brace myself for whatever it is I'm going to find. Still, knowing it—preparing for it—doesn't make it any easier when I turn the corner into the kitchen and find Councilor Mei Lantasis dangling from the ceiling.

For a second, all I can do is stare at her. Her wrists are cuffed together and bound over her head to a chain embedded in the ceiling. She's in her underwear, and instead of her having been eviscerated, her throat has been slit wide open—so wide open that her head lolls back on her neck like it's going to snap off at any second.

My stomach turns, but I force down the nausea. I'm not going to puke, not going to give in. Not tonight. Though her death was different from Alride's, quicker certainly, she, too, has been bled dry.

Unable to stop myself, I walk closer and stare up at her body. As I do, tears well in my eyes. I can't help it. Of all the Councilors, Mei is the one I know best—and the only one I've ever really liked.

She's been a member of the ACW for only ten years, which means she definitely wasn't involved in the soul-binding of Declan and me. I also think it means she wasn't involved in the plot to kill me, either, and while that might be wishful thinking, I'm going to hang on to it as long as I can. Otherwise, the betrayal might be too much to bear. After all, she's spent years intervening between my mother and me, trying to get us to see each other's side in our many and legendary battles.

She didn't always succeed, but she did try—at least whenever she was around. She was a good woman and she didn't deserve to die like this.

Not that anyone does. But I'm a hell of a lot more shaken up by her death than I was by Viktor Alride's.

I want to cut her down. It's another compulsion inside me, one that comes not from my magic but from my heart. But I can't. Everything about this scene is evidence now.

I step forward and press my palm to her bare calf. She's the first thing I've touched in this death trap of a house, and the second my skin makes contact with hers, the images bombard me, along with snippets of conversation.

Get out of my house.

How dare you.

Don't touch me.

Then a scream, terrified and soul-splintering.

Please. What do you want? I'll do anything.

Chain.

Rope.

Black-gloved hands.

A white scarf.

A silver athame with black sapphires embedded in its hilt.

Whimpers, muffled now. Unintelligible words. Pleas.

The sickening squilch as the athame is driven into her throat.

The ping ping ping of blood as it drips from the wound into a gold-plated bucket.

And those words again, spoken in an asexual voice. *Close doesn't count.*

Tears gather behind my eyes, but I ignore them. Just like I ignore the painful heat radiating from her leg to my fingertips. Mei was a fire element, one of the strongest I've ever seen next to Declan, and remnants of that power exist within her. I can feel it sizzling along my nerve endings, burning a path through my body, but still I don't let go. I can't. The familiar cadence of the three words I heard last night once again holds me in its thrall.

Close doesn't count.

Where have I heard those words before? And is it a male speaking or a female? I hate that I can't tell. That everything else is perfectly transparent but those words, that voice, this killer, locked far away from me.

Time ticks by slowly as I sort through every impression I can gather from this room and try to fit their jagged edges together. It's no use, though, not here and not now, when shades of Mei's agony color everything that I feel.

Eventually, I give up. Not for good, but at least until I can get out of here and have a shot at thinking more clearly. But I can't get out of here, can't leave, not until Mei's been found by someone other than me. She needs to be cut down, taken away, or I'm not going anywhere.

The only problem is I have no idea whom to call. This is Heka business, so I should call Witchcraft Investigations. Or the ACW, since she was a Councilor. But after what's happened to me in the last twenty-four hours, neither of those things is an option. I don't know whom I can trust in the organizations, and won't know until I can get a better handle on this killer's agenda.

Close doesn't count.

I turn the words over in my head for the millionth time. What is this person close to? What does he or she want? And why doesn't it count? Is it this person's goal that doesn't count or something else?

Frustrating as it is, I still can't get a handle on it. So I do the only thing I can do in the situation. I call Nate and let him know where I am and what I've found.

Hours later, Nate pulls up in front of my house. He's been quiet most of the ride, lost in his own thoughts, and again I wonder about how much this job takes out of him. Goddess knows, I've been at it only a couple of weeks and I feel drained to the very core of my being.

"Thanks for the ride," I tell him as I reach for the car door. I'm exhausted, completely burned out, and all I want to do is stumble up the walkway and fall into bed. I won't have long, though—dawn is only a couple of hours away, and with it comes my shift at the coffee-house.

"Hold on a minute." He reaches for my hand and I glance back at him, realizing for the first time that he looks just about as worn out and haggard as I feel. Hunting murder takes things out of a person that nothing else in the world does. It's something I'm beginning to realize more and more as my magic manifests itself.

"I'm sorry you had to see that."

I shake my head. There's nothing really to say. My gift is what it is, even when it feels more like a curse. Or maybe especially when. I don't know. All the pain and anguish is blurring together until I can barely breathe, barely think.

"I wanted to let you know, we found where Shelby was being held."

I grab onto him then, my fingers digging into his arm as I demand, "Is she alive? Did they—"

"She wasn't there. But there was a blue sweatshirt crumpled in the corner identical to the one she was wearing when she was abducted and the view from the window was exactly as you described."

"Is she—" My voice breaks. I don't want to say the word. Not tonight when the scent, the feel, the touch of death already surround me.

"I don't know." He reaches into the backseat, pulls out a plastic evidence bag. In it is a small navy sweatshirt. "I need to get this to the lab tonight, but I wanted you to see it first. I thought maybe you could pick something up—"

"I already told you. My gift doesn't work like that."

"I know." His green eyes are steady on mine. "But I figured it couldn't hurt to try."

Oh, but it could hurt. And now, when I'm already so emotionally bruised and battered, I'm terrified it will deal me a blow I'll never recover from. And yet, I can't ignore it when it's sitting right there in front of me. I'm just not built that way.

Reluctantly, I reach for it. I open the Ziploc top to the bag, reach my fingers in and gingerly brush them against the fabric.

Close doesn't count, little girl.

The voice slams through me and I'm confused—so confused—until I realize that whoever has Shelby must also be responsible for the deaths of those two Council members.

But why? What does some little girl with no connection to the Heka world have to do with two members of the ACW? And what about her makes her different from the thousands of other little girls within Austin's city limits?

Her blood.

The thought chills me, but that must be what it is. Nothing else makes sense. Two powerful Councilors bled out. One little girl, also being bled. But not all at one time.

Why not? Why keep her alive and not Mei and Alride? Because she isn't a threat? Or because they need more blood than she can give at one time? She's a small girl—her blood volume can't be anywhere near what a grown adult's is.

I'm sickened all over again. I hate what I'm thinking, hate what I've learned to think ever since my magic finally kicked in. There was a time when the darkest thing I thought about was how to escape my mother's clutches. These days, that seems like child's play.

A sob rips through my chest and I know I've reached the breaking point. Unable to do anything else, I shove the sweatshirt back at Nate and dive for the door. This time he doesn't try to stop me.

I'm halfway up the path to the house when the door opens. Declan is standing there, shirtless, wearing nothing but a pair of sweats and looking absolutely livid. I must look even worse than I thought, though, because the moment he gets a load of my face, his scowl turns to concern. Then he's rushing down the front walk toward me.

"You okay, Xan?" he asks, wrapping his uninjured arm around my shoulder and pulling me against him.

I bury my face in his chest and shake my head, hot tears leaking down my cheeks.

Declan doesn't ask anything else, just propels me toward the house. His hold is hesitant, gentle, and the sweetness of it only makes me cry more.

When did everything get so goddamn complicated? And when will it get uncomplicated? I don't want much. Just to save that little girl and to hold on to Declan so tightly that, soulbound or not, he'll never slip away.

Right now, neither of those things seems possible.

He settles me on the couch, tucks a blanket around me before heading into the kitchen. He's back in under a minute, a half-full tumbler of whiskey in his hand. "Drink this," he tells me, crouching down next to me.

I do, while one of his hands strokes my cheek and the other rubs up and down my back. "It's okay, baby," he murmurs to me over and over again.

I know he wants to know where I've been, what I've found—waves of impatience and anxiety are all but rolling off him. He doesn't say anything, though, doesn't ask any questions at all. Instead, he waits for me to finish the drink and then he scoops me up, despite his wounded shoulder and my protests, and carries me to my bedroom. Then he settles down in bed with me curled up in his lap.

We sit there for a long time, not doing or saying anything. Declan's hand tangles in my shorn hair, his fingers brushing against the ragged edges. It's barely chin length now and terribly uneven—but what can I expect considering I'd hacked it off with an ancient athame in a desperate bid to get away from those assholes this afternoon.

Tomorrow I'm going to have to get it cut properly, but I don't want to think about that now. Not when I feel so completely numb.

Eventually Declan's patience wears down and he whispers, "Tell me." His lips brush over my temple and down my cheek as he makes the demand. Though he's tender, and obviously trying not to push me, I know it's a request, so I do what he asks, spilling out everything that has happened tonight in a half-mad purging that is almost impossible to follow.

Somehow Declan manages, though, and when I'm done, he presses soft kisses to my cheeks and lips. I'm exhausted, physically and mentally wrung dry, and yet I feel myself responding to him like I always do. Because this is Declan and I'm so attuned to him that I can't not respond when he touches me.

He gentles me with soft words and softer caresses, until we're stretched out on the bed, every part of my body touching a corresponding part of his. "I already knew about Shelby," he admits to me after I rest my cheek against his chest.

"How?" I'm too tired to be suspicious. And too terrified.

"I went looking for her."

"How did you know where to look?"

"There're only so many magical signatures in this town—especially the dark ones that come with this kind of magic. I've been poking around ever since you told me about her, trying to find something that dark to trace. But it wasn't until yesterday at ACW headquarters that I found anything promising."

"That's where you were when I woke up last night? Looking for Shelby?"

"I didn't want to raise your hopes until I had something solid."

"But how did you know the room you found was where Shelby had been kept? I mean, Nate knew because of her sweatshirt, but you weren't privy to that information. You might have traced the killer back there, but they could have kept anyone in that room."

"Not really." He smooths a hand down my hair, presses more soft kisses to my shoulder and neck. "Shelby has Hekan blood. Her signature is light, very light, but it's there. Young, innocent, female. It wasn't a stretch, knowing what I did, to assume that the room I'd found had been used to hold her."

"Do you think—" My voice breaks and I have to start again. "Do you think she's dead?"

"I don't, actually. Or if she is, she didn't die in that room."

This time I don't need an explanation. Death, especially magical death, leaves its own mark, its own stench—something I've come to understand in the last few weeks.

"But whose blood was on you?" The question slips out before I can stop it. I want to trust him, want to believe in him completely, but I'm not stupid. I know Declan will always push the boundaries, because the line that is so obvious to me is too often blurry for him.

His gaze holds mine. "Shelby's. They bled her in that room."

My heart aches at the thought, but it's nothing I don't already know. "That's it? Just Shelby's?"

"There was someone else there. Whoever is holding Shelby left him behind to clean up the mess."

"That still doesn't explain how—" I break off as he

looks away. Because suddenly how he ended up streaked with blood becomes crystal clear. I don't bother to ask what he did—I'm not sure I want to know. Besides, it's hard to have sympathy for someone who would participate in the kidnapping and torture of a little girl.

"What did you find out?"

He's surprised. I can feel it, though his face never changes. But he reaches over, rests his hand on my knee. I know it's his way of reaffirming things between us, of making sure that we really are all right.

"He didn't know much. I got a couple of sketchy leads. I've already started looking into them."

I start to ask what they are, but I realize it's a waste of time before the words even leave my mouth. Declan might be willing to work together, might even be willing to share information when it suits him, but he will always try to protect me when he can. It's the nature of the beast, one I'm learning, slowly, to live with. Besides, I know if he finds something, he'll tell me. And that's enough for now.

"So what do we do now?" I ask, covering a yawn with my hand. Barely half an hour ago I was hyped up on horror and now, after thirty minutes of cuddling with Declan, I'm all but ready to pass out in his arms. There's something about him that makes me feel safe and secure, no matter how topsy-turvy the world around me has become. "How do we find Shelby?"

"We figure out what the killer needs from her."

"That's easy. He needs her blood."

Declan nods. "Yes, but why? Why her blood? Why Viktor's? Why Mei's?"

"That theory only works if this *isn't* an assassination attempt on the Council. I mean, we have to decide if they're being killed because of who they are or because of the powers they wield. The bloodletting makes me think it's their powers, yet I'm not so sure. I keep thinking that their positions as Council members have something major to do with this."

"Maybe it's both," Declan comments with a shrug. "Maybe he is going after the ACW one by one. But maybe he's doing it in a certain order—one that lets him gain the power he needs to take on the most powerful Councilors."

It makes sense. Except—"What about Shelby?"

"I don't think we're going to find out the answer to that question until we find her."

"But how are we going to find her if we don't know what we're looking for?"

"That's the tricky part."

"The tricky part? That doesn't sound very optimistic."

"It wasn't meant to," Declan tells me as he rests his forehead against mine. "But I promise you, I'll do everything in my power to find her and get her home safely."

I know he will. It's just one of the many things that make Declan who he is.

The last of the tension drains out of me at his assertion, and I relax against him, letting myself drift slowly off to sleep. As I do, I pray that whatever monster is doing this will make a mistake. Because when he does, Declan and I will be there. And he won't get the chance to make a second one.

Twenty-two

I'm yanked back to consciousness some indeterminate amount of time later by the ringing of my house phone. Fumbling for it, I answer with a groggy hello. Beside me, Declan doesn't stir, but something tells me he's awake and listening.

"Xandra?"

"Mom?" I squint across my darkened room, trying to see the alarm clock I keep on my dresser. "What time is it?"

"It's two a.m. I need you to come home."

"What's wrong?" Normally I'd be suspicious of any request she sends my way—especially since my aunt called me less than twenty-four hours ago with the same request. But she's been a little better, more respectful certainly, since I've gotten out of the hospital and I doubt she's calling just to mess with me right now. My mom might be the sneakiest witch I know, but she's also the most savvy. "I'm not sure I can leave right now. Things are just getting back to normal." No need for her to know just how chaotic life has been this week.

"It's your father," she blurts out, her voice breaking in a very unqueenly way. "He's sick."

It takes a second for her words to compute. My father

is one of the halest, heartiest men I know—I've never even seen him get a cold. The idea that he could suddenly be sick enough to warrant a predawn phone call like this doesn't make sense to me. "Where's Rachael?" I demand. "Has she checked him over?"

"She's with him now." A sob escapes. "I'm calling everyone home, Xandra. It doesn't—it doesn't look good."

Doesn't look good? Now I'm really confused. Witches and wizards live a long time—much longer than humans—and my dad isn't that old yet. Not in the grand scheme of things, where three hundred is considered the prime of a wizard's life.

"What's wrong with him?" I'm already out of bed, stumbling around in the dark as I try to find my jeans.

Declan climbs out right after me, turning on the bedside lamp before he, too, reaches for a new outfit— garments not yet riddled with bullet holes.

Just the thought has the night taking on an even more surreal quality.

"The doctor doesn't know and neither does Rachael," my mother finally answers. "We were playing cards with a few friends tonight when he suddenly slumped over. It's not a stroke or a heart attack—the doctor checked for both even though wizards don't normally have to worry about those—so everyone's clueless. Even Rachael can't figure it out. We've already called Tsura and she'll be here in a few hours."

Though my mother inherited the throne, Tsura is still one of the highest priestesses in existence, her power second only to her twin's. She's also the most talented healer in our coven.

Declan, who froze when my mother explained what had happened, is eyeing the phone like it's suddenly become a snake. "Have they checked for black magic?" he demands.

In my haste to pick it up, I accidentally hit the Speaker button, so my mom hears Declan loud and clear. "Is that Declan?" she demands.

"It is."

"Oh. I hadn't realized . . ." Her voice has gone from panicked to regal in the space of a heartbeat. The queen doesn't fall apart in front of anyone who isn't family, and in my mother's mind, Declan will *never* be family. He's too dark, too dangerous, too unpredictable. Then again, my mother and I like very different things in our men.

If Declan registers her sudden coldness, he doesn't let on. Instead, he repeats the question.

"We're looking into that as well," my mother tells him, and now she sounds downright offended. Like Declan's attempt to help is actually a slam against her competence.

"We'll be there in three hours, Mom," I say as I grab a duffel bag from my closet and toss some clothes into it indiscriminately.

"Good. So I'll expect you—"

"The two of us, Mom."

"You're not coming alone?"

I glance at Declan with raised eyebrows. He stares back disgustedly, the look on his face telling me just how stupid he thinks that question is.

"Declan's coming with me," I tell her.

Suddenly things grow muffled from her side and I realize someone else has come into the room and is talking to her. A minute later I hear a sharp cry and my sister Noora takes the phone. "Xandra?"

"What happened?"

"Hurry." It's the last thing she says before the line goes dead.

We're about an hour out of Ipswitch when Declan says, "You know this is the Council, don't you?"

He couldn't have shocked me more if he'd reached over and slapped me. I turn to stare at him, but he doesn't take his eyes off the road. But his grip is white-knuckled on the steering wheel, his jaw hard as granite.

"That's a huge assumption," I tell him when I find my voice again. "Besides, they're all running scared right now. Two Councilors dead and the rest in the crosshairs. They don't have the time, the manpower or the guts to do something like this right now. My father is an exceptionally strong wizard. To take him down like this, to bring him . . ."

I stop. I can't even say the words. My father will be fine, I tell myself, repeating the words like my own personal mantra. My father will be fine. But still, Declan's words make a strange kind of sense. "What better chance to get us to lay off them than to distract me with my father's illness? The only problem is that we're not the ones killing Council members."

"We know that, but it's pretty obvious at this point that they don't." He strokes a comforting hand over my hair. "Besides, it doesn't have to be the whole Council. It can be one or two members. The same one or two members who are responsible for the others' deaths. For Shelby. What do you think all that blood collection was for?"

"Wait a minute." My mind is boggling. "You think that the same person killing Councilors is also responsible for my father's illness? And that that person is also a Council member?"

"Think about it. What better time to make a play for the brass ring?"

"But I thought you said my father's illness was to distract us."

"No, that's what you said."

"I don't understand. There are too many variables here to keep track of. The ACW. My father. Shelby. I just don't get how all of these can be part of some master plot. Or, more importantly, why."

He glances at me, just a quick look out of the corner of his eye that is fraught with impatience. "Are you really that naïve?"

My spine stiffens. "It's not naïve to spend some time thinking things through instead of jumping to conclusions."

"I've been doing nothing but thinking things through since the moment I realized the ACW was after you, so don't lecture me in that prissy tone, Xandra."

It's the sharpest tone he's ever used with me. Not to mention, it's completely offensive. "I'm not prissy."

He snorts. "Of course not."

"What's that supposed to mean?"

"It means that you need to start seeing the world how it is instead of how you want it to be." He starts ticking things off on his fingers. "The ACW soulbound us the day you were born. They did so because they wanted to one, limit our magic and two, give me a reason to kill you. When that didn't work, they hired the job out to a sociopath of epic proportions, who not only tortured and killed four unsuspecting women, he nearly did the same to you—after you had already lived through the torment of his attacks on the other victims. And then they tried to frame me for the murders. What in the name of the goddess makes you think that they wouldn't try to kill your father if it was in their best interests?"

"I totally believe they would. I'm just not sure what those best interests are."

"Think about it, Xandra. Your parents are extremely influential in who gets appointed to the Council. If someone takes out your dad, your mom will be crippled with grief. She won't be in any position to worry about Council appointees. Or, goddess forbid, they kill her, too, and leave your brother—a completely untried king—in charge of the Ipswitch throne. You kill off a few ACW members, get the ear of the grief-stricken queen or shell-shocked new king, and it isn't that hard to control who gets the new seats. And if you control that . . ."

With those last words, everything slides into place. Court espionage isn't my thing, but once someone draws me a map, it's hard not to figure out which direction things are going. "If you control that," I continue where Declan left off, "then you control the way the laws are made and interpreted by the Council. You control everything."

He nods. "Exactly."

"Jesus. That's diabolical."

"Maybe. But it's also brilliant."

I stare at him, shocked. "You sound like you approve."

"Of course I don't approve. But if that's what they're going for, then the plan is genius."

I still don't like the appreciation I hear in his voice. Oh, I know he's not wishing ill on my parents or anything like that, but there's that dark part of him again. Able to think like a monster. Able, maybe, even to admire that monster. It's more than a little disturbing.

Still, I mull his words over for long seconds, trying my best to poke holes in his theory. But in a terrible, awful way, it makes perfect sense. Especially the bloodletting. If one of the less powerful Council members is behind this, there's a lot of dark magic that can be done with the blood of people as powerful as Alride and Mei. Dark magic that could kill my father, maybe even kill my mother if she isn't prepared for it.

I'm still not sure where Shelby's blood fits in, but as Declan's ideas rattle around in my head—and click—I know that there must be a way. There must be something she could give that no one else could. I just don't know what that is yet.

"I need to call my mother. And Donovan."

"They already know."

I gape at him. "How is that even possible?"

"I talked to Donovan about my theory when he called this morning, while you were in the bathroom packing your toiletries He was already halfway there himself, so I guarantee he's already talked it over with your mother."

"And you didn't think to tell me about it?" My voice is about three octaves higher than usual, but I can't help it. I am damn sick of Declan only sharing what he thinks I need to know. "You talk to my brother, whom you don't even like, but you don't tell me?"

"I'm telling you about it now, aren't I?"

It takes every ounce of self-control I have not to haul off and punch him. Then, because I'm not sure even that's enough, I say, "Stop the car."

"What?" He looks at me like I'm insane.

"Stop the fucking car."

When he still doesn't so much as slow down, I yell, "I

swear to the goddess, stop the damn car or it's over between us."

"I don't like threats," he tells me, even as he finally does what I asked and pulls the car over to the side of the road. "You want to fight, we'll fight. You want to yell at me for trying to protect you, you go right ahead. But you don't get to just issue an ultimatum in the middle of an argument. You don't get to threaten to walk away from me simply because you don't like something that I do."

"Why not? Because you say so?"

"Because that's not how relationships work!" He's in my face now, his eyes so dark and furious that my stomach jumps uneasily. Oh, I know Declan would never hurt me, but I've never seen him this pissed off. Then again, I've never been this pissed off, either.

"So, now you're an expert on relationships?" I ask sarcastically. "That's a laugh."

"Don't push me, Xandra."

"No, Declan, don't you push me."

I'm gearing up for a huge argument, but he stops me with a hand on my knee. If he'd tried to force my hand, to make me do what he wanted, I probably would have gone for his eyes. I'm that angry. But the gentle pressure of his palm on my leg has the anger draining out of me and tears springing to my eyes. Suddenly, I feel foolish. And petty. Two things I really hate feeling, but I know I deserve to right now.

I know Declan's not very good at relationships, know he's not very good at sharing information because he's never had anyone to share with before. Just yesterday, I'd decided that I was going to hang in, that I wasn't going to give him up no matter what we had to work through. And here I am, threatening to run away the first time he really pisses me off. I need to apologize.

I start to do just that, but Declan only smiles as he pulls back onto the highway, crisis averted. Then he asks, "So is that our first real fight as a couple?"

"If you don't shape up, it's going to be our last, as well."

Declan sighs heavily. "I know. I'm sorry. I just wanted to give you a little time to come to grips with the news about your dad before I sprang anything else on you."

"I'm sorry, too." I fidget for a minute before deciding to hell with it. I apologized, but that doesn't mean I don't have more to say about this whole thing. "I'm not a child, Declan. I don't need you to dole out information to me like candy."

"Believe me, Xandra. I don't think of you as a child." He reaches for my hand, pulls it to his lips and kisses it. "You are the strongest, bravest woman I know. I believe, really believe, that you can handle anything. But that doesn't mean I want you to."

He studies the road for long minutes, his jaw clenched and fingers so tight on the wheel that I'm afraid he might actually rip it off the steering column. I think about poking at him, getting him to talk to me, but I've learned that sometimes it's better to give him space. Or at least as much space as I can in the front seat of a car.

More time passes; my stomach getting tighter with each mile we leave behind us. Just when I feel like I'm going to jump out of my skin, he says, "It kills me, these powers that you have. I don't know how you do it. I don't know how you sleep at night or how you get up and go looking, knowing what it is you're going to find. Even worse, knowing what you're going to go through when you do find it.

"It kills me that I can't shelter you from that. That I can only stand by and watch as you live through being raped, beaten, stabbed, strangled, burned. I can't stop it, can't protect you from any of it. Hell, the fact that you're with me actually makes it worse."

His words slice right through the last of my anger, have me resting my head on his shoulder and rubbing my hand up his own leg in a gesture meant to comfort. Because I don't know what it's like for him, not really, but I can imagine how hellish it would be if I had to watch him suffer the way he's been forced to watch me.

"And yet I can't let you go, either. I've tried. I've tried so many times to walk away from you for your own safety. But I just can't do it. I love you too fucking much. I know it's selfish and—"

"Stop the car," I tell him for the second time in ten minutes.

"What?"

"I said, stop the car."

"Are you freaking kidding me? I'm pouring my heart out to you and you want to walk away from me?"

"Just pull the car over, Declan."

"Fine. Whatever." His jaw hard as granite, he once again pulls onto the shoulder. "Go do whatever you want to do."

I scoot over the gear shift, slide into his lap. "What I want to do, what I *need* to do, is this." I wrap my arms around him and lower my lips to his.

For a second, he seems shell-shocked. Like it's the last thing he ever expected me to do. But then he grabs onto me as though I'm the only lifeline he's got left, one hand

clenching in my hair while the other clenches on my hip.
And then he devours me.

Minutes later, he raises his head. I moan in protest
and he licks gently over my lips in an effort to soothe
and comfort. "If your family weren't waiting for us on
the other end of this drive, I would say screw it and take
you right here for the sheer pleasure of watching you
come. But we need to go."

Beautiful man. Sweet man, though I know he'd balk
at the description. "We do need to go. But I need to tell
you something first."

His eyes, those beautiful, beautiful eyes, turn wary
from one blink to the next. "Yes?"

"I love you, too. I love you so much that it scares me
deep inside, because if anything ever happened to you, I
don't know how I'd survive."

"Xandra—"

"Wait. I'm not done." I press gentle kisses on his forehead, his eyes, his mouth. "And if you ever try to walk
away from me for my own good, you better be prepared.
Because I will chase you to the ends of the fucking earth.
You're not getting rid of me that easily."

A deep, painful shudder wracks him at my words.
Then he grabs my upper arms, like he's preparing to
shake some sense into me, and I brace myself.

For long seconds, nothing happens and I know he's
struggling with the rage of emotions inside him. Time
stretches, elongates, until I hear only his harsh breathing
and the frantic beating of my own heart. Then, just when
I've decided to take matters into my own hands again, he
slides his right hand over my bicep and shoulder to my
neck.

He rests his hand on my chest, brushes his fingers

gently over the hollow of my throat. It's a gesture filled with tenderness, with need, with love—one that shows me his vulnerabilities even as it highlights my own and it heats my blood now just as it did then.

I bring my own hands up to cup his face, brush my lips gently against his own. He groans, a sound of desire and torment and fury, then buries his face in the curve of my neck and just breathes—harsh, ragged sounds that at any other time would be painful to hear. But right here, right now, they're absolutely perfect.

Twenty-three

"Where is he?" I demand the second my sister Willow opens the door to my parents' house. "Where's Dad?"

"In his and Mom's bedroom." She steps aside to let Declan and me in. I try to ignore how worried she looks, how drained, but I can't. She's always been the wild one, the one full of life and laughter. But right now, she just looks sad. That scares me more than my mother's phone call did, more than the thoughts that chased themselves around my head on the long drive here. "He's sleeping, so everyone but Rachael and Mom is in the kitchen. Come on back with me. I'll make you some coffee."

I ignore her invitation as I head for the stairs. I'm not going to wake him up, but I need to see my father with my own eyes, need to prove to myself that he's okay. Or, if not okay, at least alive. Yes, I think as I take the steps two at a time—Declan right at my heels—for now alive will do very nicely.

But when I get to the wing that is my parents' private quarters in the royal residence, there are four guards blocking the way—two I recognize as part of my father's regular security detail, but the others I've never seen before. And when one of them steps in front of me, as if he intends to block my path, I lift a hand, keep it at the ready. My command of Heka might be rudimentary at best, but if this guy thinks he's going to keep me from my father, then he'd better be ready to throw down. Because that so isn't happening.

Declan puts a soothing hand on the small of my back, even as his other comes up to rest atop mine and guide it back down to my side. Normally I'd be pissed at him for interfering, but the fact of the matter is he's right to step in. I'm not exactly firing on all cylinders right now.

Jared, my father's head of security, steps between the new guards and me. He's been with my family almost as long as I've been alive and is like an uncle to me.

"It's okay," he tells them. "This is Xandra." But even he looks wary, on alert, and for the first time, I realize the guards aren't focused on me at all. Declan's the one who has all their attention.

"He's with me." Figuring that's the end of it, I brush past them and start down the hall to my parents' bedroom. But I get only a few feet before I realize that Declan isn't following me. Jared and the others have closed ranks and are preventing him from passing the spot where they are stationed.

"What's going on?" I demand, retracing my steps. "I said he's with me."

"I'm sorry, Xan, but your mother issued strict orders that he's not to be allowed past this point."

"That's ridiculous!"

A quick glance at Declan's narrowed eyes shows he doesn't appreciate the situation. But he doesn't argue with my father's security. Though I know he's jonesing to teach them some manners, all he does is step back, hands raised in the universal gesture of acquiescence.

"Go check on your father," he tells me. "I'll just head down to the kitchen for some of that coffee your sister was talking about."

Love for him wells up inside me. How typical of Declan to put his own annoyance aside and focus on what I need. A part of me wants to tell the whole group of them to go to hell, but short of dragging my mother away from my dad's sickbed and having her change her orders, there's nothing I can do or say that is going to convince Jared and the others to let Declan through. In this house, in this town, the queen's wishes are all but law.

Still, it's just another annoyance, another insult, that I am determined to call her on when my dad is better. Much as I love her, she's always making it more and more intolerable for me to be her daughter.

"I'll only be a few minutes," I say. "I just want to see him."

"Take as long as you need."

I nod, then turn to Jared. "You're being deliberately awful," I hiss at him. "There's no reason for this and you know it."

For once, his face doesn't soften as he turns to walk me down the hall. "That man is dangerous, Xandra. To you and everyone else around him. I can't believe you don't see that."

"Do you really think this is the time for us to get in a debate over my choice of lovers?" I don't even try to keep the anger out of my voice.

"Maybe not, but even without your mother's order, there was no way I was letting that man get within a hundred feet of your father when he can't defend himself."

"Prejudiced much?"

"It's not prejudice if it's justified. I've known Declan Chumomisto a long while, and if there's one thing time has proven, it's that he will use whoever he needs to get what he wants."

It's not the first time I've heard that accusation— Donovan threw it at me weeks ago when he was convinced Declan was the serial killer stalking Austin and me. It probably won't be the last time, either.

But I'll be damned if I sit by and take it, not when I spend most of our time together feeling like I'm using him. And not when he's just told me that he loves me. "And you think he's using me?"

"I didn't say that, darlin'. But my philosophy is 'forewarned is forearmed.'"

We're at my parents' door now, whispering furiously since neither one of us wants to give an inch on this. In the end, I have to because I know I'm not going to be able to change his mind today and I don't have the time to stand around arguing. Not when my father might be slipping away with every moment that passes.

Shooting Jared a we'll-finish-this-later look, I knock softly on the closed door, and then turn the knob without waiting for my mother or sister to answer. I don't want to take them away from any healing they might be doing.

But when I walk in, my mom is sitting by the bed, her head in her hands. She turns to look when I come in, and I'm shocked by how terrible she appears. And how old. Usually, my mother is one of those witches who never leaves her room, let alone the house, with a hair out of place. All part and parcel of being queen, she tells me— usually as she's encouraging me to change out of my jeans into a more tailored ensemble. Just one more reason I'm thrilled Donovan is the one who will inherit the throne instead of me.

"Xandra!" she exclaims, jumping up and rushing across the room to me. As she gets closer, I realize she's crying, her eyes red-rimmed and puffy while tears slide silently down her cheeks.

Terror rips through me. It's one thing for me to get a phone call telling me that my father is in bad shape. It's another thing altogether to watch my indomitable mother shatter into a thousand pieces. For the first time, I allow myself to wonder not *when* my father will get better, but *if* he will.

"Thank the goddess you're here!" my mother says as she all but throws herself into my arms.

I return her hug warily, looking around the room for anything that could be a trap. I know I sound heartless and overly suspicious, but my mother has a way of turning any situation to her advantage. And if she thinks my father's illness can somehow be used to make me a better witch, I have no doubt that she'll try to use it. That's just how she's wired.

But the pale, shaky woman currently holding on to me as if I'm the only thing keeping her from drowning doesn't feel like she has a mercenary bone in her body. She feels fragile and on the edge of collapse.

I glance over at Rachael who hasn't moved from where she's standing by Dad's bed, her hand resting over his heart as she pours into him as much healing energy as she can manage. I can feel it crackling in the air, the charge that always infuses with the world around her when she uses her gift.

She meets my eyes for a second and answers my un-asked question with a small shake of her head. Damn.

No improvement. But hopefully the head shake also means he's not getting worse. I'll take bad but stable over bad and worsening any day of the week.

Wrapping an arm around my mother's waist, I guide her back to her chair at the head of my father's bed. Once she's seated, I lean in and give Rachael a one-armed hug. Then immediately wish I hadn't.

She's burning up, her attempt at healing our father taking every ounce of energy she has and then some. It's a normal by-product of extreme magic usage and normally wouldn't upset me at all. But the last person I was around whose body ran hot like that was Kyle. And even though I tell myself I'm being ridiculous, that I'm safe at home with Declan and my family, for a moment I'm thrust right back into those endless minutes when I was completely at his mercy.

I take a few deep breaths and do my best to ignore the part of me that wants to curl into a ball until the memories fade away. Lily swears that the only way I'll learn to deal with them is to get to the point where I accept them, refuse to let them hurt me anymore. But I don't have the time to deal with them right now and this isn't the place anyway. It's never been the place to deal with any of my problems.

"Have we figured out what's wrong?" I finally ask, my throat husky with fear and pain and unshed tears.

"His body's shutting down, one system at a time." My mother's voice breaks and she leans over until her head rests on my father's leg.

"Why isn't he in the hospital then?" I demand as visions rip through me of my father's heart and lungs and kidneys failing. "He needs to be monitored, needs—"

"It's magical, not biological." Rachael speaks for the

first time. "I am doing the same thing for him that the human machines could. Doing it better, actually."

"Where is Aunt Tsura?" I ask. "I thought she'd be here by now."

"She's due in any minute," my mother says. "Once she's here, she'll figure out what's going on. She'll find a way to stop it."

I hope so. Because seeing my powerful, dynamic father like this—so still and gray and silent—has my stomach tying itself into knots.

Settling myself into the chair next to my mother's, I reach for my father's hand, squeeze it tightly. I feel a little like Alice down the rabbit hole, like everything I know, everything I understand about the world, has turned upside down overnight.

I'd planned to take my mother to task for her ridiculous decree about Declan—the sooner she understands that we're together, really together, the better—but I can't say a word to this silent, shaken woman sitting beside me. My indomitable mother looks as if one more thing, no matter how small, will break her into a million pieces.

I'm not sure how long I sit there, holding my father's hand and praying to the goddess to make him better. It seems like both an eternity and the blink of an eye, though I know the truth falls somewhere in between.

Suddenly, my mother stiffens beside me. "She's here," she says, and there's so much hope in those two words that it almost breaks my heart. Seconds later, my aunt comes striding into the room, exuding strength and power.

Tsura is identical to my mother—long black hair, golden skin, green eyes, tall, slender build. And yet they

look nothing alike. Where my mother wears tailored
clothes befitting a queen and always has her hair twisted
into a neat chignon at the nape of her neck, my aunt
looks like every Hollywood movie's idea of the quintes-
sential sexy witch. Her hair tumbles wildly down her
back, her nails are long and painted the same bright red
as her lips and she's dressed all in black. Tight black skirt,
sexy, low-cut black shirt, fancy black cowboy boots. Even
her jewelry—of which there is a lot—is embedded with
black stones. Obsidian, onyx and black sapphires sparkle
in the light whenever she moves.

Though I have six aunts—my mother is also the seventh daughter—Tsura has always been my favorite.
When I was young, she was my playmate and, now that
I'm older, she is often the only one, besides Donovan,
who stands with me against my mother. Not that I can't
stand up to her alone—I have, many times. But some
days it's nice to know there's someone else in your corner. Of course, the flip side of that is she uses her position for evil, as well—meaning she comes down on my
mother's side almost as often as she comes down on
mine.

My mom reaches for her sister with a shattered cry,
and Tsura all but leaps the last few yards to envelop my
mother in what I know is a jasmine-and-vanilla-scented
hug. "It's okay, Alia," she murmurs softly. "Everything's
going to be just fine."

Tsura holds my mother for long seconds, swaying with
her in an instinctive need to comfort. But her eyes are
already on my father, one hand outstretched to him as
she pours healing power into him.

I know the second it hits him, because Rachael draws
back like she's been burned. And in a way, she has been.

I've been the recipient of Tsura's power more than once, and while I've been thankful for it every time, never has it been a particularly pleasant experience. There's just too much of it; it's just too overwhelming and all-encompassing to be mistaken for anything but the invasion it is. Whereas Rachael's gift is gentle, soothing, Tsura's is like an eighteen-wheeler plowing through every defense you've got.

But in this moment, I'm glad for that. Because if anyone can help my father—if anyone can ferret out what's causing this—it's my aunt.

Tsura gives my mother another minute or so, and then gently pulls away and walks to my father's bedside. She runs a hand over my shoulder in silent greeting, does the same to Rachael. And then all her focus, all her magic, becomes centered on my father.

"Leave us," she tells Rachael and me. Then, "Alia, go stand on his other side. Hold his hand but do nothing else until I tell you."

Reluctantly, Rachael and I slip out. I close the door behind us, then turn to find my sister slumped against the wall. Now that she's out of the darkened room, and away from Mom and Dad, I see how drained she really is. In fact, she's so gray and drawn-looking that I'm not sure she'll make it to her room in the adjacent wing under her own power.

"You have to stop doing this to yourself," I scold even as I wrap an arm around her waist and gently begin propelling her down the hall. "You're going to kill yourself one day."

My words fall on deaf ears, just as I knew they would. Rachael is a healer—it's in her blood, in her magic, in every breath she draws and every action she performs.

Over and over again she's sacrificed herself for the good of the coven and she'll continue to do so until the day we scatter her ashes in the wind.

"I'm fine," she says, even as she limps along like a woman fifty years her senior.

"Yeah. I can tell." I strengthen my hold around her waist, take more of her weight.

"He's sick, Xan, really sick."

"I know."

"I couldn't find the source." She sags against me, rests her head on my shoulder as we make slow but steady progress. "It's a curse, it has to be. But who could get through his defenses so easily? And Jared's? And Mom's? And then have magic so strong that I can't even find what was done let alone try to neutralize it. It doesn't make sense."

My blood runs cold at her words, though I do my best not to let Rachael see how much she's disturbed me. Because, besides Declan and my mother and a few other witches and wizards—none of whom would have any reason to harm my father—the only people with the kind of power to do something like this all belong to one group.

The Arcadian Council of Witches, Wizards and Warlocks.

It looks like Declan was right.

Twenty-four

Fury and fear rip through me as the idea sinks in. I think of all my conversations with Declan, my determination not to harm any members of the Council until we find out the truth. I could have let him end them all, but I didn't. And this is how they repay me? By trying to kill my father?

Why did it never occur to me before that something like this might happen? I've been so worried about Declan—about what he'll do and what the Council will do to him—that I never thought to worry about my family. To warn them. I didn't want them to worry, didn't want to deal with Jared and the rest of my father's security force camped out on my doorstep while he and my mother went after the ACW.

How could I have been so blind? I ask myself as I continue to move Rachael down the hall. I have a ton of faith in my parents' abilities—they are two of the most fearsome witches I know—but still, I should have warned them. I should have listened to Declan, who knows these monsters so much better than I do. I complain about him not trusting me, but I didn't trust his judgment, either. I won't make that mistake again. Because if a few rogue Council members are responsible for everything that's been happening, then chances are my father won't be the only one who suffers. My mother, Tsura, Donovan, Rachael . . . No one is safe.

Guilt swamps me, but I push it away. There's time enough to deal with that later. Right now I need to talk to Declan, need to get his opinion on what to do next. Because if he's right—if one of the remaining Councilors is behind my father's mysterious illness—then the time for being patient, for waiting to see what develops, is past. We're already at war, only our enemy didn't see fit to inform us of that fact. The only question now is what we are going to do about it.

What I want to do is go back to Austin and assassinate the lot of them myself, before anyone else I love is hurt. Now that I know where their headquarters is, I could just sneak in and take care of things before anyone clues in to what is happening. I won't be like the people who killed Alride, won't need to put on a big show for whoever finds him. I could be in and out in under an hour and the Council would never be a threat to my family again.

Because the idea appeals to me more—way more—than it should, I force myself to let it go. To put it out of my mind. But no matter how hard I try, the thought remains deep inside me, couched in blood and darkness and something else. Something black and slippery and terrifying that I refuse to look too closely at.

We're almost at the end of the hallway, and I fight the urge to rush Rachael along. It isn't her fault I've screwed things up so badly. But when one of Jared's men sees us and comes running, I don't try to stop him from scooping Rachael up in his arms.

We start moving quickly then, and as we round the

corner that leads to this wing's sitting room and the staircase, I'm already looking for Declan. It turns out he's right where I left him, looking more uncomfortable than I've ever seen him. A woman is sitting on the couch next to him, her arms wrapped around him while he tries to extricate himself from her embrace.

A bunch of different emotions hit me at once, but before I can do anything but stare, Declan pulls out of the embrace. Then he scoots back against the arm of the couch, obviously trying to put distance between himself and the woman currently clinging to him like Saran Wrap.

Considering the way she follows him across two cushions, I'm not sure she gets the message. Which is fine. I'll be happy to deliver it myself.

I start forward before I'm even aware of moving. I don't normally consider myself a possessive person—I never have been with any man before—but I find with Declan I am. Though I tell myself to chill out, there's a part of me that wants nothing more than to cover that bitch with honey and stake her over the nearest mound of fire ants in the backyard.

A quick glance at Rachael assures me she's in good hands, and after checking to make sure the guard is going to take her to her room so she can rest, I head into the sitting room. Magic is sizzling along my nerve endings—the first time that's ever happened to me when someone wasn't dead or dying—and I flex my fingers a few times in an effort to keep it under control. Inside me, the darkness gathers a little more. Throbs a little more in its bid for attention.

Once again, I shove it back down. After all, Declan doesn't look all that happy to see her, whoever she is. . . .

I've only taken a few steps when Declan catches sight of me. It could be wishful thinking, but I'm pretty sure the look that just flitted across his face is relief. Thank God. I'm not normally an insecure girlfriend, but considering who Declan is and the fact that I don't even know how to classify our relationship yet, a little insecurity seems pretty understandable. Still, he's here with me, not her, and I have better things to do than worry about some woman whose name I don't even know.

"How's your father?" he asks, climbing awkwardly to his feet. It's the first time I've ever seen him be less than supremely graceful and it raises a warning flag, despite the reassurances I'd just given myself.

"We don't know yet. My aunt Tsura's with him now."

"Oh, you're one of Tsura's nieces?" The woman who'd been crowding Declan stood up as well. "I'm Irya, Tsura's assistant."

Declan takes over, his voice as smooth and familiar as the arm he settles around my waist. "This is Xandra, my—"

"Girlfriend," I fill in for him. "It's nice to meet you, Irya." I sneak a peek at Declan, curious to see how he's handling the whole "girlfriend" thing. Surprisingly, he doesn't look the least bit shaken. Instead, he looks pleased . . . and maybe even a little smug. Maybe it's stupid to even be worrying about this stuff after we've already said the *L* word. All these semantics are just that. What's important is that Declan loves me and I adore him.

"No, the pleasure is all mine." She extends a hand to me. "It's lovely to meet another one of Declan's girlfriends."

My eyebrows shoot up at that and she blushes a little, stutters out, "I didn't . . . I just meant . . ."

Declan steps in. "Irya and I dated a long time ago. It didn't work out, obviously, but we've been friends ever since."

He's looking at me, so he doesn't notice the flash of irritation that crosses her face before she can bury it, but I certainly do. She's playing him, acting all sweet and naïve in an effort to make him feel . . . what? I'm not sure. But it's obviously working, because Declan, smart, savvy Declan, looks uncomfortable—and extremely apologetic.

I barely resist the urge to roll my eyes. I don't even know this woman and I can see through her.

"It's so nice to meet another one of Declan's friends," I say, smiling as sweetly as I can. "Especially one with ties to Tsura. I imagine being her assistant must be kind of wild."

"It's a whirlwind, all right." Her voice is flat now, the mask she's wearing for Declan's sake beginning to crack.

Declan doesn't seem to notice it. But that doesn't matter, not when Declan excuses us with an impersonal smile and a few polite words. Then we're walking away, his hand on my lower back as he propels me down the three flights of stairs and across the foyer.

"Hey," I tell him, digging my heels in before he ends up pushing me right out the front door. "What was that all about?"

He lowers his head, brushes his lips against my ear. "I don't like you near her. She's a barracuda."

A weight I hadn't even known I'd been carrying around lifts from my chest. "I wasn't sure you caught that."

He laughs. "Caught that? Xandra, I dated that. It took me two months to extract myself from her very sharp, very sticky claws. I have no intention of letting her sink them into you."

"I'm not the one she's aiming for."

"Isn't that the truth?" he mutters under his breath, sounding completely disgusted, and the last of my tension drains away. I'm obviously being paranoid. He's about as likely to fall back under Irya's spell as I am.

So what freaked me out so much? The fact that Declan dated before me? The man is more than three hundred years old. Of course he's dated. Besides, she's not the first ex of his I've run across since this thing between us started.

But she is the only one who's alive—his other ex, Lina, was the second of Kyle's victims. When I stumbled upon her down by Town Lake in Austin, I had no idea where everything was going to lead. Had no idea it was going to lead us here.

Declan finally comes to a stop in the small parlor my mother uses for guests who are waiting for a royal audience. He closes the door behind us, then pulls me into his arms. Buries his face in my hair. And just breathes.

"How's your dad *really* doing?" he asks long seconds later, his body a well of strength that I can draw from.

I shudder, press my face into his chest. And just breathe. He smells like sandalwood and cinnamon and warm, dark waters. If I could, I'd stay here forever, resting against him. Holding him as he holds me.

But not even Declan can destroy my family's current reality. "Not good. Rachael's all but killed herself trying to heal him—with absolutely no impact whatsoever. And my mother is in bad shape. I've never seen her so lost." She's so strong, so sure all the time that it's strange, scary, to see her like this. My whole life, I've always thought that she was my father's anchor, the one he holds on to when things get rough.

Yet after twenty-seven years, it's strange to realize that it's the other way around. That he's what keeps her calm and settled and sure. Even stranger when I'm in the arms of the man who has quickly come to mean so much to me. Who is settling me, gentling me, just by his very presence.

I lift my head, wait for him to lift his. Then go up on tiptoes and press a soft kiss to his lips. Unlike so many of our others, this kiss isn't about passion, about need, about the bindings that continue to grow between us. It's about gratitude. Gratitude that he's here with me now, gratitude for all the things he's done for me—in the last few weeks and in the years when I had no idea what was going on.

I've carried a bitter fist of resentment with his name on it for years, one filled with anger and abandonment issues and fear that I'd never find another person who made me feel as he did. Fear that he'll leave me just when I let myself care for him again.

No more. He doesn't deserve my distrust or my fear, not when all he's ever done is put my needs first. I brush my lips over his again and say the words that are burning inside me. "I love you." I'm so grateful that I can say them now, as often as I want.

He looks just as moved now as he did in the car. Then he drops his head so that his forehead rests against mine. Closes his eyes. Drags deep, shuddering breaths into his lungs. I tighten my arms around him, realize that he's shaking. "Declan—"

"Say it again."

"I. Love. You." I don't know why this is affecting him so much, when I've already told him.

"I thought things might change when we got back here. When you saw how your family reacted to me."

"My mother doesn't get to tell me who to care about."

"I know that. And I wouldn't let you go anyway. You're mine, Xandra Morgan." His black eyes roam my face possessively. "And I will never let you go."

I kiss him again. "Who says I want to go any—"

A huge boom—like the most vicious clap of thunder imaginable—rattles the house. "What the—"

Before I can finish, two more booms sound in quick succession. I'm still trying to figure out what's happening when Declan shoves me against the nearest wall and covers my body with his.

Seconds later, the wall disappears and we're falling.

Twenty-five

Wake up, Xandra. Please wake up.

I come to slowly, Shelby's voice little more than a whisper in the corner of my mind. *I'm awake, Shelby.*

I'm scared.

Are they back? Are they hurting you?

No. Nobody's here.

You're alone?

Yes.

I'm sorry, honey. I try to focus, to remember what I want to tell her. But my head hurts and I feel groggy, out of it. Like I'm sinking into a pit of quicksand. No matter how hard I struggle to get free, I only end up sliding deeper and deeper under the surface. *Is it dark?*

Yes.

Are you okay? Does anything hurt?

A sad little whimper. *My leg.*

I know, baby. I'm so sorry. There's more to say, but I still can't remember what it is. Not while I'm drifting.

Xandra?

Xandra?

Xandra!

I'm here, Shelby!

I can't feel you.

What do you mean?

Normally I can feel you inside my head, ever since the first time you talked to me. But I can't now. You're going away. She starts to cry. *I don't want you to go away.*

I'm not going anywhere. The words sound funny even as I say them, all the syllables slurred and running together. *Pretty soon we'll get to meet in person. I can't wait to talk to you face-to-face.*

I don't think that's going to happen.

Why not?

I'm tired, Xandra. I'm tired and it hurts and I don't want them to come back. I don't want to do this anymore.

Alarm rips through my lethargy, reminds me of what I need to say. *Shelby, I swear, baby, we're looking for you. Do you know Nate? He lives on your street.*

Officer Nate?

Yes, Officer Nate. He's a friend of mine and he's the one who asked me to help look for you. I told him what you showed me yesterday. The top of that building outside your window.

Officer Nate is looking for me?

He is. But he needs some help. When he got to the room you showed me, you weren't there anymore.

I know. They moved me yesterday.

Did you see where they moved you?

No.

Do you have a window in this room? Maybe you can—

There's no window. Her little voice sounds completely forlorn.

"Xandra!" Another voice interrupts our conversation. "Xandra!"

I listen for a second, try to figure out who it is, what he

wants. But the voice drifts away and so does my attention.

It's okay, baby. We'll find you.

I want my mommy.

I know, Shelby. She wants you, too.

The woman, she says my mommy doesn't love me anymore because I'm not a good girl.

Anger stirs. *Don't listen to her. Your mommy loves you very much and she really wants you back at home.*

I want to go home.

Soon, Shelby. Soon you can go home. I pause, give my pounding head a chance to settle down some. As I do, I think of the seven Councilors who are still alive. And wonder, again, what they want with Shelby. Obviously she has power—she wouldn't be able to connect with me if she didn't—but is that power worth bleeding her for? Worth killing her for?

Shelby, do you want to play a game with me?

I like games.

I smile at the childish enthusiasm in her voice. It's so much better than the hopelessness I heard a little while ago. *Me, too.*

What's the game?

I want you to think really hard about the people who have been hurting you.

I don't like this game.

No, no. It's a good game. I'll list something about them and you tell me if I'm right or wrong. If I'm right, I get a point. If I'm wrong, you get a point. If you can tell me why I'm wrong, you get two points. Sound good?

What do I get if I win?

Hopefully freedom. When I asked before, Shelby couldn't remember anything about what her captors looked like, except that they were mean and scary. Now that I'm pretty sure she's being held by a Councilor, I'm hoping I can help her remember more about who has her. Not that there's any guarantee that she's actually seen her captor as opposed to just his or her servants, but still, it's worth a shot.

If you win, once you get home, I'll take you out for the biggest hot fudge sundae ever. And if I win, I'll still take you out for that sundae. How does that sound? It's a win-win situation.

I like caramel sundaes.

Caramel it is then. Whatever you want, the sky's the limit.

Silence for a moment, then, *Okay.*

Great! I think about the Councilors for a moment, remember what she said about the woman being the one who gave the orders. There are currently two female Councilors, so it seems as good a place as any to start with them.

The woman who comes to your room sometimes.

Yes? I hate how scared Shelby suddenly sounds, any excitement she had in playing this game with me completely gone.

Does she have long red hair?

No.

Okay. That's a point for you.

Shelby giggles. *This is easy.*

It is, isn't it? You can get another point if you tell me what color hair she does have.

It's black.

Good. That's another point for you.

Two for me, none for you.

You're right. I need to get on the board soon. So, if the

woman actually is a Councilor, then we're down to Vera Alradano—she's the only one with black hair. *Is her hair short?*

No. It's long and curly like my mommy's. But it's not as pretty as my mommy's.

Damn it. Not Vera, then. Unless she's wearing a wig, but I can't imagine that she would be. Not when every instinct I have is screaming that there is no way she plans to let Shelby go. And if she doesn't plan on letting her live, then there's no reason to worry about a disguise.

That's another point for me, Xandra.

I know. You're really good at this game. Are her eyes brown or black, like her hair?

No.

No? Are you sure?

They're green, like my cat's. I don't like her eyes. They're mean and scary.

Wow. She sounds ugly.

She is! Like Cinderella's mean old stepmom. And she smells funny, too.

I latch onto that description, even though it might not mean anything. A lot of witches smell funny to nonmagical people, because of the herbs and incense used in rituals. *What does she smell like, sweetheart?*

Like chewing gum from my mommy's purse. Shelby starts to cry a little and I immediately backtrack.

Do you want to stop the game, honey?

I don't like this game.

Okay. Then it's done.

"Xandra!" The voice is back, more impatient—more frantic—than before. This time I can hear it better, can tell that it's rough, masculine. And it belongs to someone much older than Shelby.

Wait! She calls out. *Don't go!*

I'm not going anywhere, I tell her. Except that doesn't feel exactly true. Already, my head is hurting worse and it's harder to hear her than it was.

Xandra, please. I'll play the game. Don't go! Please don't go!

She's crying again in earnest now, and, strange as it may sound, I can feel her clutching at me with her little hands. She's trying to hold me to her with every ounce of strength she possesses. I try to reach out, to hold on to her, but my hands won't move.

"Xandra!"

Every second that passes makes it harder and harder for me to hear her. The voice calling my name is getting louder now, more insistent. More anxious. I can't fight it any longer.

Xandra, please! Don't leave me.

I'll come back, I tell her. *As soon as I can, I'll come back.*

"Xandra! Goddamnit, Xandra, where are you?"

I wake up completely disoriented. I feel like I'm missing something, like I'm forgetting something important, but I can't figure out what it is. Instead, all I can focus on is the sound of Declan calling my name. Or to be more accurate, screaming my name. He sounds completely frantic, though I can't figure out why. The last thing I remember is telling him that I love him.

He calls my name again and this time I try to answer, but nothing comes out. It's as though my throat has forgotten how to work. Which doesn't make sense—weren't we just talking? I know I was talking to someone. I open my mouth, try again, and abruptly become aware that my lungs hurt, too.

What the hell is going on? I cough a little, attempt to draw air into my lungs, but nothing happens. My chest doesn't move; my lungs don't inflate. Declan isn't the only one panicking now. Something is sitting on my diaphragm, slowly, painfully squeezing the last remaining drops of air from my lungs.

"Xandra!" Declan roars my name this time. "Come on, baby. Give me something. Move something. Where are you?"

Move something? He's not making any sense. What am I supposed to move? And why? The only thing I'm really concerned about moving right now is whatever's sitting on top of me, keeping me from breathing.

There's a strange scrabbling sound above me, like someone is tossing things around. Then, suddenly, an electric charge rips through me. My whole body sizzles— something new to go with the aches—but at least I know what this is. It's Declan's magic, searching me out, though I still don't know why he's looking, or what happened to rip me out of his arms in the first place.

I can't help responding to his power—it clears my head, makes it impossible for me not to respond to the desperation I hear in his voice. Though it hurts, and every nerve ending I have is screaming at me not to move, I force my eyes open. Then really wish I hadn't. Because whatever is sitting on my chest is also covering my face. I'm buried alive in . . . I don't know what.

Panic finally sets in as I try to figure out how I got here—and how I'm supposed to get out. Though it threatens to overwhelm me, I beat it back. Right now, Declan is doing enough panicking for both of us. Besides, freaking out isn't exactly going to help my present circumstances. Not that I have any idea what will help at this point, but I know losing my head certainly won't. Especially when the dark is threatening again, my lack of oxygen making it harder and harder to think.

Knowing I have only one shot at this, I press my head farther into whatever I'm resting on and rock it back and forth a little. There's not much give, but I don't need much. Just enough to turn my head so I can try to take a breath.

For long, desperate seconds, I rock and turn, rock and turn, as my fingers start to claw at the rubble above me.

"Xandra!" Declan's voice sounds directly above me. "I've got you, baby. I've got you."

Another shot of electricity rips through me and I finally manage to turn my head, to gasp in precious gulps of air. "Dec—"

I don't even finish saying his name before the rubble is gone, lifted off my face with one flick of Declan's powerful magic. A little while longer and the rest of me is free as well.

For long seconds, I just lie there gasping for air. Then Declan is kneeling next to me, his face dark and dangerous and more livid than I have ever seen it. He looks ready to kill something—or someone—but the hands he runs over my body are gentle in the extreme.

"Are you okay? Are you hurt? Can you move?"

Though my body aches all over, none of the pain is worse than the rest. Which I'm going to tell myself is a good sign. "I'm okay," I gasp. I'm still sucking oxygen in like I've never seen the stuff before.

I reach out and grab onto his arm, use it to pull myself up.

"You shouldn't move," he tells me severely, but in the end he supports me instead of fighting me. I think he's as desperate to hold me as I am to be held.

As his arms wrap around me, I ask, "What happened?"

"There was an explosion."

"An explosion?" I know I'm looking at him like he's lost his mind, but his words just aren't making sense. "What exploded?"

He glances around the room. "If I had to hazard a guess, I'd say the whole damn house."

This time when panic hits, there's no holding it back. My parents, my sisters, Donovan, my aunt Tsura—I try to scramble to my feet, but my legs feel like rubber. It doesn't help that Declan's grip has gone rock solid and immovable on me.

I shove at the arms I had welcomed only minutes before. "I need—"

"You need to sit here for a few more minutes. You've got a bump on your head the size of a racquetball and so many cuts and bruises that I don't even know where to start with trying to heal you."

"My parents were upstairs."

"I know," he tells me grimly. "Give me a few minutes to take care of you and then I'll go check on them."

He probes at a very tender spot on my scalp and I yelp, glare at him. He glares back. "That would be the racquetball. Now sit still and take it like a big girl."

I grumble at him, but in the end, I acquiesce. Partly because I know I don't have a choice in the matter and partly because I feel absolutely awful. I won't be much help to anyone in this condition, so if Declan can help even a little bit, I'm willing to give him the few minutes he requested. As long as it's a very few.

As the familiar tingle starts on my scalp, followed by an icy heat, I try to relax. To give myself over to it. It's more difficult than usual because I'm freaking out about my family, but I know that the less I fight him, the faster this will go. All magic is like that. As in most things in life, it works best with compliance.

Seconds tick by with excruciating slowness, but in less than two minutes, I can feel the effects of what he's done. My headache has dulled considerably and the dizziness is almost gone. Thank the goddess I have such a talented lover.

Once I realize the room is no longer spinning, I start to get up, only to settle right back down when he snarls at me. More heat. More tingles. Then finally a reluctant sound from Declan that I know instinctively means he's willing to let me up.

He stands first, then helps me to my feet. I'm still feeling a little unsteady, but I do my best to mask it. He's watching me for any sign that I'm in trouble and I don't want to give it to him. If I do, I know that no matter how hard I argue, I'll end up sidelined.

He doesn't handle me being hurt very well at the best of times, and I can tell he's barely hanging on to his control by a thread right now. If he had his way, he'd whisk me away from here, take me someplace where he could wrap me in cotton. And while I appreciate his concern, if I don't get to my family soon, I'm going to completely lose my mind.

"Let's take it slow," he says, wrapping his arm around my waist as he leads me carefully through the rubble.

I don't want to take it slow. I want to run screaming through what's left of my house until I know everyone I love has escaped this living nightmare. But since my legs are barely supporting me now, I go along with him.

As we step into the foyer—or, should I say what once was the foyer—I'm stunned, horrified, by the piles of rubble that cover the marble floor in all directions. In some places the walls have caved in completely, giving me a perfect view of the outside woods that border my mother's gardens in all directions. But not all the rubble is from the house's exterior. I look up to where the third-floor landing used to be and realize there's nothing there but a gigantic hole.

Mom. Dad. Tsura. Rachael. Jared. Their names run through my head like a mantra and I start scrabbling over the piles of debris, desperate to get to the back stairs. Desperate to get to them.

Declan is right behind me, moving aside piles of brick and stone and plaster with little more than a thought. I'm running by the time I hit the kitchen, end up plowing straight into my brother, Donovan, who is bleeding profusely from a head wound.

Stretched out on the floor beside him are Willow and two more of my sisters, Noora and Nadia. All three of them look shell-shocked, but at least I don't see any blood—which is either a very good thing or a very bad one.

I choose to think positive as I grab onto Donovan and line his face up with my own. "Have you seen Mom or Dad?" I demand.

He squints at me as if trying to figure out what I'm saying, and I realize that all four of my siblings have blood coming out of their ears. They must have been closer to the explosion site than Declan and I were.

"Sit down," I tell Donovan, clearly enunciating my words so that he can read my lips. I lead him over to the closest wall, prepare to sit him on the ground. But Declan has seized a few pieces of debris and—using transubstantiation—has fashioned them into a chair.

Donovan sits heavily, and before I can do anything more than stroke a hand through his hair on the uninjured side of his head, a small group of policemen bursts through the back door, a door that is currently hanging by only one hinge. They're quickly followed by Witchcraft Investigations—I recognize them from their gray jackets and sour expressions—and two sets of paramedics.

I leave Donovan and the others in the EMTs' capable hands and, after grabbing Declan, start up the stairs at a run.

"There are more people up here," I yell over my shoulder. I hear them relay the message via radio and I know that Declan and I are on our own, at least for a few minutes.

I make it to the fourth floor in seconds, start to sprint down the hall to my parents' bedroom. But I only manage to take a few steps before my already shaky legs go out from under me and I hit the ground, hard.

Declan's right behind me, but I shake him off. Try to struggle to my feet. Shout, "Mom! Dad!" at the top of my lungs. If something happened to them, I'm not sure what I'll do. Much as my mother drives me insane, she and my dad mean more to me than I've ever contemplated before. I can't handle the idea of their dying. Don't want to think what it will mean to me—or to our coven.

There's no answer. The panic grows, especially when I see what it looks like up here—I don't know how to describe it except that it appears as if a bomb went off. Which, I realize with a sinking feeling, is exactly what happened.

I start running, scrambling, down the hallway toward my parents' wing. I'm not thinking now; I'm acting purely on instinct. Behind me, Declan curses and starts moving things out of my way so that I don't hurt myself as I stumble forward.

I don't pause until I get to the makeshift security station Jared had set up right at the beginning of my parents' private hall. I freeze when I get there, my heart dropping to my feet as icy dread whips through me. Forget panicked, I'm terrified now and Declan's muttered, "Oh fuck," certainly doesn't help matters.

Stretched out on the ground in front of us are the bodyguards Jared had stationed at the start of the hall. They're all covered in varying degrees of rubble and none of them are moving. I want to stop and check on them, but I want to find my parents as well.

For long seconds, I'm paralyzed by indecision. It's an unfamiliar state for me, made more powerful by the renewed throbbing in my head and my desperate desire to pretend none of this is really happening.

"Go!" Declan shouts to me, as he crouches down next to two of the fallen security guards. With a wave of his hand, he clears away the rubble in front of me, creating a path straight to my parents' door.

Flashing him a grateful look that he doesn't see—he's already checking for survivors—I take off down the hall, screaming for my parents. Right before I reach what used to be my parents' room and is now just a blown-up shell of a place, my mother stumbles to the doorway. She's streaked in blood, covered in dirt and grime, but she's alive. She also looks more like my mother than she has since I got here today—she's as calm as I am frantic, as in control as I am crazed.

"Dad?" I demand as I stumble to a stop in front of her.

"Tsura's with him. Even with this"—she gestures to the disaster around us—"he's doing better than he has been since this whole thing began. How is everyone else?"

"I don't know how many people were actually here, so I don't know who else I'm looking for." I tell her about Donovan and the others I found in the kitchen. Which is when it hits me. *Rachael.* She's in her room, in the part of the house that has been absolutely decimated by the explosion.

I take off back the way I came, this time with my mother at my heels. Emergency services have arrived en masse and are swarming the place—there are more members of the royal family security detail, more cops and paramedics here now than I've seen in one place ever.

A few glom on to us as my mother and I sprint down the hallway. I'm inclined to wave them off, but with just a few words she has an entourage following behind us. Declan is still with the security guards, talking to the paramedic who is taking care of the lone survivor. But one look at my face has him springing into action. Just not the way I'd like him to.

He grabs my arm just as I'm about to step into the hallway for the other wing, the one that leads straight to Rachael's room. "It's dangerous," he tells me when I try to wrench my arm from his grip.

"Let me go!" I demand. "Rachael's down there."

"Fuck." He drops my arm. "You stay here. I'll go."

I look at the chasm yawning in front of us, the uneven boards on the other side of it that used to be my mother's hardwood floor. There's smoke drifting down the hallway, which means there's a fire in that part of the house. I can't let Declan go, can't let him risk his life for my sister.

When I say as much, he shoots me a fulminating glare. Then looks at one of the cops standing near us, points to me. "Watch her."

"Yes, sir." The cop steps in front of me. "I'm sorry, Your Highness—"

I blast him out of my way with a surge of magic I didn't even feel coming on, one I had no idea I even had in me. "She's my sister!" I scream at Declan. "I'm going with you."

He locks his jaw so tightly that I'm shocked he doesn't break a tooth or three. But after a good look at my face—and the shell-shocked cop who is now on the ground at our feet—he doesn't waste time trying to argue. Instead, he grabs me and hurls me (with a little help from a spell, I'm sure) over the five-foot chasm that stretches between us and the other wing.

I land on my hands and knees and scramble to my feet, ignoring the jarring pain that comes with every move I make. By the time I'm standing again, Declan is beside me, looking as grim as I have ever seen him.

Now that we're over here, I can hear the fire crackling down the hall, can feel the residual heat of it creeping through the air. Declan turns back to the others, yells at them to get the fire department up here. One of the cops assures him they're on their way.

Declan nods, then turns back to me. "Are you sure about this?" he demands.

I nod. Who knows how long it will be before the fire department gets up here. Rachael could be dead by then.

"Okay, then. Stay behind me—follow my footsteps exactly." Then he's grabbing my hand and we're running straight into hell.

Twenty-six

Declan has an instinctive knowledge of which boards are shaky and which ones will hold our weight. I stay directly behind him as he runs across them, making sure to place my feet exactly where his have just been.

But the smoke is getting heavier the farther down the hallway we go and it's getting harder and harder to see. Fear ravages me from the inside, my body recoiling from what we have to do. Where we have to go. I ignore the warning signs from my brain and keep my feet moving forward. My already abused lungs are protesting, aching, at the sudden influx of smoke and toxins.

Ducking my head, I pull the collar of my shirt up over my nose and mouth to try to filter out some of the smoke. It doesn't work very well, but it's better than nothing. I think about what I learned in school years and years ago, about dropping to the ground and crawling to avoid the worst of it.

But the floor beneath us is way too uncertain. I'm scared enough balancing on a board here and there. I can't imagine what would happen if Declan and I tried to spread our weight out into so many different spots.

When we get to the corner, Declan stops, looks back

at me. "Are you okay?" he demands. "Are you sure you want to do this?"

I'm not sure of anything at this point, but my sister is somewhere in the middle of this smoke-filled mess and I can't just leave her here. I nod, because my throat feels raw . . . and because I can't trust my voice not to shake. If Declan had any idea how scared I am right now, there's no way he'd let me go through with this.

"Which room is Rachael's?"

"The second on the left." I'm shocked at how ravaged my voice sounds and can tell from Declan's narrowed eyes that he is, too. I squeeze the hand I'm still holding, a sign that it's okay. That I'm okay.

"Do you trust me?" he demands.

I nod more vehemently this time. If I didn't, there's no way we'd be on the fourth story of a burning house, attempting a rescue that even I know is damn foolhardy.

"Okay, then," he says. I can feel him bracing himself, his muscles tensing up until it's a miracle he doesn't snap in half. "It's going to get ugly."

Uglier than this? I bite my tongue at the last second to keep from spewing the words out, but he knows what I'm thinking.

He smiles grimly. "Way uglier." Then, making sure he has a tight grip on my hand, he rounds the corner, pulling me after him.

I gasp at my first sight of the corridor, recoil instinctively. Because this one isn't just smoke filled. It's covered in wild flames bent on devouring everything in their path. There's no way we're going to get through this without being burned to a crisp. It's not possible. And while I'm willing to die for my sister, I can't ask the same of Declan.

"Let's turn back," I tell him. "Get the firemen." I'm terrified doing so will end up being a death sentence to Rachael, but I also can't sacrifice Declan for her. I won't.

That's when I learn just how crazy the man I've fallen in love with is. Because instead of beating a fast retreat, he just grins at me—a flash of brilliant white teeth in a soot-streaked face. "You're not giving up that easily, are you?" he yells over the voracious roar of the fire.

"You'll die!" I scream at him, trying to hold him back as he takes his first steps down the inferno-like hallway.

"Have some faith!"

He throws one hand out to the side, the other above his head, and starts walking steadily down the corridor. I follow tentatively, expecting the flames to leap onto us at any moment. But I've underestimated Declan. From the moment he walks into this fiery hell, he is in control.

Fire is all around us, and though I feel the heat from it closing in on me, never does one spark from it so much as brush up against me. Declan holds it back—with magic or with the sheer power of his will, I'm not sure. Either way, it doesn't touch us. Even the smoke seems to retreat. It sounds ridiculous, and maybe fear is making me hallucinate, but I swear, it's easier to breathe here than it was on the other side of the stairs.

I start to relax, start to believe that we have a chance to get Rachael out of this alive. At least until we turn the corner toward her personal hallway and I get a glimpse of what hell must really look like. The entire hallway is engulfed in fire, so much so that nothing—not the walls, not the carpet, not the art—nothing, is distinguishable from the flames raging completely out of control.

Declan curses viciously. Turns to me and says, "Go back. Now."

I can barely hear him over the roaring in my ears. Terror is a wild animal inside me—terror for my sister, terror for Declan, terror for my entire family. Because if the fire is this rapacious up here, I can only imagine how little time it will take for it to engulf the entire house.

"Did you hear me, Xandra?" he demands. "Move it!"

"Only if you come with me." I grab his arm, start to tug him back even as I send a silent apology to Rachael. I love my sister, would die to protect her, but I can't ask Declan to do the same.

He has other ideas, however. With another muttered curse, he shakes me off. Sends me stumbling several steps away from him. Then, without a backward glance, he turns and hurls himself straight into the fire.

I cry out as it swallows him whole, an insatiable, insensate beast that he has no hope of battling. That strange tingling starts deep inside me again—my magic welling up in a panicked burst. The only problem is, I don't know what to do with it. How to wield it to help Declan or my sister.

Even knowing it's probably suicide, I plunge into the fire after Declan. I can't—I won't—let him face this alone like he's faced so many other things in his life.

I expect the worst, expect the fire to tear through my flesh and burn me alive. But amazingly, it doesn't. Heat—stifling, overwhelming, omnipresent—surrounds me, but the flames never touch me even as they surround me on all sides.

It doesn't make sense, at least not until I see Declan up ahead of me. The fire has attacked him, surrounding him completely as it licks at his hair, his clothes, his skin.

I nearly scream at the nightmare of it, but then I get closer and realize that it's not burning him. That, in fact, he's *letting* the fire do that to him.

I'm terrified and in awe all at the same time. Sure, I've seen Declan play with fire before—just the other day, in his house—but every other time he's done this, it has been fire of his own making. Fire created and sustained through one's own magic is easy to manipulate. But this fire is different. This is the result of a bomb, of malicious intent and probably black magic; it should be completely uncontrollable. No matter how strong a call a witch or warlock has to an element, he or she can only influence, only really control, the manifestation of that element if she or he created it. At least, that's what I've always been taught and it's what I've always seen. Until now.

Because now, right in front of me, Declan has seized control of the flame and he isn't letting go. He hasn't extinguished it yet—I don't even know if he can. But he's definitely controlling it, stopping it from getting to me or down the hall to Rachael.

I've caught up to him now, and though the heat is nearly unbearable, I don't move. I just stare, hypnotized as he manipulates the fire like it's nothing more dangerous than a soft spring rain.

He holds his arms out in front of his body and the flames shoot up and out, into a fiery arc that meets directly above his head. And then he slowly, arduously, begins fighting the power of the fire.

More than once, the flames fight back, pushing against him, licking over him until he is completely flamebound. Horror rips through me and it takes every ounce of control I have to keep from screaming at him to just let it go. But it's too late for that now—even I, who know nothing about the fire element except what I've learned from my sister Noora, can see that.

If he lets go, if he loses control—even for one second—of the beast he's grabbed onto, it will be too late. Too late for Rachael, for me, and definitely too late for Declan. I'm scared to death that it's already too late for him. One wrong move, one lapse of concentration, and he'll be incinerated.

I hold my breath, squeezing my hands so tightly that my fingernails dig into my palms, all in an effort to stay completely still. I don't want to distract him. My lungs ache from fear and the dark haze of smoke that hangs in the hallway. The smoke isn't nearly as heavy as it should be with this much fire—it's not pleasant, but I'm nowhere close to coughing up a lung—and I know it's because Declan has found a way to control that, too.

Behind me, I hear people clambering up the stairs—from the noise they're making and the words I can make out, I'm pretty sure they're firemen. My knees nearly go weak with relief, but then I realize it doesn't matter. Even if they are here to fight the fire, Declan is still at risk. He can't just let go, can't just walk away because the cavalry has arrived. The flames will jump, swallow us all whole.

Closing my eyes, I offer a whispered prayer to Isis. Not for me, but for Declan. *Please, goddess, keep this brave, beautiful man alive. Keep him safe.* But when I open my eyes and look again, my worst nightmare comes true.

The fire slips out of Declan's grasp, shoots straight at the ceiling and explodes outward, completely engulfing everything around him.

I do scream then, and behind me the firemen's voices

become a million times more urgent. Even knowing it's too late, knowing there's nothing I can do, I rush straight for my lover.

"Declan!" I shriek, my voice scratchy from the suddenly thick smoke. My power is welling up in me, strong and electric and surprisingly painful as it courses through my body. I'm shocked by it and furious at myself for being so. If I knew what to do with it, if I'd spent the last few weeks trying to harness my magic instead of running away from it, maybe I could be of help to Declan now.

He's directly in front of me, his entire body aflame—and this time none of it is under his control. Shrugging out of my hoodie with some distant thought of smothering the flames around him, I leap forward—only to crash into nothingness. Into a wall that shouldn't be there. A wall that I can't see. That doesn't exist.

Maybe it's because we're soulbound, or maybe it's just because I've gotten to know Declan over the last few weeks, but I know what he's done. He's the one responsible for the invisible wall between us. Even as he burns, he's determined to keep me safe.

Behind me, the firemen have finally caught up. Though many of them are fire elements themselves, they carry huge extinguishers with them—there's only so much they can do against nonmagical fire. They aim the extinguishers at the fire that surrounds Declan, but the magic-infused mist stops in midair and falls harmlessly to the ground. They look at one another, astonished, and continue to shoot.

I don't have the heart to tell them it's no use. All around me, the hallway is blackened, but there's no sign of fire, no smoke except for the lingering wisps from earlier. Declan has walled up all the flames—all the danger—on his side of the barrier.

I fall against the wall, hysterical. I beat against it with my fists as I watch, impotently, as the only man I've ever loved burns. "Declan!" I scream. "Declan!"

Next to me, the firemen mutter to themselves. A few of them dash back down the hall as they shout into their radios. They want to come at the blaze from the other side, to attack from the windows at the side of the house. I don't have the heart to tell them it won't do any good, either. Declan has sealed himself up perfectly. Too perfectly. I can see that the other end of the hallway, near Rachael's room, looks much like my end does. Burned out, blackened, but with no fire in sight. No one will be able to get to where Declan battles the fire, at least not until his magic fails.

Until he dies.

I'm on my knees now, dizzy, devastated, nearly deranged with grief. The firemen try to help, try to pull me to my feet, but I don't even acknowledge their existence. I'm too busy clawing at the wall. I can feel my magic leaking out, feel it pressing against the barrier as it, too, searches for a way to reach Declan. But there's nothing, no weakness in the barrier to exploit, no flaws to capitalize on.

I want nothing more than to curl into a ball and pretend none of this is happening, but I can't look away from Declan. I won't. He's doing this for me, sacrificing himself so that my sister and I can live. There's no way I will give in to my weakness, not when he is so filled with strength.

I force myself to watch as Declan falls to his knees in front of me. He's still burning, the fire somehow even more ravenous than when we first entered this hellish journey. His eyes lock with mine and he reaches a hand out, presses it right up to mine on the other side of the barrier he's thrown up between us.

"I love you," I mouth to him, refusing to look away.

At that moment, all the magic that's been bouncing around in me explodes outward. I feel it slam through me, out of me, and right through the wall and into Declan.

The flames around him falter for just a moment and I push against the barrier, determined to reach him. Determined to help him.

The barrier holds against me, but I feel more magic slipping through it. I have no idea what I'm doing, but I reach deep inside myself, harness whatever power I have left and shoot it straight at the wall. Straight at Declan.

It connects—I know it does because his whole body bows up at the sudden influx of power. I watch as he staggers to his feet. Spreads his arms wide, just as he did before, and begins once again to compress the flames into a fiery arc.

Long seconds pass—the longest of my life as I continue to funnel my power into him—but even through the tears and smoke clouding my vision I can see that it's working. The fire is narrowing, compressing, under the weight of Declan's will and our combined power. Growing smaller, weaker, all the flames in the room flowing into that arc of fire even as Declan pushes his hands closer and closer together. Pushes the fire into a smaller, tighter area until finally all the flames are gone, pressed into a spinning ball of flames that Declan hurls to the ground at his feet.

The flames dissolve into nothingness.

The barrier between us dissipates at the same moment Declan collapses onto the ground. I fall forward, barely able to catch myself before I plummet onto his raw, blistered skin.

Twenty-seven

"Declan. Oh my God, Declan." I swallow back the sobs that are ripping at the back of my throat. Try to concentrate on what needs to be done to help him. He's in bad shape—though not nearly as bad as he'd be if he weren't a Hekan warlock and a fire element. His skin is red and blistered, and though there are a few deeply raw and open places, most of what I can see looks like second-degree burns. Blistered, raw, even charred in places. But still treatable.

I don't know how that's possible—I saw him burning—but I'm not going to question it. Neither, it seems, are the firemen and paramedics who rush to his aid. Then again, maybe they've seen this before. For all I know, this is what happens to a fire element when the beast gets loose. In which case, I've never been more grateful for Declan's powers.

Trying to keep my head, I direct some of the firemen down the hallway to Rachael's room, but the majority of them stay with us. As they start to work on Declan in the middle of the hallway, I get shuffled out of the way. It's hard for me to step aside, especially when every instinct I have is screaming at me to get him out of the house and as far away from this nightmare as possible. I know that's just my fear talking—with the fire obliterated, thanks to Declan's magic, we're actually pretty safe for the moment. Provided the floor beneath our feet doesn't decide to cave in.

The paramedics must be a little worried about that, too, because they mutter a few spells to reinforce the buckled wood. I try to give them room as they put in an IV—I want them to do whatever's necessary to help Declan—but it's a physical pain deep inside for me to be separated from him even by a few feet. The newness of sharing my magic with him is still a raw space inside me.

I wonder if he feels the same way, hope he doesn't, but when he turns his head, his eyes tracking me, I know he's suffering at our separation just as I am. When he finds me, he struggles up into a sitting position. Reaches for me.

"We need you to lie back down, sir," one of the paramedics says, but Declan ignores him.

"Xandra," he rasps out, his hand connecting with mine and squeezing tight.

I wince at the contact. Not for me but for him. Blisters are already starting to form on his fingertips and I know touching me must be making the pain worse. "I'm here, baby. Let the paramedics do their work."

"No pain medicine," he tells them with a glare as one starts to inject something into his IV.

"Sir, you're blood pressure is really high. We need to—"

"No pain medicine." He looks at me, his eyes black with discomfort and a demand not to be ignored.

"Declan, please," I tell him, reaching out to stroke his hair back from his face. It's a miracle to me that there's any left, but with the exception of some singed edges, it's as long and silky as ever. "I can't stand to see you in pain."

"I can handle the pain." An arrogant statement from a man who has suffered far worse in his life—I'm not sure where that thought comes from, but looking at him now, I know it's the truth.

"In case you haven't noticed, someone is trying to kill your family. There's no way I'm going to be so out of it that I can't protect you."

His blunt words, like arrows to the very heart of me, strike at the knowledge I've been trying so hard to ignore in the heat of the moment. But now that the fire is gone and Rachael is walking unsteadily down the hallway with the help of two firemen, it's hard to ignore the obvious:

My father's grave and inexplicable illness bringing everyone home.

A huge explosion that rocked the family seat—and that of the coven—once the last Morgan made it through the doors.

A fire that seemed just a little too powerful and just a little too convenient to be simply a by-product of the explosion.

It doesn't take a brain surgeon, or even an incredibly powerful warlock, to figure out the obvious. That this is more than just a bid for the Council. Someone meant to end us all. Right here. Right now.

"We need to transport him to the hospital, Princess."

"Of course."

Declan's fingers tighten on mine. "I'm not going anywhere."

"Declan, please. Be reasonable."

Rachael stops a few feet away. Her eyes are wide and

wild in her too-pale face. "I can help him here." Her voice sounds like she's swallowed an entire quarry's worth of gravel. Or the equivalent of that in smoke.

"Excuse me, Your Highness, but you need to be taken to the hospital as well."

She gives the paramedic the same look Declan had just a few minutes before. "I'm fine here."

"Rachael, let them take you in and check you over. Then, if your lungs are okay, I'll bring you back here."

"My lungs are fine. Every time the smoke damage got too bad, I healed them. Between that and Dad, I don't have much left to give Declan right now, but I'll try." She starts to sink to her knees beside him.

Declan stops her by taking matters into his own hands. He gets to his feet in one long, smooth movement that belies the amount of pain he must be in. "I'm fine, Rachael. You should conserve your power for someone who really needs it. Besides," he says, looking around at the paramedics, all of whom are staring at him in varying degrees of shock, "I think we should get out of here, don't you?"

I've been doing my best to ignore the ominously creaking floor beneath us, but if Declan and Rachael can walk, I am all for getting the hell out of Dodge. It isn't safe in here anymore. Besides, the sooner we get out of here, the sooner I can get Declan to see reason about medical help. Not to mention, now that the most immediate crisis is over, I'm dying to see my family. To make sure they are all healthy.

Declan takes my hand in his and, ignoring the paramedics and their gurney, starts propelling me toward the stairs. I grab hold of Rachael and drag her along with us, determined to keep an eye on both of them. My sister is walking slowly, painfully—like there might be something more to her injuries than smoke inhalation—but the only sign of the nightmare Declan just lived through is a small hitch in his stride. Well, that and all the red, blistered, angry skin. I still don't know how it's possible. I plan to ask him at my earliest opportunity, but for now I decide to just be grateful.

Wrapping an arm around my sister's waist for the second time today, I take as much of her weight as I can. It's not nearly as difficult to move her now as it was earlier, and I don't know if that's because of the adrenaline flowing through me or if Declan is doing something to help things along.

I look at him sharply—the last thing he needs to be doing is expending more energy, especially considering how miraculous it is that he's alive and not in severe shock—but he just looks at me as though he has no idea of my suspicions.

It's a long walk down the three staircases to the front door. My head is throbbing from the bump I took earlier and I'm starting to feel more than a little nauseated. I don't know if the nausea is a sign of a concussion or if it's from the smoke inhalation or if it's just reaction to the abject terror I felt for Declan. Whatever it is, it's getting worse with every step I take. I fight it, just as I fight the strange lethargy sweeping through me. I focus simply on putting one foot in front of the other. It's harder than I ever imagined it would be.

All around me, my parents' house—the house I grew up in—has been reduced to rubble. Walls are missing, ceilings have caved in; whole chunks of floor have simply disappeared. There is colored glass everywhere from my mother's beloved stained glass windows, and remnants of furniture block our path.

We're almost at the front doors, or what's left of them. Outside I can see my mother, Donovan, my aunt Tsura, my sisters. The paramedics have even managed to get my father out. Beyond them is a ring of people, members of our coven and citizens of Ipswitch, who have gathered to help ... or simply to watch the spectacle.

My headache is getting worse and I close my eyes, trying to get control of the pain. Just a few more steps, I tell myself. A few more steps and I'll be out of here. Once clear, I'll make sure my family is okay and then I'll convince Declan to go to the hospital to be checked out. I'll go with him, let someone check me over, too. Make sure this headache isn't a sign of anything more serious. I'm sure it isn't, but still ...

Declan steps through the doorway, my hand still firmly gripped in his, and I start to do the same. But that's when it takes me over. A compulsion so powerful that I pause midstep as it winds itself around me and yanks me backward.

I stumble, start to fall.

Declan whirls around, catches me before I can hit the ground. He sweeps me into his arms despite the burns covering his upper body and heads through the door. "Are you okay?" he demands. "What happened?"

The second we make it outside, I start to scream.

Twenty-eight

Every instinct I have is telling me to hit, kick, bite, claw, to do whatever I have to do to get out of Declan's grip and back inside the house. I have enough control not to do it—I can't, won't, do anything to make his pain worse—but I do struggle against him until he lets me down.

The paramedics and firemen have stopped behind us, frozen in place by what I'm sure looks like a total mental and emotional breakdown by one of the members of the royal family. But even though I can't stop myself from screaming, I know that isn't what's going on. I've felt like this before and not once has it meant that I'm losing my grip on reality.

I dive through the paramedics, shoving and clawing my way back into the house. One of them wraps an arm around my waist and tries to stop me. I punch him in the face as Declan barks out, "Don't touch her!"

Behind me, I can hear the confusion my insane behavior has caused. My mother is calling to me, my sisters and aunt demanding for someone to stop me. Even the crowd has gotten into the act, and I know that there will be articles and photos of me acting like a crazy woman on the front page of every Hekan newspaper in the country.

It doesn't matter, though, because I know something they don't. I can feel it inside me, building, building, building, as strong as anything I ever felt on the rain-slicked streets of Austin. Stronger, even, because I know—I know—that wherever this compulsion takes me, I will end up at the feet of someone who shares my blood.

There's no way I would resist even if I could. Not now, with that certainty burning inside me. This is only the seventh time I've ever felt like this, but that doesn't matter. It's not a feeling I will ever forget.

Dread sits heavy in my stomach, on my heart, as I close my eyes and block out the frantic shouts and clutching hands of those around me. The certainty is a sickness inside me, all around me, as it wraps me up in strands of electricity and starts pulling me forward, forward, forward.

I don't try to resist, even knowing what's waiting at the end of the invisible rope I'm caught up in. Or maybe I don't resist *because* I know. Either way, I surrender myself to the inescapable pull. Let it lead me instead of fighting it at every turn as I am wont to do.

There's a part of me that's aware of Declan moving beside me, his hand resting gently between my shoulder blades. He doesn't say anything, doesn't try to dissuade me, but even as injured as he is, he won't let me do this alone. There's a part of me that wishes he would—I don't like the person I become when the compulsion takes a hold of me, the zombiclike creature fixated on only one thing. But at the same time, I understand. I couldn't leave him alone as he burned, as he faced down his demons. There's no way my big, strong, alpha warlock will ever leave me alone as I face down mine.

I'm drawn through the foyer and back up the stairs to

the second-floor landing. The stairs are precarious in this section—more than one of us almost fell through on our journey down just a few minutes ago. Beside me, Declan tenses, but I don't pay him any more mind than I do the shaky stairs. It's as if the compulsion recognizes the danger and somehow tells me where and how to step.

The farther up the stairs I move, the worse the burning gets, until my entire body feels like it's being electrified. The hair on my arms is standing straight up and my skin feels tight, achy, and so sensitive that the slight breeze blowing past me—let in by all the new holes in the walls—actually hurts wherever it touches me.

I turn to the left, head down the hallway to the guest wing. The fire marshal tries to stop me as I head into the rubble-filled hallway, as do three police officers. I don't even acknowledge they exist—I can't. Every molecule of energy I have, every ounce of concentration, is focused on what's waiting for me at the end of this corridor.

Somehow Declan takes care of the authorities. Not that it surprises me. Even covered in burns and blisters, he is the most formidable man I've ever met.

We're at the most badly damaged section of the hallway now, where the walls have caved in under the pressure of the floor above. Piles of bricks and wood and furniture litter the floor—some of them shoulder height or even higher—having fallen down from the third floor, which is pretty much decimated. It's a miracle of engineering and witchcraft that the fourth floor didn't collapse right along with it.

For a moment, just a moment, something squeaks through—a brief understanding that at least one of the bombs must have been planted on this wing of the third floor. Near Donovan's quarters.

My blood runs even colder, though I didn't know that was possible. If one of the bombs was left up there, then my earlier conclusions are right. This really *is* an attack on my entire family—and, even more importantly, on the Ipswitch crown. Donovan is the oldest child—and the most powerful and gifted of all my parents' offspring—and as such he is the natural successor to the throne. Killing him means killing my coven's greatest hope for the future.

The chill becomes a solid block of ice inside me, even as I remind myself that it didn't work. That Donovan was down in the kitchen when the explosion blew. That I saw him outside just a few minutes ago, safe and sound except for a few ugly bruises.

It doesn't matter, though, because the intent to kill him—to take over the monarchy—was there all along. My family isn't safe. And neither is whoever is buried in these piles of rubble.

"Xandra? Are you all right?" Declan's voice is soft, tentative, loaded with his own version of let's-not-upset-the-crazy-person. That's when I realize, compulsion or not, I've stopped here in the middle of the hallway. Frozen. Numb. Unable to go on.

I know what's on the other side of the rubble. I may not know who yet, but every instinct I have warns me that it's going to be bad. That it's better if I just stand here for a little longer and pretend. Because once I know, things will never be the same.

The only problem—the compulsion is getting stronger, like rusty nails raking along my skin from the inside. Declan's voice speaks to my magic, and the push deep inside me. It gets me moving again as the electricity kicks in, ribbons of painful sparks shooting along my every nerve ending.

I start to run, to claw and climb and dig and fight my way over the hills of debris until I slam to a stop on the other side. This is it. I know it. I can feel the surety of it bouncing around inside me like one of those rubber balls from childhood. It hits up against something—my fear, my revulsion, my hatred of this aspect of my power— then bounces off again. Every slam is another emotion, every moment another reason for me to just do it. To just rip the bandage off and see what I've been so desperately trying to hide from.

It's harder than it sounds. I've spent so long—most of my childhood and early adulthood—wishing for magic. Now that I have it, I want nothing more than to give it up. For so many, many reasons.

But now, this moment, isn't the time for wishes. I stumble forward, aware—once again—of Declan at my back. The compulsion guides me to just the right spot. Then I drop to my knees and begin to dig.

Seconds later, Declan follows suit.

He uses magic to lift as much of the debris as he can, but the balance is precarious up here and if he lifts too much, we risk all of it caving in on whoever is trapped below. Though there's a big part of me that knows it's too late—that whoever it is is dead or the compulsion wouldn't have kicked in—there's a small part of me that won't let go of the hope, the prayer, that we'll find him or her alive.

So, for the most part, we use our hands to dig through the debris—the wood and rock, glass and plastic. I'm not being careful enough. My attention is focused on what, who, is below the rubble, and I end up slicing my thumb open on a particularly jagged piece of glass.

Declan curses, tries to heal me, but I block him. He has so much healing to do on his own, so much damage to repair, that there's no way I'm letting him waste any of his power on me.

Only he doesn't seem to care what I want. At least, not in this matter. He grabs my hand in his, wraps his long, magician's hands around my thumb.

It takes only a second for the metallic stink of blood to reach my senses, only a few seconds more before I see a pale hand, fingers scratched, blue-painted nails cracked and broken from where she tried to claw her way out of the rubble.

I go light-headed at the sight of those blue-tipped nails, start to tremble as my entire body alternates hot and cold. "No, no, no, no." I'm not even aware that I'm speaking out loud until Declan wraps an arm around my shoulders and hugs me to his chest.

I cling, even knowing how much pain I must be causing him. I can't help it. I need his strength, his focus, his center, if I have any hope of getting through the next few minutes.

The two firefighters who followed us through the broken labyrinth my house has become pull up short when they see the hand. They radio for help, then start to dig her out.

"Do you know who it is?" one grunts out as he lifts a wooden beam off her.

I don't answer, I can't. Now that I've found her body, now that I've touched her, I'm locked in the nightmare of her last moments alive. The electric shocks have stopped ripping me apart, but in their place is the terror she felt. The desperation. The pain.

And finally, the hopelessness.

I curl into a ball against Declan and let the memories swamp me. I won't be able to think clearly until they do.

The second I surrender, she grabs onto me, pulls me deep. Confusion comes first, shock as the sound of the explosions registers. Followed by fear.

A mad dash for the door.

A jarring fall.

Pain radiating up from her hands, her knees.

A loud crack. The ceiling falling in.

Pain, pain. Can't breathe. Can't breathe.

Have to get out. Have to try—

Can't breathe.

Panic.

Heart racing, head pounding, fingers screaming in agony as they scramble for purchase.

Can't breathe.

Heavy. So heavy.

Chest . . . hurts.

Oh goddess, please. Please don't let me die.

Try again.

Fingers raw. Hurts.

Can't breathe.

Can't scream.

Tears.

Please, find me. Please, someone find me. Donovan. Rachael. Xandra. Please, find me. Please.

Can't breathe.

Can't . . . breathe.

Can't . . .

"Do you know who it is?" the fireman asks again, more impatiently this time.

With that last thought, the memories fade into nothingness. In their place is a soul-searing grief because, yes, I do know who it is. My sister, whose fingernails are always painted a sparkly blue. My sister, who always has a laugh and a smile. Hannah, my sister, who, with her sunny personality and happy-go-lucky approach to life, has always been the family favorite. Even mine.

Especially mine.

I mumble her name, my face still pressed against Declan's chest.

He stiffens—he knows her well because she dated his half brother, Ryder, for years—and mutters a particularly vile curse. Then he starts to rock me. "I'm sorry, Xan. I'm so sorry, baby."

The firemen are working with even more fervor than they had been—no one wants to hear that a member of the royal family is trapped under piles of rubble or that they missed it on their first tour through the house. I start to tell them that it's too late, that I wouldn't have been able to find her if she hadn't been already gone, but in the end I don't have the strength to speak, let alone answer the inevitable questions that will come with my certainty.

It doesn't take long for more help to arrive, firemen, policemen, paramedics, piling in with shovels and other tools that will make excavating her easier. I want to help, the gaping hole inside me demanding that I take some kind of action, but Declan holds me back.

Then he just holds me, crooning nonsense words in my ear as he cuddles me closer and closer. I want to scream, to rage, but that won't do Hannah any good. Won't do anyone any good. More than once, one of the policemen tries to convince Declan to take me out of here, back to the front where we can both get medical attention. Where I don't have to see them excavate my sister's dead body.

But that's not the way this godforsaken magic of mine works. Once the compulsion kicks in, once I start on the path to find a body, I can't leave until the body has been recovered and is on its way to the morgue. Only then does the compulsion release me. Only then am I free.

Except I'm not. I haven't been free since I found that poor girl's body three weeks ago. I'm not free of the magic, not free of the nightmares, and most certainly not free of the guilt that comes with always being too late.

Declan tells me that I can't be so hard on myself. That my magic manifests how it manifests and that there is good in finding people who have been discarded, hidden, forgotten. But I don't see it. All I see is that I'm never there in time. If I knew earlier, if I felt their suffering before it was too late, I would embrace the burden. Difficult, painful, as it is, I would deal with it. Because there is something valuable in being able to save a life, in being able to stop it from ending prematurely.

But this—this ridiculous compulsion that draws me to mangled and abused bodies, that has me reliving the person's dying moments, is no gift. It's a nightmare, one that gets worse every time I endure it.

And now, with Hannah. Knowing that she cried for help. Knowing that she cried for me to save her before she died . . . I can't bear it.

There's a commotion behind us and I look up just in time to see my mother—my regal, always-in-control, always-aware-of-her-duty-to-her-subjects mother, screaming my sister's name as she scrabbles over the piles of rubble. Tsura is with her, and though she lays a restraining hand on my mother's arm, my mom doesn't seem to notice. She just shrugs it off and keeps scrambling over the debris as she tries to get to Hannah.

"Mom, stop." I croak out the words. "It's too late."

I can see from her face—from the way she looks at me—that she already knows the truth. She knows what my power is, knows that it was too late the moment I could sense my sister's distress. And yet she can't go there, can't—

At that moment, the rescue crew manages to unearth the upper half of my sister's body. Even though I know what's coming, it's a shock to me—her eyes wide open, her mouth frozen in a silent scream, tear tracks still damp on her cheeks.

My mother takes one look at her and falls to her knees, starts to scream. Tsura grabs onto her, turns my mother's face into her chest and rocks her much as Declan is rocking me.

I watch as my mother collapses into her sister, her body shuddering with sobs. I try to push away from Declan, to stand so that I can make my way over to her, but the moment his arms fall from around me, the nausea returns tenfold.

The room spins, and then suddenly I'm on my knees again, vomiting up what feels like my stomach lining. Declan pulls my hair back, holds me, but even his touch can't make the sickness go away.

This time I don't think anything can.

Twenty-nine

It's been a long night, maybe the longest of my life.

I spend most of it sitting next to Declan's bed. Watching him heal a little bit more with each hour that passes. We've moved to my family's ranch, about ten miles outside of Ipswitch. My dad originally bought the land—which surrounds Ipswitch on all sides—for safety reasons. When Texas started developing a couple hundred years ago, he didn't want to have to worry about human towns springing up too close to our borders.

About twenty years ago, he built a house on the land for our family. Protected by the most powerful Hekan charms in existence and under constant surveillance by my parents' security, it still provides us with a lot more privacy than the house in town does. Did. For years now, he and my mother have used it a couple of times a year as a kind of retreat. Now, however, it's become the seat of our coven's government. The home of the royal family.

I wanted Declan to go to the hospital in town, but he insisted on coming here instead. He told me it was because he didn't like hospitals, but I know the truth. It's because he wanted me here, surrounded by security, safe. Or at least as safe as I can be right now.

He stirs in his sleep, moans a little, and I stroke a

soothing hand over his hair. Murmur a few words to him. At the sound of my voice, he settles back into sleep. And I get up from the armchair I've been sitting in for the last eight hours.

I cross to the window that overlooks the pastures and horse barns. Normally, it's so dark out here that you can see every star in the sky. But tonight, the whole area is lit up. Jared has rolled in security troops by the dozen to ensure that the house—and, more importantly, my family—are secure. Or as secure as we can be right now.

As I look out over the land, I relive every second of the day. Of the last few days. And wonder what I could have done differently. I'd do anything, give anything, to have a different outcome than the one I'm living.

Declan, badly burned. Hannah, dead. My father gravely ill and not responding to treatment. My family in shambles. My coven in chaos.

I'm so sick with sorrow and anger that I can barely breathe. Barely think. The darkness is creeping up on me, getting worse with each impotent moment that passes. There's a part of me that wants to fight it, but it's a small part. Because there's strength in the darkness. There's control and power and action. And right here, right now, I want to embrace all of those things.

Is this what Declan feels? I wonder. When he performs his magic? When he walks in the shadows? Is this what it feels like? If so, I don't blame him for embracing it. For craving it. I know the dangers, know how easy it is to be seduced. And still I want to give in. To take the vengeance that is due to me and mine.

There's a soft knock on the door and my aunt Tsura pokes her head in. "How's he doing?"

"He's sleeping. I slipped him a tranquilizer in the

healing draft Rachel made him. He's been resting pretty comfortably ever since."

"Good girl."

She crosses to the window, wraps an arm around my shoulders and pulls me into her embrace. "How are you doing?"

"I'm fine." I shrug off the concern I hear in her voice. I'm not the one she needs to be worrying about right now. "How are Mom and Dad?"

Tears glaze her green eyes, and she looks away. Takes a moment to compose herself. "There's been no change in your father's condition. He isn't getting any worse, which is good. But he's not getting any better, either, no matter what I try."

"And Mom?"

"I slipped her a tranquilizer, too. She's a wreck. Not that I blame her. Losing Hannah like that. Maybe losing your father." She sighs heavily. "Your mother is the strongest woman I know, but what happened today is enough to break anybody."

I nod because I know exactly what she's saying. I feel more than a little bit broken myself.

"Why don't you take a break? Go downstairs and get something to eat. The housekeeper made some soup. It'll do you good."

"I don't want to leave him alone."

"I know. That's why I came up. I'll sit with him, do some healing while you stretch your legs. Maybe check on your mother and Rachael—I can see that you want to."

She's right. I do. Even more than that, though, I want to talk to my brother. See what Donovan has to say about all of this.

"Thanks." I lean over, brush a kiss across my aunt's cheek. She smells like lemons and spearmint, the same as always. Somehow it isn't as comforting a combination as it usually is. But when she squeezes my arm and I feel the wave of heat where her fingers wrap around my bicep, I find myself relaxing despite myself. Which is exactly what she intends, I'm sure.

While she takes up vigil next to Declan, I slip out of the room as quietly as I can. I don't want to be gone too long, but there's a lot I need to cover in these next few minutes. I can't afford to dawdle.

First stop is to look in on my mother. Rachael and Noora are in her sitting room, talking quietly. I take one look at their red noses and swollen eyes and feel the darkness grow. Feel my resolve stiffen. Whoever did this to my family is going to pay.

Next stop is the kitchen for that bowl of soup. I don't really want it, but I'm determined to try to eat. With everything that's happened in the last three weeks, I've somehow managed to lose twelve pounds—pounds I can't afford to lose if I plan to take on the bastards who did this to my family.

And I do. Dear goddess, do I ever.

Besides, my head is back to its painful throbbing and I need something in my stomach before I pop some Advil.

Donovan walks in while I'm ladling up a bowl. I hand it to him, then pour another bowl for myself. Then grab a couple of chunks of bread from the basket sitting on the counter before sitting next to him at the breakfast bar that runs the length of the back wall.

We don't talk as we eat. Instead, we spend the time looking out over the ranch. Down here, I can see things so much more clearly than I could on the third floor. There's a security guard posted at every point of entry around the house—including the window where we're currently sitting. Others are patrolling the acreage while others guard the borders from inquisitive reporters and unknown threats.

Even more are at the house in town, working with the police and firefighters to comb through what's left of my parents' home.

When I've choked down as much soup as I can—which turns out only to be a few bites—I push my bowl away, then wait for Donovan to finish his. Considering his appetite isn't much better than mine, it only takes a couple of minutes.

He starts the conversation. "How's your head?"

I reach up, trace gentle fingers over the golf-ball-sized bump that's sprung up at the crown of my head. "It hurts."

"I bet. You should let Tsura take a look at it."

"She's got enough to do. Besides, Declan already healed most of it."

"Yeah, well, if it gets any worse, I want to be the first to know about it."

His voice is so full of command that I can't resist. "Yes, Your Majesty. And shall I curtsy while I inform you?"

He retaliates by tugging on a lock of my hair from the uninjured side of my head. "Brat."

"Bossy."

We grin at each other, enjoying the few seconds of normal before everything crashes back in on us. Finally, Donovan stretches out his legs with a sigh and asks, "What are we going to do about this, Xandra?"

"The only thing we can do. Find out who did this. And make them pay."

For long seconds, he doesn't answer. Just stares at me through narrowed eyes as if trying to sense my resolve. "Is that you talking? Or Declan?"

I don't take offense—it's a valid question, after all, considering that this darkness isn't characteristic of me. "Oh, it's me. It is, very definitely, me."

He nods. "Okay, then. So how are we going to go about doing that?"

"My first thought is to get rid of the bull's eye that seems to be painted over every single one of us. We need to restrict access to the royal family, especially to Mom and Dad and you."

"And you," he reminds me. "You are right behind me in the line of succession to the throne."

"I try not to think about that."

"Yeah, well, maybe you should start. These are dangerous days."

"In my opinion, that's just one more reason to keep you alive."

"I'd like to keep all of us alive, if possible."

At his words, my thoughts turn to Hannah. From the look in his eyes, so do his. "Where is she? Where's Hannah's—" My voice breaks. I can't bring myself to say the word *body*. Hannah's body. It just sounds so final and I can't go there yet. Can't accept the idea that my beautiful, carefree big sister is really gone.

"Jared and I arranged for her to be taken to the Kasseras'. We agreed an autopsy wasn't necessary considering we already know . . . how she died."

Another benefit to having me around. Who needs a coroner when I can tell you in excruciating detail, exactly how people die? Admittedly, being in a witch town—with citizens who generally live for centuries—we don't have much need of coroners or mortuaries anyway. Hannah is only the second member of our family to die in my lifetime, though I have dozens of aunts and uncles and cousins. My mother's family, especially, believes in big families.

"Makes sense. When will we—" Again I can't bring myself to say the words.

"That's up to Mom. And hopefully Dad. When she's ready, we'll talk about the funeral." He pauses, thrusts a hand through his hair. Drums the fingers of the other hand on the counter in front of us.

"Just spit it out," I finally tell him, exasperated.

"Sorry." He grimaces. "I spoke with Declan this morning."

"I know."

"Do you agree with him? That the Council is behind all of this?"

"Not the whole Council, since two of them are dead. But, yeah, I think someone's gotten way too power hungry. And it only makes sense that it's one of them."

"I was afraid you were going to say that."

"Do we know anything yet? About what actually happened at the house?"

"We know more than I thought they would at this juncture, actually." He crosses to the coffeepot, pours himself a cup, then lifts an eyebrow in my direction. I shake my head—I'm exhausted, but caffeine is the last thing I need right now. "All four of the bombs—"

"Four? I thought there were only three?" I was sure I'd heard only three explosions.

"There were four," he tells me grimly. "One was set in

the middle of Mom's garden—it took out the ceremony circle, along with the cabin that houses all our tools. Mom's plants were also decimated."

Dear goddess. I fall back against the chair and try not to think about what he's said. How could anyone be so malicious? So evil? It's one thing to bring the house down—that is more than awful enough. But to go after the ceremony circle? Our wands and athames? The plants my mother and sister use to work magic and heal people? "It's vile."

"Yes," my brother agrees. "But it's also stupid. Whoever did this was so worried about taking everything down that they didn't do enough to cover their tracks."

My heart beats more quickly. "You have a lead?" While I'm thrilled at the thought, I can't help wondering if maybe our suspicions are misplaced—because careless, rushed, sloppy work just doesn't sound like the ACW. When they want to cause damage, they do, but they are masters at covering their tracks. I know this from intimate, personal experience.

"Well, whoever created the bombs didn't bother to hide the magic woven into them. It's all over the fragments. They probably thought the bomb would destroy all traces of the spells that were used, but it didn't. Particularly the one in the gardens. It was such a wide-open space—nothing for the bomb fragments to decimate themselves against—that WI managed to piece together a bunch of shards. Those shards, when combined, have given Jared a partial magical thumbprint.

"He's running it through the database right now, waiting to see what pops up. It won't be definitive—there isn't enough to make an absolute call—but they have five partial matches already. Once the program is done running, they'll have a list of suspects. And we'll go from there."

I think of my assumptions earlier, the conversation I had with Declan. And feel the prickles of unease get worse. Could the ACW really have been so incompetent? All my knowledge, every instinct I have, screams, "No way." If they're found culpable for this, then they are all dead—witches, wizards and warlocks aren't exactly known for their ability to forgive.

Even if my parents don't eviscerate them—which I have no doubt they will—the covens will never tolerate being governed by these Council members again. Even the Council structure itself would be in jeopardy if such a thing came out. This isn't to say that one Councilor wouldn't be this stupid. But more? Suddenly the conspiracy we've been looking for seems awfully shaky.

"Would any of the Councilors really be that stupid?" I ask Donovan. "Would one of them really be careless enough to leave a magical imprint?"

"They were stupid enough to hire Kyle," he answers.

"Or so he claimed. There's no actual proof of that."

"Except for your torture and near-death experience?" His fists clench with a rage that clearly hasn't abated in the last week and a half.

"What if this is just a setup?" I ask, voicing the suspicion that's just taken hold inside me. "What if all this is just an elaborate ruse to pit us against the ACW?"

"You don't really believe that."

A few hours ago I didn't. But here, now, in the bright lights of the kitchen, I'm not so sure. My arguments just aren't standing up. "Think about it. We're on hair triggers over here—even before the bombing. Declan is just looking for an excuse to go after them and I know you are, too. Hell, if I'm honest, so am I.

"But think about what would happen if we were wrong? If we act against the Council—even formally—and then get proven wrong, we're finished. There's no way they wouldn't be compelled to make examples of us. No way we could save ourselves or any of our citizens that stand with us.

"Now look at it from their point of view. Someone is killing Councilors one by one. And who's got a bigger grudge than we do, right now? Hell, it's all I've been able to do to keep Declan from going after the lot of them. They know they're guilty, know that we have reason to want them dead. So why wouldn't they be waiting for an attack from us, some overt action that they can hold up as treason?"

Donovan still looks resistant—like Declan, it won't be easy to get him to think past his hatred for the ACW—but at least he's listening. So I continue. "If we've got a non-Council enemy, pitting us against them would be a pretty impressive strategy. There's a good chance we'd end up destroying each other before we stop to figure out whether or not we *should*."

"By that logic, the bombing could be retaliation for what they perceive as our actions against the Council."

"You're right. It could be a warning to back off before all hell breaks loose. But I have to tell you, that didn't feel like a warning. It feels like a declaration of war."

Thirty

"Shit, Xandra."

"Tell me about it."

"If it is the ACW and we don't act, then we risk being perceived as weak."

Donovan's logic appeals to the growing darkness inside me, the part of me that wants to strike first and ask questions later. I'm trying to ignore that part. To do what's right for my family and my coven. But it's hard to do that when there are still so many questions. And so many answers that could be right or wrong.

"If it isn't them, and we do act, then we risk a lot more than perception. We risk the lives of our entire family and all of our people. We can't afford to do that. No one else needs to die senselessly."

For some reason, a picture of Shelby flits through my head as I say that. I haven't given her much thought today, not with everything going on. But if there was ever an innocent victim in the middle of all this, it's her. Whoever is holding her against her will—

I freeze, my water glass halfway to my mouth as I remember, for the first time, what happened after the explosion knocked me out. The dream that wasn't really a dream. The one where I played a game with Shelby and asked her to describe her kidnapper to me.

Curly black hair. Mean green eyes. Smells like her mommy's chewing gum. It's a childish description, but it's the only one I've got right now. And, as I realized earlier, it doesn't fit either of the female members of the ACW, or the wives of the male members. I wish I'd been able to ask her a few questions about the man who was holding her as well. Because as it stands right now, her captors could be anyone.

Frustrated, angry, afraid, I drop my head onto the counter, close my eyes. And try to fit all the different puzzle pieces together in a way that makes sense. It doesn't work. Right now, I feel like I have all the pieces, that they're all spread out in front of me. But no matter how hard I try, I can't get them to form the right picture. Instead, everything is a little mixed up, a little out of focus.

It's maddening, especially considering how many people have already lost their lives. And how many more people's lives are at stake.

"So what do we do? Mom's going to be awake in a couple of hours and I want to have a recommendation for her. She's in no shape to think all this through on her own."

"She's the queen—"

"The queen who just lost her daughter and might very well lose her husband in short order. She's going to need something to hold on to."

"Yes, but—"

I break off as Rachael comes racing into the kitchen. "Have you heard?" she demands, flipping on the flat-screen TV hanging on the wall opposite us. "Councilor Marquez has been killed. His head of security found him in the family room, his throat and stomach slit wide open. He'd been completely bled out."

I close my eyes, suck in deep breaths to hold at bay the nausea that has resurfaced at her words. Another Councilor dead. Killed violently. The news on TV for the whole Hekan community to see. This—on the heels of the explosion—is going to light up the entire witchcraft world.

The news flashes a picture of him across the screen— alive, smiling, but with the coldest eyes I've ever seen. And as the newscaster starts recounting the accomplishments of the man who had served as an ACW Councilor for nearly eighty years, my heart stutters in my chest. Because even though I know we weren't involved in it, even though I know that no one in this house had anything to do with it, his death smacks of retribution.

I glance at Donovan, see the realization in his eyes as well. We're one step closer to a war that we might not be able to win. A war that we don't want to be any part of but one that we're being forced closer to with each hour, each minute, that passes.

"Why Marquez?" Donovan asks into the ensuing chaos caused by Rachael's announcement and the subsequent newscast. "He has almost nothing to do with Alride or Lantasis. They vote the issues differently, aren't friends, don't have anything in common that I can see. So why kill him?"

Trust Donovan to get to the heart of the matter with only a couple of simple questions. Too bad I don't have a clue how to answer him—and judging by the looks on the others' faces, neither do they.

I mean, we all know Marquez was a total bastard—and power hungry, to boot—but if someone had asked me which Councilor might be involved in blowing up our house, Marquez's name would have been one of the last on the list. His moves are usually much more passive-aggressive, and more smoothly plotted. In fact, the only person I would suspect less than him is Callie. And that's mostly because she's the youngest Councilor—she hasn't been around long enough to have been corrupted the way the others have.

Silence hangs over the lot of us until finally Donovan answers. "Maybe whoever did this knows something we don't."

"And maybe whoever did this is looking to cause the most damage in the smallest amount of time." This from my sister Noora, who entered the kitchen while we were all gathered around the TV. "We know Marquez was an asshole, but he always put on a good show with the covens. The people love him—he has the highest popularity ranking of any of the Councilors."

My eyes meet Donovan's, lock. Because there it is again. Another nudge into war.

The doorbell rings before anyone else can add their two cents. Seconds later, our ranch housekeeper enters the kitchen. "Excuse me, Your Highness." She addresses my brother. "Witchcraft Investigations is here. They'd like to apprise the queen of their progress."

"Send them in, Leandra," Donovan says, then puts on his poker face and straightens up to his full height. As he does, I can see the future—and the monarch he is going to be. It's a good look for him.

As Leandra heads back to the front parlor, the tension level in the room—already high—escalates. I can feel myself bracing for the worst, know that my brother and sisters are doing the same. Whatever WI has to say, it's bound to be bad news. Either they know who did it and we'll be faced with finding out who betrayed us, or they don't know, in which case we'll still be in the dark, trying to figure out whom we can and can't trust.

Only a minute or two passes before Leandra leads three detectives into the kitchen. I nearly groan when I recognize Moira. She's a good cop—or so my family keeps trying to convince me—but since she spent our formative years making my life hell, it's hard to see past that to the person she's become. Especially since my loathing for her is definitely mutual.

I don't recognize either of the male cops with her, but I'm pretty sure they're the best the department has. This is because, first, my brother knows both of them by name, and second, because lousy cops don't get assigned to the royal family detail.

"What do you know, Kal?" Donovan asks, jumping right in. The fact that he doesn't bother to explain to them where my mother is shows just how agitated he is.

The tall cop with the rumpled suit and exhausted eyes answers. "Not enough. But we're getting there." He glances around the kitchen. "Should we wait for the queen to join us?"

"No need. She's here." My mother steps into the kitchen, escorted down the stairs by none other than Declan. Tsura is trailing behind them, like she's waiting for one of them to collapse at any moment. Still, I have to bite my lip to stifle my cry of relief at seeing Declan up and about under his own power. He's still a far cry from looking like himself, but at least he's doing okay. And when he comes over to stand beside me, I can't help but lean into him. In response, he strokes a gentle hand up and down my arm. Not enough to distract, but more than enough to soothe the agitation I know must be pouring out of me.

"What have you got for us, Kal?" my mother asks once she's reached him.

"Not enough, Your Majesty," he says with an obsequious bow of his head. "As you know, four charges were set in strategic places around your house, next to or underneath structural elements, which caused the worst of the damage. The fire department and bomb squad are looking into the actual, physical components of the bombs — tracing where they were bought, who bought them, and so forth.

"We're focusing on the magical side of things. Whoever did this has certainly got a lot of talent. They've managed to do a very good job of obscuring their magical thumbprint. But we've got some real skill of our own and we think it's only a matter of time before we unravel the safeguards."

"How much time?" my mother asks. "I have to cremate my daughter next week, and before I do, I want to know who's responsible for her death."

"We understand, Your Majesty." Moira bows her head with a respect she's never shown to me. "And I assure you, we're working with the utmost diligence and speed. The entire department has taken a piece of this investigation. We're close and I believe it will only be a matter of days before we run the people who did this to ground."

"Close doesn't count," Tsura tells her. "This is my niece we're talking about. My sister. We need answers."

"Of course, ma'am. We understand."

"Are there any other leads?" I ask, trying to move the

conversation along. My aunt is in superprotective mode and the detectives don't need the added stress of an inquisition. "Or are we completely dependent on figuring out whose magic is on the bombs? I mean, that only works if whoever wanted my family dead did it themselves instead of hiring it out."

"Actually, we do have a couple of really good leads," Kal answers when it becomes obvious that Moira won't. "We've interviewed your entire staff and one of the assistant housekeepers—a woman named Elsa Vinnick—has admitted to letting her boyfriend into the house early yesterday morning. Her boyfriend claimed that he wasn't feeling well and needed to use the restroom. He was out of her sight for about twenty minutes and he was carrying a dark green backpack. She didn't think anything of it at the time."

"Where is he now?" Donovan growls.

"Dead. We found his body two hours ago, about three miles out of Ipswitch. We're running down his bank account, known associates, anything that might tell us why he planted the charges and who he was working with. By morning, we should have a well-fleshed-out profile on him."

"Excellent work," my mother tells him. "Thank you."

"I wish it were more. We all cared deeply for Princess Hannah."

My mother nods, but she doesn't say anything. Probably because she's too choked up at the reference to sweet, laughing Hannah. I know I am.

Leandra shows the detectives out, and after a quick strategy session that doesn't yield any results, we all watch as Tsura leads my mother off to bed. My sisters soon follow, and then even Donovan heads up, though the look on his face tells me he won't be getting much sleep tonight. He'll be too busy doing his own research on the only suspect we have.

I recognize the look because I plan on doing exactly the same thing.

After too many hours of research and discussion, Declan lures me to bed with kisses . . . and a few, well-placed threats. To be honest, it feels good to be beside him, especially when it was less than twenty-four hours ago that I thought I'd never be able to hold him again.

I'm exhausted, physically, mentally and emotionally, and yet I can't fall asleep. Every time I close my eyes, images of my sister, my father, Declan, fill my mind until I can't breathe, can't think. Can't do anything but feel the horror swamp me over and over again. Declan holds me through it all, stroking and petting me—loving me—in a way I never imagined he had in him.

And when that doesn't work, he strips off my old sweats and tank top and licks me to orgasm again and again and again. Then, when my muscles are like butter and my brain like mush—and I can't even think about fighting him—he returns the favor I did him earlier in the day. Only instead of slipping me a tranquilizer, he murmurs a rest spell that sends me into a soft, dreamless sleep.

I wake up a few hours later to daylight streaming in the edges of the blackout curtains. But it isn't the light that wakes me; it's the temperature. It's hot. Stifling, really, and it takes me only a minute to figure out that I'm buried under what feels like fifty pounds of blankets. I kick them off, fight my way to the surface, only to find out that it's not the covers making me so hot. It's Declan.

He's lying beside me, his body radiating enough heat to light up the whole room.

"Sssh, Xandra, you're safe," he murmurs. "You're with me."

"I know." My sister's death comes back to me, followed by images of Declan on fire, the explosion, the house collapsing around us. I sit up quickly, then wish I hadn't as the dizziness I've been fighting off since the explosion tugs at me once again.

It doesn't stop me from trying to get out of bed, though. Pushing down the last of the covers, I swing my legs off the bed and plant my feet firmly on the floor. Before I can stand, however, Declan wraps an arm around my waist and pulls me back against his torso.

For long seconds, neither of us speaks. I lean into him, then stiffen as I remember his burns, try to pull away. But he doesn't let me go. Instead, his arm tightens around me, encouraging me to rest against him. And I do. Even knowing I'm probably hurting him, I can't bring myself to move away. Right now I need him. I need the strength he wears so effortlessly and the comfort he offers so selflessly.

When I can't take the silence any longer, I ask, "How long have you been up?" My voice comes out sounding distinctly froglike and I wonder how long I've been out. Is it lack of use, exposure to all that smoke or just sadness that's making me sound so hoarse?

"I got enough sleep earlier." He gestures to the laptop beside him on the nightstand. "I've been working."

"Did you find anything?"

"I don't know yet. I'm tugging on a few strings, waiting to see how they unravel." His hand strokes gently up and down my back as we talk. "How are you feeling?"

"Like I plummeted twenty feet through a wall to the floor below."

"Then you're right on track." He lowers his forehead to mine in a gesture I'm coming to love. "I'm sorry."

"Me, too." I reach for the lamp on the nightstand, flick it on. Then turn to look at Declan. His skin is still red and blistered in spots—particularly on his hands and arms—but he looks better than he has any right to, especially considering that he nearly self-immolated not very long ago. "And you? How are you?"

"Better now that you're safe." He sits up, presses soft kisses to my right shoulder and the side of my neck. "You frightened me."

He pushes the last words out from between gritted teeth and I know it took a lot for him to get them out at all. For a warlock like Declan—so strong, so powerful—admitting fear is akin to slicing off one of his limbs and then dousing the wound in alcohol. Only about a million times more painful. But he's done it. For me.

I can do no less. But there are many ways to be strong and the last thing he needs right now is to catch a glimpse of my utter vulnerability. Not when he has to concentrate on recovering. And not when I'm so screwed up inside that I can barely tell which side is up.

"How are you feeling?" he asks after the silence stretches too long between us. This time, I know he doesn't mean the physical stuff.

"I'm okay."

He twists so those crazy onyx eyes of his are looking straight into mine. "Yeah?"

No, not even close. But he doesn't need to hear. Nobody does right now, not when we're all drowning in our own shades of grief. "I'll be better once I find out who's doing this to my family."

"We'll find out. I promise." He eases me back down onto the bed. "Rachael stopped by while you were sleeping. She says you need to get as much rest as possible. She worked on your concussion for a while, made sure there wasn't any dangerous brain swelling or bleeding, but she says you need a lot of rest for the healing to take effect."

"I don't think I can sleep any more."

"Try." He pets my hair, my cheek, silently urging me to relax.

"How are we going to find the people responsible for this mess?" I ask after a long pause. "If it's not the ACW, if it's someone playing us off against each other, how are we going to find them? There are hundreds of thousands of witches out there. Any one of them could be trying to mastermind a coup."

He strokes a hand over my hair. "Why don't you get some more sleep and we'll talk about this in a few hours?"

I narrow my eyes at him. "That sounds remarkably like 'Don't worry your pretty little head about this, little lady. The big boys will take care of it.'"

"Don't be ridiculous. You'll worry you're pretty little head no matter what I say."

I gape at him. "Good answer," I tell him sarcastically.

He leans down, brushes his warm lips against my own. "Xandra, much as I'd like to take care of this for you, I am well aware that you should be involved. That you *need* to be involved."

And just that easily my annoyance abates. In its place is the sorrow I've been holding at bay through sheer force of will. Declan sees, and the impartial mask he's been wearing for the last few minutes melts away. "Oh, baby, it's okay," he tells me as tears seep silently down my cheeks. "It's okay."

"It doesn't feel okay."

"I know." He presses soft kisses against my forehead, my eyes, my cheeks.

"I loved her so much."

He shifts so I'm cuddled up against him, his entire body wrapped around mine in his effort to shield me from my pain.

Somehow his care only makes the agony more acute. I start to cry in earnest now, huge, wracking sobs that feel like they're going to tear me apart from the inside out. I can't believe Hannah's gone, can't believe I'll never get to hear another one of her lame jokes or listen to her recount some ridiculous thing that happened to her when she went to the bank or the supermarket or the zoo. Hannah had a gift of seeing the absurd in everyday situations, and more often than not, she used that gift to keep the rest of us in the family from taking ourselves too seriously.

I can't imagine what we're going to do without her. Don't want to imagine it.

Just the thought has me crying harder, until I'm all but gagging under the onslaught of pain. Declan tenses against me and there's a hitch in the soothing sounds he's making as he tenderly rubs my back. I know I'm worrying him, just as I know that my agony is also causing him pain. I regret it, but there's nothing I can do to stop the tears.

It just hurts too damn much to keep them in.

I'm not sure how long I lie there in his arms, weeping. Long enough for my eyes to swell under the onslaught and for my head to start pounding with renewed vigor.

But somewhere in the middle of all that bawling, I become aware of a warmth spreading through me. It starts in my back, in the exact spots where Declan's burned and battered hands are resting. Continues up to my shoulders, across my chest before running down my arms to my own hands. From there it spreads to my stomach, my legs, until every part of my body is filled with the comforting heat.

It's Declan's magic; I know it is. Instead of arrowing it into me like he usually does, he's taking his time, letting it seep in and slowly, *slowly*, comfort me. My own magic rises up without my bidding, tangles with the shimmering strands of his until the warmth turns to flame.

Instinctively, I shy away—I've had enough experience with fire to last a lifetime—but Declan won't let me go. He wraps his power all around me until I can't feel anything but safe, anything but loved. Then he uses those feelings to coax my own power back out from behind the hasty barrier I'd slammed into place.

Part of me wants to resist—on some levels, this sharing of our magic is a million times more intimate than sex. And while I've felt Declan's magic inside me before, it's never been like this. Never been so much a part of me that I feel it in my every nerve ending, my every cell. Never been so overwhelming that I can't tell where his power leaves off and mine begins.

There's a part of my brain screaming for me to shut this down. That it's too intimate, too dangerous. That it will only speed up everything that comes with being soulbound—the bad parts as well as the good.

I ignore the warning. There's no way I'm giving this up. Not when I have a direct pathway to the fiery beauty of Declan's soul. For once, the darkness that seethes between us is nowhere around and I'm grateful. I want to relish every second.

Time passes and still he doesn't withdraw. Neither do I. Instead, I savor the heat rippling through me, touching me in places I never imagined another human being would ever be able to reach.

My headache—nearly blinding in its intensity just a little while ago—is all but gone. My eyes feel much less swollen and gritty. Even the pressure in my chest, partly from crying and partly from grief, feels lighter.

I'm not sure how I feel about that last one—my sorrow over Hannah's death is an intensely personal thing, one I'm not yet ready to share with anyone else. And yet I can't deny that I feel more able to see clearly, more capable of moving beyond my own emotions to see the big picture.

Feeling a little drunk on all the power that's still bouncing around inside me, I open my eyes slowly. And stare in wonder at Declan's face.

In just the last few minutes, his skin has lost most of the red burns. I glance down at his hands, realize the blisters are gone as well. "Did you . . . ?" My voice trails off, as I don't even know what it is I want to ask.

"Actually, you did," he tells me.

"I don't understand."

"It works both ways. I can heal you, partly because I have some talent for it and you can heal me—at least partially—because of the binding. The stronger your magic gets, the more you'll be able to do. It's how I got out of that inferno with only second-degree burns. Once you started pumping your magic into me, the flames couldn't do that much damage."

Astonished, I touch his face with soft fingertips. Trace

the wicked curve of his lips and the tiny little dimple to the left of his mouth that few people ever get a chance to see. It took me forever to get a glimpse of that dimple—smiling is not something Declan does on a regular basis—but now that I have, it's become one of my favorite places to kiss and touch and lick. Partly because it makes him look sexy as hell, but mostly because that dimple means Declan trusts me in a way he trusts almost no one. He opens up to me when normally he goes out of his way to be as closed off as possible.

Because I can't help myself, I lean forward and press a light kiss directly over that dimple. And think about just how much my life has changed since this man found his way back into it.

Long minutes pass in silence, both of us locked in thought. But eventually the corners of my mind start to crumble in on themselves and I know that I've tackled too much. Hannah. Declan. The ACW. A concussion. The pain comes back, as agonizing as ever.

Declan shifts, stretching out on the bed before pulling me into the curve of his arm. His hand tangles in my hair, his fingers massaging my scalp until my eyes drift closed despite myself.

Before I go under completely, I force myself to ask, "What's our next move?" I need to be prepared.

He kisses my shoulder, lingering on the gold seba tattoo that sprang up a few days ago—and that marks me as his as surely as his new tattoo marks him as mine. Then, in a dark, hard voice I haven't heard since our first days together, he answers, "We find the people who did this to you and then we set their world on fire."

Exhausted or not, headache or not, after that revelation, it takes me a long time to fall back asleep.

Thirty-one

Xandra! The scream rips through my sleeping psyche like an explosion.

"Shelby!" I sit straight up in bed, shoving the strands of my still-mutilated hair out of my eyes. Beside me, Declan stirs and wraps an arm around my waist. He doesn't wake up, though—my first clue that Shelby's scream was all in my head.

For long seconds I wait in the dark, heart pounding and terror coursing through my bloodstream. *Come on, Shelby,* I urge her mentally. *Give me something to go on here.*

Silence is my only answer.

I glance at the bedside clock. It's four in the morning and though I should probably try to get some more sleep, I know that's not going to happen. After disentangling myself from Declan, I push out of bed. I grab my robe and Declan's tablet, then quietly slip out of my room and head down the hallway. I don't want to take a chance on disturbing him. Though he's definitely recovering, he needs as much rest as he can get to help speed the healing process along.

I'm almost to the sitting room at the end of the hall when the shout comes. *No! No! No! Xandra!*

I freeze, terrified of losing the nebulous connection between us. *I'm here, Shelby.*

Make it stop!

Is the woman hurting you again?

An image of Shelby burying her face in a stained sheet, sobs wracking her little body.

Talk to me, Shelby. Tell me what's going on.

The man. She's going to kill the man.

Who?

I don't know. He's screaming and it's scaring me. Make it stop.

I want to, honey. But I can't sense anyone else there with you.

They're here. In the next room. She's cutting him.

Damn it. *You can hear what's going on?*

I can feel it. Inside me. I can feel what he feels. It hurts. Xandra, it hurts.

Impotence burns inside me as I realize what she's suffering. This poor baby, this poor little girl, can somehow connect to the victims in much the same way I can. That's why they want her blood, why they need her. Because in connecting to the dead, especially the Councilors, she's capable of amassing great knowledge. Knowledge that they need.

The thought of her suffering nauseates me. I'm a grown woman and can barely take it—how horrible, how utterly vile, must it be for Shelby to have to experience something like this without understanding any part of what's going on.

Xandra! Another panicked scream. *Are you still there?*

I'm right here, baby. Do me a favor. I know you said you couldn't see anything before, that there were no windows in your room.

There aren't.

I know. But can you look around anyway? See what's in the room with you? See what's in the room with you? Maybe describe it to me?

Whatever she tells me won't be much, but maybe it'll give Nate something to go on anyway.

It's dark.

I know, Shelby. If you can't see anything, that's fine. But if you can, you need to tell me what it is. Maybe it will help me find out. Maybe—

The walls are blue. Dark blue. And there are funny pictures on them.

Funny pictures?

Yes. Some look like birds. Or cows. And there's a cross with a kind of circle on top of it—

Hieroglyphics? My heart starts beating double time. *Are there hieroglyphics on the wall?*

I don't know what those are.

I tamp down on the surge of impatience that rolls through me. She's just a little girl, after all. How can she be expected to understand what she sees?

They're pictures, sweetheart, just like you said. I concentrate really hard on forming an image of my marks in my head—the symbols of Isis and the sebas that decorate the different parts of my body. *Do any of the pictures look like these?* I ask her.

For long seconds she doesn't answer and my fear grows. *Shelby!*

I'm here. I'm looking. More silence, then, *Yes, Xandra! Yes! There are a bunch of symbols like that on the wall across from me. Only they're bigger and there are more of them.* She must be concentrating really hard, because suddenly a picture comes back to me—one of midnight blue walls covered in hieroglyphics in varying shades of gold and silver.

My first good look at them has the tablet tumbling from my suddenly lax fingers and crashing to the hardwood floor. I stare blindly at it for long seconds as more and more images bombard my brain. Some of them come from Shelby, but the majority come from my own memory.

I know that room. I know that room. I. Know. That. Room.

I clutch at the wall for support as everything realigns in my head, all the jagged puzzle pieces shaping and reshaping and fitting together in a whole different way.

Close doesn't count.

Curly black hair.

Green eyes.

Witch.

Blood magic.

Smells like chewing gum.

Close doesn't count.

The words echo in my head, the cruel female voice that I first heard say them replaced by another tone. One that's just as hard, but less psychotic sounding.

Close only counts in horseshoes.

No prizes for close.

Close doesn't count.

No, dear goddess, no.

I start to run then, flying down the two flights of stairs and into the kitchen. The Peg-Board near the garage door has a bunch of keys on it and I grab for my dad's. Then I'm out the door and flying through the huge garage, looking for the car that my dad keeps exclusively for use on the ranch.

I climb into it, fumbling the keys into the ignition before I've even got the door closed.

I'm in a panic now, so freaked out that I barely re-member to open the garage before putting the car in reverse and backing out.

Then I'm speeding down the ranch road that will let me out onto the main highway in about seven minutes.

It can't be. It can't be. It can't be.

The words run through my head like a mantra, one that picks up speed and urgency with every repetition. I'm flooring the gas pedal, which is making the SUV bounce like hell over the rugged dirt road. But I barely feel the bumps. I'm too caught up in my fear that I'll be wrong about all this—and my absolute terror that I might be right.

I'm so lost in thought that I nearly plow straight onto the highway without looking. At the last minute I slam on my brakes, and narrowly avoid being creamed by an eighteen-wheeler blasting past.

Heart in my throat, I tell myself to concentrate. To slow down. But in only a couple of minutes I'm back up to ninety miles an hour. Right now the only thing that matters is getting there. Finding out the truth.

Please, goddess, let me be wrong. It can't be her. It just can't be.

And yet, there's a part of me that already knows it is. The sorrow is a crushing weight on my chest . . . and on my soul.

I press down harder on the gas pedal. The SUV growls, but the needle on the speedometer continues to climb.

I'm about halfway to Ipswitch when a blinding surge of heat flashes through me, the power of it slamming me back against the car seat so hard that I give myself a headache. The blast of heat is followed almost immediately by the shakes—a precursor to the convulsions I can already feel building at the base of my spine.

Horror works its way through me, along with the insidious knowledge that I'm too late. Someone's already dead—either Shelby or the man being tortured in the next room. I'm so scared, so empty, that I don't even try to reach out to Shelby, to connect. If she's dead—if I didn't make it in time—I don't want to know. Not yet.

The first convulsion hits me and I start to seize— which is pretty much the worst thing that can happen when I'm speeding down a dark, winding road in the middle of the night. But I can't stop. One person might be dead, but that means that one person is still alive. I can't let her kill again. I can't fail again. I just can't.

Using sheer will alone, I battle back the convulsions. Flat-out refuse to give in to them. It's a million times more painful than seizing on my kitchen floor was—and that was no picnic—but somehow I manage to do it. Flames ripple under my skin, but they never actually break out, and slowly, torturously, I get them—and everything else ripping through my body—under control.

At least until the compulsion hits. It wraps itself around me, pulling me forward. Faster, faster. Pulling me into the abyss of darkness that waits for me at the end of this rabbit hole to hell that I've fallen into.

Finally, I'm there. I pull into the driveway and stumble out of the car, punch-drunk on the powerful vibes that fill the air all around me. I'm so wrapped-up in getting into the house, I don't even bother to close the SUV's door behind me before I'm lurching up the front walkway.

The closer I get, the more the power hums over me, through me. The compulsion is a live wire now, shocking me with every step, every breath, I take.

I stumble on a rock, fall flat against the door with a resounding thump. The powerful vibes in the air around me stutter and for a moment, it's like the whole world around me is holding its breath. Then the magic surges hotter and higher than ever.

That's when I know for sure. This isn't a bad dream, isn't a mistake. Murder has just happened here. Dark magic. Blood magic is happening still.

It's been under my nose the entire time and yet I'm still shocked, still traumatized, when the front door swings open and I meet my aunt's eyes, gleaming with an unholy light.

Thirty-two

"Xandra." Tsura is lit up from the inside, the power she's just ingested making her all but glow as she looks at me in confusion. It's strange how doing something so vile can make her so beautiful. It's not supposed to work that way.

But then again, none of this is supposed to work this way. Because only in a turned-around, upside-down, fucked-up world would I be standing on my aunt's doorstep minutes after she murdered a man and used dark magic to claim his power.

"What are you doing here?" she asks.

I have absolutely no idea how to respond to that.

"Xandra, darling, are you okay?" She reaches a hand up as if she's going to feel my forehead but stops at the last second. I'll never know if that's because I lurch away or if it's because she realizes that she's glowing. And that, no matter how much she wants to pretend it is, that just isn't normal.

"Can I come in?"

"Of course." She doesn't hesitate and I'm suddenly assailed by doubts—and hope. Maybe Tsura hasn't done the things I think she has. Maybe I've got this all wrong.

But the moment the door closes behind me, I know

that I'm not. The stench of death is all around us, similar to what I smelled beneath the Capitol grounds, but worse. That's when I realize that it's not only death I'm scenting. There's fear here. Panic. Someone is still alive.

Shelby? The cry echoes through my mind as I frantically push against the barriers of my mind and try to find her.

Xandra!

Oh, thank the goddess. She's still alive. That means someone else is dead, which is awful, but at least I haven't lost Shelby. Not yet anyway.

"Would you like a cup of tea?" My aunt is watching me closely, her eyes gone narrow and night-glow in the dim light.

"No, thank you."

She's acting so normal, so civilized, that I don't know where to start. How do I go about asking my mother's twin sister—my favorite aunt—and the most powerful *healer* in my clan what turned her into a murderous bitch?

"Well, come sit down, then."

Sitting is the last thing I want to do right now, but I follow her into the living room. As I do, a spatter of blood on the rug catches my eye. My stomach pitches and rolls.

Tsura is in front of me, so she can't see what I'm looking at. I blink, stare harder as I try to convince myself that I'm wrong. That it's not blood. But it is. It's real and so is this. I just don't know why.

And that's the question I end up asking her as she settles herself on the sofa. A million thoughts are floating around in my head, but only one word comes out. "Why?"

I expect excuses, prevarications, but my aunt surprises me again. She looks me straight in the eye and says, "Because close doesn't count."

It's so not what I was expecting to hear—though I should have been, obviously—that I stare at her for long seconds before asking, "What does that even mean?"

"You of all people should know, Xandra. Aren't you second in line for the throne behind Donovan?"

I'm totally confused now, but I answer anyway. "Yes." Thank the goddess. Being queen is not something I've ever wanted.

"That's the position that I occupied for years. Second in line to the throne. Second best to my beautiful, talented sister."

"You're identical twins."

"Yes. And I was born first. That throne should have been mine. It *would* have been mine if not for the archaic rules of inheritance this coven is governed by."

I don't bother pointing out that most thrones are inherited through some archaic laws—Ipswitch's throne is no different from a hundred others. But I don't want to push her completely around the bend, no matter that it seems she's already there.

"So you kidnap a little girl? You kill four Councilors? How does that get you the Ipswitch throne?"

She doesn't answer right away, but there's something about the way she looks at me that makes the last puzzle piece snap into place. "You're the one who put out those bombs. You tried to kill all of us."

Again, she doesn't answer. But then she doesn't have to. The horror of everything she's done sweeps through me and I want to scream. Hannah. Sweet, gentle Hannah is dead because of her.

I leap to my feet, prepared to do I don't know what, but before I can so much as lift a hand, a tremendous force knocks me off my feet and slams me to the ground. I lie there, staring up at Tsura, who is standing now, towering over me—her chest heaving and hands out in front of her.

Even though I can see it in every line of her body, in every breath she takes, it still takes me a moment to understand. My aunt, whose only magic is the soft, selfless art of healing, is long gone. In her place is this creature, bloated with its own power and sense of self-importance.

"Why?" I ask again. Although I'm not really looking for a reason. Not anymore. Because there is no reason, at least none that doesn't speak of a life of bitterness and jealousy compounded by the kind of corruption that only comes from throwing oneself headfirst into darkness.

Tsura's eyes harden at the question, her face frozen in a mask I've never seen from her before. But then her lips curl upward and she hisses, "Because I can."

She extends a hand toward me, her mouth moving rapidly in a spell I have no hope of comprehending. Lightning dances across her fingertips as she gathers the power, condenses it, and I brace myself as I scramble to my feet. I don't know if I can fight her, but I know that I don't want to die lying on the floor staring up at her.

Electricity is arcing through the room now, dancing across the ceiling and skimming down the walls. It feels like it's going to blow up at any second and I only pray that it doesn't take the whole house—and Shelby—with it when it goes.

Tsura tosses her head back, lifts her arms above her head, and screams the last few words of the spell. I dive for the couch, hoping to get behind it before she lets loose all that power, but I'm a few seconds too late. With a shout of triumph, she lets the electricity loose—all of it headed straight for me.

I brace myself for the hit, but it never comes. One second I'm leaping toward the back of the couch and the next the electricity slams into something in midair and dissipates in an instant—the way fire winks out in a vacuum.

Tsura screams—this time in outrage—and we turn in time to watch Declan stride into the room.

Tsura howls, starts spinning a spell even as she leaps across the room at him. Terror, rage, determination explode through me—it's been less than a day since Declan was nearly burned alive because of her. He may look fine, standing there, but I don't believe he is fine. Not yet. And there is no way that bitch is taking anyone else from me. And certainly not Declan.

But my powers—seeing the dead, connecting with them—don't lend themselves to this kind of magical showdown. I have nothing to hurl at her, no spell to stop her in her tracks. So, in the end, I do the only thing I can. I grab one of the heavy, stained glass lamps off an end table and leap after her.

She's already attacking Declan, and though he manages to dodge her assault, I know it's only a matter of time before something gets through. Tsura has the power of four Councilors running through her veins; their magic is sparking so violently inside her that it's miraculous that she can even contain it.

Declan sends some of his own power back at her, and she's not fast enough to get around it. I gasp as the blast hits, and I wait, expecting to see her stumble. Or fall.

Declan packs a powerful punch and I can't imagine anyone standing up under a full assault from him. But Tsura merely latches onto the power he exudes, and pulls it into herself.

That's when I know for sure that he's holding back — either because he's too weak or because he doesn't want to hurt my aunt, doesn't want to hurt me. I want to scream at him to finish her, that this power-crazed woman in front of me bears no resemblance to the woman I knew in my childhood. But it's too late, there's too much going on. Already, I can see her preparing to turn that added breadth of power back on Declan.

I leap through the air, brandishing the lamp like a baseball bat, and crash it into the back of her skull with every ounce of rage and strength I have inside me.

Tsura drops like a stone.

For long seconds, I can't believe it. I stand over her, lamp at the ready, prepared to beat her to death at the smallest provocation. But she doesn't move, and eventually I allow Declan to pull the lamp from my numb hands.

I stand there, staring down at her, and feel a darkness take over me in full force. I want to injure her, to kill her, to rip her limb from limb for what she's done to my family and to Shelby. I don't give a shit about the Councilors and am not about to pretend that I do, but Hannah? Rachael? Declan? My father? I want nothing more than to make sure that she never gets the chance to do this again.

I reach into the small of Declan's back, pull out the athame he always carries. Slowly unsheathe it. He watches me with steady eyes and I know — I know — he wants to be the one to kill her. To plunge the dagger through her chest and end her for everything she's done. Everything she's put us through.

The thought calls to me, his darkness seducing mine out of hiding until it fills me up, until it seeps into my every pore and envelops all that I am. All that I stand for.

There's a part of me, a small part, that is screaming for me to stop. To wait. To think. I'm not interested in listening, though. Instead, I lean forward and prepare to commit murder.

"Xandra." Declan calls my name moments before I plunge the dagger straight into my aunt's chest. I turn my head toward him and for the first time since he showed up to rescue me, our eyes collide. His are wide, dark, churning with power and the need for vengeance. In them, I see all of my own feelings reflected back at me. My need to hurt her, to make her suffer. And the small, insidious thrill that comes with all this power—the understanding that in this moment I have total control over whether she lives or dies.

I take a deep breath, pull the knife back and prepare to end this—to end her—but Declan's hand flashes out. Stops mine. Electricity arcs between us at the first touch and I gasp in surprise. He steps closer, and as my head tilts up to maintain our eye contact, I see something else in his eyes: love, devotion and an acceptance of me however I am, whoever I am—the Xandra he fell in love with or this new one who's trapped in the darkness and can't seem to find her way out.

Somehow, it's exactly the grounding I need. I step back, let the athame slip from between my fingers. Declan plucks it out of midair, shoves it back into its scabbard. He's still watching me, solemn, steady, waiting. I know what he wants, what he needs, and I reach for him.

Only then does he smile, really smile. And as he gathers me in his arms, I understand—for the first time—the battle he goes through. It's a battle between darkness and light, between wrong and right. It's a battle I've never had to fight before, but now that I've faced it myself, it gives me faith in his strength, his power, his goodness—an understanding that I might never have had otherwise.

"You okay?" he murmurs, stroking a gentle hand down my cheek.

I shake my head. I'm a long way from okay and I think we both know that. But for now, in Declan's arms, I feel like I'm going to make it.

"Shelby?" he whispers in between pressing tender kisses to my cheek, my forehead, my eyes.

"She's here somewhere," I tell him. "She's alive, but I don't know much more than that."

"I'm sorry I couldn't spare you this. It's why I tried to find her on my own, so that you wouldn't have to go through all of this."

I can see the torment in his eyes, and it slays me. It really does. I brush a hand down his cheek, watch his eyes darken. "I think I had to do it. I had to see."

He knows I'm right—I can see it in his face. But that doesn't mean it's easy for him to accept. I understand, though. I hate the idea of his being in danger as well.

"Let's go find Shelby," he says after a moment.

"What about my aunt?" I stare down at Tsura, a new wave of hatred and rage welling up inside me at the sight of her.

Declan rubs soothing circles on my back even as he

murmurs a spell that binds her. "She won't be going any-where until the police get here."

"We should call them."

"I already did."

For a moment, I don't believe him. The Declan I thought I knew would never step back like that, never hand over to the police so easily the woman who had tormented him and me. But the man standing before me isn't the man he's always been. Just like I'm no longer the woman I've always been.

And that's when I know. Really know that things are going to be okay. This soulbound thing isn't going to be easy. It's going to pull us into the shadows more times than it doesn't. It's going to show me things—about my lover, myself, and the world I live in—that I never wanted to see. Never wanted to know.

But in the end, it's going to be as much salvation as punishment. As much joy as sorrow. As much light as dark. And that—that is all I can ask for.

Well, that and Declan. Everything else can take care of itself.

About the Author

Tessa Adams lives in Texas and teaches writing at her local community college. She is married and the mother of three sons.

CONNECT ONLINE

www.tracywolff.com/tessa-adams

Read on for an excerpt from Tessa Adams's

Soulbound
A Lone Star Witch Novel

Now available from Signet Eclipse

Prologue

I was born on a dark night, under a Dark Moon in a sky turned bloodred with power and prophecy.

Some say it was a less than fortuitous beginning to a new life of power, but as I squalled my way into the world, none of those bound to love me were disturbed by it. Why should they have been? Magic was everywhere.

It was burning in the wall of flames that surrounded the birthing bed.

Bubbling in the vases of sacred water positioned at North, East, South and West.

Trembling in the blessed earth sprinkled all over my grandmother's prized Aubusson rug.

Even spinning in the air that whipped around the room in a frenzy.

Yes, magic was all around me. How could it not be when hundreds, thousands, of members of our coven were there, gathered right outside the walls of my grandmother's garden, straining for their first glimpse of the enchanted one? Of me.

The news of my imminent birth spread quickly— which was no surprise as it was the most anticipated, most celebrated, occasion the coven had seen in many years. Since the birth of my own mother some two hundred odd years before, probably. After all, it's not every day that a seventh daughter bears a seventh daughter, let alone does it on the seventh day of the seventh month. In fact, our historians swore that it had never happened before.

Tales of my expected power spread until they became a thing of lore. Or even worse, until all those stories—all those whispers—became the norm. The expected. I would be great, powerful, untouchable by nearly all witch standards.

It was one hell of a birthright for a scrawny, five pound baby, but my family was convinced I would live up to it. As were my coven, the Council and the entire magical world.

And when the sky split straight down the middle, when it was rent in half by the most powerful forces of Heka—of the goddess Isis, herself—I moved from creature of lore to portent of legend.

Lightning spun through the sky like a whirlwind, whipping around and around as it tore through my grandmother's roof and through the third and second stories of her house until it found me tucked safe in my mother's arms on the ground floor.

And that's when it hit, lighting up my mother and me—the whole room, really—in a strike of such brilliance that it could be seen for endless miles. It disappeared as quickly as it had come, leaving the two of us untouched—except for the golden mark that appeared on my neck and collarbone.

A circle with the outline of a pointed half circle above it, it was Isis's most sacred symbol—a magical tattoo that nothing could remove and one that no one had been gifted with before me.

The legends and the expectations grew. And grew. And grew. Until no mortal could possibly live up to them.

Especially not me.

One

My humiliation is complete.

I can see it in their faces, in the way some are trying desperately not to look at me while others can't stare long or hard enough.

I can see it in the embarrassed flush on my father's cheeks and the clenched hands, wandering gazes and tapping toes of my sisters.

And, most of all, I can see it in the way my mother's amethyst eyes have glazed over with mortified tears. In the way she keeps clicking together the heels of her favorite, ruby red pair of cowboy boots—like if she hits the perfect spot she'll spiral out of the room just as Dorothy did all those years ago.

Too bad there's never a tornado around when you need one.

I try to tune them out, to close my eyes and pretend that I'm up in my room, practicing, instead of standing here in the middle of my Kas Djedet—my magical coming out party—making a complete and total ass of myself. If I can do that, if I can just forget my audience of legions, then maybe this once I can find a way to make the stupid spell work.

The fact that it never has before is utterly inconsequential to me now. Everything is, except making fire.

Please, Isis, just this once. I beg of you.

There's no answer, but then I didn't really expect one. Except for the day I was born, Isis has been notably absent from my life. You'd think, by now, I would have learned to stop asking.

Still, I concentrate on the spell as hard as I can, repeating the words over and over again in my head like I've been taught. The charm itself is child's play—or at least, to a certain kind of child. But I've never been able to do it. Never been able to do *anything* when it comes to magic, no matter how much I study or how hard I try. Why I let my family talk me into believing tonight would be different, I'll never know.

Maybe because I wanted to believe it as much as they did.

Still, I'd warned my parents, weeks ago, that this party was a bad idea. Told them that I was going to fail. That I absolutely, positively could not do what they so desperately wanted me to.

They'd refused to listen.

"You're simply a late bloomer," my mother told me. "Your powers will unlock on your nineteenth birthday and you'll do fine. Isis knew what she was doing when she marked you. Trust me."

"You're just nervous," my dad concurred. "Once you're up there, the magic will come."

"Performance anxiety," my oldest sister, Rachael, commented with a smirk that was a long way from sympathetic. "Good luck with that." Still, despite her amusement, it was obvious that she hadn't expected me to fail, either. But then, why would she? No one in my family fails. At anything. And certainly not at magic. There hasn't been a latent witch on either side of my family tree for seven generations. And if there *was* going to be one, it certainly shouldn't be me.

After all, with my birthright, I should be loaded with power. Showered with it. It should be leaking out my pores and lighting up everything I touch.

Instead, it turns out that seven is *not* my lucky number. I can't do even the most basic spell.

I try again.

Nothing.

Again.

Nothing.

In the audience, someone clears his throat, coughs, and the small amount of concentration I've been able to muster shatters. I glance around—I can't help myself— and once again see the shock, the horror and disgust, rolling off the witches and wizards gathered in my family's ceremonial ballroom.

Even my own family looks ashamed, like they can't believe I'm one of them.

It's the last straw and more than enough to get me moving, to have me jumping off the circular stage set up in the center of the room and zooming out the French doors that lead to the patio.

Behind me, my mother shrieks my name. In a booming voice, my father demands that I return to the ballroom at once. But I'm running full out now, scrambling to get away from the pity and the revulsion radiating from so many of the guests. They've come from all over

our territory, all over the *world*, to witness the Kas Djedet of the youngest, and supposedly most powerful,
Morgan daughter. What they've witnessed instead
doesn't bear thinking about.

No, I tell myself, nothing can make me go back there.
Not when the joke that is my nineteenth birthday party
is still in full swing, and maybe not even when it's over.

My black designer cowboy boots, bought by my
mother especially for tonight, pound over the hard,
packed earth as I flee my yard for the safety and comfort
of the peach orchard behind my house. The sweet scent
of the fruit tickles my nose but I'm too busy sprinting
down row after row of trees to notice. The only thing
clear in my head is the need to get away.

I don't come to a stop until I'm at the lake at the very
end of my family's property. It's my thinking spot, the
place I've been coming to brood and cry and reflect since
I was a little girl. As far as I know, I'm the only member
of my family to come here, and if I'm lucky, it will be the
last place they think to look for me.

Frustrated, fuming, I yank off my eight hundred dollar
boots—which are supposed to help me channel magic
and instead have only aided in channeling mortification—
and hurl them, one after the other, into the lake. As they
sink, I feel an incredible surge of satisfaction welling up
inside of me. The first satisfaction I've felt all day, all
week. All year.

Screw magic, I tell myself as—mindless of the Dolce
& Gabbana party dress I'm wearing (again courtesy of
my mother)—I sink down onto the moist dirt surrounding the lake so I can dangle my feet in the water. Being
a latent witch isn't the worst thing in the world. It just
feels like it now because of the party.

Most days, it's actually a relief not to be able to practice magic. After all, who needs the hassle? The responsibility? And who actually wants to touch all those gross potion ingredients, anyway?

A couple of tears roll down my face and I brush them impatiently away. I will not feel sorry for myself. I. Will. Not. Feel. Sorry. For. Myself. It's stupid and useless and utterly selfish. My life is better than a lot of people's, even if it doesn't feel like that right now.

Leaning back on my elbows, I gaze up at the beautiful night sky above me. And repeat the admonishment again and again, until I almost believe it.

I lay there until the heat of the summer night sinks straight through the cold brought on by nervousness and humiliation. Until my arms fall asleep from resting so long in the same position and my neck gets a crick in it for the same reason. And still I don't move. I can't. I'm transfixed by the idea of what comes next. Or, to be more specific, what doesn't.

What am I supposed to do with my life now that it's clear, once and for all, that I am *never* going to follow in my family's boot steps.

College?

Backpacking through Europe?

Getting a job—a regular, run-of-the-mill *job* with no magic involved?

Is it too much to contemplate all three?

The possibilities stretch endlessly in front of me, not nearly as disappointing as they should be. I'm actually a little excited, to be honest, at least until reality comes crashing back down. There's no way my mother will let me do any of those things. No way my parents will just let me walk away from centuries of coven tradition to lead my own life somewhere else. It simply isn't done. At least not for me, the youngest princess in Ipswitch's royal family and second in line to the throne, right behind my only brother. Latent witch or not, my place is with the Ipswitch royal family of witches. No other choice will be tolerated.

Depressed, I pick up a handful of rocks, then skip them across the surface of the lake, one after the other. I'm lost in thought, not paying much attention to what I'm doing even as I'm doing it—at least not until the last stone goes spinning out of control. Instead of jumping harmlessly across the water, it starts to glow, to spin. Then it rises straight up from the lake—about ten or fifteen feet in the air—and hangs there, whirling, for long seconds before it explodes outward. Hundreds of small, burning red pebbles fall harmlessly back into the water.

Eyes wide, heart pounding, I scramble back from the edge of the lake. *Did I do that?* I wonder frantically. But if so, how? I can't even light a candle using magic, let alone make a rock levitate and then explode. It simply isn't possible. No matter how much I want it to be so.

I glance wildly around, looking for some explanation, some *reason* for that rock to have done what it did. But there's nothing, no one, on either side of me.

Just to be sure, I turn to look behind me . . . and that's when I spot him. Dressed in black, he blends completely into the surrounding trees. I wouldn't have seen him at all except for the small flames dancing back and forth along his fingertips.

The show-off.

"What are you doing out here?" I demand, keeping my voice steady with an effort. "This is private property."

I can't see his face, don't know who he is, but the

power rolling off him is unmistakable. Not because of the rock or the fire—both are simple spells for someone who can wield magic. There's just something about him, an electricity that fills the air between us, that overwhelms the peace and quiet of the lake with the unmistakable aura of potent magic ruthlessly leashed.

"Looking for you." He walks toward me slowly and as he does, he extinguishes the flames that have moved from his fingertips to his upturned palms. I can still see him, though. Away from the trees, the light of the full moon silvers over him.

He's tall, with broad shoulders, a narrow waist and long, powerful legs. I strain to see more of him, to figure out who he is though I am certain I've never met him before. I would remember the aura of raw power that surrounds him—it's not something anyone could easily forget.

With that realization, suspicion whispers through me—an idea so outlandish I can't begin to credit it. But then he takes a few more steps and I get my first good look at his face. Razor-sharp cheekbones where they peek through his dark, chin-length hair. Full lips curled into a sardonic smile. Midnight eyes rimmed with impossibly long lashes. And a face so beautiful, so distinctive, that it's impossible to forget.

I don't know who he is and while there's a small part of me that wants to swoon at his feet, the majority of my brain is screaming for me to run. To get as far away from him as fast as I possibly can.

I choose not to listen.

Instead, I start to ask his name, but he's even closer now. So close that I can see *his* mark. It's a stark black tattoo in the shape of Seba, the Ancient Egyptian star, and like mine, it has been magically cast into the left side of his neck. It's an unusual place for a mark and seeing it has me stumbling, though I haven't moved an inch. I catch myself, force my knees to hold my weight when they want nothing more than to buckle.

Two thoughts hit me at once.

First, that I was right about the power. The man who is even now slowly, inexorably, crossing the last few feet between us, is a warlock of almost unimaginable skill. One who straddles the line between light and dark, white magic and black. One who even my very powerful parents speak about only in whispers, despite the fact that his brother has been dating my sister for years now. Though Ryder celebrates most holidays with us, Declan has never before been invited to our house. I'm not sure he was even invited this time. After all, my mother is adamant that we don't associate with his kind of power.

And secondly, that he's even better looking than the stories proclaim. And that's saying something.

He stops only a foot or so from me and though I want to look away, I force myself to meet the burning gaze of Declan Chumomisto, the man many consider the most powerful warlock living today. Some people say that he's losing it, that he's not nearly as formidable as he once was, but the rumbles only feed the rumors about him. Especially when he can still do things that most witches can only dream of. Standing here, across from him, I see no hint that he's lost any of that power. The air around us all but throbs with it.

Which, unfortunately, makes holding my ground even harder than I expected. Being near him is intense, overwhelming. So electric that I can feel every cell in my body vibrating with the strength of it. It's also scary as hell.

"What are you doing here?" I whisper, when what I really want to ask is *why me?*

Why am *I* reacting like this to you?

What did *I* do to attract your attention?

And why did you come out here to talk to me when there are so many more interesting people back at the house?

But reading minds must not be one of his gifts, because his smirk grows more pronounced as he answers my original question. "The same thing everybody else is, I would imagine. I came for Xandra Morgan's Kas Djedet."

Of course he had. My cheeks burn with shame and I want nothing more than to duck my head and run away yet again. From him, from home, from the whole nightmare of my nineteenth birthday. Still, I might have fled earlier, but I wasn't raised to be weak. Tilting my chin, I ask, "Did you enjoy the show?"

He laughs as predicted, but there's no mockery in the sound—which is totally not what I expected. "Your family will get over it."

"You know my family?" This is news to me.

"Not really. But isn't that what people are supposed to say at times like this? When royalty screws up, royally?"

Now I'm the one who's laughing. At least he's honest. "Yeah, I guess they are."

He glances down at my muddy feet. "You want to sit?"

Do I? With *him*? I don't know. His laugh has calmed my earlier terror, but my heart is still practically beating out of my chest. Declan Chumomisto is talking to me.

He extends a hand to help me settle, but I don't take

it. I don't move at all for long seconds, just stand there watching him. He's a grown man, powerful beyond my comprehension, and I'm a nineteen-year-old screwup. We don't exactly have a lot in common, even if it's only midnight conversation that he's after.

"Is something wrong?" he finally asks, letting his hand fall back to his side. There's no impatience in the question, no condescension. Just an honest concern that has me forgetting the whispers about him. Or at least putting them aside for a while. Despite my best intentions, I lower my guard.

"You mean besides the fact that I just humiliated myself in front of my entire coven?" I answer, settling down beside him as he takes off his socks and shoes.

"And what looks like a fair amount of outsiders as well, don't forget."

"Gee, thanks. I was totally in danger of forgetting that, so I appreciate the reminder."

"I do what I can."

"And not a thing more, I bet." I narrow my eyes at him. "You need lessons on how to pretend to give a damn."

"Oh, I give a damn, Xandra. I just didn't think you'd want me to lie to you. I can try, but I warn you, I'm not very good at it."

"Someone like you doesn't have to be." I, on the other hand, have spent my whole life living a lie. Trying to be who my parents want me to be no matter how hopeless I am at it.

"Someone like me?" There's a dangerous note in his voice now, but I don't care. I'm feeling reckless.

"I'm not stupid. I know who you are. Someone like you doesn't have to answer to anyone."

This time it's his eyes that narrow. "You'd be surprised."

To the side of us a peach tree bursts into flame. For a moment, Declan looks stunned, like he can't imagine how it happened. I wonder what that would be like, to have so much power that it could just leak out like that without me even noticing. I don't think I'd like it—I'm too much of a control freak.

A second later, the fire goes out as suddenly as it started. He doesn't say anything else and neither do I. Instead, we just sit here, the tension between us ratcheting up with each minute that passes.

"So, why did you come?" I finally ask. "You don't know my family, don't know me. You aren't even part of our coven. So why did you travel halfway around the world—"

"Halfway across the country, not the world. I was in New York before this."

"Whatever." I couldn't care less about semantics when there are questions I want answers to. "So why, out of all the places you could be right now, did you choose to be here?"

"Because you're here."

My gaze jumps to his. I've been careful not to look him in the eye since those first moments, scared of what I might find. Now, I know that fear is justified. Power— overwhelming, unimaginable power—swirls in the obsidian depths and I can't look away. I'm pinned, as trapped here as I was back there on that stage. More so, really, because here it feels like there's no escape route. No back door to scuttle out of. Nowhere to run.

I desperately want to look away. But the pull is intense, like he's reached out and grabbed me and there's nothing I can do about it.

I'm playing prey to his predator.

Even worse, there's a strange lethargy pulsing through me. Pulling me into him. Pulling me under. I start to fall . . .

No! I don't know what game he's playing, but I won't be anyone's pawn. Not anymore. When I jumped off that stage tonight and ran away, I started a new path for myself. A new life. Instinctively, I know that this isn't it.

I finally find the strength to wrench my gaze from his and as I do, I feel this pop, like I've ruptured something deep inside. I gasp, wrap my arms around myself in an instinctive bid for comfort. Declan doesn't react at all, doesn't move a muscle, but I think he felt it, too.

When silver sparks of energy whip through the air around us, I'm sure of it.

Reaching a hand out, I capture one of the sparks. I can't stop myself. I want to know, for just a second, what that kind of power feels like. It sizzles against my skin, crackling and spitting, burning me, until I open my fingers and let what's left of the spark fall back out into the air.

My palm throbs where it touched me, white hot and painful. It takes all my energy not to flinch, but I manage it. It's my turn not to react. Except, Declan knows—just as I did with him. He reaches out, gently cups my hand in his own. Strokes the fingers of his other hand lightly over the burn.

It should have been smooth, easy, but the second his skin brushes against my palm, the entire world ignites. Fragments of memories I shouldn't have rush at me— terrifying, fascinating, *compelling*. I close my eyes, try to block them out, but they're still there behind my eyelids.

Still there, deep in my mind as every nerve ending I have lights up like it's Christmas at Rockefeller Center.

I order myself to pull away, to break the connection this one last time, but I can't do it. The pleasure, woven as it is amidst the pain, staggers me and I can't do anything but sit there and soak it all in.

The pain dissipates as suddenly as it came, but in its place . . . in its place is a silver Seba, identical in all but color to the one on Declan's neck.

"What did you do?" I gasp, looking at the new mark on my palm. It shimmers in the moonlight, is the most beautiful—and frightening—thing I've ever seen.

"That wasn't me, Xandra." But he looks shaken as his fingers close around mine in a grip so possessive it makes my breath catch in my throat. I start to pull back—this is too weird, even for the daughter of witch royalty—but then I realize his hand is shaking even worse than mine. It's enough, that hint of vulnerability, to keep me here when every instinct I have screams at me to flee.

"What—" My voice breaks and I clear my throat, try again. "What's happening?" The sparks aren't stopping. In fact, they're spinning all around us like a freak midsummer snow flurry—growing hotter, more plentiful, the longer we're touching.

Declan doesn't answer, just shakes his head. I get the impression, right or wrong, that for all his power and experience he doesn't know what's going on any more than I do. I take a step back and electricity arcs between us, flowing from him into me and back again.

Every cell in my body is vibrating with it, every nerve ending screaming with the agony of it. Just when I think it's over, that the electricity is going to rip us apart, he does something even more unexpected. He leans forward, and slowly lowers his mouth to mine.

Rockefeller Center turns into Mardi Gras, the Fourth of July and New Year's Eve all rolled into one. Too bad I never thought to wonder what happens after the ball drops.